THE MERCENARIES OF ATLANTIS:

VOLUME ONE—THE INCEPTION

By

John Aylwin

NOTEBOOK | PUBLISHING

First published in the UK, 2011, by Notebook Publishing, Suite 13320, Lower Ground Floor, 145–157 St. John Street, London, EC1V 4PW.

www.notebookpublishing.co.uk.

ISBN: 978-0-9565539-1-1

CIP catalogue record for this book is available from the British Library.

Typeset by Notebook Publishing.

Printed and bound in Great Britain by Lightning Source, UK. Please visit www.notebookpublishing.co.uk for details of titles published by Notebook Publishing along with online store. The website also features details of upcoming author events, interviews and new titles.

ACKNOWLEDGEMENTS

My dearest Sue, without whom life would not be worth living: I thank you for your unselfish and undying affection which sustains me throughout.

My children: your love and support has been and always will be greatly appreciated.

Hayley: my heartfelt thanks for all your patience and professionalism in editing this book, and also for a valued friendship developing in the process.

Allan and Tracy, from a friend in need: you are true friends indeed.

And my sister Judy: we shared two wonderful people who might be surprised by our calling—but no more so than us, perhaps? I dedicate this book to their memory.

CHAPTER ONE

Wing Commander Jack Bannerman and Squadron Leader Mark Calloway were flying their last patrol of the day, seated once more in their Spitfires high over the Sussex countryside. This was the fifth sortie they'd flown, and they were tiring.

Just half an hour earlier, Jack and Mark had climbed into their planes. 'Well, this is the last time today we've got to risk our bloody necks up there, which I suppose is something to be grateful for,' Jack had said.

'Certainly is, Wing Co. Another quick bash round the old county, enjoying the sunshine, a pint up the local, a couple of hours' kip, and then we get to do it all over again. Really something, eh?' Mark had replied sarcastically.

Cruising through the crystal-clear air at three hundred miles an hour, the duo hunted the Luftwaffe, which had been constantly pouring across the channel for the past several weeks, mercilessly bombing the cities and airfields running along the south coast. The evening was drawing on but, after a blisteringly hot summer's day, the air was still warm as they prowled over the county at ten thousand feet.

Wing Commander Bannerman was just twenty-five, a tall and handsome farmer's son with jet-black hair and deep blue eyes. Already, despite his young years, he'd proved to be an outstanding pilot and a highly competent leader, attributes which had earned him the unwavering respect of his peers. He was considered by all who knew him to be good humoured, intelligent and utterly fearless—which were attributes which had, much to his delight, proved to be rather appealing to the ladies.

As a young teenager, Jack had joined the local flying club. There, he had quickly learnt to fly the club's only old Tiger Moth. Taking his test in the same machine, he had gained his pilot's license just four days before his seventeenth birthday. As a young boy, his ambition had been to join the Royal Air Force and become a fighter pilot, and such an achievement virtually ensured he'd be given the opportunity. This subsequently proved to be the case, as he enlisted without difficulty and was directly posted into fighter-training school. 'Ambition fulfilled at eighteen years old. Not bad, eh?' he'd said to his father at the time, pride and joy glistening in his eyes.

Despite flying somewhat more advanced aircraft, Jack nevertheless continued to sail through his training, and was subsequently posted to his first squadron where he was ranked as Pilot Officer. From there, after three more postings—each with a considerably higher rank—he'd achieved his present commission in a total of just five years. Soon after the start of the Second World War, his was one of the first squadrons to be allocated the coveted new Spitfires—an aircraft with which he had instantly fallen in love.

Jack and Squadron Leader Calloway had arrived at Tangmere in West Sussex, one of the airfields along the south coast of England, which was bearing the brunt of the Luftwaffe's aggression. They'd immediately joined the desperate daily-waged air battles with the ambitious objective to halt a full-scale invasion by Germany's prodigious war machine. The conflict was approaching its climax, and the endless fighting consequently induced was pushing all of the front-line pilots from both air forces to their limits.

From the outset, the RAF was outnumbered by the Luftwaffe; an unenviable position considering they were a highly capable and utterly relentless foe. Daily, the two air forces traded heavy losses, with numbers on both sides quickly reducing, thereby increasing the load on the survivors.

On August 11, 1940, the outcome wobbled in the balance: no amount of warmth or sunshine could dispel the approaching darkness. As with the many preceding, the outcome lay in the hands of the air force, which was now quickly dwindling away. The only certainty for all involved was that the battle couldn't continue at this level for much longer. Coming down to the wire, the result would be dictated by the force left standing.

Jack looked down as they flew along the coast. He knew the area intimately as his new posting was, coincidentally, only seven miles from his family farm. Passing over Selsey, the seaside town near his home, he could clearly see the farmhouses and buildings far below. He wondered if his mother and father would be looking up at him right now.

Seeing the familiar fields, ditches and ponds, and the old meadows with the rife flowing through them, precious memories from his early years stirred: he remembered falling in those ditches whilst playing soldiers with his friends; making rafts to float on the ponds; and, a little later in life, shooting ducks beside the rife in the meadows. Endless summer days—like this one—had been spent kicking up stones from the dusty farm tracks and attacking beds of stinging nettles with sticks, beating back the invading armies. Jack also recalled preparing picnics with his mother to take to the harvest fields. He laughed to himself as the memories continued to surface; it would take a good hour and a half to put everything together and to carry it out to the fields. Then, if they were lucky, his father would stop work for five minutes—never more— to eat the carefully prepared food before affectionately patting his son on the head and pressing on again.

He thought of the great many times he'd wandered those fields with his father, slowly learning from him the intricacies of farming. He realised now what a privilege it was that he'd been born to a place which offered such freedom and happy memories, each day passing with its own individual lesson on life. By its very nature, the farm encompassed each of the fundamental principles of life: these principles had presented themselves daily throughout his young life—not that he'd really appreciated it at the time. Nevertheless, just living there had unconsciously broadened the mind. One such example was the seed that, once planted, grew strong and fresh, matured, seeded, and then died; slowly passing through every phase of life, following the natural order of all life forms. That, in itself, wasn't surprising at all, but to be able to influence the seed's growth, the journey through life and the ultimate demise—and all to the benefit of mankind—was the real skill. Such skills couldn't be learnt from textbooks or lectures, but were achieved only as a result of years of experience and by constantly becoming frustrated by the fact that no season is ever the same as another; a frustration which, with the passing of time, calmed and was embraced.

Undoubtedly, however, every year lived there presented its own unique challenges; nevertheless, owing to a lifetime of farm-work, the solutions would always present themselves to his father. 'Work with the land, not against it,' had always been his father's philosophy—and it usually did the trick.

The livestock side was similar in principle, but Jack still had to understand what he was doing, as with the plants. He understood, even as a young child, that no animal is ever the same as another, even within the same species. Undoubtedly, the learning curves were endless, aggravated by so many variables. Insidiously, his knowledge had developed until—becoming ever more like his father—he began to instinctively feel how to react to the ever-changing patterns of a farming life, and that feeling was like the first time he kept his balance on his first bicycle: suddenly, without rhyme or reason, he simply knew what to do—and it felt fantastic.

As his Spitfire droned on high above the neighbours' farms and out towards Portsmouth harbour, the western extent of their current patrol, Jack felt grateful for the hugely practical life skills the farm had bestowed upon him. A fountain of knowledge he'd draw from for the rest of his life—both consciously and unconsciously; that was the gift given to him by his family and the farm, and he dearly loved them all for it.

And it was this last thought that caused a savage anger to surge through him: it was obvious a deep threat, posed by the enemy he now fought, had been inflicted upon the pastoral setting he remembered so fondly and all he loved. He'd spoken with his family on this subject and appreciated the frustration they endured being in a reserved occupation: precluded by law from enlisting, they were instead forced to watch others fighting the battle, not having any influence over it. However, his job allowed him to influence some things and, much to his delight, he'd quickly discovered the new Spitfire was also good at influencing things, and his style of combat had complemented its effectiveness. As a result, the partnership between the two had recently confirmed they were likely to be pretty influential, each and every time they encountered the enemy together.

Originally designed as a racing aircraft, the Spitfire had been reconfigured in such a way to meet Fighter Command specifications: already fast and now deadly, it encompassed all key attributes of the ultimate fighter aircraft. Its performance had saved his life on more than one occasion, and he'd already killed with it many times—he also resolved to go on doing so until it was over, one way or another.

For Jack, the battle arena was very personal: by virtue of being based at Tangmere, he was not only fighting for the greater cause but also to protect his own family.

Squadron Leader Mark Calloway, on the other hand, had a completely different life story: he was the son of a West Country doctor and a year younger than Bannerman. Shorter and carrying a little more weight, he had an unruly shock of blonde hair and chocolate-brown eyes. As a young boy, he had developed a wicked sense of humour and was viewed by his peers with a certain amount of trepidation. He was the ultimate prankster, and was the first to be at the receiving end of a pointed finger following a practical joke: if a mouse was found in a lunch box at his school, Mark was most likely responsible; along with spiders down blouses, flat bicycle tyres, stink bombs and the like. He was also renowned for his verbal dexterity, and very few ever bested him when it came to a war of words. Nevertheless, he was ever popular and retained a large circle of boyhood friends. He had subsequently grown into a man portraying the clown who, in reality, was quick-witted, gregarious, caring and kindly, and who had come far with great merit.

Mark was an only child and his parents adored him. He, in turn, would do anything for them—a situation he could never envisage changing. His parents had always supported him, which he returned by working hard to achieve all he could. When he expressed an interest in flying, his parents helped him through and, like Bannerman, had qualified at a private club. Without doubt, Mark's first love was flying, with fast cars, good wine and women now vying for joint-second place in his affections. A brilliant pilot, flying came naturally to him. He'd never looked back from his first flight to the present and, much like Bannerman, had gained rapid promotion.

As a result of both differences and similarities, the two men had formed a lasting friendship at RAF Fighter Training School, during which time they'd become inseparable. Disappointed to have been posted to different squadrons after they'd qualified, they were delighted to have been recently reunited at Tangmere.

Suddenly, Jack heard Mark's voice over his r/t, which abruptly ended his reveries.

'Look out, Wing Co., we've got company. There's a Jerry Bomber at six o' clock low, heading out towards the Isle of Wight.'

'Got him. Looks like he's all on his own for a change, but just in case his pals turn up, cover my wing whilst I knock him down.'

Normally, it wasn't this clear-cut but, lacking fighter escorts, the bomber was in deep trouble. There was nothing to stop them from going straight in for the kill, and so the two fighters eagerly pounced on the lone Dornier.

'I'll come in low and behind. With luck, one pass should do it,' radioed Jack, who was now flying close enough to note every detail of the German warplane: a large grey twin engine aircraft with black crosses stark on the wings, swastikas emblazoned on each side of the tail plane, its crew darkly silhouetted against the setting sun through metal-latticed perspex screens. The crew of the Dornier had the odds stacked against them, but they weren't completely defenceless.

Both attackers and defenders prepared to do battle, and the question as to who might survive would be answered in only a few short seconds. To the fighters, however, time seemed to pass by in a blur, seconds feeling like minutes as hearts raced and adrenaline pumped.

With engines snarling, the Spitfires closed right in, at which point they were greeted by the bomber's tail gunner, who sprayed a disturbingly accurate burst of heavy machine-gun fire directly in their path. Tracer, appearing lazy as it approached, flashed around both Spitfires and disappeared behind them. Hearing several thumps and feeling his fighter lurch to the right, Jack was forced to acknowledge the accuracy of his foe. Fortunately, however, despite his plane having been painfully peppered, his controls nevertheless continued to respond perfectly.

'Fuck, that was close, you bastard! Now it's my turn,' growled Jack, locating the bomber in his sights. With his thumb already covering the firing button, he pressed down sharply. Eight machine guns reacted simultaneously, spewing bullets forward from the wings of the fighter.

Taking only a split-second to reach their target, the missiles sprayed from the guns and smashed through the rear of the German plane. Debris flew from the stricken bomber and flames spurted from its starboard engine. The unfortunate tail gunner had sat unwittingly obstructing the maelstrom, his head consequently reducing to bloody pulp until it was finally torn from his riddled body along with the remains of his left arm. Alarmingly red, his blood ran through the tortured bomber. Leaking from the fuselage, it mingled with flaming fuel in the slipstream, pouring from the shattered engine. The bullets flew swiftly along the main body of the bomber, filling the cockpit and up through the nose, remorselessly harvesting the remaining aircrew in the process, ripping and tearing through everything in their path.

The burning nightmare skewed to the right before it eventually nose-dived towards the ground. Flames gained in intensity until it became a fireball before crashing to Earth, only one field away from Jack's parents' farmhouse. Crumpling, rending, screeching and tearing apart, it ploughed the hard-baked summer earth; its hideous landing terminating in a tremendous explosion, and the concussion consequently breaking some of the farmhouse windows.

'Amen,' whispered Jack, pulling a four G-turn up into a steep climb as he viewed his handiwork. With his wingman shadowing, he shot up through the failing evening light. The Merlin engines sang happily as the pilots slammed on the throttles, pulling their loads ever higher behind them, the screaming notes providing a twisted requiem for the dead.

Levelling off at ten thousand feet, Mark called over his radio. 'Nice work, Wing Co. Spoiled their day a bit, though, I reckon. Still, I trust you're in better shape than your kite. You are okay, Jack, I take it?'

'Not really,' Jack sighed over the radio. 'I don't feel that great, to be honest. I still can't get my head round this war—look at the poor bastards. I know they'd have happily done it to us but, just the same, they didn't really have much chance, did they?' Jack looked down at the black smoke whirling upwards from the field below. 'Maybe that's not the whole problem, though; I think it's *where* it's happened more than what's happened. That's my home down there. For God's sake, I've sowed that field many times, Mark—only it was with wheat, not corpses.' The shock of the battle continued to stir Jack's emotions.

'Steady on, old boy. You had no choice, and at least it was quick. I reckon they were going home, so just think how many people they've murdered with their bloody bombs in Portsmouth just tonight. Thanks to you, they won't do it again,' Mark reassured his friend. 'It was bloody terrifying, though. Like I said, your old kite looks like a colander! They nearly got you this time, you know.' Mark laughed nervously. 'I know you like to come close but, hell, do we always have to land on the buggers before you'll shoot at them?'

Jack smiled, knowing his approach of getting so close before firing unnerved his fighting companion, but his heavy heart remained as he observed the fields below them.

Though still struggling with his emotions, Jack was however forced to cast aside his sentiment as he noticed a strange cloud formation literally appear out of nowhere, which quickly positioned itself in front of his plane. It had a cube-like shape and, deep within, sheet lightening flickered. More alarmingly, the cloud was quickly moving towards them.

'Mark!' called Jack over his r/t. 'What the hell's that coming at us?'

'Shit!' replied Mark. 'Where did that come from? There was nothing there a minute ago! Best we get out of here—I don't like the look of that at all! Let's head for home now; it's getting dark anyway and you've got a date with that new WAAF, which might cheer you up a bit.' Banking their planes away from the weird phenomenon, they headed off, not taking the cloud as any real threat—not until they realised it was actually following them.

The two Spitfires flashed across the sky, racing toward Tangmere with the cloud-like object closely pursuing. Hardly believing what was happening, the two pilots pushed their planes to the limit, but the strange cloud nevertheless drew closer.

Suddenly, white light engulfed the two aircraft; the engines cut out and silence pressed in on them. Losing the horizon, the pilots rapidly became disorientated. The controls were soggy and unresponsive, and the radios quickly died. Frustratingly, although the airmen could still see each other in the strange illumination, they were unable to communicate. Deeper into the alien cloud the planes sank, the light turning from an angry red before mutating into a vortex of dark swirling colours. The men watched in horror as the aircraft began to dematerialise from the propellers. And when the effect reached the cockpits, they too disappeared.

Like their Spitfires, the men stretched, warped and flew apart, instantly reduced to atoms that went spinning wildly before being sucked through the vortex, right into the heart. Once there, they slowly reformed. When their senses returned, everything was restored like nothing had ever changed. With engines growling contentedly, the Spitfires dropped out from the cloud like a flicker of light. Soaring into an overcast sky and completely baffled by their experience, the two pilots could only breathe sighs of relief that they were alive. Appreciation soon passed, however, when, beneath their rain-lashed aircraft, appeared an endless wave-tossed ocean, an extensive island, and a large naval convoy.

CHAPTER TWO

Far out in the Atlantic, the English convoy, call sign L-405, ploughed on ponderously, heading for home. The ships had left America several days before, their cargo and personnel destined to assist England's war efforts against Hitler's Germany. The sea was a flat calm and the visibility endless, which was unusual in these waters.

The aircraft carrier Victorious, accompanied by the heavy cruiser Arcadier and the destroyers Plymouth and Hastings, were escorting five heavily laden cargo ships carrying a vast cache of various weaponry: two troop carriers, each with two thousand men aboard; one hospital ship; and three large oil tankers. On the bridge of Victorious, Captain Paul Rowsell lent against the armoured bulkhead overlooking the flight deck and scanned the surrounding ocean through powerful binoculars. A short, stocky man with thick chestnut hair, deep blue eyes and sporting a full Sir Francis Drake beard, he was the epitome of an English sea captain. It was a testament to the captain's abilities that he'd recently been assigned command of the truly awesome Victorious—the largest and most modern carrier in the English fleet. Following the Plymouth's earlier report, all his ships and crews were now on full-alert.

Whilst patrolling the rear of the convoy, the destroyer had briefly sighted a German U-boat. As he quickly scanned the sea around him, the captain considered the current state of the war: the army had suffered a major defeat in France, which had consequently ended with evacuation from Dunkirk. That had, at least, been highly successful, bringing many more troops home than expected, but they'd returned minus most of their equipment. He knew how vital it was that his convoy reached England— the cargo they carried was urgently needed in order for them to continue on with their defence. Being located by U-boats had been his worst nightmare which, it seemed, had now come to pass.

His thoughts were interrupted by the voice of Petty Officer Peter Pierce on the bridge close to him.

'Captain, a signal from Arcadier. Contact confirmed five miles ahead and to starboard of convoy, three U-boats in attack formation.'

The war had sought them out far from England's shores, and a desperate struggle now seemed inevitable. 'Right, Peter, let's go and get them. Send the Plymouth to join the Arcadier; they can depth-charge them together—that'll put them off a little for a while. We'll send our Swordfish to assist them and we'll immediately break formation of the merchant ships. The Hastings will remain at the rear of the convoy to cover our backs; there may be more of them behind us,' the captain said, strongly issuing his commands.

Through the periscope of the U35, Commander Kurt Galland watched with frustration as the sudden activity of the enemy convoy unfolded before him, suspecting that his small force had been sighted. 'Signal U79 and U82: crash-dive and prepare for attack by depth charges,' he instructed Paul Heinz, his radio operator. 'In this cursed calm, we've no chance of pressing home an unseen attack now.'

Commander Galland, the classic tall, blonde, handsome Aryan, was the son of a German trawler man. Unfazed by his humble origin, he had enlisted in the Navy with full intentions of eventually commanding a submarine. Single-mindedly, he'd worked his way through submarine training and gained his first commission. Serving in three submarines prior to reaching his goal, he'd been given command of U35 a year before. Already, his list of achievements comprised sinking three merchant ships and one destroyer—and all with this boat—thereby making him the top-scoring young commander in the U-boat fleet of present. Galland rotated the scope through three hundred and sixty degrees before submerging his boat. Fixing the image of the impending attack in his mind, his attention became diverted as he viewed something inexplicable approaching from behind the boat. A green-coloured fog crept up with a flickering pale yellow light simultaneously rolling in towards them. Leaving no time to react, the fog swirled over the U35. Galland felt the boat start to slowly turn under him, spinning faster and faster, until it was eventually pulled into a gigantic whirlpool, concealed within its maw. The control room swam before Galland's eyes, an increasing pressure overcoming his lungs until he felt unable to breathe.

In a boat filled with air, the captain was drowning and, within mere seconds, the darkness of subconscious consumed him.

From the bridge of Victorious, Rowsell watched as the strange, green fog appeared from nowhere. Rolling across the flight deck, it engulfed his ship. Immediately, the carrier was overrun by a gigantic wave, throwing her onto her beam ends. Spinning like a child's play top, the giant ship dropped into turbulence. As the ship sank deeper and deeper, Rowsell's last memory was the bizarre sight of Galland's U35 swirling over the flight deck, far above him.

When Galland eventually regained consciousness, he was still grasping the controls of the periscope but was slumped against its mast. Gathering his shattered senses as quickly as he could, he fixed his eyes to the lenses. At first sight, everything appeared to be normal: the boat seemed intact and the crew seemed nothing more than confused and disorientated, all still standing at their posts in the control room. However, considering the swearing he heard, what had just occurred clearly hadn't been a figment of the captain's imagination.

Turning back to the scope, Galland looked through the lenses once more, jumping back and rubbing his eyes in confusion. He stepped forward and looked around again: the British Navy was still out there, in more or less the same position relative to his boat. All previous similarities, however, ended there: the sea was now rough, with spray and rain streaming down the scope, consequently obscuring his vision; the sky was filled with black clouds, all racing behind the hills of a large landmass which now confronted him as if from nowhere.

The land was the biggest shock: Galland knew they should be far out at sea—hundreds of miles, in fact. It was this more so than anything else which caused him to question his eyes.

To his dismay, Galland saw that the U35 was about to run straight into a series of jagged rocks which had accumulated together, thus forming a reef just off-shore. White water smashed amongst the jagged teeth, jutting above the waves. With adrenaline coursing through his veins, Galland realised that his vessel was far too close to the bed of rocks. 'My God!' He exclaimed, to nobody in particular. 'It's happened to us as well!' Issuing a barrage of orders to the helmsman, Galland desperately steered the wallowing boat away from the rocks, attempting to head it back out to sea, narrowly missing the reef by mere yards.

Meanwhile, on Victorious, having also come round, the captain wasn't entirely convinced that he wasn't dreaming, instead holding the belief that what he was seeing couldn't possibly be any form of reality. From high up on the carrier, his view comprised a much greater area than Galland's, which didn't really help him as all he could see were more bizarre surroundings, thereby leaving him no wiser than the German commander. However, much like Galland, the proximity of the reef gave Rowsell little time to reflect on their general situation. Reacting instinctively, he issued an urgent command to his petty officer beside him on the bridge. 'There's no time to lose, Peter! Signal our ships to turn away now! We'll worry about regrouping out at sea later. Bugger the bloody U-boats—or anything else, for that matter; that reef is the biggest threat to us all right now!'

Pierce rapidly issued the relevant orders as the captain gripped the chart table, willing his charges to cooperate. Knowing everyone would be as disorientated as himself, Rowsell was grey with worry.

Having attended to his duties, Pierce returned. Taking up station beside the captain, he watched as the almost impossible task began of quickly rerouting the many pitching rolling ships in the hands of confused men.

Due to their present course, not all the Royal Navy ships were in immediate danger but, those which were, even having the advantage of the great power of their engines, were struggling to change course in enough time. The heavily laden merchantmen headed directly toward disaster, lacking the more responsive engines of the Navy boats. They were responding, the two men realised, but agonisingly slowly.

The captain continued to speak. 'If any of our ships end up on the reef, what's happened to us is academic; I don't see much chance of anyone surviving in that surf. But just what the hell has happened to us, Peter? I have to say, at the moment, I don't quite know where to even start on that one!'

Reacting swiftly, the helmsman had already come about, turning the huge ship back out to sea. With its size and inertia, however, the great ship responded ponderously. With all the enthusiasm of a geriatric snail, her bows swung to starboard, the jagged rocks disappearing from sight beneath the leading edge of the massive flight deck.

'Stop mucking about, old girl! You're taking far too long about this!' The helmsman muttered through gritted teeth. Although the reef had apparently disappeared under the ship, the height of the flight deck above the water and their position relative to its leading edge created an illusion. All on the bridge were aware of this, of course, but it nevertheless indicated how close they were.

Currently, the captain thought, they had only a fifty/fifty chance of saving the ship. But, as his thoughts swirled and his palms sweated, a movement in the sky distracted his attention. His mouth gaped open as two Spitfires banked and flew across the carrier above him. 'Where the hell did they come from?' he exclaimed.

As they flew above the fleet, Mark called over the r/t, 'Oh, bloody hell, Jack! What's going on? This all looks pretty bad to me! Where are we and what in heaven's name is the Navy doing pissing about in the rocks down there?'

'Search me! There's nothing familiar about any of this! Let's face it, Mark, we're up shit creek without a paddle here. It looks like a bloody disaster down there, but just what we're supposed to do about it all, fuck knows!' replied Jack. 'One thing's for certain, though: I'm running out of fuel. I've got to land somewhere pretty soon. It's not going to be easy, looking at this lot, but let's try to keep calm and take one thing at a time. For a start, I'll try to raise that carrier on the r/t; maybe they'll let us land on her; if not, perhaps they might know what's going on and tell us something useful! Actually, if they don't watch where they're going, there'll be nothing left to talk to anyway, let alone land on!' Jack contemplated attempting to land on a carrier, which would be a huge challenge as they simply weren't adapted for such a task and, more to the point, he didn't really know if it was even technically possible—neither of them had ever landed on a ship before, and no training they'd previously received had prepared them for such a manoeuvre. As a result, Jack wasn't unduly put out when his friend had an alternative suggestion.

'If we can stay in-flight for a little longer, Jack, it'd be better to fly to that island and see if there's anywhere there we can land. We'd probably have enough fuel to come back with if there isn't, and then I'll opt to ditch near the boats and hope to be picked up rather than commit suicide on that ship.'

'Okay, Mark, let's head for the island then. The Navy probably wouldn't want us to scratch their nice new carrier anyway!'

'They're likely to do that all on their own by the looks of it. God, they're close to those rocks now.'

They banked their planes toward the land and, approaching the island, both spotted the long, wide, crescent-shaped sandy beach nestling in the arms of a range of cliffs. 'Perfect emergency landing ground if you ask me,' said Mark, relieved he was now unlikely to get wet.

'Piece of cake,' replied Jack.

Turning their planes into the wind, the two men set them down together on the beach, the sand proving to be firm and reasonably level, achieving a successful, though albeit somewhat bumpy, landing. The airmen climbed from their cockpits, dropped onto the beach, and walked over to one another. 'Well, that's that bit over with,' said Mark with relief. 'Now, let's find the nearest pub!'

Jack shook his head and looked around them; although they were still alive, he was far from pleased with their surroundings. In front of them, the cliffs rose sheer for several hundred feet, and behind them the ocean tumbled and roared. The beach curved round to a promontory at either end as the cliffs ran into the water. Effectively, they were trapped on the beach with no way out other than to climb the cliffs or swim in less than desirable sea conditions.

'I hate heights almost as much as I hate water. You don't see any fuel around the place by any chance?' Mark asked with a grin.

'Just my luck to be stuck with the village idiot when the chips are down,' replied Jack with a smile. 'I'd like to run through this nightmare together in case we see something that might help us because, quite frankly, I don't know what else to do. Maybe when we discuss what's happened something will turn up. To be honest, Mark, I really think we're in deep shit this time—there's no way this is an everyday occurrence! I mean, just look around us! And not to mention the quite extraordinary way we got here in the first place.'

'I agree, including the shit bit. But, yes, let's go through it then. I can't see we've anything to lose,' replied Mark.

'Okay, let's give it a go. First, we were on patrol over Sussex. It was late in the evening. We had successfully attacked and destroyed a German bomber headed for France. We'd just returned to our operating height after the fight when a cube-shaped cloud with strange emanating pyrotechnics simply appeared out of nowhere.' Jack smiled and rolled his eyes with disbelief that he was telling the most unbelievable, yet accurate, tale. 'Not liking the look of it,' he continued, 'we turned away and dived down at full throttle. At close to four hundred miles an hour, the bloody thing still managed to overtake us, whereupon everything literally fell to pieces. The next thing we knew, we were flying above an ocean when we saw an island ahead of us. The Navy were also there. Oh and another thing: we weren't that low on fuel when the cloud got us.

'Anyway, it's safe to say that we're not in Sussex and, likewise, it's definitely not evening. I've just noticed something else as well: I'm not a botanist but I was raised on a farm and, looking at the plants around here, I can safely say I don't recognise many of them—and I really should. I've seen a plant like that one over there before, though; I'm sure it's the three-headed wheat—which, I might add, hasn't been grown since the time of the Egyptians! I know this because an archaeologist we knew had some seeds that he'd found in one of the Pyramids of Giza and asked my father to plant them in a small area on the farm to see what would happen. Unbelievably, after three thousand years, it grew just fine. I saw it growing and it looked just like that.

'Mark, I think the bottom line is that we don't know where we are, we don't know how we got here, and I honestly wonder if we are still in 1940. More to the point, I wonder if we're even still on Earth!'

'Well, I'm glad we went through that little exercise, Jack!' Mark said with a nervous laugh. 'I think it's answered all our questions. Sorry,

I meant it's raised quite a few more, which I didn't think was really the point. But, I pretty much agree with your account of events, although I have to say I hope you're wrong about the time and place observation! I think we could discuss this till the cows come home—but we still won't solve anything by ourselves. Anyway, before we get carried away, let's try our radios and see if we can contact anyone who can tell us what's happening and save us the bother. I'll transmit over the emergency wavelength and hope someone responds who *does* know what's going on.' Mark climbed back into his plane and turned on the r/t.

The carrier's bridge was in chaos: not only were they struggling to avoid the rocks themselves, but just about the whole convoy was trying to contact them all at once, each trying to communicate their own specific problems. Totally shot away by events, the captains and crews of the convoy were all looking to their commanders to magically devise solutions. Trying manfully to provide the lead they required in these unheard of conditions, the captain began to assess their status. Starting from the basics, he established that everything mechanical on Victorious was working as it had been. With the exception of the compasses— which were spinning uselessly—all equipment appeared to be working satisfactorily. In both instances, he found that to be the case right across the fleet.

Preventing some of the ships from continuously broadcasting mayday calls, which interfered with the immediate need for local communications, the captain proved two more things: only local communications were functioning, and any attempt at contact further afield resulted in heavy static. He stopped the reports from coming in regarding submarine attacks; he felt these were erroneous, fuelling the panic and confusion, and were preventing the reef from getting the ship's full attention, consequently adding to the fleet's troubles.

In actual fact, the German U-boats were in no shape to attack, suffering the same problems as the British ships. At least Galland didn't have the numbers to contend with, and now, having narrowly avoided wrecking his submarines on the rocks, he led his boats away from the British fleet. With the immediate danger eradicated, he ordered his captains to attend a conference aboard U35 to consider an emergency plan; any thoughts of hostilities had long left his mind.

Things slowly improved for Captain Rowsell. His ship, which had brushed the rocks as it came about, had sustained no appreciable damage and was safely away from the reef. His destroyers and the cruiser had never been in any danger as, coincidently, they were sailing away from the reef when they arrived. Nevertheless, he could see that, unless he could regain command of the merchantmen immediately, they were headed for one of the worst naval disasters in British history. Proactively, he took personal control of the radio, sending messages to each of the craft. 'For the captains of all merchant ships: you must comply immediately. I repeat: comply immediately. Follow my original directive: turn away from the coast and head out to sea. Keep all surrounding shipping in sight, and only use your radios if absolutely necessary. Post lookouts to warn of rocks and U-boats, and then stand by for my further orders.' He then concentrated on his warships: 'Plymouth and Hastings: take up stations in-board the merchant fleet and shepherd them away from the reef. Get those ships together and form them in line astern. Arcadier, take the lead and steam at eight knots; Victorious will take the rear and deal with the stragglers.' He then dispatched the torpedo bombers due to leave before the fog engulfed them all, commanding they fly off immediately and ordering them to provide continuous air cover above the fleet.

As he watched his planes leave the ship and begin circling the convoy, Rowsell knew there was nothing more he could do for the moment.

Gradually, the fleet overcame their problems, painfully reforming in line astern and heading out into the ocean and away from the rocky coast.

Between them all, they'd avoided creating a new naval scrapyard as their initial contribution to this strange place, with thanks mainly to the shepherding skills of the two destroyers. The ships tore about amongst the merchant boats like two berserk terriers, each with dense black smoke flying from their funnels, bullying and cajoling them into shape.

Finally, Captain Rowsell relaxed a little as he realised the immediate danger was subsiding: short of an attack by the U-boats, as far as he could imagine in this strange location, his command was safe for now.

However, like the airmen now imprisoned on the island, no one in the fleet knew where they were or how they had got there. Totally overcast and with no compasses, the navigators were unable to confirm their position or where to head to next. With only local radio communications functioning, the fleet was undoubtedly trapped, and its commander was in a quandary.

CHAPTER THREE

Myriddian Amis, Chief Science Officer to the King of Atlantis, sat devastated at his desk. With his eyes unfocused, he stared at his communicator. He'd just had a conversation with Joel Barr, his deputy, and now his mind was reeling with the extraordinary news. Amis, a thin, weedy man with a pointed face and grey, balding pate, stared sightlessly, his narrow, pale-green eyes flickering with concern.

For many months, Amis and his team had been striving to reactivate an alien machine left on Earth by his forebears' ancient benefactors. He now knew that this tool, in the hands of its creators, transported matter from place to place instantaneously. In his hands, however, it had proved time and time again not to be quite that simple. To add salt of the seas to his already raw wounds, Barr had just given him the results of today's test, and Amis was now having great difficulty coming to terms with their findings.

It had been intended that a batch of weapons be transported from Atlanta, the capital of Atlantis, to a floating platform on the sea near to Kira, a medium-sized, lightly inhabited island two hundred miles to the south. This was to be the first of yet another series of tests which Amis had thought, up until this moment, would be considerably more satisfactory than any of their previous attempts. He again reconsidered the situation.

Under Barr's supervision, the machine had been activated, and the weaponry he'd stated to transport had duly disappeared from Atlanta, as intended. Monitoring the platform from his recording equipment, Barr expected to see the weapons they'd just sent materialise but, whilst still displaying an empty platform, the equipment picked up something he hadn't expected: appearing out of thin air, a large military force had materialised on the sea; this force had apparently been complete with flying machines, undersea craft and surface vessels. Despite being barely recognisable in appearance to Barr, it was nevertheless clear as to their purpose. Of their own weaponry, however, there was no sign at all. Panicking, Joel Barr had screamed at his team to turn off the machine and to stay well away, at least until he'd consulted with their chief. At that point, he had contacted Amis and totally spoilt what the Chief Science Officer had, up until that point, believed had been a quite satisfactory day.

Amis knew the king was becoming impatient with him, and this new set of events was now likely to cause a reaction much like a petulant child who hadn't got his own way yet again. Unlike a child, however, the king would be likely to visit upon Amis something extremely nasty, thereby making it even less likely he'd ever receive the considerable financial gain he'd been promised for the overall success of the project. After all, bringing a large, apparently well-armed and potentially hostile force to the king's doorstep was possibly not what the king had in mind considering Amis's diligent and expensive research.

Stung by the thought, Amis became annoyed with the ancient benefactors whom he now felt were actually highly responsible for his current predicament, bearing in mind the unnatural evolution they'd foisted upon his ancestors. The God-like creators of the equipment—which was causing him so much trouble recently—had pre-historically inhabited the earth. Now long departed, they still briefly returned from time to time, continuing to influence its affairs. He considered at this moment that he, personally, might have been far better off without their blasted interference. With this thought in mind, he reflected upon his own knowledge of history, considering these timeless aliens and their involvement with his people in the past.

When occupying the Earth, the ancients had created a power source to drive their machinery and run their society. This source utilised a force produced by crystals which had been brought to Earth from another dimension. The multi-faceted complex structure remained fully functional to this day—presumably as did the few machines they still required for the purposes of their infrequent visits. During their last visit two centuries ago, they'd chosen to share some of this technology with the newly emerging Atlantien society.

Although at the time still primitive, the Atlantiens were nevertheless the most advanced society on Earth: the people were intelligent and innovative, and actively enjoyed a rudimentary society. Obviously wishing to advance these traits, the Ancients donated some of their existing technology—and subsequently created new technology—specifically tailored to the Atlantiens' needs. This had radically altered the lives of the citizens, and short-circuited centuries of natural evolution. With the benefit of these gifts, the ancestors had evolved at a prodigious rate, and today they commanded a highly technological society with an all-encompassing infrastructure of their own.

It would seem the Ancients had left artefacts hidden on Earth, holding secrets they'd not shared, and all possibly with a view to employing them again at some time in the future. Nevertheless, that point, Amis recognised, was highly speculative; to date they'd only found one of these machines, although it would appear that the infernal resistance had found another similar. He hoped to Ra they'd find no more, as this one—which had been recently unearthed by archaeologists working for the king—was more than enough, in his opinion. Following its discovery, it had been immediately passed on to Amis, and now the whole bloody mess was sitting right in his lap.

It had been clear from the outset that the Ancients had produced it, but its overall purpose or how to bring it to life had proved to be frustratingly elusive. Technologically, this machine was radically different from anything ever encountered before, and was of such complexity it reached way beyond their comprehension. Having been produced by a non-human race, combined with the fact that its creators had kindly omitted any accompanying instructions, would, in all probability, mean that the finer points of the machine's operation would always be incomprehensible to them. Dammed inconsiderate, in Amis's opinion, when one considers just how precise the operating instructions were for the fantastic machines they had handed over to his people.

In any case, it had been only a fluke that had led to the identification of this particular artefact's purpose; a fluke, he sadly remembered, which had cost the lives of the three scientists Amis had originally assigned to its study. Having spent some months with the artefact, these people remained at a loss when striving to ascertain its function. Four months into their research, they were still of the opinion that, if it was indeed a tool of some kind, it must be possible to activate it, which spoke volumes as to the great progress they were actually making. Ultimately, however, they unknowingly activated the machine, and were completely unprepared for the resulting disaster which befell them. Blissfully unaware that it was now functioning, the three men had walked onto the machine's primary chamber emendator. At that time, none of them knew of the primary chambers or their functions—and whether they knew much more now was a point up for considerable debate. But, irrespective of the knowledge Amis's team had acquired during their academic journey up until that point, nothing could have prepared them for the results which subsequently ensued.

That fateful day, a green cube of energy—resembling some sort of fog or mist—had begun to seep out from the emendator, immediately dematerialising the men. In the blink of an eye, as if they had never been there, Amis's men had disappeared without a trace, never to be seen again.

Learning from the unfortunate experience of the original scientists, Amis had, at least, discovered what this machine was originally designed to do. Now focused in the right direction, he and his team had finally unlocked more of its secrets, succeeding in moving small objects over short distances—but they were still nowhere near achieving its full potential. Driven by the king's military leaders and their own scientific curiosity, which was further encouraged by their minor successes, they had nevertheless pressed on with the research. The team worked day and night, without concern for the tides, focused only on the king's brief: use the machine, adapt it as necessary, instantly transport ordnance and men to any battlefield (as his military desired), and transport away again when military missions are complete. Amis, undoubtedly frustrated and pressured by his leader, felt the brief was a tall order under the circumstances. In addition to the already overwhelming pressures, the situation was helped less by the resistance movement of Atlantis, which had resulted in the recent defection of three of his top people, all of whom he had considered crucial to the project. Ultimately, losing Lara

Freyr had been the greatest loss, as she had had the sharpest mind of them all. Notwithstanding losing her, Amis was fully aware he must still meet the king's expectations—in spite of this setback. Furthermore, Amis acknowledged that, should he succeed in fulfilling the king's brief, it would negate the need for expensive and time-consuming logistics, quickly expanding the king's dominance across the remainder of the free world. Amis and his team realised that, fully operational, this machine could greatly assist the king in devastating the remaining far-flung pockets of resistance, and would subsequently further his desired goal of world domination: the ability to have his forces instantly appear at any place, with the means of conquering any resistance within the locality, would quickly put his enemies out of business.

The main reason for why they'd currently failed to achieve battle success—in spite of their vastly superior strength—was largely attributable to the enemy's ability to attack the king's overextended supply lines. However, with the transporter operational, there would be no supply lines for the resistance to attack, no waste of personnel and vehicles in the logistics of it all—and, in the king's military opinion, subsequently no problem remaining. This, of course, was easy for him to say but not quite so simple for Amis to achieve.

Nevertheless, Amis felt that, although they were clearly struggling with the Ancients' science, he and his team had done pretty well to grasp as much as they had of the principles involved in the transporter. Simplistically speaking, they'd discovered that, in order to produce the desired effects, the process required employing the power produced by the Ancients' crystals in conjunction with electromagnetic influences and the natural force of earth's gravity. The balancing of these elements, however, was absolutely critical, and the frustrating thing was that the machine undoubtedly embodied everything required to perfectly complete the task. Unfortunately for him, it had a set of controls which, amongst other things, involved positioning different sized crystals into varying receptacles at varying depths, providing an almost infinite combination of possible settings which completely defied human logic. All they'd ever needed was to discover how to set it up and then everything would be fine; however, they'd not managed to succeed in this area so far, instead having to conduct various experiments and trials—some of which had produced some very bizarre results.

With so much time behind them and their portfolio of past empirical researches growing thick, a great many of Amis's fellow scientists were expressing their concern at the wisdom of continuing on their currently experimental path; indeed, even before the Big Event two weeks ago, some had claimed the king might opt to warp time, playing with this unknown and potentially hazardous technology. It was just after this bizarre event that the three scientists had defected. In truth, clearly frightened by what had happened, Amis couldn't blame his staff.

Revisiting the events in his mind, Amis pondered the occurrence for a moment. Two weeks ago, they'd intended to transport a Hovertak fighter aircraft from Atlanta to a tiny uninhabited island owned by the military, located fifty miles to the east of Atlantis. Amis himself had been overseeing the test, and had, as he'd thought at the time, correctly configured the crystals within their receptacles and adjusted the remaining myriad of balancing controls to perform the task. Moving across and inspecting the primary chamber emendator prior to placing it beneath the aircraft, he'd noticed a small stone lying on it. At that point he'd been distracted by one of his colleagues who'd needed his assistance and, with his attention averted to other tasks, he'd left the stone where it lay. Having dealt with his colleague's query, Amis had returned to the transporter's controls, aligned the largest crystal, and switched it on. As he'd not yet touched the crystal which activated the primary chamber, nothing else should have occurred. Unfortunately, however, something most definitely did, and that precluded his next step.

Had the process been simple and had it gone as planned, Amis would have slid the emendator beneath the aircraft and placed its twin inside for the return journey; naturally, he would have removed the stone in the process—although that probably wasn't the point, really, as it turned out. This time, however, when he switched on the machine, the primary chamber discharged from the emendator, and the stone being the only object encompassed within it was transported away. Instantly, the stone arrived on the island where it exploded with a force so great the landmass was entirely obliterated, and a great tidal wave was consequently stirred, which smashed into the eastern shores of Atlantis only a half-hour later. This caused untold damage to the shipping in Atlanta's harbour and to the waterfront properties running along the coast. In mere seconds, the shock wave had reached Amis in Atlanta, closely followed by the sound of the gigantic explosion. Dreading the consequences and virtually certain he was the cause, he'd shut down the machine in a panic, accidentally realigning the crystals as he did so.

Worryingly, Amis's recording equipment on the island appeared to have failed, and he subsequently had no visual record of what had occurred. Absolutely desperate for information, he'd dispatched the Hovertak—which he'd previously intended to transport—with the hope of surveying the area, instructing the pilot to keep him informed throughout the flight. Through the communication system in the lab, the pilot's voice had constantly updated the remaining team of the damage to the island, his tone taking on a note of hysteria when it became obvious that the military installation was no longer there. Shortly afterwards, Amis had been summoned before the king, convinced he'd be terribly punished for the damage he'd caused to his personal property—let alone everyone else's. As he'd left to attend the king, Amis remembered how hard he'd tried not to dwell on the small matter of vaporising sixty square miles of important military testing grounds and another rake of Land Forces' Chief Maltor's precious equipment.

Dreading the immediate issues, Amis had been totally unprepared for the reception the king had given him. On the way to face what he was sure would be dire consequences, he'd convinced himself that his reputation was now irrecoverably damaged and that his very survival was highly questionable. The king's affable and friendly attitude, however, had initially left him totally nonplussed. Returning to his laboratory some time later, he'd been able to reflect on this meeting with the king—and that was exactly what he'd been doing ever since, albeit with ever lowering optimism. In truth, at that time, he'd not expected to return anywhere ever again, and although still ecstatic in that respect, his new orders from the king made his original brief look simple by comparison. In his panic, he'd missed the point—which the king clearly hadn't: although the experiment had caused general mayhem and loss of life, it had also quite inadvertently produced a potential weapon; a weapon of prodigious power, and one which the king thought, given the circumstances, was acquired without significant cost—provided Amis could now manufacture it for him.

Seeking to find a way of wriggling out of his immediate problems, Amis had taken the cowardly way out and adopted the age-old method of self-preservation: he'd lied. He'd assured the king, without any real basis for such a statement, that he could fulfil the brief, qualifying his words by requesting more time to safely produce such a weapon. He'd lied knowing all too well that the chances of replicating the settings which had brought about the explosion were remote at best. In his mind, he berated himself for the umpteenth time for not being more careful when he'd shut it down. Ultimately, he'd lied to temporarily save himself, to extend his existence as much as possible, and all in the hope that he'd get lucky and be able to do what he had stupidly promised. Then, the thought that his whole future rested upon luck had given him some degree of comfort, though it ran down his spine like a cold sliver; now, however, mere luck seemed remote and foolish, and the feeling had since become positively artic.

Quite simply, Amis had lied because he'd no choices left.

Now, with time quickly seeping away, this current circumstance had topped it all off. No further forward with the weapon—today's fiasco was just about the final straw. His reveries were interrupted by the arrival of Barr, bringing with him the visual recordings from the laboratory.

'Well, Myriddian, I hope you're satisfied now? We should have left the bloody thing alone after the last time! You knew how concerned we all were,' Barr said, having brought up the visuals on Amis's office viewer.

'You assume, Joel, that I have the luxury of choice in the matter— an assumption which is far beyond accurate, may I add. I'll thank you in future to restrict your comments to something more constructive, or to otherwise keep them to yourself.'

'I'm sorry, Myriddian, but this just gets worse. The island was bad enough, but what happened, happened, and it was over. Unless that fleet disappears again, it's probably here to stay. What if those people out there turn out to be hostile?'

'We don't know anything yet, and even if they are, there aren't that many of them.'

'There may not need to be—and then what happens?'

'Look, Joel, I don't like it either. It's a matter for the military now; we can't do anything about it ourselves because I can't see any way of sending them back with our machine.'

'Even if we could, back to where?'

'I don't care *where*, Joel, just as long as they aren't here! That would do me just fine right about now. Go back to the lab, get everyone together, and study those settings between yourselves. If it was us that brought them here, maybe, just maybe, we can get rid of them again. I'll join you as soon as I've spoken with Chief Maltor, and hope to Ra we can do something about this.'

Amis watched Barr leave his office, the set of his shoulders telling Amis he'd given up before he'd even started. And who could blame him? Amis was at a loss himself. In theory, it should have been impossible for the machine to produce such a result and, quite frankly, the more he thought about it, the more he realised it *was* impossible—but the notion gave him little comfort. However, there was an alternative: he knew the resistance were working with a similar machine and were pursuing similar researches. With that in mind, he was now pretty sure that *they* were the ones who were actually responsible for such a catastrophe; they'd probably even timed the whole thing to coincide with his latest experiment, thereby making it appear it was all his doing. He thought it unlikely that they'd done everything solely to ruin him, but it almost certainly would.

The dreams of power and wealth to which he so strongly aspired crashed down around him. Aside from the personal damage they may have inflicted upon him with their actions, just what had the resistance brought into the world off the coast of Kira anyway? And, more to the point, why?

Realising he couldn't delay further, Amis contacted the king's military Chiefs of Staff. Aware that he wasn't their favourite person due to his constant problems with the machine, he also had the added concern that he was particularly unpopular with the chief of Land Forces, Rak Maltor. Maltor had suffered not only the major losses of men in earlier malfunctions, but also equipment—losses which culminated in the total loss of his island testing ground and all it contained. With events only occurring two weeks ago, the wounds of mourning were still raw, and so Amis's heart had dropped into the vast ocean when Chief Maltor demanded he immediately attend a meeting at his headquarters.

Amis left the scientific administration building, climbed into his Hovertrans, and embarked upon his journey towards what would undoubtedly be a very difficult—and, quite possibly, disastrous—discussion.

Floating through the streets of Atlanta as he headed for the meeting, he contemplated the city surrounding him. Thronged with the capital's citizens, its innumerable streets were crowded, with people travelling in all directions, all busy with their daily activities, exuding a sense of purpose. Hovertrans vehicles of all sizes drifted through and over the city, ferrying commercial and domestic requirements. The high hills surrounding the capital were, in the main, lush and bright green, only occasionally broken by freshly ploughed fields of fertile dark brown earth. Hung in an azure sky, the bright sun highlighted the soft yellow stone of the buildings, and shadows danced beneath the many trees that stood elegantly swaying in the light warm breeze. Construction was evident everywhere, and the attention to detail of both the partially completed and newly finished buildings was outstanding.

The king was developing the city, and Amis thought it successfully reflected his enormous wealth. Actually, he'd missed the point a little, as the king used the ill-gotten gains raised from the heinous taxation of his own people coupled with the riches of the lands he had conquered to fund it. Dominating all other structures, new or old, was the overwhelming golden pyramid built by the Ancients at the dawn of time. One-third down from its peak, and exactly in the centre of that space, it housed a huge crystal that gave its power to the city and way beyond. The power it generated provided lighting, heating, communications and transportation—power he'd tapped into in order to pursue his questionable experiments.

As usual, Amis had completely failed to recognise the worried expressions on the citizens' faces, all of whom were rushing around him. He was oblivious to the general disrepair some of the once beautiful older buildings had fallen into and to the ever-present sinister black uniformed heavily armed police. Being one of the king's favoured subjects—at least for now—he was insulated from the oppressive taxation and other repressive practices the king imposed on his normal subjects. Although clearly now threatened, Amis still had a privileged life for the moment. He had been looking forward to a huge reward from the king—both in wealth and position—when he had achieved the objective of perfecting the transporter; a bonus which became eye-watering if he could also produce the super weapon he'd promised the king. However, in light of the day's cock-up, he felt the cold wind of change blowing his way, leaving him feeling distinctly uncomfortable. 'Bugger the bloody resistance. Whether they meant to or not, they've finished me this time,' he muttered to himself.

Eventually arriving at the Land Forces headquarters, Amis parked his Hovertrans and approached the building, an imposing structure upon which no expense had been spared. It achieved an air of menace which had delighted the designing architect, thereby fulfilling his brief—and probably saving his life.

A heavily armed soldier awaited Amis's arrival, and he escorted him through a labyrinth of passages to his meeting with the Chiefs of Staff. They travelled down passages hung with priceless works of art and glistening gold and silver statuary. Marble tiles adorned the floors across which soldiers moved busily in all directions.

Finally arriving at their destination, the accompanying soldier pushed open a door, leading Amis into a large meeting room. Dominating the room, a picture of the king gazed down from high up on the wall opposite the entrance door, his cold, calculating eyes watching the proceedings. Seated around a fine, highly polished wooden table sat the three Chiefs of Staff; Amis couldn't fail to notice they appeared to be somewhat less than happy to see him. His heart instantly began to beat faster as his palms sweated and his hands trembled. Next to the king himself, these three men were the most powerful people on the planet. Seeing their general demeanour now, he knew for certain that this meeting wasn't going to go well for him.

CHAPTER FOUR

'**H**ey, Mark, get back down here! You won't believe this!' called Jack urgently before Mark had time to operate the radio. Directly over their Spitfires, Jack had seen something moving above the cliff.

Jumping down from his cockpit, Mark stood beside him, looking up to where Jack was pointing. Something was definitely moving. A stunned silence fell upon them when it became clear that the *something* was, in fact, some*body*—somebody who appeared to be standing in thin air at least ten feet above the cliff top. The figure was dressed in a tight-fitting one-piece garment of a silver hue, and seemed to have a square object resembling a parachute rig strapped to its back. A slight heat haze seemed to be emanating from the pack's base. In the person's hands was a silver rod which flattened out at the front and connected to the backpack with a flexible tube at the rear. The figure wore a domed helmet encasing its head, complete with a black-tinted visor.

'Herman the German that isn't,' said Mark, recovering first, 'but God only knows what it really is. It's armed, though, I reckon. Whatever it's holding looks bloody dangerous to me. It looks more like a spaceman than anything else! I think we'd be wise to defend ourselves, you know.'

Reaching into their flying suits, the two men produced their pistols which, aside from the planes' armaments, which were clearly useless to them in this situation, were the only weapons they possessed. Crouching down beside Jack's Spitfire in anticipation of a confrontation with the apparition, the duo peered up from under its wing.

Suddenly, with the men watching, the figure slowly descended in front of the cliff face until its feet finally came to rest on the sand. Lowering its weapon, the being unplugged the tube from the backpack, and set it down on the ground. Stepping forward, the figure then raised its hands to the helmet, removing the headwear and cradling it beneath one arm. The 'spaceman' appeared to be a normal—although surprisingly extremely attractive—young human female. Her long silver hair framed her stunning face and the tight suit accentuated her curvaceous body. The airmen relaxed, viewing her as being far from hostile.

'Jack, you're right, old boy; this isn't 1940 or Earth. We died in that fight with the German bomber and we're obviously in heaven,' said Mark.

'Maybe, Mark, but it looks like she wants to talk, so hide the guns and we'll go and hear what she has to say, shall we?'

'Okay, Wing Co., let's do it, but I hope that lovely creature speaks English. My Angel's a little rusty, you know.'

Stepping carefully from under the wing, the two pilots slowly approached the woman standing beneath the cliff.

As they approached, she held up a hand in greeting and, in perfect English, said 'Hi! I'm glad you've arrived safely. You may be pleased to know I can tell you exactly what's happened to you and why, though I fear you probably won't like it much at first. I've come to welcome you here on behalf of my people and, as I've said, to explain everything to you. We mean you no harm; in fact, quite the contrary. I can help you through this, and I'll make it as easy as possible for you—if you'll be kind enough to allow me.'

'Blimey, old chap, that's handy,' Mark whispered incredulously. 'She *does* speak English.'

'I'm Jack Bannerman,' Jack began. 'My companion here is Mark Calloway. We're both officers in the Royal Air Force. I suppose we're pleased to meet you since we've no idea what's going on, but that rather depends on what you're going to tell us. Anyway, we'd certainly appreciate knowing just what's happened to us. Since you're clearly expecting us, I can only assume you know a lot more than we do at this point, so I think I speak for both myself and Mark when I say we'd be more than happy to discuss what's going on.'

'I'm Rema Sark, a scientist and field commander within the resistance movement of Atlantis. You've just landed on Kira—an island two hundred miles from the island of Atlantis itself. You're far from your own timeframe and are now thousands of years before it—living in the past, as it were.'

'Holy cow! Break it to us gently, why won't you, Miss Sark? You really expect us to believe that load of old codswallop, do you?' Mark cried. 'Sorry, Jack, we were both wrong; we've obviously landed on Planet Idiot here.'

'I'm telling you the truth, though I'm not surprised at your reaction,' replied Rema. 'I can, of course, prove the point, but it's going to be difficult to do so right here. Currently, we've big problems in the world, and we're actually hoping you'll be able—and willing—to help us solve them. You've obviously seen the ships out there; we also brought them for the same reason.' Rema looked from Mark to Jack and considered their bemused expressions. 'Our reasons are genuine and warranted, but these will become clear later; I would rather move away from here before discussing them. I don't think we're in any immediate danger but, nevertheless, we need to get off this beach. I'd prefer it if you'd accompany me to my base where we can talk in comfort, and I'll explain everything fully when we're safely inside. If you'd care to stand either side of me and put one arm each around my shoulders, the anti-gravity pack will take us to the top of the cliff, and then we can get under way.'

Jack and Mark exchanged curious glances.

'Atlantis? Anti-gravity?' Mark mouthed to Jack, shaking his head in disbelief.

Despite their reservations, the two men silently conceded that they had no more appealing options than journeying with the woman, and so they did as she asked. Rema replaced her helmet and picked up her weapon, reconnecting it to the pack. She activated a control and, within moments, they were lifted from the beach before slowly floating up to the top of the cliff. Upon arriving at the top, Rema used her backpack's controls once more which moved them away from the cliff's edge, and lightly set them down onto firm ground again.

'That was the strangest sensation I've ever felt. Flying without wings and all that... somewhat disconcerting,' Mark mumbled.

'You got that right. Still, you've got to admit: it's an amazing gadget. Makes me wonder just what else these people use.' Jack turned his attention to Rema. 'Okay, Miss Sark, that was unusual, I have to say.

Whatever that equipment is, I'd say it clearly isn't from my world. I really don't want to believe you but there's obviously something in what you're telling us.' Jack glanced to Mark and then back to Rema. 'To be honest, I'm more concerned right now about us just coming along with you without question. We could be walking straight into a trap. Maybe we won't like it here, maybe we'll love it—but either way, it would be good to stay alive long enough to find out. How do we know you'll let that happen once you've got us inside your base?'

'I appreciate your concerns, Wing Commander Bannerman, but if killing you was our aim, I could have already fulfilled that objective. Oh, and by the way, it's Rema.'

'Thank you, Rema, and we're Jack and Mark. However, you might not have found it that easy to dispose of us. We were ready to defend ourselves, you know.'

'I'm sure you were, Jack.' She lifted the silver rod, pointing it at the cliff top two hundred yards away. A bright purple ball flew from the end and exploded against the cliff edge with force akin to a five hundred pound bomb. It blew a large section away, causing a significant landslide which tumbled angrily down to the beach below. Rema turned and smiled at the men, striding off into the forest, beckoning the airmen to follow.

'I'm glad you didn't say "you and who's army?", Jack, or you'd look a bit silly now, I reckon,' Mark said grinning. 'But, on the whole, I'm not sure whether I found that demonstration particularly comforting either.'

'Well, she's either on the level or a bloody psychopath. In any case, we've got to find out now, haven't we?' Jack replied.

The trio walked for some time, penetrating the green wilderness deeper and deeper until they eventually came upon an entrance to a cave beneath a small hill, through which Rema led them. The cave floor sloped downwards, twisting into a narrow passage with a low ceiling. As they moved through the cave, the darkness became more and more dense. Rema reached for her pack controls, and a bright light burst from the end of the silver rod. The men could now see that the walls, floor and ceiling of the passageway were completely smooth, like glass. It appeared the passage was manufactured rather than a natural formation, and again Jack wondered what forces had been employed for its excavation.

Eventually arriving at the end of the passageway, the men were confronted by a solid stone wall. Rema moved another control on her pack, and the light from the silver rod deepened to a dark, furious red. She directed the light at the rock face, which lost its solid appearance. Wavering and shimmering before them, the rock's face dissolved away, revealing a small room behind. The room, which was comfortably warm and illuminated by a soft pleasant light, contained several exits. In the room, another pretty young woman was sat at a desk, speaking into a communication instrument whilst writing on a notepad in front of her. The woman also wore her hair long, but it was a deep shiny chestnut colour which matched her large, oriental eyes. Clearly curvaceous, Jack was amused to see Mark craning over to observe her body concealed beneath the desk.

As they entered the room, the wall behind them returned to its former solid state. 'Just as you feared, it looks like we're trapped good and proper now, Jack,' said Mark, staring in dismay at the thickening wall behind him. 'I hope this lot really are on the level, or I reckon they've just taken in the most gullible pair of idiots this side of wherever we are.'

'I'm sorry, Mark,' Rema said, turning to the pair of nervous men. 'I should have prepared you for that. As I've said, you're not a prisoner.' Rema turned to the girl behind the desk. 'Tiea, please open the portal to prove the point.'

Tiea reached beside her to a small control consul and operated a control, which dissolved the rock face as before.

'You're free to leave if you wish but, obviously, I'd prefer that you stayed, at least until you know what you're facing here,' said Rema to the airmen.

'Well, seeing as there's nowhere else for us to go that we know of, I think it best we stay with you and clarify the situation, but I appreciate knowing we're only here because we want to be,' said Mark, instantly feeling a little more relieved. 'But please don't spring things like that on us again if you can help it, Rema; it's not good for the old constitution.'

'I agree with Mark,' began Jack, 'we must stay and listen to your story, but try to remember if you can, you may be comfortable with unconventional doorways and the like, but things like that will upset us a bit, bearing in mind we're new here. Judging by what we've seen already, it's going to be something of a problem to us around here.'

'I'll try to bear that in mind, Jack, but if you've any problem, please ask because, of course, I'm comfortable with my own technology; explaining to you what seems perfectly natural to me is going to be difficult to remember. I'm bound to miss things as we carry on but, nevertheless, you'll soon pick it all up, I'm sure. Anyway, if you can bear with me, I must get out of this gear before we begin.'

Rema crossed to the nearest door. Opening it, she revealed a storeroom containing racks of equipment, all of which were identical to hers. Entering the storeroom and leaving the door ajar, she undressed without embarrassment, removing her suit and backpack and placing them on an empty rack in-line with the rest. Partially undressed, her white silky undergarment showed off a deep even tan and accentuated her jutting breasts. The skimpy one-piece admirably set-off her slim waist, perfect behind and long, slender legs. Ignoring the bizarre situation, Jack felt a surge of desire for this half-naked stranger, but curiously felt he recognised her from somewhere which succeeded in disturbing him somewhat.

Noticing his interest, Rema smiled coyly, reaching behind her to remove a short light-brown dress from a peg on the wall. Donning this and stepping into a pair of sandals, she returned to the reception area.

Whilst she was changing, Mark had wandered over to the girl at the desk and was engaging her in one of his—in his opinion only, of course—best chat-up lines. 'My dear girl,' said Mark, 'I'm the best and bravest pilot in our King's air force. Because of this, I'm constantly called upon to face terrible dangers. Sadly, my life may therefore be short. Come with me now and we'll make mad passionate love together. I offer you this opportunity whilst I'm still around. You will, of course, experience ecstasy which will far exceed your wildest dreams.'

The young woman giggled at Mark's outrageous comment, but surprisingly showed little inclination to accept his generous and clearly selfless offer.

'Mark, you'll have no more success with that old chestnut here than you did back at home,' laughed Jack.

Mark wore a hurt expression and grumbled, 'I don't see why. After all, I'm only telling the truth. It's not my fault they can't see it, is it? What's so difficult about it anyway?' Mark shrugged as the room filled with laughter.

'Would you like anything to eat or drink before we settle down to talk?' asked Rema.

'Thank you, Rema, that's a great idea,' replied Jack. Mark nodded his head.

Rema took them to another room containing six long, trestle tables, all surrounded by many upright chairs. In the corner stood a large square cabinet, on the face of which were images of various refreshments, each with its own selection button.

Rema led them to the cabinet. 'Just press the button under any picture of food or drink you fancy, and it'll appear in the tray there at the bottom of the machine.'

'You must have some pretty small chefs working in there then,' said Mark, grinning.

Having made their choices, Mark and Jack settled down to eat around the nearest table. The airmen found the food they'd chosen to be surprisingly good considering it had apparently been instantaneously produced by a machine. They were particularly impressed with the drinks; they had no idea what they were made from, but they were alcoholic and chilled and hit the spot nicely. When the meal was finished, Mark said, 'That machine is definitely the best piece of kit I've seen around here so far.'

'Yes, I agree with you there,' said Jack. 'It'd go down well back home, that's for sure. Maybe can we take it with us when we leave or, better yet, show us how to make it, Rema; that thing would make us a fortune, eh, Mark?' Jack smiled.

'Sadly, Jack, neither will be possible, I'm afraid,' said Rema. 'Now we've eaten, please sit back and relax and I'll try to put you in the picture. Try to save any questions you may have until I've finished, if you can. You'll find it hard to accept some, if not all, of what I'm about to tell you, but it'll probably be easier to explain if I'm not interrupted.'

The airmen glanced awkwardly at one another before nodding in agreement. Sitting back in their seats, they sat silently, wondering what tall tales were about to unfold.

CHAPTER FIVE

Kurt Galland watched from the conning tower of U35 as U79 and U82, the other two boats within his command, slowly emerged from the depths, one to port and one to starboard of his position. He watched the green water slide from the superstructures of the submarines, spilling down until they'd fully surfaced. Although they were his comrades, he still felt menaced as their black forms slowly rose from the depths. Two powerful war machines, their sleek lines now exposed above the water, each with their deadly torpedoes aboard, were capable of destroying the strongest ships afloat.

If he were to be completely honest with himself, he'd never been entirely comfortable with the dictates of his job, which primarily required him to sink as many enemy ships as possible, sending fellow mariners to a watery grave. The principles of submarine warfare required him to sneak up on his prey, unseen, and destroy them, always in a rain of fire and terror. Such principles and methods of attack were not necessarily his own, but he had to accept that he was nevertheless good at implementing them just the same. That aside, the current situation was extraordinary, and he hoped he'd be as good when it came to resolving the problems he now faced. He had his own theory explaining their plight, and he'd commanded the other captains to meet with him on-board the U35 to discuss their future plans. In the meantime, he'd been trying to raise the German naval command on his boat's radio, but all that he'd encountered so far was static. He'd tuned his radio to the English frequency and, from that, he'd gathered they were currently experiencing the same problems. It seemed that all communications in the local area were using plain speech with nothing encoded; obviously, not a soul on-board any vessel had a clue—and all were clearly just as spooked as he was.

He had ordered a course laid in to return them to Germany, but his navigators reported the compasses were non-functional. With the lack of sun, they couldn't even attempt to fix their present position, let alone map a way home. Although the situation wasn't entirely surprising, it was nevertheless disconcerting—for not only himself but for all under his command.

The two submarines slowly came up alongside Galland's boat. Their crews threw lines across to his sailors who made them fast, tethering the submarines together side by side. The captain of U79, Hans Moulder, and the captain of U82, Erwin Gould, scrambled on to the deck of Galland's boat. They climbed the sail and stood beside him in the conning tower. They'd carried out their training together and were already acquainted prior to coming under his command.

'Hello, Hans, Erwin, please come below and we'll discuss our problems,' said Kurt. They descended through the conning tower and gathered in the control room of his submarine. 'Firstly, can you both tell me what you experienced just after we broke off our attack on the English ships?' asked Kurt.

Erwin Gould spoke first. 'I was looking through my periscope and saw the English ships break formation. I saw the English cruiser and destroyer altering their positions to attack us and, like you, Commander, realised we were in trouble. I received your signal to abandon our attack, dive and prepare for a depth-charge attack. I retracted my scope and gave the order to crash-dive, whereupon my boat felt as if it were spinning around, faster and faster. The lights went out, and I remember no more until I regained my senses some time later. At that point, I ordered my boat to come to periscope depth and raised the scope. When looking out, I saw that landmass over there, a rocky reef alongside me, and the British Navy clearly in complete disarray. That's probably the most I can tell you at this point.'

Hans Moulder spoke next. 'Like Erwin, I saw the impending attack and received your order to break off, but before I dived, I saw through my scope a thick green fog approaching us from behind. It was coming fast. Like Erwin's, my boat began to revolve, and I also lost consciousness. When I came to, I did pretty much the same as Erwin, but I noticed the clock in the control room had moved forward an hour.' Moulder broke off, clearly upset and confused with the current predicament and their lack of knowledge surrounding recent events. 'Have you any idea what's happened to us, Commander? What can we even do about it?'

'My friends: whatever has happened, it's possibly not totally unprecedented. Strange fogs, large ships spinning around like children's toys, the temporary loss of our own faculties… all of these experiences have been rumoured before. Land appearing where there should be no land, compasses spinning uselessly, no contact with the rest of the world, some doubt as to the reality of time, not to mention the different weather conditions and sea state… I've reason to suspect others may have experienced these phenomena before. We must carefully consider our options at this juncture. Firstly, we must take stock of our resources. We're getting low on fuel and food. We were, of course, expecting to be re-supplied shortly by our support ship and we have about three days' worth remaining for full operational duty. At that time, we must withdraw anyway as there will be nothing left to fight with. So, with that in mind, we could continue to stalk and attack the English convoy for a short time. I think it's true to say that, in the state they're in, our chances would be much improved. However, realistically, I don't think we'll be re-supplied. Over the years, I've researched cases of ships disappearing at sea without a trace; there have been several well-documented accounts of which there has been no reasonable explanation concerning what's happened to them. Furthermore, none of these disappearances have ever been satisfactorily resolved. Of course, ships are subject to freak waves, storms, general disrepair, mechanical failures, enemy actions and the like—any one of which could result in the loss of a vessel. But, my studies reveal accounts of ships sailing in calm waters, in contact with other vessels in the area, their exact positions well-known, but which nevertheless suddenly send out distress calls reporting spinning compasses, the sea and sky 'not looking right', and the appearance of strange fogs. In some cases, rescue ships have arrived at their last known positions in a very short time—only to find nothing: no sign of wreckage, no survivors, no further contact. These unfortunate souls simply vanish off the radar—forever.

'To a degree, our circumstances do seem to mirror these incidents. I'm sure we've become another victim of whatever causes these strange events. Personally I'm not expecting any assistance from our own Navy and I don't expect to return to our normal lives from here either.

'If I'm right,' continued the commander, 'the only source of supply for us is the English convoy. They're carrying enough fuel and food to last us all for some considerable amount of time. We don't know what we might face in this place. We might have to fight to survive: our U-boats combined with their warships and aircraft would make a formidable alliance. I've thought very carefully about this, and now I think we should contact the English: in our present situation, neither we nor they need the further complications of continuing the hostilities between us. Ideally, we must call a truce, combine our forces, and go forward from there. Should they be agreeable, that would allow us all to concentrate on getting out of here or, if that's not possible, living here— wherever *here* is! With that in mind, I intend to proceed with this course of action. Do either of you have any comments?' asked the commander.

'I have also heard the rumoured stories, Kurt,' said Captain Moulder. 'If you're right and there is truth in what you say, I would seriously consider agreeing with you: the English are the superior force here, and they possess all the required resources—there's no argument about that. Again, if you're right and we can expect no help from our own people, we can't function for much longer on our own given our depleted state. If we continue to harass them, we can only do that for a short time but then, when we run out of fuel, we'll be sitting ducks and they'll inevitably destroy us anyway. I'm with you: we need to try to reach an arrangement with them now. If they don't agree, then we'll at least still have the resources to get out of here and consider our next options.'

'I don't believe what I'm hearing,' said Captain Gould, shaking his head. 'Neither of you are sure of your ground here. You want to commit to what is nothing more than total mutiny based upon fairy stories and ridiculous superstitions perpetrated by lunatics and drunken sailors' gossip. There's no proof whatsoever that anything supernatural has ever occurred. The cases you refer to could be explained by any number of natural causes. I admit that our situation is very strange and, to be fair, I've no other explanation at this point. But, until we can prove beyond any doubt that what you say is right, I believe the correct route is to continue on with our original orders—to the letter—and continue to fight until we can fight no more.' Captain Gould looked towards Galland. 'If you order me to support your actions, I'll obey your commands, of course, but I want it recorded that I strongly object to such a plan.'

'Very well, Erwin, I'll enter your objection in my ship's log,' responded Galland. 'Nevertheless, I'm in command here, and it's my responsibility to protect us all in any way I see fit. I'll contact the English and attempt to negotiate terms with them. Return to your boats now, men. We're very vulnerable at present. Stand-off half a mile on either quarter of my boat and we'll all submerge to periscope depth. When we've done that, I'll contact the English fleet.'

Captain Rowsell, trailing his fleet in the carrier Victorious, was contemplating his next course of action. Following preventing his ships from running onto the rocks and having re-established order to his command, he now needed to devise a workable idea to further improve their current predicament. By this point, he was all too keenly conscious of the responsibility laid upon him: he was the overall commander of fifteen ships with over six thousand people aboard; it was vital any decisions made were the right ones, but he lacked the information on which to base any long- or, for that matter, short-term plans. Furthermore, he'd no idea how to return them to their original location or employment. He knew realistically that he couldn't simply steam-off into the unknown sea in the hope of finding the correct way back, particularly when he had no idea where to head for in the first place. However, there seemed little point in remaining where they were either. Nothing in his training or his career could have prepared him for an event like this and, for the first time in his life, Rowsell felt at somewhat of a loss as to what to do next. He was worried about the U-boats, but thought they'd be having their own problems right now and would be possibly less inclined to attack him, but he couldn't even be sure of that. He would like the fleet to heave-to and give him the chance to consult with his captains, face-to-face, but if he did that, they'd be easy prey to the submarines.

On top of the current predicament, night was now falling.

In the back of his mind, Rowsell remembered the two Spitfires which had landed on the beach immediately after their arrival. He decided that, for now, they should continue to steam ahead at the slowest practical speed for half the coming night, then come about and return to land, maintaining movement in order to reduce the German threat. Then, in the morning, he'd send out a landing party to seek out the planes and pilots—both of whom could quite possibly know more than he did.

His thoughts were interrupted by his radio officer, George Smith, who leaned out of his radio shack into the bridge saying, 'Captain, I've a communication from a Commander Kurt Galland of the German submarine U35. He requests a truce and an urgent meeting with the commander of the fleet. He says he feels the situation to be so extraordinary that he wishes to cease hostilities immediately, and would be prepared to discuss putting his submarines at our disposal. He asks for your urgent response.'

'Well, there's a turn-up for the books,' said Captain Rowsell, his spirits improving instantaneously. 'Clearly they've no idea what's going on either. Peter, what do you make of that?' he asked his petty officer on the bridge.

'He could be laying a trap for us, Captain, but I don't see how. If we allow him to come in amongst us, he'd have to be on the surface, and although he could fire maybe a couple of torpedoes, we'd reduce him to scrap in an instant. With our combined deck guns, he'd have no chance whatsoever. If he insists on approaching underwater, then it would be clear to me that he was intending to attack us, which is their *modus operandi* anyway, so why bother to let us know he was coming? I think he's a clever cookie, this one. If we are, indeed, stuck here, he'll run out of fuel and provisions pretty quickly, and we're likely to be the only source of both in town. On balance, I think he's probably on the level, Captain,' replied Peter.

'I agree with you,' said Captain Rowsell. 'Mr Smith, send the following reply: 'Message from Captain Paul Rowsell of the aircraft carrier Victorious, and overall commander of His Majesty's convoy L405, replying to Commander Kurt Galland of the German naval submarine U35. Your message has been received and understood. I agree to a meeting between us. I suggest we hold it on neutral territory and request we meet at first light on the beach under the cliffs, opposite our original insertion point. We'll both come to this meeting unarmed and with only our landing boat's crew in attendance on both sides. In light of the fact that you requested this meeting, and until I'm sure that you're truly seeking an alliance, I'll have a squadron of fighters continuously fly over the beach with orders to attack at any sign of treachery. However, you have my assurance that these fighters will not attack you under any other circumstances. If you agree to the aforementioned, please confirm.'

'Message from Commander Galland to Captain Rowsell,' said the radioman. 'Agreed. I'll meet you on the beach on your terms, as stated.'

Intrigued but nevertheless still erring on the safe side, Captain Rowsell then sent an order to all the ships' captains, instructing them to continue on their present course at six knots for four hours in current formation. All ships were to keep lookouts posted to watch for enemy activity, then were all to heave-to and await further instructions.

'Maybe we're getting somewhere,' said Rowsell. 'At least we have a purpose for the time being. For now, I'm going to try to get my head down. Wake me in four hours' time when we heave-to, please, Peter— unless anything arises in the meantime.' Rowsell then left the bridge and headed for his cabin.

CHAPTER SIX

Jack and Mark sat back, waiting for Rema to begin her story.

'Firstly, I'll start off by telling you that you've deliberately been brought here from your own time. Your place in history is just under ten thousand years in the future from ours. Our resistance movement was responsible for bringing you here, and you are currently on an island called Kira.

'Kira is part of an island chain situated roughly in the middle of what you know as the Atlantic Ocean. Atlantis is the largest island in the chain and is the capital of the Atlantien race. I'm one of them, and most of our world is now ruled by the kingdom of Atlantis. Like you, we are a technological society. Two centuries ago, we were the most advanced civilization on the planet which, although sounds grand, actually meant we'd moved slightly from hunter gatherers like the rest of the tribes sharing the world. We had produced a more ordered society, which had developed a basic agricultural system for the production of food, and had built permanent though simple dwellings. We'd developed a rudimentary form of politics and had devised an alphabet which allowed us to record and pass on our knowledge in a written format. Evolving artistically and architecturally, we'd also created a military to defend our evolving culture. However, although well-ahead of the pack in technological and social terms, we were still only a tribe with aspirations; technologically, we couldn't have been considered significantly advanced compared to any others.' Rema took a moment's pause before continuing. 'You'll need another leap of faith with the next part, no doubt, but it was the hinge point in our development, completely changing everything for us virtually overnight. I can show you proof later, but please try to accept what I say for now as it's fundamental to everything else.

'Still active within the universe, there exist aliens of unfathomable intellect. They are incredibly ancient and, in pre-history, lived here on Earth for a short time. Although they've long left for reasons of their own, they do, from time to time, revisit this world and influence its development as they see fit. We've little concept of the science they've developed which allows them to achieve this. These beings are so far advanced in terms of the technology they use that it is completely unrecognisable to us; their technology appears supernatural, and so we're incapable of understanding most of it. They're following an agenda of their own, and we strongly suspect we're being employed within their overall strategy—which now also includes you.

'Two centuries ago, these beings made contact with our forebears, at which time they gave us everything we required to transform our rudimentary society into a fully functional political, scientific, agricultural, architectural and technological civilization. Their knowledge allowed us to short-circuit any natural evolution and to accordingly achieve the entire process in literally a few short years. Naturally, the Ancients were using their own technology when they lived here on Earth—probably all of which is still functional; however, they were quite specific in just how much of it they allowed us to employ. Advanced cultures must develop a power source of some kind to develop and move on; here, they allowed us to utilise theirs. They used a crystal which they called Diathydril. These crystals generate power when exposed to the earth's natural magnetic field. This power loosely resembles the electricity which you currently use. In pre-history, they'd installed a grid system for the purpose of storing and distributing the power. You have some comprehension of this in your time. In addition, a few of your people are aware there is something unusual throughout the world and have called this grid system 'ley lines'. To generate the power in the first instance, the crystals are positioned within a pyramid, exactly one-third down from the peak in the exact centre of that space. Two sides of the pyramid must be precisely aligned to the north/south axis of the planet. The power produced then flows into the grid. The system is completed with a series of units positioned throughout the grid, all of which together draw the stored energy and transmit it like radio waves. The engines of all the machinery on the planet receive and utilize this power system. The grid requires many generators to keep it supplied. The power is not provided throughout the whole world from one source, and so the amount of power available and the distance from the generator that it can be accessed from is directly related to the size and number of generators used. We can set up small portable pyramid/crystal generators anywhere to feed the grid and increase the power locally where it's low due to distance from the principle much larger generators. Their output is limited and only enhances a small area around them.' Rema took a sip of water and looked from Mark to Jack, considering how many of her words were being believed. She continued when satisfied they were openly listening. 'The main power to the grid comes from the large static pyramids which house enormous crystals. The Ancients built several, all of which were located across the world as their influence continued to expand. The largest is sited in Atlantis, our capital city. From that, we are able to draw almost limitless power for a circumference of around one thousand miles. This all sounds very logical and it does work very well, but there is a more supernatural element.

'I've tried to explain the system relating to your electricity so that you may understand the general principles as we do. In fact, this system is totally alien; the crystals they use do not naturally exist here on Earth; they may have been manufactured or come from another world. We don't know—and the Ancients wouldn't tell us. We do, however, know that there are no more of these crystals in existence, other than those remaining here. The pyramid/generators only work if they are precisely set up in the format explained but, again, we don't know why. The grid I refer to is just there, as are the power transmitters. There's no physical manifestation of their existence, like the pyramids. We were taught to use the system and that's more or less how it's remained ever since.

'What's more, nothing requires any maintenance: the system never needs repairs; it could be that the system is self-repairing. Furthermore, the power produced from the crystals never diminishes. This, of course, is just as well because, if it did, we couldn't replace them, and our society would inevitably collapse. The gift and subsequent utilisation of this technology has given our people a massive advantage: in our generally primitive world, we subsequently became like gods to the other tribes existing around us. Nevertheless, in spite of the new technology, we were, at the time, a benign society, merely using the power we possessed to stabilise and enhance the world. We were, however, responsible for great advances spanning across a large spectrum of industries, from farming to medicine and construction. What's more, in every area, we strived only to improve and enhance, and although the other races at the time paled beside our forefathers, they all benefited from them, subsequently improving their own societies along the way. Our leaders were wise and wished only to advance the world. They gave their inherited gifts freely to all, never subjugating their neighbours or forcing an issue. As neighbours, they assisted others and were welcome wherever they travelled. Essentially, the world was better for their influence—and the future was looking good for everyone.

'Time passed. The Ancients left and, having presumably achieved their purpose here, have not returned since. Our forefathers, who'd directly worked with them, passed away. And, somewhat predictably considering the hard-earned principles and life-long lessons being lost to time and the cycles of life, the following generations began to abuse their superior power and became ever-more predatory; lacking in the desire to better the world for all as our past generations had done, the wish was only to dominate the rest and become the ruling class. Greed overcame any wish to compromise, and they slowly withdrew their help from all other races. Everything they possessed—knowledge, wealth and compassion—they kept firmly to themselves and, before long, they'd become territorial, jealously guarding their lands and deporting from them any not of their race, stealing their land and possessions into the bargain. Completing their fall into the abyss, they developed more advanced weaponry and proceeded to wage war upon their neighbours, taking for themselves everything they conquered and enslaving the occupants.' Rema took a moment to steady her now quavering voice. Her eyes shone with sad tears as she struggled to remove herself from the past and continue on with the story. Taking a deep breath, she smiled at Mark and Jack—both of whom were now leaning forward in anticipation and concern, awaiting the next instalment.

Rema continued. 'Alongside this sad scenario, they developed even stronger and more terrifying weapons to use against their enemies. Following a long line of slowly degenerating rulers, our present King is the worst Head of State our people have ever had rule over them. He's the epitome of absolute power corruption: a fat, ugly man whose cruelty and perversion know no bounds. He's totally committed to furthering his own pleasures, power and wealth above all other considerations. He's an arrogant and selfish individual who will, unless we can stop him, ruin all that's left of our once-proud nation. Possessing a low animal cunning, he knows that he's incapable of achieving his goals in his own right and has subsequently recognised the need to surround himself with a group of high commanders and political leaders who have the capability—but who are ultimately as unprincipled as he is. Unfortunately, these individuals are, in the main, highly intelligent and are able to carry out the king's wishes. They're all good strategists in their fields, and if you want commanders to fight your wars for you or politicians to economically subjugate the populace, they're the best around. They have, up until now, proved to be pretty much invincible on both counts, but then again, they've so far not come up against any force capable of thwarting them.

'Essentially, there is a number of us now who are trying to reverse this situation. Our team mainly comprises scientists with a smaller number of military and political advisors. Our allies consist of people from the conquered races who have escaped the king's tyranny and who wish to regain their lands and, during the process, free their enslaved compatriots. We also have a large following within Atlantien society, who also wish to be rid of this administration.

'The only sovereign nation remaining unconquered is the kingdom of Mu, the land of which lies far to the west of Atlantis. They're outclassed by the Atlantien forces, although we, in the resistance, supply them with some modern weapons. Their army has been swelled by escapees from previously conquered lands, but they're mainly only tribesmen fighting with primitive armament. They've little idea of the tactics, discipline or strategies required for success in such major conflicts. Predominantly, they carry out hit-and-run attacks on the king's forces and his supply lines. They're bravely resisting and are making life difficult for his soldiers; however, he'll undoubtedly soon overcome them.

'Our resistance movement strives to achieve one aim only, and that is to reintroduce order to the world. We're totally committed to the goal of removing the present King and his henchmen from their position of power, thereby allowing us to recreate the utopia our ancestors once provided.

'As you'd undoubtedly—and correctly—assume, the king and his commanders are well aware of our presence and are equally committed to destroying us. Should they succeed, they'll not only finish us but will also change the entire future of the world to follow, which could disastrously affect your world also. With this in mind, we've brought you here in the hope that you'll assist us in our struggle. I'll explain why we think you will, especially when you understand how it will affect your world if you don't.

'Importantly, the king has recently discovered a machine left here by the Ancients and, at this point, his scientists have managed to partially reactivate it. This artefact is potentially so dangerous that, if misused, it has the capacity to destroy the world. Unfortunately, they're not put off by this lethal element; the terrible danger it poses to the world doesn't faze them. Alarmingly, they continue to experiment with it. Amongst other things, following a recent unexpected result during one of their trials, they're now trying to produce the super weaponry we fear from it the most. The scientists in charge, whilst undoubtedly gifted, are greedy and unprincipled: they won't see anything they don't want to and are rushing to complete the project without completely understanding their actions. They're under huge pressure from the king to complete his new toy, and have apparently been offered massive rewards to deliver it to him without further delay.

'Simplistically speaking, their artefact is a basic matter transporter: it has two emendators, which create the primary chambers used to transport materials. You've experienced a primary chamber; it was what brought you here. Anyway, using the grid to set the coordinates, one emendator supplies the primary chamber, which looks like a cloud—as you'll no doubt remember—which can be expanded to encompass whatever volume of material you wish to transport. By selecting a location on the grid at which you would like the material to arrive, you

54

can then send the material to the specified location, sending the second emendator with it for the return journey.' Rema smiled at the two pilots' confused expressions. 'Don't worry, I know it's a lot to take on-board, but you will understand in time. Anyway, the primary chambers reduce the material to atoms, sending them through the ether at the speed of light and subsequently reassembling them at the pre-set coordinate on the grid. Both chambers reverse their functions, which permits a return but only to the point of origin. This allows the almost instantaneous transport of matter from one place to another, and applies equally to organic or non-organic materials, i.e. men and their machinery. In order to operate the transporter, critical balances between the power of the Diathydril crystal coupled with the earth's gravitational force and supplemented by an exertion of electro-magnetic influence are utilised in unison. Provided that everything remains perfectly harmonious, the machine will do exactly what it was intended to do: matter will disappear from one place and reappear in another with no ill effect; in the hands of its creators, it undoubtedly always did.

'Obviously, I understand that all of this means little to you, perhaps aside from better explaining how you got here. I've described the general principles involved because I want you to understand that, should the combination of these forces be only slightly out of balance, the consequences are horrendous: an excess of power from the crystals results in the recombinant atoms being mixed up, resulting in, for example, a man reappearing with part of him combined into either someone else he was travelling with or, equally as nasty, something inanimate he was travelling with, consequently resulting in instant death or unimaginable living mutations. Too much gravitational force and, although matter disappears, it never reappears, and we've no idea where it goes—we only know we can't get it back.

'Here on Kira, the Ancients had built a large installation which the resistance quite recently discovered. Within this complex, there's a similar unit to the one in Atlantis which I've been talking about. Since accidentally and, by great good fortune, stumbling upon this bastion of the Ancients, we've been constantly working on this unit and have achieved a far greater understanding of its capabilities than the king's men have done so far with theirs. This machine is far more advanced than the one on Atlantis; it's much bigger and, although it harnesses the same forces in a similar manner, its capabilities are incomparably greater. I told you earlier that the machine on Atlantis is a basic transporter, which may seem a peculiar description of a machine able to do what it does; however, it is ultimately basic compared to the unit here. I must digress a little now, for you need to understand more of our artefact here before I can successfully describe why we're so worried about the king's.

'The machine here transmits matter but otherwise requires no receiving unit at the other end. Its controls can be set to send and return matter both to and from any place on Earth, upon which time it reappears, perfectly reformed, and with no ill effects either way—a feat incredible enough on its own, but it's also possible to control the unit to send and return from another time. In addition, we're also able to send matter from here through time and accordingly return it or otherwise bring things back to here from the future. Recently, three of the king's scientists defected to us—they'd been working with Myriddian Amis, the king's Chief Science Officer, and his team, on the king's machine.

'Another slight deviation is required here. One of them is a plant; she's an agent of the king's military. She obviously doesn't realise that we're aware of this, nor is the military. She's not been here long, and we're very careful to keep her away from anything sensitive. This is not particularly relevant to this conversation, but it's an issue for later which I won't belabour for now. In any case, their knowledge has allowed us to replicate the set-up of the king's machine, and we have reset ours accordingly. By doing this, we have discovered that, in its present configuration, the machine has a terrifying flaw: due to the scientists' approach to reactivating the unit, they've unknowingly affected its primary control mechanism, which has subsequently now made it incapable of the degree of accuracy required in order to adequately combine the forces it is handling, consequently causing the repeated failures witnessed in their trials so far. With this in mind, it is only a matter of time before they realise their mistake.

'In our experiments, we've also discovered what the king's scientists are looking for. Having modified our unit to mirror theirs, and with our greater understanding of this machine, we can produce what they're after. They require just a few simple modifications made to their machine, and it will then return matter as antimatter; combine this with normal matter and you then have the most destructive force in the universe. Fundamentally, matter and anti-matter can't exist in the same vicinity; quite simply, they'll obliterate each other in an incomprehensible burst of pure energy. A tiny amount of each coming together will destroy a country, whilst larger amounts will destroy the world. If they discover how to do this—as we have—they'll attempt to make the weapon they're seeking for sure, and will, in all probability, destroy the planet. Remember, this planet is also to become *your* planet.

'At this stage, we know they're very close to achieving the required knowledge. Clearly, if we can do it, obviously, so can they. Time is running out.

'Two weeks ago, they accidentally destroyed a small island. They've already created their super weapon but, thank Ra, they don't know how they did, nor can they replicate the trial at present—but they will. During our research, I used the transporter here to visit your century, arriving in the period of your present World War. There, I learnt your language, studied your societies, and gained a sound understanding of your technology. Adolph Hitler and his regime are akin to our king and his people; you'll soon appreciate the similarities—they're both outstanding megalomaniacs. For what it's worth I'll tell you that your people finally overcame Hitler and, for the sake of your society, of course, it was essential they did—and essential they do, although the cost in lives is horrific.

'We've used the Ancients' machine here to search through time, trying to find a race with the right attitude and technology to assist us in our battle against the king and his forces. Beyond our time and right up until your period in history, the world hadn't achieved the capabilities needed to help us defeat him. A few years beyond your time, your world develops weapons so destructive, and the people who control them are so predatory that we'd probably be worse off than we are now if we'd been foolish enough to bring them back here. We brought you to us simply because we consider that, with your help, we can defeat our version of your Hitler, and thereby allow your history to remain unaltered.

'Finally, before I finish, there's a vital piece of information you have to know: everyone we've brought back was about to die pursuing your war—either at the time of transportation here or soon after transporting them back here. On the one hand, I appreciate that we've kidnapped you all, but I hope you'll appreciate that you're still alive because of our actions too. In your case, as you attacked the German bomber, you were unaware of a squadron of enemy fighters arriving in the vicinity. Their pilots watched your attack. Too late to save their comrades, they were positioning themselves ready to attack you in turn as you were climbing away from the battle. As you levelled out, they were nearly upon you. Seeing the cloud or, more correctly, the primary chamber approaching, you unsuccessfully tried to avoid it, which subsequently distracted your attention. When it overtook you, the enemy fighters were close behind you—they actually opened fire but you'd already been transported out. Those pilots will never understand how you and the cloud just disappeared in front of them. Their gun cameras recorded your disappearance and, when later questioned by their superiors, not one could explain what happened and it became yet another mystery of your time. Had we not brought them here, the English naval forces and the German submarines—who are also here, as you have probably seen—would have totally wiped each other out in a bloody battle lasting a period of three days. I tell you this for two main reasons: firstly, so that you can appreciate that, had we left you where you were—in your then-present time and location—your fate was sealed with only moments of life left to live between the two of you and, secondly, by our actions, we've ensured that the future of your world remains unchanged and totally unaffected by your disappearance, as you all would have ceased to exist there in any case.

'Ultimately, however, travelling through time brings its own specific problems, for any changes made will have massive repercussions in the longer term. We're very aware of this and, because of this fact alone, you cannot return to your own time: quite simply, with your death imminent, you shouldn't be there and, therefore, anything you did shouldn't have been done, and so on.

This explains, as comprehensively as I can, all the facts. The floor is now yours. Please ask me anything you want.' Rema sat back, clearly drained, after concluding her incredible story.

The airmen had visibly paled during this long briefing. Both sat in shock, clearly unsettled and unsure where to start. The silence extended for several more moments.

Finally, regaining his voice after some time, Jack spoke first. 'Rema, you must know what you've told us is difficult for us to take at face value to say the least. Amongst all the information you've given us, the overriding factor is obviously this ancient race, which is behind all your abilities and, by using their technology, you can work miracles. I suppose the fact that we're here—and if *here* really is thousands of years in our past—then, clearly, supports the fact that you really can work miracles—by our standards, at least. You say you need us to help you but you possess the power of gods: we're only human, and our technology is clearly inferior to yours. I'm at a loss as to understand why we're even here at all, and what we can do against your king and his armies that you can't. The king's forces use the same systems; surely they'll just transport us away to somewhere else, disintegrate us or something equally as nasty if we're stupid enough to attack them. We've nothing with us which, as far as I can see, has the potential to resist powers like those you've described, and, with respect, how do we know for sure that the king is really the villain here? It could be you.'

'That occurred to me, too,' said Mark, now having gathered his thoughts. 'If you can play around in time, why not just go back to your forefathers' days and eliminate the problems that your rulers' declining standards have caused before they decline? If you do that, then this situation will never arise.'

'Indeed,' said Jack. 'And another thing: the fact we're here must mean that your king did not, or will not, destroy the world or, following your theme, we'd not be here anyway as we'd not have existed at all.'

'Another point,' said Mark. 'As you appear to be so far in front of us with your technology, why if we've come from the future are we still so far behind you technologically? With ten thousand years of development-building from here, we should have reached the stars and way beyond by now.'

'Just another thought,' added Jack. 'You've gathered together a substantial complement of men and armaments, present within that convoy. Among everything else, they have planes and pilots on-board the carrier. Why then do you need us? We're only two guys with two planes—which are out of fuel anyway, I might add,' Jack stated.

Waiting for a moment to ensure the two men had posed their questions for the moment, Rema then began to answer. 'Of course, I can appreciate that you'll have difficulty in accepting the facts I've given you. Realistically, I wouldn't expect anything else, given the circumstances. I'll answer your questions so far, and hope the answers satisfy you to a degree,' said Rema. 'Our abilities derive from the Ancients' technology, which underpins our entire society; Jack, you've clearly appreciated that. Using their machines gives us the means to support our culture, to travel through time and the like, and yes, it endows us with God-like power to a certain degree. You are thousands of years in the past, but I think you'll need to experience more of our time before you'll totally believe that. We're not gods, however; we're simply human—like you. We have the gift of a different technology, but we're tool users, nevertheless, just as you are.

'The king's machine is limited: it can't transport you anywhere, nor can it disintegrate anything. First, you're contained within its primary chamber; since they can't presently control it properly, they can't use it as a weapon in its own right. You do, however, face his more conventional weapons; however, with that said, although extremely dangerous and more than capable of inflicting major damage upon you, they're nonetheless vulnerable to your technology. In a fight, you'd stand as much chance of success as they would, but you'd have the advantage that he's never encountered any force equal to him and, what is more, you'd ultimately have the edge because they've never lost a major battle or ever encountered really heavy losses before. I think his soldiers and commanders would, initially anyway, not expect the damage you're likely to inflict upon them; however, if you hit them hard enough and pursue your attacks constantly enough, you'll likely defeat them. With that said, I don't actually believe it will ever come to that, simply because we've got things to contribute which will make it a whole lot easier. If you decide to join us, we can discuss those considerations later.

'With regards to the villains here, I must ask you to reserve judgment, but try to accept for now what I've told you as fact. I intend to take you to Atlanta, our capital, to prove the point as soon as possible. When you see what's going on there, I'm sure you'll be convinced.

'Mark, you asked why we can't return to our past and rectify the problem at its source. In answer to that question, there are two fundamental problems with that. Firstly, that would require our interference in another time, which then changes all time from then forward, including the time from which we've come, and thereby lays the conundrum. The cardinal rule when time-travelling is that there should be no interference with anything that has the potential to change the timeframe you're visiting, simply because it can have far-reaching effects on the future from there. The permutations are, of course, endless—we could talk forever considering different scenarios. We've just brushed on one example, so let's investigate another which is pertinent to us here. I've told you that you were both about to be killed as we transported you away, and I've also explained how, by doing so, we've changed nothing in your time by taking you, as you wouldn't have existed any longer there anyway. If you were to return now, at exactly the same time you left but in circumstances that accordingly allowed you to survive, then any actions you make from that point must cause discrepancies to the future you didn't exist in. There are thousands of you here. Should you all go back and continue your lives, it's not hard to imagine how great the changes would be. The future of your world would be unrecognisable in a very short time span. Bringing you all back to our time at once is the biggest operation we've ever carried out, but you all were due to die, so we've not changed anything in your future by doing this.'

'Oh no of course you haven't because we weren't supposed to be there now, or so you say,' Jack said angrily, 'but do you really believe we're supposed to be here? If we help defeat your king—who, by the sounds of it, is top-dog around here—we'll change everything completely. With that in mind, using your logic against you, we must therefore change our future from here probably even more radically than if we had returned! So, what's the difference, Rema?'

'The difference is, Jack, that we really do believe you're meant to be here, and it's only your influence that will keep the current course of history true. The Ancients are involved at present more than they've ever been. The things they've recently shown us and given us have made it possible for us to bring you here. We're as sure as it's possible to be that your being here is essential, and the changes you'll make must happen. If this wasn't the case, the Ancients would never have allowed things to get to this point, let alone helped orchestrate it.'

'I'm damned if I know what to say. It's about as clear as mud. It might help if we had some proof of something. For a start, can you prove your claim regarding our deliverance?'

'Hold on a minute,' interrupted Mark, 'I temporarily forgot about that small point. I also want proof that our redoubtable flying circus was so ignominiously removed from the Sussex skies, particularly as we're in the prime of our lives and you're trying to tell us we're technically dead.'

'But you're not dead, Mark. We pulled you out before it happened. However, you would have succumbed in the ambush by the German fighters. However, proof I can certainly provide: I've copies of the gun camera photographs from the German planes which I can show you,' said Rema. She reached across the table to a file and took out a sheaf of photographs which she promptly handed to Mark.

Somewhat hesitantly, Mark began to flick through the images before handing them over to Jack, grumbling as he did so. 'I was always telling you to keep a better lookout, Jack. There's no excuse for your allowing the world's ladies to be deprived of their pleasures through your inattention.'

In spite of the shock which the photos inflicted upon Jack, he couldn't help smiling at Mark's comment. He wondered just how bad things would have to get before his friend's sense of humour deserted him. Irrespectively, Jack could clearly see that they'd been caught napping and were sitting ducks, and there would have been no way out from an attack like that. Undoubtedly, there would only have been one possible outcome. 'Okay,' began Jack, 'I have to say these photographs seem to support that part of your story, so continue with answering the rest of our questions.'

'Jack,' continued Rema, 'you've observed that the king hasn't destroyed the world or you wouldn't be here. I agree, but you're here now, and the probable outcome is that, with your help, we'll indeed defeat him and prevent him from doing this. As I've already said, we believe this to be the most likely case; however, in spite of the Ancients' influence, we still have to defeat him ourselves or there will undoubtedly be a different outcome. We think there is the potential of any number of possible scenarios, all of which could ultimately determine different futures for our world—and the fact that things are as they are now doesn't necessarily mean they have to remain that way. Remember: any changes made here change everything in the future. We must win now to preserve the status quo. If we succeed, the world will remain as it is; but if we fail, the entire planet's future will change and will, in all probability, not include any of your loved ones in it. As much as it is a difficult concept to grasp, we're certain it's a fact nonetheless.'

'You said you had two problems with going back to your forefathers' days, and you've told us of one. What's the other?' Mark asked.

'The second problem, Mark, is the machine won't go back in time anyway. From the point in time it's activated, it can take you forward but can't return you before the present you left. We don't know if it can't or we just don't know how to make it achieve such a task. I think it's a fail-safe function because, if you were to go back before the machine had been built and inadvertently alter anything then, quite possibly, due to it not having been built, you therefore couldn't be there and, presumably, would cease to exist yourself, and so we loop around the thorny issue again,' replied Rema.

'Okay, I accept you can't go back, which is just about all that is logical in this discussion, but you can go forward, so this begs another question, Rema,' said Jack. 'Why don't you use your machine to travel forward to see what happens now we are here? Why don't you already know what transpires when you can just go and look?'

'We had a real problem with that, Jack. The Ancients' machine initially made a jump of five hundred years. From then, we were able to control its progress through time and direct us to any period we chose. As I've said, we're not gods and we are therefore limited to the extent that we'd gained control over the machine's capabilities. With the machine, we were dealing with an alien concept and, although we were working to solve this problem, we didn't overcome it, and so we just don't know what happens in the near future. I'm sure the reason for the machine not going to the very near future has been in-built by the Ancients. If we could see exactly what to do, then the Ancients would effectively be directly controlling events: they always leave an element of chance. They don't run things and, because we can't see exactly what to do now, there's an unknown factor remaining. We have to come up with a solution ourselves—and that's what interests them, I'm sure,' replied Rema.

'"*Were* dealing with", "*were* working to", "*did* not"... Rema, you're speaking in the past tense all the time now. Is there something you're not telling us?' asked Mark.

'Yes, Mark, there is.' Rema took a deep breath and eyed the two men. 'As soon as you all arrived, the machine ceased to function. We have no idea why, and we're trying to fathom out the reason—to no avail, as yet. It had been our intention for a while that we eventually destroy it ourselves unless we are able to gain complete control over it— and I have to admit, it was becoming more unlikely that we ever would.

'We still can't really comprehend the technology that originally created the device; like grabbing smoke, it's very elusive. The need to destroy it—or to otherwise fully understand it—became more pressing when we also discovered it could be made to produce antimatter. However, it wasn't our intention to lose it right now. I have to say, the coincidence of it failing as you arrived leads me to believe that the Ancients are behind it, in some way or another,' admitted Rema.

'That bit of information won't please the senior service when they find out they can't return and, now I come to mention it, I'm not sure it pleases me much either,' said Mark.

'Well, what is, is, I suppose,' said Jack. 'If we accept we can't return anyway, that side of it is probably mute. We can always come back and discuss that one later if we want to but, for now, please continue with our original questions, Rema.'

'Very well. Regarding our technology—an issue you raised, Mark—you asked why you're not living amongst the stars in your age. Well, we discovered in our journeys to the future that everything to do with our present technology had virtually disappeared from the consciousness of the people we encountered there. We're only remembered in legends and rumours. All physical traces—aside from a few—were gone, and even the pyramids weren't attributed to us—which, in the case of the ones the Ancients built, is quite true, of course. Furthermore, Atlantis had completely disappeared from the ocean, and none of our machines had even survived. Whatever happened to our technology will happen very soon, as this was the situation we found to be the case only five hundred years from now. It would appear that our technology is about to be eliminated; that being the case, there's absolutely nothing left to build upon, and any following technology will have to start from scratch which, of course, it did—and the standard of advances you have come to know was the result,' Rema explained.

'Hmm,' Jack contemplated. 'By bringing us here and, assuming we succeed, it would seem that you'll have brought about the annihilation of your people, Rema. Although I see the inherent dangers with your society as it stands, I don't really know or understand how you can even consider this? Surely there has to be some hope for your people? I simply can't justify being part of the extermination of your entire race. I refuse to even be involved in this unless there's some chance that the decent people of your society will at least survive. We were fighting a monster in our own time—and, quite frankly, I won't become one here,' said Jack passionately.

'Jack, I was addressing the technology issue only. In answer to Mark's question, I'm sad that we've perverted the Ancients' science, twisting it until the point that it has become threatening and malignant, but we have—and now it must be stopped. However, some of our people did survive and they established themselves on the mainland in a place you now call South America. I believe they purposely abandoned our previous technology and destroyed all traces of it. It's a double-edged sword, simply because it's so hugely dangerous if misdirected. It had its own benefits, of course, but it also has the potential to destroy everything. It was they who buried the facts about their past; they who left small clues creating the legends of Atlantis as a warning to others following. No species should possess power in excess of their ability to control it. The Ancients are not necessarily benign—of course they may be, I'm not sure—but by giving us their technology, they've not really helped us much as we obviously weren't ready for it. However, if we could have used it as it was possibly first intended, this world would have become a paradise.

'My personal opinion is that the Ancients are conducting an experiment, and perhaps they've learnt something from it, who knows? Maybe we will too, which is possibly the point of it all. Either way, one thing's for sure: it's still on-going, and probably always will be, but in any case, we're all a part of it at the moment and we must therefore make the decisions ourselves.

'That having been said, I'll return to the subject of my people. It was the survivors of whatever's due to happen now who have set the world on the course along which it has evolved ever since. You're not being asked to kill a race, Jack, but to assist in the birth and development of the world they'll create, protecting the course of history to follow and ensuring the people you love within your own time will continue to exist,' Rema explained.

'My God, Rema, this conversation gets more and more bizarre by the minute. I can't begin to grasp the principals involved, let alone take on-board your blasted Ancients and their schemes.' Jack rubbed his temples with frustration and confusion. He took a deep breath. 'Strangely, though, I'm more comfortable with our part in it now. My last question, Rema: why do you need us specifically? What can we do that the others you brought can't?'

'To answer that question, Jack, I'm going to leave you for a while; I've something to show you when I return, which I hope will help you to accept the reality of your situation more easily.' At that, Rema rose from the table and left the dining room.

'Bloody hell, Jack,' exclaimed Mark. 'What do you make of all this? I'm almost inclined to believe what she says, though; bizarrely, it all ties-in with our experiences so far. I wonder just what she expects us to do and how difficult it will be. I can't say I'm not excited by the prospect of fighting the evil king and his merry men—it'll be some challenge. Anyway, if Rema and her people really did save our lives—and, looking at those photos, they probably did—it would be somewhat ungrateful not to help them, don't you think?'

'Yes, on balance, I'm getting there, too, I suppose,' replied Jack. 'And, if we've got to stay here, we might as well be useful. I'd like to see a bit more of what goes on in her world before I totally commit myself, though. Let's hope we get to go to Atlanta soon, like she promised. For the sake of argument, though, if we do join in, we'll need to carefully analyse and evaluate the enemy's strengths and weaknesses and, if possible, we'll need to fully understand all their weapons before we take them on. But, of course, Rema still has to persuade the Navy to get involved. Judging by the size of that convoy, there must be thousands of them! If we're going to be an effective force, they'll obviously have to join us. But if they do, we'll take some stopping then,' Jack observed.

'Just to further complicate matters,' Mark responded, 'she mentioned German submarines. I didn't actually see them but it sounded to me rather like they could be here too. That could be interesting, Jack. I hope we don't have to fight them as well.'

'Yeah, that would be great, wouldn't it? All we'd need right now, I reckon. On the other hand, we appear to be accepting the situation rather easily, you know, Mark. When you really think about it, it's so fantastic—how could anything we've been told be right? I'm still completely fazed by the whole thing but, unless we're dead and this is what happens when you are, it's real and we've just got to accept it.'

'No, Jack, I don't think we've passed on! There's too much which suggests the contrary. I agree, it's all weird and in the extreme, but I think it's real and we've to deal with it somehow.'

As they were talking, the door to the dining room opened and, through the doorway, entered a young WAAF officer in full dress uniform.

Jack's eyes widened as he said, 'Good lord, Patricia, whatever are you doing here? Once again, I can't believe what I'm seeing!'

'Hi, Jack,' the young woman replied with a smile, her cheeks turning a dusty pink. 'Remember you asked me to go out with you tonight? I wouldn't want to miss our date so... here I am.' Her eyes glistened.

Jack had indeed asked her to go out with him. He'd intended to take her to the Anchor Blue at Bosham that night, to wine and dine her when he'd completed his patrol. Patricia Young had recently been posted to Tangmere from Biggin Hill where she was working as an Intelligence Officer.

When they'd first met, Jack had instantly liked Patricia, and had intended to develop a relationship with the lovely newcomer. Tonight, this was to be their first date, and he'd been excited by the prospect of an evening alone with her. This, however, was not quite the venue he'd been considering.

'I'm here to complete your briefing and answer your last question,' said Patricia. She removed her cap and then she reached up and removed a wig from underneath it. She turned away with a smile and, from where the men sat, appeared to be pulling something away from her face. She shook her head and long silver hair fell about her shoulders. She turned around again to face the two men.

They both did the classic and expected double-take, totally unprepared for the sight that greeted them. 'Rema!' They gasped in unison.

'I hope this last revelation has removed all doubt in your minds,' Rema said. 'And I hope you can now see that I was in your time, and accept that you're now in mine. This is the answer to your last question, Jack. It was my personal decision that you're here. I was impressed by you both in my short time at Tangmere. You're a great team and you have the ability to independently make your own judgments. You're both mavericks in your own ways, but you have the respect of your men and your commanders. You can certainly fly and you have both shown fearlessness in combat. In truth, people like you are in very short supply. I know that, if you join us, you'll make a big difference. Remember: I also knew you were both to die, and I couldn't have accepted that.' Rema turned her attention to Jack specifically. 'Jack, I know you had chemistry with me—well, with Patricia, anyway—I feel that with you. I hope who I really am doesn't change things. I know it will take time...'

'I hope I'm not here only because of old Casanova there,' interjected Mark. 'I feel a bit left out now,' he said with a good-humoured smile.

Rema smiled and said, 'Mark, you're here because you're a leader and a good person, no other reason. Anyway, I'm sure you'd rather be here than your alternative location.'

'The only question I have left for now,' said Jack with a self-satisfied smirk, 'is do I call you Patricia or Rema? That aside, the rest sounds pretty good to me now.'

'Rema's fine, otherwise it'll get complicated,' she said with an ironic smile. Now, if neither of you have any further questions for now, I think we should turn in; it's getting late and we're all tired. I can give you beds here in our quarters where you can sleep. We're monitoring the radio traffic from the Navy: the English commanding officer and the commander of the German submarines are having a meeting on the beach at dawn where you landed. Even though we're not invited, I want the three of us to be there too. We can discuss this and your trip to Atlanta before we leave tomorrow.'

'Well, I'm exhausted and more than a little disorientated,' yawned Mark with a stretch. 'I'm more than happy to leave any more talking until tomorrow. Sleep sounds like a far better plan right now.'

'Suits me just fine,' said Jack. 'Please lead on then, Rema, and we'll continue our deliberations in the morning.'

Rema led them from the dining room and back into the main hallway. Three doors down from the dining room, she entered a small square room in which were two single beds and a wardrobe. The floor was covered with a kind of rush matting, and it was lit by the same soft lighting as they had encountered elsewhere in their limited tour of Rema's base. The airmen noticed that the walls and ceiling were like everywhere else: perfectly smooth and glass-like.

Adjacent to the room was a large communal bathroom complete with all the usual fittings. There, Rema provided them with a wash kit each, which she took from a cupboard. Leaving them both, she promised to wake them early the next day, wished them a good night, and told them the reception area where they'd first arrived was always manned should they need anything else. Before leaving, she reassured them that, whilst there, they'd be well looked after.

CHAPTER SEVEN

'We'll not waste our breath with formalities, Amis. You've properly messed up this time.' Rak Maltor, the Land Forces chief spoke. 'You assured us that your infernal contraption was going to work just fine from now on. And now, seemingly not content with losing countless numbers of my men and machines in your past bungling experiments, not forgetting blasting my island from the face of the earth, you've now completely excelled yourself.' Rak Maltor eyed the pathetic Amis from across the room, tapping his long fingernails on the desk. 'And so I find myself wondering how you might even try to explain what you've done now. What have you brought here and where are they from, Amis? And, perhaps more of a concern to myself: where's my latest batch of weapons which you appear to have lost yet again?'

Amis hopped from one foot to the next, nervousness running down his spine and turning his legs to jelly.

'The king is finally—and rightfully, I might add—pissed right off with you this time, Amis. He's continued to pour money and resources into your damn fooled enterprise. You should know: this is the last time any of us will listen to your lame excuses. You'll come up with a very good reason for your latest debacle or I'll personally remove your testicles and shove them up your arse.'

Rak Maltor was not known for his diplomacy, nor was he known for his patience or suffering of fools. A giant sporting a huge black beard, he was a born soldier and man of action. Always successful in his own field, he couldn't tolerate failure in others, rarely disguising the fact.

Amis realised that his worst fears had come to pass as he acknowledged he possessed no answers to Maltor's questions. And now his gut churned and heart racing, remembering how he'd previously witnessed the testicle scenario before—and that the man wasn't necessarily joking. With bile filling his mouth, Amis shakily replied. 'Sir, as I've always said, we're dealing with completely alien technology. Only by continuous experimentation can we ever expect to move forward. Considering we've no parameters to work from, I would say that no experiment has so far proven to be a failure; we're constantly learning lessons. In this instance, I must say that we truly believed we'd eliminated the problems with the machine. Nevertheless, I must admit that, at this stage, I don't yet know what went wrong with your weapons.' Amis rubbed his sweaty palms together, nervously watching for any glimmer of mercy in Maltor's expression, but so far saw none. 'However,' he continued, 'I actually don't think our machine was responsible for bringing the foreign forces to Kira's coast. I strongly suspect that Rema Sark and her colleagues are responsible for such a stunt. I've told you before: I've reason to believe the resistance has been researching in the same sphere as us, undoubtedly aided by the scientists who recently absconded.

I must stress: our equipment was only set to send your weapons to the platform off Kira. On the low power settings we employed, it simply isn't possible that the effect witnessed could have been induced. In fact, there's no setting I'm aware of that has the capacity to transport anywhere near as much mass as that represented by the navy that's now appeared. We wouldn't even know where to look for such a force!'

Amis paused for thought, carefully choosing his words. 'I warn you, Sir, that if Sark and her colleagues have managed to pull this off, they're way ahead of us in terms of research and developments, which could prove to be highly dangerous to us all. If they've caused this, they must expect this fighting force to be able to match yours—or to possibly exceed it—or they wouldn't have brought it here.

'At this stage, Sir, I don't know what else to say to you. All I can suggest for now is that you allow us to continue our research into the bomb we're currently working on. You've seen what it can do, and you may actually need it sooner than you expect.

In my honest opinion, we should put the transporter project on hold as, in the short-term, we're clearly still unable to rectify the problems we have with it.'

Land Chief Maltor's face visibly darkened, turned an angry shade of purple as he shouted, 'Amis, you astound me! You don't even have an excuse, you bastard, other than the obvious old cop-out of "let's blame the resistance for our crass stupidity". I made it perfectly clear that we wouldn't accept any more of your nonsense. You've failed and, by your failure, may have put our entire empire in extreme danger!' The chief took a breath and paused for a moment. He considered Amis, stroking his coarse beard and smiling menacingly. 'I intend to arrest you for treason, Amis, and then we'll let the king decide your fate. Furthermore, we'll suspend all activities at your research facility. You must think we're as stupid as you are if for one moment you actually think we'd let you fool around with any further complex projects!'

'May I say something in my defence, Sir?' asked Amis.

'Absolutely not! You'll remain silent until you're removed from my presence!' stormed Maltor. Calling up his Sergeant at Arms on his personal communicator, Chief Maltor ordered an armed guard be sent to take the scientist to the holding cells. Within minutes, the guard arrived and led Amis from the room.

'Well, Rak,' said Sol Aharmer, the Chief of Air Forces, 'I don't think he was left in any doubt as to your feelings.' A slight but athletic man, Sol was approaching middle age but remained handsome—looks which stood in stark contrast to a ruthless, uncompromising nature. 'However, have you considered that he may have had a point? Judging by his past performances, I actually think he really is incapable of pulling off anything quite as dramatic as producing tens of thousands of tonnes of equipment and personnel from thin air. That being the case, who else but the resistance could've achieved such a result? Of course, this could be a natural phenomenon, but I seriously doubt that.' Sol looked off into the distance, contemplating the situation and its potential magnitude. 'My own personal view, Rak, is that we're in trouble, and my instinct is to attack these intruders without delay and remove any threat they may pose as soon as possible. In any case, the king will expect us to address this problem at our earliest convenience....'

'Actually, Sol, I just think the man's an idiot,' remarked Maltor. 'But I agree with your assessment of his capabilities, of course—and possibly with the rest of what you say. Nevertheless, the fool aggravates me; I simply had to remove him before I lost my temper.' The chief smiled wryly. 'If the resistance are responsible for this, I'm surprised our agent on Kira doesn't know about it; according to her they aren't much further ahead than us with their research. But, it's possible they're on to her, or maybe this is something to do with the Ancients, which could be even more alarming.' Maltor banged his fist down on the table in frustration. 'I wish we'd taken this whole Kira situation more seriously. We've known the resistance have been up to something for a while, haven't we?'

Sol opened his mouth to speak but was interrupted with a dismissive wave of Maltor's long hand.

'I know what you're going to say, Sol, so save your breath. I know you feel we held off because of the transporter issue, hoping they'd discover something of use which Freyr could relate to us. And I suppose, to be fair, we were going to attack Kira until those bloody scientists defected and changed our plans. Nevertheless, when Freyr told us just how extensive their operation on Kira actually was, we should have destroyed them immediately.'

'Which, of course, is something we would have done if we hadn't been commanded to wait owing to that infernal machine the king holds in such high regard!' fumed Aharmer. 'I'm afraid we've now gained nothing of use out of it, and it looks like waiting may have ultimately cost us dear. Still, whatever our prior reasons—and however misdirected they actually were—we've now got to deal with it.' Aharmer looked from Maltor to Neda and nodded his head. 'Certainly, the king won't tolerate this incursion into his realm; I therefore don't doubt he'll have a change of heart concerning the matter.'

'Probably,' responded Maltor, 'but it's a bit late now. Attacking Kira is no longer feasible until we deal with this new development. We could take them on, and maybe we should, but we don't know their capabilities.'

The two men nodded in agreement.

'With that in mind,' Maltor continued, 'let's try to draw them out so that we can get an idea of their strength. I suggest we send in a small task force, quite possibly an assault from the air in the first instance. We'll hit them fast and, if there's a problem, we'll turn away in the same manner.

This should satisfy the king in the short-term and might possibly provide us with some indication of the enemies' abilities without initially committing serious resources.' Maltor turned to the Chief of Sea Forces. 'And what's your opinion, Cesa?'

'I'm comfortable with that plan,' replied Cesa Neda, the youngest of the commanders. A short and vastly overweight individual, his thin, plastered-down hair and piggy eyes combined to create the most ghastly face. But his physical appeal was of no concern considering his extremely agile mind, which made him an extremely valuable member of the king's force. 'I'd rather not commit a larger force to engage them, not until we're certain of our position.'

'Fair enough,' nodded Aharmer. 'Provided we can get the king's approval, I'll order an attack by a squadron of our uprated Hovertaks to arrive over Kira at first light. Then we'll see what these interlopers are made of...'

'In the meantime, gentlemen, we must decide what to do with Amis and his research,' continued Maltor. 'I still feel his position has become untenable. He said himself he can't control the effects of the machine, and the facts remain that we've lost too many people and too much precious equipment during the course of testing this unreliable thing. On balance, I think we should suspend any further active tests at the facility and instead give the scientists a chance to reconfigure the equipment. We may have a problem persuading the king, but we should put pressure on him to sanction this or I'm sure we'll only lurch from disaster to disaster with this project—and probably with no appreciable gain.'

'Very possible, Rak,' responded Neda. 'I'll support you on that one. However, I must say, I'm keen to develop the bomb Amis thinks he can produce. Our existing weapons are powerful, but we've nothing in our arsenal that has the capacity to take out large concentrations of hostile forces, or their population centres, in one hit. If we had this weapon, we could destroy the navy we're facing with just one strike.'

'I agree,' stated Aharmer, 'but I also agree with Cesa: we should continue with the bomb and concentrate all our efforts in that direction. I think it's time to meet with the king, brief him on tomorrow's attack, and try to resolve any other issues at the same time.'

With the meeting concluded and an agreement reached between them, the other chiefs departed, leaving Maltor to contact the king. He sanctioned their plan to attack the invaders, but stated he would be unable to provide them with an audience until later the next day owing to pressures from his 'affairs of state'.

Maltor was somewhat annoyed with the king's attitude; as he was perfectly aware, 'the affairs of state' to which the king referred had absolutely nothing to do with the state itself, but was more to do with his desire to participate in his never-ending orgy of eating, drinking and perverted sexual practices. Nevertheless, Maltor arranged to meet Aharmer later wherein they'd refine their plan for the next morning's attack on the force off Kira Island.

Owing only to their united thirst for war, not one of them had even considered a peaceful approach to the strangers before opening hostilities.

The fleet steamed on, wallowing along at six knots, ploughing through a strange sea. Pierce looked from the bridge of Victorious in command of the graveyard watch. Under clearing skies, ragged clouds scudded across a watery moon, with stars flickering in the ever-widening spaces between them. The north-westerly wind was blowing at a gentle force three, which had halved in strength over the recent four hours, and the previously troubled water, calmer now, rolled beneath them in eight-foot undulating swells.

Captain Rowsell was awoken from a deep sleep by a naval rating sent by Pierce to awaken him in accordance with his earlier order: the time had arrived for the fleet to heave-to. Quickly reaching full awareness, the captain dressed and returned to the bridge of Victorious.

'Good morning, Peter,' he greeted Pierce. 'It looks a little different this morning. It's nice to see the storm front has finally passed. I think it could turn out to be a reasonable day—for weather only, I suspect. Oh well, back to it, I suppose. You'd better hold this position, Peter. We should be only approximately thirty miles from the island, and when dawn breaks, you should be able to see it. We can't have you lost out here, you know. I presume the compasses haven't miraculously repaired themselves whilst I was sleeping?'

'No such luck I'm afraid, Captain, but when this clears a bit more, we can at least take star sightings, and no doubt we'll get a glimpse of the sun later.'

'Back to basics then, Peter, the navigators should enjoy that. Nevertheless, it would be rather nice to know where we are on the planet if nothing else! Anyway, I intend to transfer myself to the Plymouth and return in her for the meeting with Commander Galland. Whilst you're holding here, keep the Hastings and the Arcadia on patrol around you and provide some cover with the Swordfish. I don't think we need to worry about the submarines, but we can't be a hundred per cent sure at the moment. And, of course, we've no idea if we need to worry about anyone else getting bloody minded! I'll contact you from the island with further instructions when I've something to report.'

'Of course, Captain.'

'Oh and one more thing: I want a squadron of Seafires to cover the beach and the surrounding area for the full duration of the meeting, as agreed with Galland. They must arrive over the area just prior to first light. Instruct Flight Sergeant James Roberts to assume command of the squadron; he's as level headed as anyone. I want someone I can completely trust up there. Instruct him to attack if the Germans don't keep to the terms, as dictated to them earlier. You will of course personally fully brief him on those terms, Peter.'

'Yes, Sir,' responded Peter.

'Should I be incapacitated in any way, my command will immediately transfer to Captain Ford on the Arcadier as per our original directive from the Admiralty. Please inform the Plymouth of my requirements, Peter. I'll stand by for her boat to arrive to take me across.'

Several hours later, after having successfully transferred to the destroyer and returned to the island in good time, Captain Rowsell ordered the

Plymouth to anchor off a mile from the beach, just beyond the reach of the reef, which had earlier given them all such problems.

Captain Rowsell stood on the bridge with two officers and Alan Bartlett, the Plymouth's captain, a competent and reliable man with a lifetime's experience at sea. Whilst assisting with the evacuation from Dunkirk, he became one of the few to date who'd already sunk a German U-boat.

Dawn was breaking when the squadron of Seafires appeared in the sky above the boat. In loose formation, they began to circle the beach in accordance with Pierce's orders.

Within minutes of their arrival, the Plymouth's radio man had relayed a message to the captain from the Germans. 'German submarine U35 requests permission to anchor off and disembark Commander Galland onto the island, Sir.'

'Reply permission granted. Instruct them to hold-off approximately half mile from us and make it quite clear they're to anchor on to the Plymouth broadside,' ordered Rowsell. 'I don't want to give them any opportunity to launch torpedoes without warning. But, if that's what they intend to do, they'll have to come about to line-up their tubes. When she anchors up, train your guns on her. Alan, should the sub attempt to come around, sink her. There's no point in taking any more chances than necessary.'

A disturbance in the water a mile to starboard of their position heralded the arrival of the submarine, which rose from the sea with her running lights flickering. Captain Rowsell watched as Galland's submarine slowly approached the destroyer. Coming to a halt, it anchored broadside to and approximately half a mile away.

'So far so good,' commented Rowsell. 'They're not threatening us at the moment then. Prepare a boat and I'll land on the beach as arranged.'

The small launch drew away from the Plymouth with the captain and the boat's crew aboard. They slowly motored towards the beach with all unarmed and carrying only a radio set with them.

Commander Galland's party left his submarine in a small inflatable dingy. He also headed towards the island.

The sun rose, refracting through a thin mist that lay over the island. With the sea calmer, only a light swell rocked the boats. The heady fragrance of salt mixed with damp earth and vegetation enveloped the sailors as they approached the beach.

The cliffs appeared daunting. Shear black rock stood darkly, high against the early morning sky. The two abandoned Spitfires sat parked together on the sand created a completely surreal backdrop. Thin, high cloud lightly masked the sun, but its light penetrating through, promising warmth. The storm completely dissipated, it was, as Captain Rowsell had predicted, developing into a beautiful day. Undoubtedly, had it not been for the harsh crackling of the Seafires' engines and the thudding of the launch motor, the location would have proven to be idyllic.

CHAPTER EIGHT

Thala Stowal, a flight commander of the Atlantis Air Arm Unit 767, walked purposefully across the lush grass towards the seven Hovertaks, all of which stood in a line at the far end of the airfield, just beyond the city limits of Atlanta. The planes had been prepared earlier by the base's flight mechanics in readiness for the sortie over Kira Island. Alongside him strode the six other pilots, all set to accompany him on the attack on the strange fleet currently situated close to the island's shores.

The Hovertak was the main attack aircraft of the Atlantien Air Arm, and as such, several of the models had undergone various modifications with the aim of further enhancing their performance. Unmodified, they were propelled by a single impeller unit powered by the energy transmitted from the Diathydril crystals. The craft were undoubtedly fast and extremely agile, and were armed with one deadly pulse beam projector. During the course of their implementation, they had proved to be undoubtedly effective, and a weapon which excelled in the role of ground attack.

In the modified versions of Stowal's planes, however, the manufacturers had increased the power of the impeller units, providing them with all round improved performance. In addition, the projectors had a longer range, sustaining a higher rate of fire. Stowal looked forward to trying them out in a real air battle.

With the exception of a few stolen Hovertaks operated by the resistance forces—who apparently avoided engaging the king's forces in the air—it had yet to be tested in combat against another air force, let alone one with totally alien technology. Stowal and his companions were to be the first to experience this, and they were all questioning how they'd perform in this situation. During the briefing they'd received, prior to the mission, they'd been shown images of the force they were to attack, sent to the scientists in Atlantis via their own recording equipment. They could see from the pictures how strange the aircraft and ships appeared to be, although their capabilities were somewhat of a mystery.

The pilots boarded their Hovertaks and, leaving the well-lit airfield, rose up into the pre-dawn darkness and headed out towards Kira and their unknown fate.

Commander Galland was the first on the beach. Drawn to the two spitfires, he then turned to watch the English launch as it grounded alongside his dingy.

Rowsell climbed from the launch and walking towards the German commander. 'Good morning, Commander,' he greeted. 'I'm Captain Rowsell. We meet under very strange circumstances, as I'm sure you'll agree.' The captain offered an unsure smile, still trying to establish whether they were, in fact, on common ground. 'However, since we're here at your request, would you care to open the discussion?'

'Good morning to you also, Captain, and thank you for agreeing to meet with me,' replied Galland. He looked to Captain Rowsell, unsure of exactly how to approach the situation. 'I'll be blunt, Captain. I've a feeling we're in another time. I can't absolutely prove the theory at the moment, but I think that events are currently so strange that you may be forced to admit it's unquestionably a possibility. It's obvious we're in another place. Certainly, when we arrived, we had gone from night to day. I do believe, however, that the situation is much deeper and far more complex than simply a change of the time of day.' Commander Galland paused for breath, weighing-up Rowsell's reaction, which so far provided no indication of whether he was taking any of this on-board. 'I'll also add that I've been unable to contact any of my command chain and my mechanical navigation equipment is completely defunct. I'd willingly wager that you're experiencing something similar?'

Captain Rowsell smiled and nodded his head in agreement.

'At this stage,' Galland continued, 'we've encountered no other inhabitants and, although our radios are fully operational, we're only able to send and receive signals between our two forces. Seemingly, there's no other radio traffic, which of course there should be.

'When the skies cleared earlier this morning, we took some star sightings. You'll probably be a little sceptical when I tell you this but, considering the configuration of the constellations we observed, it would seem that their position is the same as that of several thousand years ago.'

'Several thousand years ago?' Rowsell whispered.

'Yes. In brief, I feel that continuing the hostilities between us now would be extremely unwise; after all, we may be the only people from our time here, in which case I feel we must join forces. Whatever has gone before must bear no relevance here. If I'm correct in my assessment, Captain, I would say that our respective governments and their policies are no longer applicable. At this point, we've no idea of the challenges and dangers potentially facing us, and I've no wish to destroy anything we currently possess between us which may ultimately prove to be essential for the survival of us all.'

'Commander Galland,' Rowsell began, 'I have to admit that I'm completely at a loss to explain the situation myself. As I'm sure you can appreciate, your theory is a little difficult to grasp, but I'm willing to discuss it further. I don't have one of my own to offer; all I'm currently sure of is that the lives of thousands appears to be my responsibility. I can't argue with your logic, but what I need is absolute proof in order to make the right decisions.'

'Well, I think I can help you out with that one,' said a voice coming from the cockpit of one of the beached Spitfires.

Both men jumped, and with their eyes searching upwards, they saw the smiling face of an RAF officer looking down on them from the cockpit of the aircraft. 'May I join you, gentlemen?' asked the man.

'Please, be our guest,' replied Galland, hoping he hadn't been foolish enough to walk into a set-up of some kind.

Climbing down from the aircraft, the RAF officer addressed the two sailors standing before him. 'I'm Wing Commander Jack Bannerman,' he started. 'I arrived here yesterday in this Spitfire and, if you'll excuse the pun, I was in the same boat as yourselves not too long ago. I'm afraid

I do have an advantage over you gentlemen: I already know who you both are. I am also aware why you're meeting here, having listened in on your communications.'

Galland and Rowsell looked uncertainly at one other, considering whether trouble was lurking.

'You're pretty much correct in your assessment of the situation, Commander Galland and I'm genuinely impressed. I don't quite know how you worked it out because all that's occurred recently made no sense to me until it was explained by a local. I'm afraid, however, that when everything has been explained to you, you'll undoubtedly have great difficulty accepting the unacceptable. Nevertheless, you really do need to meet with Rema Sark—she's the local oracle, a scientist and a leader in the resistance movement of Atlantis.'

'Atlantis?' gasped Captain Rowsell. 'You're joking, of course, Wing Commander.'

'Unfortunately not, Captain. Miss Sark and my fellow officer, Squadron Leader Mark Calloway, are both waiting at the top of the cliffs behind us, and I suggest you allow them to join us.' Jack looked at the two men, both of whom were visibly shocked, unsure what to make of his tall tales—and further unnerved that such a story seemed to be perfectly aligned with Galland's own theory.

'With your permission, Commander Galland,' Rowsell began, 'I think we probably need them to join us. It sounds like they might be able to answer some of our questions.'

'Hmm...' Galland contemplated. 'Either that or blow us into the next century—whenever that may be.' The commander sighed, considering his options and, when deciding his choice of other routes was limited at best, he nodded curtly in agreement.

'Call them down then, Wing Commander,' said Rowsell, looking up at the sheer cliff and wondering what path—so far invisible to himself—they intended to use to reach the beach.

'Be prepared for the initiation ceremony,' Jack said with a smile, a hint of amusement in his voice. 'I think you'll find it somewhat entertaining.' He waved his arms above his head, signalling Mark and Rema.

On the cliff above the three men appeared two figures clad in silver suits, helmets and wearing backpacks. Unlike the previous day, however, silver rods were nowhere to be seen.

The two sailors could not believe their eyes, both stepping back in amazement, their mouths open in disbelief as the silver-clad figures floated from the cliff-top and slowly descended to the beach.

Removing their helmets, Rema and Mark walked over to join the rest of the party.

'I could grow to like this silent flying malarkey, I really could,' quipped Mark with a smile. 'Pleased to meet you both,' he said, smiling at Rowsell and Galland. 'I'm Flash Gordon, Saviour of the Universe, at your service, no job too small.' He outstretched his right hand towards them.

'Please forgive my friend,' Jack interrupted, laughing. 'He's had a nasty shock in the past day or so, and I fear it may have affected his sense of occasion somewhat!'

Rowsell reached for Mark's hand but, before anyone could say any more, a high-pitched whine broke through the skies and, quick as lightning, seven unearthly flying machines passed low over them in an arrowhead formation. Jet black, the aircraft had bright yellow insignias blazoned across the sides of their fat, stubby bodies and wings which were, on the face of it, far too short to enable flight. Blue-tinted cockpits blistered the fuselages roughly four feet back from the noses, and domed heads peered down on all below them.

'What the hell are those things?' called Mark in surprise. 'They look like pregnant bumble bees! And *they* aren't supposed to fly either, so I'm told!'

Perfectly aware of their origin, Rema shouted, 'We're in big trouble now! Those things are Hovertaks—they belong to the king's Air Arm and they're deadly! Take cover behind those fallen rocks and get the men away from the landing boats before it's too late!'

Calling the open-mouthed boat crews over, everyone dived for cover behind the large rock-fall which Rema had created the previous night. Last to arrive was the captain's radio man. Encumbered by the heavy equipment, he struggled to keep up with his comrades. Now peering out from their inadequate shelters, squinting against the strong sunlight, the men watched as the peculiar aircraft turned over the sea and headed back towards them.

James Roberts and his squadron appeared high above the cliffs. They were approaching the bay from the north when the new arrivals shot beneath them, flying low across the water, heading for the shore. By pure luck, they had been above the flight of the Hovertaks and were virtually invisible to them, hidden in the day's bright sun.

Roberts watched as the craft flew across the land, banked around, and made another pass towards the beach. Dumbstruck by the appearance of such strange flying machines, he barely considered the possibility that they were, in fact, hostile: they clearly weren't German fighters and, being confused as to their origins, initiating an attack against them seemed somewhat unnecessary.

Still puzzled by the Hovertaks, he continued to watch as they persisted to fly towards the defenceless group, which was now huddled behind the landslide under the cliff face. And then suddenly, without warning or provocation, the lead aircraft shot out a bolt of white light, a glowing sphere of iridescent purple flaring from its nose. Almost simultaneously, the other six aircraft followed suit, and seven bolts of pure malignant energy immediately struck the area surrounding the beach party. The landing boats blew apart instantaneously as if struck by a gigantic hammer, as did both Spitfires.

Two German seamen hiding behind a large boulder were instantly killed as the bolts obliterated the rocks in front of them, reducing them to mere fragments.

In only one pass, the attackers had destroyed all the equipment on the beach and killed two German submariners.

Furious with this unprovoked attack, and now in no doubt of their intentions, James Roberts ordered his squadron to dive on the intruders—and destroy them.

Meanwhile, Thala Stowal delighted with the success of their first run. Speaking to his flight over his headset communicator he congratulated his team. 'Nice work, men! We'll attack those ships next and mop-up the survivors on the beach later. Then we'll deal with those out at sea. Taks two, three and four follow me; we'll take the largest ship. Five, six and seven engage the smaller one.'

As per their commander's instruction, the formation split into two groups and streaked towards the destroyer and submarine lying anchored off the shore. Importantly, however, Stowal had failed to notice that his flight wasn't alone—his first mistake.

Too late to prevent their attack on the beach, Roberts's squadron dived out of the sun behind the Hovertaks just as their formation split. Adjusting their flight to suit the enemy's manoeuvres, each pilot proceeded to select a target and, without hesitation, pressed their gun buttons. The whining scream of the Hovertaks and snarling roar of the pursuing Seafires mingled with the staccato thudding of multiple machine guns, which persisted to hurl furiously flowing rivers of bullets at the unsuspecting attackers. Two of the Hovertaks were torn apart as the Seafires' guns struck with unimaginable force, causing the Hovertaks to fall into the sea, flaming and broken. Another Hovertak, now badly damaged, slow banked round, fire streaming from its superstructure and losing height rapidly. Within mere moments, the craft went smashing into the cliff face, the dying pilot oblivious to his fate.

Stowal watched in horror as the craft exploded in a shower of debris, hot, white fragments of aircraft blending with the remains of its pilot, subsequently showering the beach. Stowal was devastated; he'd not seen these planes when his flight arrived over the island. In his haste to attack what he saw, he'd not even looked for trouble elsewhere. He'd failed. Worse still, he'd known these invaders had aircraft from the visuals he'd seen at the briefing, but he'd allowed himself to become excited at the prospect of fighting them, unaware of the tactics required.

His heart sank within him, acknowledging the irreparable damage. He should've been more cautious—and his error of judgement had proven to be a fatal error for three of his comrades.

Having never encountered enemies in the air before, Stowal had not been threatened in the sky and lacked the instincts born from experience. Aside from his minimal training in aerial combat, this was his first genuine air battle he had ever experienced—which, to be fair, was the real reason for his mistake. Quite simply, he hadn't been ready for it and all it entailed.

Taking evasive action, Stowal threw his aircraft into a ninety-degree turn and, applying full power, shot straight up into the sky, still appalled by the ease with which his comrades had been dispatched. And perhaps worse, for the first time in his professional career, he was also terribly afraid.

'Remaining Taks, break off. Watch your backs and let's get the Hades out of here!' Stowal commanded. The four remaining aircraft spilled across the sky, each desperate to gain height and shake off their tormentors.

Roberts and his pilots, having untold hours of combat experience, were ready for this manoeuvre. Hauling their planes around with the rudder bars whilst pulling back on their control sticks, and already at full throttle, they soared up into the sky, keeping pace with their quarry.

From their shelter on the sand, the beach party watched as the fight developed above them, their eyes permanently fixed on the sky. All of them knew: their lives depended on the airmen's protection, and their concentration was absolute.

'They're giving those bastards a sound beating at the moment,' commented Galland.

'Damn right they are. Those goons will think carefully before sailing in like that again, the arrogant bastards,' replied Mark.

'They've got to keep behind those buggers, though. That gun affair they're using looks nasty—look what it did to our poor old kites,' Jack said, looking sadly at his ruined aircraft.

'Don't worry about your bloody plane, Wing Commander,' said Captain Rowsell. 'That's the least of our worries right now. If we get out of here, I'll gladly replace it for you—we've plenty more of those on-board our merchantmen.'

~*~*~*~

Up in the air, flying officer George Knowles was right on the tail of a Hovertak. Through an almost vertical climb, he'd jockeyed his Seafire into a perfect position. Pressing the button on the side of his control stick, he felt the kick of his guns as they disgorged their missiles into the fleeing enemy. 'Right up his arse!' he shouted triumphantly. Unfortunately, however, his victory cost him dear as, unbeknownst to him, he'd hit the beam weapon's initial firing chamber located at the tail of the Hovertaks. His bullets instantly released the stored energy of the shattered chamber in an uncontrolled surge of power. The machine subsequently exploded with the force of a magnificent bomb. Knowles was flying much too close, and the shattered Hovertak ripped into his plane, shearing off the propeller, a large section of the port wing, and peppering his cockpit with shrapnel. Although now badly wounded, Knowles was nevertheless able to slide back the canopy of his doomed aircraft and bale out.

Releasing his chute, Knowles drifted down towards the sea far below him. In spite of his pain, he was relieved to see the fight had ended right above the submarine, making it more likely he'd be rescued sooner rather than later. He needed treatment urgently, and now he hoped they'd get to him in time.

Back in the air and instantly aware he'd been hit, Stowal felt his craft veer out of control. Without stopping to think, he activated the emergency systems. The canopy above him melted away, and his seat rose from the aircraft as it disintegrated beneath him. Fitted with the same mechanism as Rema's backpack, the seat allowed him to escape from the aircraft, remain in the air, and subsequently control his descent, selecting a landing place of his choice.

Below him, Stowal witnessed his aircraft explode, and watched as the pieces descended, crashing into his attacker's aircraft, which then partially dismembered, rolled over, and went into a dive. He was surprised to see the pilot leap from the stricken plane, which seemed to him to be just as suicidal an action as staying in it. He then watched as a dome of material connected to a mass of ropes emerged from a pack on the pilot's back and spread out above him, slowly arresting his fall.

He now understood why the man had jumped from his plane.

Looking around, Stowal saw the remaining Hovertaks madly gyrating around the sky with their adversaries still in hot pursuit, seemingly unable to shake them off or position themselves to retaliate. Stowal had, in spite of everything, controlled his fear, although this had since been replaced with a demonic anger, directed solely at the strangers. Unable to exact vengeance on anyone else, he manoeuvred himself above the one who'd destroyed his Hovertak and followed him down towards the sea below.

Undoubtedly, the king's air force had never been damaged like this before, and their first major action against these intruders didn't bode well for the future. In blind rage, Stowal realised that, even if he could return—which he clearly now couldn't—he would be stripped of his rank, imprisoned, or possibly worse, and so he decided that the man responsible for his downfall would pay for his misfortunes.

Steering himself closer to Knowles, who was now hanging beneath his parachute, Stowal concluded that the man would be unarmed. Hatred burned as he lifted a silver rod from its holster in the side of his seat and pointed it at the wounded, defenceless pilot.

Stowal had made yet another miscalculation and, as a rapid thumping began to emanate from the sea, Stowal sensed his death was imminent. The sound mutated to the buzzing of large angry insects. With blind panic engulfing him and with the passing of only a second or two, a hail of gunfire was released from the submarine below, ripping him apart. The German gunners at their post beside the anti-aircraft gun had guessed Stowal's intentions and had intervened, putting a conclusive stop to his murderous plan.

Knowles watched in horror as the enemy pilot was dissected by a stream of bullets, tearing him limb from limb in front of his eyes. In a split second, Stowal was reduced to a lump of bloody gore, which dropped to the sea like a stone, shredded by the submarines guns.

'Four down, three to go,' smiled Mark, clearly enthralled with the on-going competition thriving above him.

'Good shooting by your men, Commander!' exclaimed Jack. 'They saved our pilot's bacon there.'

Tane Scala, flying Hovertak No.7, was pulling away from his pursuer. His machine had a faster climb rate than the Seafire tailing him and, having gained some thousand-yard advantage, he levelled out, allowing his adversary to line-up behind him in straight and level flight.

Pilot officer Richard Barns, currently engaged with Hovertak No.7, couldn't believe his luck. Faster than the Hovertak in level flight, he rapidly closed-in for the kill. Suddenly, without warning, the machine slowed appreciably and rose vertically, remaining horizontal. Barns was completely unprepared, and flew straight under the enemy plane which, returning to horizontal flight, now pursued him.

Scala delighted with the complete reversal of fortunes he'd gained by implementing the most textbook of strategies. Now the pursuer, he unleashed his weapon on Barn's Seafire. Barns' last earthly memory was a glowing purple ball engulfing his plane, a burning sensation, and utter darkness. The Seafire disappeared in a flash of brilliant white light and vaporised, leaving little trace it ever existed.

Having successfully disposed of his foe, Scala was now slowly flying forward. Using his hovering and vertical lift capabilities, he'd lost most of the forward momentum and now needed time to accelerate away, which ultimately left him vulnerable.

Roberts and his wingman, observing the wallowing Hovertak that had just killed Barns above them, flew in behind it. One on either side, they delivered a withering burst. Sixteen machine guns quickly sent it to join the unfortunate Barns, ensuring Scala's victory was amongst the shortest lived of the day so far.

'Oh hell! Did you see that?' cried Mark, still totally immersed in the unfolding drama above him. 'We'll have to watch that one when we fight this lot!'

'I thought we had the edge until I saw that little trick,' replied Jack. 'It was a clever stunt, but then again, it really did him no good in the end, did it?'

'Hmm…' contemplated Mark. 'I think we'll definitely need to revise our strategies to allow for these machines' little tricks or we definitely won't survive for long up there.'

The remaining two Hovertaks, now hopelessly outnumbered, made their attempt to escape. Flying low at maximum speed and hugging the waves, they sought to flee the fight. In their panic, they flew directly between the Plymouth and the U35, which subsequently put them in range of every gun on both ships, which naturally brought the whole lot to bear on the fleeing aircraft. With a sound like thunder, smoke and flame belched from the combined armaments, propelling a flying wall of steel to greet the departing raiders. At almost point-blank range, the two surviving Hovertaks flew straight into the barrage, both of which exploded in mid-air, their remains disappearing into the ocean in a sheet of spray. Their demise concluded the initial engagement between the Anglo/German/Resistance alliances versus the king's Atlantien Air Arm.

The entire savage battle was over in less than ten minutes and had cost, in total, an equal number of lives.

Roberts sighed in relief. The last of the raiders had been destroyed by the ships' guns, and he knew everyone involved here today could be proud of their performance. Undoubtedly, however, his thoughts were understandably tinged with sadness of the loss of Richard, who had been a dear friend. 'Damn this fucking war!' he said to himself, before wondering exactly what war they were supposed to be fighting.

His attention redirected, Roberts watched as George Knowles was picked from the sea by the Germans and taken on-board their submarine, hoping he'd not lose yet another friend here today.

Now climbing from the shelter of the rocks, the beach party watched the Seafires as they departed, their battle now won, giving silent thanks to the retreating pilots who, with skill and courage, had unquestionably saved their lives.

Galland looked sadly at the two dead sailors, both of whom had been members of his crew for some time, were keen and efficient in their work, and fearless in action. He knew he'd miss them. Using the captain's radio, Galland contacted his boat, promptly ordering his crew to collect the bodies and prepare them for a sea burial later on in the day.

Meanwhile, Rowsell instructed Victorious to return with the fleet as soon as Roberts's squadron had landed. Now wary of the king's forces, he ensured all of his aircraft would be ready to scramble should they be attacked again. He ordered the fleet to maintain full alert, and instructed his second in command on-board the carrier to debrief the returning airmen.

Returning to their meeting, which was now plus three more, the captain and commander resumed their discussion which had been so savagely interrupted.

'Commander,' began Rowsell, 'considering we haven't agreed to amalgamate our forces yet, we made a pretty good team in that unpleasant little interlude.'

'Indeed we did,' responded Galland thoughtfully. 'With that said, I think my original thoughts have just received evidential proof as to why I believe we should make this a permanent arrangement.'

Rowsell nodded his agreement.

'Mind you,' continued Galland, 'we were lucky this time. The enemy was clearly unprepared for the reception they got here. If your planes hadn't been on station when they arrived, or if they'd seen them before they attacked us, the outcome may well have been very different.'

'If we'd had no aircraft,' Jack commented, 'they'd have done a hell of a lot of damage. I don't think the two ships here could've stopped them on their own. But, judging by their performance against our pilots, it probably would've turned out much the same if they had seen us. I don't think they have had much experience in air-to-air combat.'

'It would appear that way,' replied Galland.

'If all their airmen are at the same level as the ones sent here today, we most definitely have a distinct advantage. But,' continued Jack, 'I'd be more concerned if those machines were flown by the Luftwaffe Commander… those aircraft in the hands of your fighter pilots would be very hard to beat indeed.'

'They were the latest version of the Hovertak,' Rema volunteered. 'There aren't many of them in service yet, and their performance has been greatly enhanced. I can tell by the markings I saw on their tails that the pilots belonged to the king's elite 767 air arm. You've just fought the best he has. And, to be honest, I'm stunned by the result.' She smiled at each of the men.

'If I'd not seen it with my own eyes I wouldn't have believed it myself,' commented Mark. 'Such flying abilities—and in the Fleet Air Arm of all places! I think I might show them more respect in future!'

Captain Rowsell scowled at Mark, well aware of the rivalry between the services. 'We need to get back to business! Will somebody tell Commander Galland and me what the hell's going on around here?' The captain barked at the group, turning to look at Rema, Jack and Mark.

'Very well, but I suggest you find somewhere to sit down and let Rema tell the tale,' said Mark. 'Firstly, it's a long story, and secondly, you'll need to sit down when you learn the truth anyway. The Wing Commander and I are leaving you shortly. We're off to Atlanta with one of Rema's colleagues. When we arrive, we'll check out the opposition; hopefully we'll satisfy ourselves that the facts Rema gave us yesterday— and what she's about to divulge to you here today—all stack up.' Mark looked at Jack, smiling slightly. 'By the end of the story, you're bound to need the same reassurance as we do—which, with any luck, we'll be able to pass on to you when we return.'

'There's no point in us hanging around whilst we wait for her to reiterate the whole thing, so we'll go off and do something useful,' said Jack. 'I'd say time seems to be of the essence at the moment. Who knows when the next attack will take place.'

That morning, before they had left for the beach, Rema had arranged for Jack and Mark to be collected by a resistance member in her family's private Vertlyn—a fast four-seat flying machine considered to be extremely popular amongst the Atlantien hierarchy. Rema would call her onto the beach at a convenient point in the coming meeting, which would therefore allow the two airmen to depart, at which point she'd fly them to her family home on the outskirts of Atlanta. From there, Rema's colleague would act as their guide and give them the opportunity to see life there for themselves.

Rema decided now would be the best time to make her call and so, using a handheld communicator, she called her pilot, receiving the reply that the two men would be collected within the next few minutes.

'Unfortunately for some of us, we've encountered your military now, Rema,' Galland said after the call was made. 'Obviously they're airborne, so what else have they got?'

'Like you, they've three main services, all with subsections specialising in various types of warfare,' Rema began. 'The army is the greatest of the three. At this point in history, there's little opposition on the sea and virtually none at all in the air. The air arm and navy support the armies in the field, who do the bulk of any actual fighting. The main duties of the navy involve escorting the vast merchant fleet which the king uses to distribute supplies to his armies and conquered lands. They're also used to attack the shorelines of the lands he's currently invading. The lands have many large rivers which are navigable for thousands of miles, and so the navy is used in many of the king's campaigns—even if they're far from the main oceans.'

'It sounds like your monarch's a fan of war and bloodshed,' remarked Galland.

Rema nodded. 'Our lands have vastly changed.'

'And, judging by the equipment they brought here, am I right in assuming all of the services have weapons equivalent to ours?' Rowsell asked.

'You are. All their equipment is as advanced as yours, although it works on different principles. In some cases, it's incomparably more so. I'll cover that subject in more depth when I give you the rundown of the situation later,' Rema replied.

Within a few minutes, a small white aeroplane with red flashes along the fuselage appeared round the cliff buttress as it entered the sea to the left of the beach. The high-pitched whining indicated a similar engine to those which powered the fighters that had attacked them earlier. Turning towards them, the little aircraft quickly reduced its speed and settled on the ground in front of them in a welter of whirling sand, its motor sighing to silence.

A young woman climbed from the cabin and stood on the short triangular starboard wing. 'My Ra!' she exclaimed. 'We heard the racket and saw something of the scrap from the base. Looking at this lot, I'm guessing you've had a visit from the king's lot,' Tiea said thickly. Turning her attention to Mark and Jack, she smiled. 'Are you boys ready for the trip across the old briny?'

Anticipating a kindred spirit, Mark was delighted to see Tiea again, and flashed a dimpled smile. 'I knew you couldn't resist me! Well, I guess it was only a matter of time really.'

Tiea couldn't help but return the smile, having looked forward to seeing Mark again since meeting him the previous night.

'Well, girl, take me to paradise, I'm ready,' Mark added, his eyes sparkling.

Rema laughed whilst the two seamen exchanged curious and somewhat disapproving glances.

'I apologise once again, gentlemen,' Jack remarked. 'As I told you before, I'm afraid my colleague here has had a bit of a shock; he's really not himself at the moment,' he lied.

Mark glanced to Jack and gave a knowing smirk.

The two airmen bade their farewells and climbed up into the aircraft's small cabin behind Tiea, Mark ensuring he sat beside her.

Once the three were safely harnessed in the craft, Tiea lifted the trim little plane from the sand, rapidly gaining height and speed, and headed off towards Atlantis. At nine thousand feet, Tiea levelled off.

Back at the beach, the remaining shore party watched as the Vertlyn departed. Accelerating rapidly, it soon became a speck on the horizon.

With the airmen gone, Rema had quickly settled down and reiterated her information for the benefit of the two sea captains. They listened intensely, immersed in her words as she passed on the facts, as she had with the airmen the previous day. Both Galland and Rowsell asked much the same questions and expressed the same doubts, but once their queries had been answered, the captains were seemingly satisfied that what they had been told was probably sound.

Informing the seamen and answering their seemingly endless string of questions had taken several hours but, nevertheless exhausted, the two sailors felt that they were now in a better position—completely aware of what they now they faced and what decisions could be made in light of such information. However, reserving their final judgement until the airmen returned with the results of their investigation in Atlanta, they'd agreed that they would work on the basis that the facts were as Rema had presented.

Captain Rowsell continued the conversation. 'Well, as I'm sure you can imagine, Rema, it is somewhat of a fantastical tale to us mere seamen. Nevertheless, I think I speak for both of us when I say that I'm convinced enough to pass this data on to our people; I'm sure it won't be the simplest task to achieve, but having listened to your account, I accept—even though I don't much like it—that we've travelled back in time.

'Incidentally, the commander here also suspected the same thing when he took note of star sightings earlier, and so you've managed to sell that one to us without much effort. I hope I'll make as good a job of it myself when tackling my crew.' Rowsell looked out to the ocean, contemplating the situation and how he'd ever begin to inform his men of the situation—and the time!—in which they now found themselves. 'Having said that, however, I feel the time travel is the most difficult element to overcome. If I can get my men on-side with that notion, I'm sure we'll be fine. But I must say, Rema, you've had a somewhat simple task, convincing four men of this predicament; I have to appeal to six thousand!'

'Quite so,' agreed Galland. 'The human mind is an unpredictable thing, and who knows how these men will come to terms with not only the current state of affairs, but probably more importantly, the fact that they'll never return to the lives they knew or the people they cared for. This is a whole new life for everyone concerned, and we're going to have to set out all of the parameters clearly; we're going to have to try to sell these circumstances, offer them a package to make this obligatory situation as appealing as possible. We've one chance, and so we need to ensure we get this right. Who knows what would happen if the men can't or won't accept how things stand.' Galland shook his head, dreading such a situation arising.

'I wouldn't want to even consider what we'd be facing if they won't accept the truth,' Rowsell sighed. 'Anger, possibly an ambush. They'd undoubtedly feel trapped or that we are trying to fool them, possibly holding them hostage…' Rowsell straightened his back and poised himself. 'When I tell them the news, it will mean all their deep-rooted concepts and beliefs regarding life as they once understood it will have to change radically. Obviously, not one single member of the crews have chosen to be in the Kingdom of Atlantis, let alone have any influence in its affairs. In fact, I doubt many of them have ever before considered the bigger picture or its endless ramifications, let alone having an involvement in such. Somehow, I've got to make them want to rebuild their lives here.'

Rema nodded her head in agreement, and looked from Galland to Rowsell. 'Gentlemen, I agree you face a challenging task, much like I have done. And you're correct when you state my own task in this arena has been much simpler, tackling significantly lower numbers. But this can be done—it *must* be done. We all know now exactly what's at stake here.'

'Of course,' Galland continued. 'But we must not neglect to acknowledge that there are some pretty fundamental considerations to take on board here. Firstly, none of our military laws realistically apply in the new order, not unless a new agreement is devised and implemented, and so none of our men are under any obligation to serve. In reality, we'll become mercenaries if we fight for you—which, of course, is something quite different to our previous occupation. As I'm sure you'll both agree, this could prove to be somewhat problematic.'

Rowsell continued. 'I'm sure, within our ranks, we'll have a number of well-versed professionals in the legal arena who aren't likely to miss such a fact. If I can't persuade them all to accept everything you've told us, I've at least to convince them that this new enemy is dangerous to them personally. That being the case, I personally consider the best way forward is for them to continue to serve within the fleet, just as before. This would of course require that they obey all the standard protocols and laws which formerly applied. They must continue to act on the directives of their superior officers and my overall command. I believe, after what you've said, Rema, that they will, in all probability, be killed by your king should they not cooperate. If I can influence my men along those lines, we'll be halfway there.' Rowsell turned to Galland and eyed him cautiously. 'Commander, I do believe that we need to stick together, form an alliance from hereon in, at the very least until we fully understand how everything works in this world. We've little hope individually.'

Galland acknowledged Rowsell's sentiment, leaving him to continue.

'And, Rema, both Commander Galland and I are forced to trust you when you say we can't return to our time, although I must admit that the evidence you've given us regarding the potential outcome of our battle in the Atlantic was pretty conclusive. It would appear we all owe you our lives, and I can see that it wouldn't be right for any of us to return to our world now—even if we could. Ultimately, although it was rather one-sided as deals go, you've saved us, and now we must help you.'

Commander Galland now steered the conversation. 'Unfortunately, the choices of our men are now zero. Frustratingly for them, if this had been just a foreign country seeking mercenaries, those that disagree with any such proposal could simply discharge themselves and journey home. Since they can never do that, however, I only hope they'll come to terms with the situation and stay with their comrades out of choice, rather than wandering off on their own and facing whatever ghastly fate this war-zone has to offer.

'Assuming we get that far, it's going to be undoubtedly more difficult to communicate some of the further revelations,' Galland continued, speaking directly to Rema. 'Suggesting that your fight is, by association, *our* fight, in which we must join as the only way of preserving our own futures, whilst compelling in its logic, this could still prove to be a difficult concept to sell to some of our compatriots.'

Galland chuckled to himself in disbelief. 'Rema, you're asking us to transform from logical, rational men to those who miraculously live in a world of ancient aliens, super weapons with planet-destroying capabilities, energy-producing crystals... However, I feel the impossible could be achieved, but it's important to highlight to you, Rema, that one cannot be expected to give for nothing; greed is a good motivator here, and I'd therefore appreciate it if you could consider how our men and their services could be compensated.'

'A point I was intending to raise myself,' Rowsell stated. 'Without question, personal gain will be the only reason a number of our crew will feel the need to fight for you instead of running for the hills, or the ocean, or the skies. To be fair to them, they've lost their world now and all they'd built within it. An appealing package would give them something else to aim for in this world—*their* new world.'

'Quite,' nodded Galland. 'I suppose one of the more predominant advantages is, of course, that we are only asking them to continue on with what they were already doing, insomuch as they're all fighting men. We were fighting a war in 1940, but their skills still apply here.'

'Yes, that's perfectly true,' stated Rowsell. 'Providing we are able to retain the full and unquestioning support of the vast majority of our people in this war—*your* way, *our* way, *whoever's* war—we can do as you ask. And assuming we can rely on their support, irrespective of their reasons for giving it, I think we should join you.

Rema looked out to the vast ocean and the marvellously blue sky, considering how, only mere hours ago, the sky had been greyed with attack and defence, bloodshed and destruction, but had since returned to its magnificent glory. She contemplated how her world might end if the king was able to wreak any further havoc, and knew that, without question, she needed as many thousands of fighters on her side if she was to achieve the ultimate objective of the resistance. 'I do understand all of your concerns,' said Rema, finally breaking her silent contemplation. 'I trust you'll find a way to resolve all of the issues you'll face, and naturally we'll do all we can to assist you. I'm relieved that you agree in principle and have at least accepted the reasoning behind our desperate action in bringing you here.

'On the practical side, I'll deal with your request for compensation immediately. We'll ensure everyone's well paid for their services, allowing them to enjoy the full range of essentials and pleasures on offer in our world.'

Seemingly pleased with Rema's response, Captain Rowsell turned to Galland. 'Commander, in light of this meeting, and assuming we'll both keep the support of our officers and men, I now agree unreservedly to combine our forces, as per your suggestion. I'd be delighted to welcome you and your men into my command. Do you still wish to proceed?'

Galland nodded enthusiastically. 'Most certainly, Captain, probably even more so now than before. I'm sure it's the right thing to do, especially if we're going to continue fighting here, as Rema expects. I've no doubt we'll need to draw on each other's strengths before this is done with.'

'Then so be it,' Rowsell smiled, holding out his hand. 'I'll inform my command of our agreement, and issue a fleet directive confirming that your boats and men are to be accepted into our service with immediate effect. You'll hold an equivalent rank within our navy and will be part of all decision-making processes in line with our other senior officers. How does that sound?'

'Perfect,' Galland responded, taking the captain's hand and shaking on the agreement. 'Thank you, Sir. I'm pleased to accept your generous terms, although I must state that it will feel very strange for us all to be fighting together rather than against each other—at all levels, no doubt! We'll have to watch our men carefully for a time, I fear; I'm sure we don't want our past animosities to ruin this alliance.'

'Quite so, Commander.' Rowsell turned to address Rema. 'A small point possibly, but do you know where the RAF men stand in all of this?'

'Well, we had a discussion about this prior to gate-crashing your meeting,' smiled Rema. 'Should you wish, I'm sure they'll accept you as their Commander in Chief, as has Commander Galland. We assumed for the sake of our discussion that you'd probably join forces and would presumably wish them to be included. However, we felt they'd be best employed acting as liaison officers between the resistance and yourselves. I hope you see advantages in that arrangement. If you agree, they'd be on secondment to the resistance for the foreseeable future.'

'I agree that's possibly a wise route to take, Rema,' Rowsell replied. 'I'll happily go along with that. Now all we have to do is convince everyone else to join us!'

'Well they're still with us at the moment, Captain,' said Galland, nodding towards the ocean. Looking up, they saw the fleet spread in a wide formation across the calm blue waters, heading for the Island.

'So it would appear, Commander,' acknowledged the captain with a small smile. 'Rema, we obviously need a better location than this from which to operate our fleet. And to be perfectly honest, I'd rather not stay any longer than necessary. If we anchor up here we'll be easy targets if we're attacked again. Any suggestions?'

'Our base here would be ideal, Captain,' Rema responded. 'Amongst other things, it already has a well-defended anchorage that we use for our own boats. It's not far from here either.'

'Would it be adequate for our fleet?' Rowsell asked.

'Well, there's a large sheltered cove on the North coast, surrounded by high cliffs, which form a perfect outer harbour. Leading through the cliffs is a navigable natural chasm which opens out into a large deep inner lake. The lake's surrounded by hills on three sides, all of which are covered in tall, dense forest. The lake would provide a safe place for your fleet to anchor—it's easily defended from either ground or sea attacks due to the terrain. Air attacks are not so easy either because of the height of the cliffs and the surrounding hills. It's where we operate from and where we anchor our own vessels. We already have pulse weapons in position to defend it, but the king's forces so far haven't attacked it.'

Both Galland and Rowsell looked pleased with Rema's description of their potential new operating base, and smiled satisfactorily.

'In addition, we also have underground facilities there which would enable you and your crew to relax and mix with our people, should they wish to do so,' offered Rema.

'Well, that sounds exactly what we need. A safe harbour from which to operate and a place to belong for the time being. If you're sure there's room for the entire fleet, it sounds to be far better than I'd have hoped for,' said the captain with relief. 'Well,' he continued, clapping his hands together, 'the sooner we leave, the sooner we'll be there, I suppose. I'll call the Plymouth and get us picked up. But, as we've no idea how to get to your base and no compasses or charts either, I guess we'll need you to show us the way?'

'Of course, Captain, I'd be only too pleased. I'd recommend allowing an hour or so to get the fleet organised and under way again, and assuming we can then steam ahead at about twelve knots, we should be there just before dark.'

'Perfect,' replied Rowsell.

Having all been duly collected from the beach by the launch, Galland was promptly delivered to the U35. He ordered his remaining submarines to join them on the voyage to the harbour whilst Captain Rowsell and Rema sailed on to the Plymouth and climbed aboard.

Not wishing to further delay their departure by transferring himself to Victorious, Rowsell directed his fleet from the destroyer's bridge, leading the fleet around the island and towards the harbour, guided by Rema.

CHAPTER NINE

In the control dome of the Air Arm landing field near the city of Atlanta, Sol Aharmer was following the course of the attack he and his colleagues had planned yesterday. Sat by a communicator, he'd been listening to his men as they struggled with the Seafires over Kira. As the fight progressed, it soon became apparent that things were not going well for his men. From a promising start with the achievement of a couple of victories, they were now being decimated as the action continued. In spite of sending his very best men and machines into the battle, it nevertheless appeared that they had been quickly—and, from his perspective, all too easily—despatched by the opposition.

Given the absolutely disastrous outcome of the battle, he now wondered whether he and his colleagues had made the right decision when they'd sent his airmen on this mission.

Unquestionably, with the benefit of hindsight, the plan was still sound in parts; it was, after all, only a hit-and-run raid carried out by a small and expendable force for the purpose of assessing the enemy's capabilities. Essentially, insofar as that went, the mission had succeeded. Now at least they knew just how capable their opponents had turned out to be.

Whilst that knowledge provided Sol with little comfort, it was nevertheless better to have sacrificed a small force rather than wasted a more significant one. Judging by today's events, it was almost guaranteed that, had they opted to send a larger, more valuable army and thereby invested more aircraft, the result may have been much worse.

Of course, despite looking on the bright side and considering the mission a success, Sol was nevertheless forced to acknowledge one very disturbing fact: never before had his pilots been defeated. Although, of course, it had to be noted that there had never before been much in the way of air battles to provide any form of experience; in fact, stolen

Hovertaks operated by the resistance had been their only adversary in the sky, and even they wouldn't engage unless they had no other choice.

One fact remained pretty clear, and that was that his pilots and not his machines had failed. Without question, his men were far more suited to air to ground operations, in which they'd received plenty of practice. It was clear that, ideally, he must retrain them all in air-to-air tactics before they took on any of the strangers again—but it seemed unlikely he'd have the time.

Without question, he'd been expecting at least some of his aircraft to return. In truth, it never crossed his mind that none of them would.

The Hovertaks had been equipped with visual recorders. These showing the morning's detailed action coupled with the pilot's reports would have given him a much needed insight as to the direction their training should take. In this, the mission had totally failed, and he was more upset by this than the loss of a few men and machines.

Maybe the king would be objective about the raid and take it, as he had, as a lesson learnt—but this would depend on his mood at the time rather than any future tactical advantages the loss of the flight may have given them. Irrespectively, he was sure he'd soon find out.

Having been previously rejoicing in the title he'd now bestowed upon himself—His Undefeated, Invincible and Most High Majesty, Ruler of Atlantis, Ramma the Thirteenth—the king was now highly annoyed. His temper was not improved by the severe hangover and chronic indigestion from which he now suffered, caused by yesterday's overindulgences—which, even by his standards, had been excessive. Never one to take setbacks in his stride, having been informed only yesterday of the failure of his transporter machine and the invaders in his realm, the defeat of his air force over Kira island this morning was simply more than he was willing to accept: he was now actively looking for someone to execute to satisfy his need to release some frustration. In fact, he comforted himself with the thought that he'd probably execute a lot of people.

Without question, his High Commanders were responsible for their current predicament; it was they, after all, whom had been charged with looking after his interests. It was *their* fault that things were now going so wrong. He debated whether he should have their wives whipped in public, whether such actions might succeed in forcing them to focus their minds a little better towards their duty.

In actual fact, the king—much like any other bully—was frightened of strength and power, and was therefore secretly wary of his men. Whilst he knew that their own fear of him would ensure they'd never dare cross him, he nevertheless understood that, should they choose to do so, their power would outmatch his own and he would be done for.

Despite such an acknowledgement, the king was nevertheless an exceptionally cruel individual; a man who commonly partook in fantasies of causing pain and loss to those vulnerable and enjoying the absolute power bestowed upon a King, knowing he was in a position to carry out whatever he deemed necessary, which to his female prisoners, wives and serving girls poor behinds and backs painful knowledge, he often did.

Restlessly wandering through his sumptuous palace, the king contemplated the potential threat posed by the events of the last two days. His ultimate priority was to ensure his own safety—a priority which, given the recent events, required urgent attention.

Having already conquered a vast area surrounding his native island, the only local threat had been the resistance, and their attacks had been mainly confined to his factories and distribution centres. Of course, such issues had proven to be a thorn in his side, and the damage inflicted during such instances was undoubtedly disruptive and expensive to repair, but the fact remained that the resistance considered themselves to be *good* and held no belief in bloodshed, and so posed no actual threat to him. Nevertheless, he always ensured he was guarded within his fortressed palace, utilising several hundred hand-picked troops. In addition, he was also surrounded by a reasonable contingent of armed forces, all of which were permanently based in Atlantis. With that taken into account, had the resistance ever considered casting their morals aside and pursuing a full-blown war against him, they would simply have been outnumbered, with inadequate firepower to secure any hold over him.

Before now, the king realised, there had never been any opportunity for any significant incursion into his homeland, and so he'd so far been well protected. Now, however, its local defences didn't seem quite so adequate. Now, if the intruders decide to attack him before he could return the bulk of his armies, he might not have the power to resist them—and where would that leave him? Considering the outcome of the first instalment—which, he recognised, had been sprung without warning—he was inclined to doubt that he would experience success if *they* were to mount a surprise attack.

He would be finished.

With this realisation, the king's anger reignited as his thoughts wandered to his campaign in Mu. The battle had been going well, and he'd expected to conquer this last remaining bastion by the end of the year, therefore making him king of the entire world. Annoyingly, however, the only reason for the defeat taking so long was Mu's vast area coupled with the mountainous and heavily forested terrain, which made it significantly less vulnerable to his war machines. As a result, more reliance had to be placed on his foot soldiers who had been backed-up by seemingly ineffective air support. Nevertheless, although an unquestionably difficult and time-consuming exercise, the forces were making steady progress—but that didn't help him much in the current predicament; now, he needed every last resource he could lay his hands on.

He could be on the verge of losing everything—everything he'd ever fought for.

The three high commanders approached the thick fifteen foot high stone wall surrounding the outer perimeter of the palace grounds. They were on their way to an appointment with the king—one which had required meticulous preparation.

The three men had just left their Council of War to attend this audience, during which they'd reached the same conclusion: the short-term threat posed by the resistance and their potential new allies could turn out to be grave in the extreme. This sombre realisation, combined with knowing their defences were inadequate until they could be reinforced, the men felt as if they were walking to their deaths. Undoubtedly, the king wouldn't like their assessment of the situation, but they'd no choice but to give it to him anyway.

Upon approaching the vast wall, the guards patrolling the grounds opened the massive steel gates covering the only entrance to the king's residence.

The three men entered the lair.

The palace was vast and glorious, covering eleven acres. Built in honey-brown stone, the building comprised four storeys, complete with soaring towers, penetrating the cloud cover, and covered in burnished gold. Large ornate windows graced each elevation, the heads elegantly curving and perfectly set into the matching stonework. All doorways had thick timber doors, complete with black iron bands, with the masonry above each archway depicting intricately carved battle scenes. Surrounding the palace was a raised terrace covered with white stone, which comprised an imposing stone balustrade and handrail fixed to the perimeters. Marble statues, earthenware and stone pots filled with a multitude of flowering plants decorated the surroundings. Wide and sweeping stone staircases led up to the terrace at intervals around the building. The grandest of all the staircases approached the huge double gold-sheathed doors gracing the main entrance.

Without question, each line and intricately designed curve of the entire palace was unflawed and was the ultimate fairy tale castle—had it not been for the king with the black heart, seated on his majestic throne.

The commanders drove up towards the palace, their Hovertrans gliding just above the wide driveway, with only a muted whine emanating from the propulsion unit.

Aharmer considered how the plethora of military equipment starkly contrasted with the otherwise peaceful surroundings of the palace and its grounds: batteries of pulse weapons were positioned around the outer wall and scattered within the grounds; four Hovertaks were parked alongside the workshops, ready for immediate take off; soldiers patrolled the grounds whilst others guarded every stairway and entrance; ten Hovertancs—particularly large and menacing—were stationed around the curtilage of the buildings. The steel, the armour, the guns and weaponry, all surrounded by lush green gardens and flower beds providing oceans of colour, created a sorrowful picture—a picture which spoke volumes concerning the king's paranoia and his now seemingly urgent need to protect himself with the most threatening and dangerous of all the land's resources.

The three men alighted from Maltor's Hovertrans and crossed over to a staircase at the side of the palace, climbing the stairs onto the terrace. They approached a door leading into the king's waiting room—a small reception area where those waiting sweated and worried and contemplated the very worst outcome to be determined when their meeting was concluded.

The guards inspected the men's passes and admitted them into the palace.

The commanders stood in a cavernous hallway leading to a wide corridor, stretching right through reception area and ending at a staircase which subsequently rose up into the palace's main entrance. Doors opened up from both sides, leading into a vast number of rooms required to house an army of administrators who ran the king's realm, ensuring strict accordance with his instructions, assigning him as the main beneficiary of any endeavour.

The men walked along the corridor until they reached the king's private office where their meeting was to take place. Neda knocked at the king's door and waited for his command to enter.

Upon entering, the men had barely a moment to greet the king before his blasting began. 'In the last two days, we've encountered more problems than we have in the last five years!' stormed the king, discarding any need for standard pleasantries. 'I demand to know exactly what you intend to do about it—each and every one of you.' He eyed the men individually. His eyes were wide and furious, his temple creased with concern and self-pity. 'It would appear, gentlemen, that you've given up on the transporter. And surprisingly, it still refuses to function in spite of the money you've forced me pour into the damned contraption! I knew you'd never sort it out, but you insisted you were capable of mastering the technology. Against my better judgement, I allowed you to continue with this project which has now brought great danger to me.

'Sir—' began Aharmer.

'Fool, I'm speaking!' raged the king. 'Not only have you wasted my men and aircraft in an ill-conceived raid on the invaders your malfunctioning transporter actually brought to Kira Island, but now you have put my life—your own leader—in harm's way! Only my forces should ever be in such a position! Quite clearly, I should never have listened to you. And now I am forced to admit that it was pure stupidity to fail to send overwhelming forces against these new intruders! You said you sought to draw them out; assess their strengths; lead them to their deaths. Well, you've succeeded in nothing but showing them *our* weakness—and that weakness is *you*! You've also shut down the research project developing the most powerful weapon we've ever contemplated—which has obviously precluded any opportunity of getting it now, during a time when we really need it!'

The men stood nervously waiting, wondering what conclusion this meeting would have, whether they would live or die—and hoping that, should the worst outcome prevail, the king would not seek to inflict unnecessary pain.

The king rubbed his chin. 'I want the solutions immediately! When I say *immediately*, gentlemen, I mean the clock is ticking! Start speaking!'

'Your Majesty,' Maltor responded, 'what's happened has happened, unfortunate as it is. Quite simply, Sir, we can't change it now. We can discuss the reasons later if we survive the next few days, but I must stress to you that we're facing a potential disaster, and I suggest we concentrate on the best available means of defending ourselves.'

The king turned puce. Not used to being subjected to such insubordination, his temper instantly flamed. About to rage at Maltor, the full force of his words then hit the king like a blow to the stomach. His emotions began to swing from anger to panic, causing him to feel physically sick. 'Did you really just say *if* we survive, Commander Maltor?'

Maltor nodded. 'Your Majesty, in preparation for this audience, the three of us met to discuss the issues raised by the intruders off Kira Island. We've been forced to re-evaluate the resistance and their involvement in light of this event. As a result, we have been forced to acknowledge another albeit disturbing possibility which we must ask you to consider.'

'Go on!' shouted the king, becoming increasingly panicked as the seconds passed.

'Yes, Sir,' continued Maltor. 'We're sure the resistance brought the intruders here at a time that coincided with our transporter's latest test. This made it seem like we were responsible for bringing the masses of men here, but this is looking less likely to be the case. With that said, I'm sure you'll agree, even without this apparent boost to the resistance's forces, they were becoming an increasing problem. And, granted, they're gaining advantages here and there. However, up to now, we've managed to successfully counter most of their schemes in one way or another, and we've pretty much kept them under control. We thought that, following the conquering of Mu, we would be able to bring all our efforts together to bear down on the resistance—we considered it wouldn't take long to wipe them out. At that point, summing up the opposition as it was, they had proven to be disruptive and their actions ultimately affected our progress, but we believed they were never going to pose a significant threat.

'It's true that we don't yet know what the strangers intend to do but, as the resistance appears to have brought them here—intentionally, I might add—it therefore stands to reason that they expect the forces to join their campaign. With that said, the conclusion to be drawn here is that our previous summing up of the opposition has now drastically changed.'

'I'm not liking this one bit, Maltor,' responded the king. 'You'd better be laying a winding path here and soon be divulging some pleasing news!'

'I wish I could, your Majesty, but if the intruders do join the resistance, our opposition would have a considerable military capability situated only two hundred miles from us. The men they brought here, Sir, are in their several thousands, and the fact that they've managed to raise such a force, from Ra knows where, itself indicates they have abilities far in excess of what we had considered or could otherwise have predicted. Following on from that, it's not beyond the realms of possibility to suggest that these warriors may also have abilities reaching way beyond our own.' Maltor mopped his brow, mentally chastising himself for feeling threatened at such a time, when the current situation was just as much the king's doing as anyone else's.

'If I may be permitted to speak, your Majesty,' continued Aharmer, 'we feel that, taking into consideration the abortive attack earlier, we might actually be faced with a serious fighting force in our opposition, and the threat is very real—right here, right now. We, on the other hand, have the greater part of our fighting men and equipment located five thousand miles away in Mu; it would take weeks to move sufficient numbers here so as to absolutely guarantee we could defeat an attack on Atlantis itself.'

'Surely we could return the bulk of your air arm within a day or so, Aharmer?' asked the king, unusually quiet, a tremor apparent in his voice.

'I'm afraid not, Majesty. We've a power gap of at least a thousand miles in the grid between Mu and Atlantis, regardless of the route selected. As you're aware, although we're currently building another large pyramid generator to cover this area, it's not yet completed and is therefore useless in this scenario. Furthermore, the concept of portable generators is far too risky in this instance; we would be able to provide no guarantee they'd cope with the demands of a large number of engines drawing their power at one time over such a vast distance. Our aircraft would need to be brought through this either by land or sea transports, each of which would require on-board generators to be fitted.'

The king seated himself down in a huge leather chair and rubbed his temple. 'How can this be?' he whispered.

'As you may recall, your Majesty,' continued Maltor, 'you restricted us in the production of these vehicles due to their prohibitive cost. As a result, we have only a small number available, and so it would take time to amass sufficient aircraft back here—which similarly applies to our heavy land-based fighting equipment. Using our troop ships, which are all fitted with generators, we could return approximately fifty thousand men in a week or so, but only with their personal weapons and equipment. The timescale of such a task couldn't be improved.'

Bile gushed into the king's mouth. His heart racing and his eyes wide, panic completely overtook him. 'Is my fate sealed?'

Neda continued. 'Sir, we have nine warships here in the harbour and five on patrol at sea. We've five alpha class beam weapon carriers not too far away, and of course we've approximately one hundred and fifty aircraft already based here. Using the troops we do have in conjunction with the civilian police and your guards, we've upwards of forty thousand men on Atlantis. We're not defenceless by any means, your Majesty, but we're not invincible either.

'As has been highlighted by Commander Maltor, our resources were more than adequate for defence purposes given the situation as it stood a mere forty-eight hours ago. Unfortunately, no one could have foreseen this, but we've badly underestimated the resistance and we're now very much on the back foot. Conceivably, using their allies, they'd defeat us if they attack before our reinforcements arrive. In their position, it's what *we* would do—we'd attack within the next two days before the window of opportunity closes. And we're convinced that's exactly what they intend to do.'

The king's mouth visibly dropped open.

'With that in mind,' Neda continued, 'with your Majesty's permission, I feel we should prepare for the defence of Atlantis by utilising our resources to the greatest extent we can. Ultimately, need for such a defence might not even arise but we'd be foolish not to prepare for it.'

The king, now ashen-faced and visibly shaking, stared at his commanders. He didn't know how to deal with this. He, the most powerful being on the planet, he who wielded limitless power only two days ago, he who was within an ace of fulfilling all his desires, was now looking decidedly exposed.

'Your Majesty, we need your commands urgently please,' requested Maltor who, in spite of the crisis, was hugely enjoying the king's apparent discomfort.

With great effort, the king rallied his reeling senses. He knew now that the most fundamental of priorities was to ensure his own protection, and that if the worst was to happen, he needed these men more than he ever had. Notwithstanding all that had occurred, they were the best at their jobs and, if anyone could get him out of such a dire situation, it would be them. As long as their plans didn't require him to fight any form of battle but would ultimately enable him to escape before there was any real danger posed to him, he didn't much care what they did.

The king finally addressed the commanders. 'Your first duty is to your leader, your monarch, your king. You must protect His Highness above all other considerations. I command you to provide me with a completely safe exit from here, and you have my permission to use as many resources deemed necessary to achieve that end prior to any other action you take. Of course, although I would like to stay and assist in the upcoming hostilities, my duty nevertheless remains to my loyal subjects who, without my leadership, would be at a complete loss. Accordingly, and for their wellbeing alone, I must reluctantly ensure my own survival.' The king's clear self-importance was growing ever greater by the second. Warming to his theme, he continued, 'I intend to temporarily move myself and all my retinue to my second city, Rammath, from where I shall rule until Atlantis is considered to be secure beyond doubt. I will detail my requirements and send them to you within the next few hours. Only when you've fulfilled this directive will you be permitted to arrange your defences here as you see fit. You have until eight tomorrow morning to present your plans.'

'As you command, your Majesty,' responded Maltor. 'We'll return tomorrow with our proposals.'

With their audience with the king concluded, the three commanders left his office and returned to their vehicle.

'I swear that man gets worse by the day,' grumbled Aharmer. 'Despite knowing we need every resource we can possibly get our hands on, he's more concerned with us directing a significant portion to covering his own arse, which leaves us even more exposed! If that wasn't bad enough, he gives us a generous fourteen hours in which to do it!'

'As infuriating as it may be,' Maltor responded, 'can you honestly tell me you're that surprised by his approach?'

Aharmer shook his head. 'If only the king would pleasantly surprise us!'

'Exactly. Well, the fact remains that we've no choice, so let's get on with it and pray we can cover all angles. I personally think that any effort to rid us of his presence will be worth it. Can you imagine the headaches he'd cause us with his panicking if he was to be present during an attack!' said Maltor.

'As selfish as it is, he's chosen wisely selecting Rammath,' mused Neda. 'Providing we can get him there, it has a strong garrison and is well within range of our forces in Mu. It's inconceivable that the allied forces could threaten him there immediately. The city's hundreds of miles from the sea and thousands from here. We're much better able to protect him there, which he's clearly deduced for himself.'

'Undoubtedly, the king has always had a talent for seeking the best solution to his own problems,' observed Maltor. 'Now, let's head back to our base; it's going to be a long night.' And with that, the commanders headed out of the palace and towards the Land Forces headquarters.

CHAPTER TEN

'**N**ippy little kite isn't it, Tiea,' Mark observed, clearly impressed with the aircraft. 'How long do you expect the flight to take?'

'About three quarters of an hour, as long as I don't get lost on the way,' she replied with a smile.

'Great. That leaves us some time to relax and take in the scenery then. Incidentally, how do you know where we're going? I don't see a compass, and you don't appear to have a chart either.

'I've sort of got both, Mark, you just don't know what you're looking for. If you lean over, you'll see the chart projected on a screen by my right knee on the instrument cluster. The white dot moving across the screen is us, and the red stationary one is where we're headed. It's another benefit of the Ancients' technology. Much of it is interrelated, which is why it's so versatile and effective.'

Mark looked dumbstruck at Tiea's answer.

'Okay, let me explain. Obviously, in order to navigate, you need to know where you are and where you're going. Rema will have explained in general terms about our principal power source. Part of the power source is the grid, which distributes power on a near-enough worldwide scale. That's already in place and complete. With that in mind, the grid acts like a map as it's global and all encompassing. To use the power held in the grid, our engines draw it from the point closest to the grid. Right now, we're taking our energy from directly beneath us, which is actually always the case. Quite clearly, we're moving, which therefore means we're constantly pulling energy from a different section of the grid. Effectively, our navigation system relates where we're taking power from the grid geographically, and subsequently translates this data onto the actual chart here in the aircraft. Land vehicles and ships use the same principal.'

'Impressive! Very impressive, in fact! How much easier than our method is that, Jack?'

'It's fantastic, of course—like so many things around here. But when you say energy is provided near-enough worldwide, what exactly isn't covered?' asked Jack.

'Well, the grid itself is worldwide but it isn't yet completely powered across its entire area. It's possible that some of the pyramids have been destroyed since the Ancients built the system or that, for some reason, they were never built in the first place. I'm sure Rema explained that the large pyramids generate the power which they feed into the grid? However, they would need to be spaced equally across the entire world in order to ensure power could be consistently supplied across it. At the moment, we've got many dead spots in the grid. Ultimately, we can build more—and indeed we are—but there currently aren't enough to run the entire system.'

Jack and Mark nodded their heads in acknowledgement as they followed her explanation.

'As the king conquers more and more lands,' Tiea continued, 'he builds pyramids in them if required, thereby giving him the power he needs to hold the new territories and move on to the next. Each one is a massive project but, without reliable and consistent power, his war machines can't function effectively—in fact, nothing in our society can. But, to our advantage, building new pyramids has seriously slowed down the king's progress as he's moved further and further from Atlantis.

'The good thing is, though, his newly built pyramids make great targets for sabotage. Nothing pisses him off more than us fucking up his building plans by constantly destroying their materials!' Tiea said with a wicked grin.

'I'm sure, old girl,' replied Mark warmly. 'Nothing like knocking-up the old mortar and polishing the trowel only to find someone's nicked all the gear and consequently upset your entire day!'

The group spent a little time discussing Tiea's aircraft, the two airmen fascinated by the alien propulsion and control systems employed by the Vertlyn to fly it. To the two experienced pilots, the technology it employed to achieve such incredible capabilities differed so strikingly to the technology implemented in their own craft.

As they flew along the chain of small islands, a more significant landmass appeared on the horizon. Initially a hazy indistinct blur, as they drew closer, they were greeted with a green-brown chequered landscape with high snow-capped mountains at the extremities of their vision. A few miles out, the coastline sharpened and they could clearly see waves breaking on wide sandy beaches, and towns and villages dotted along the coast and beyond. Judging by the number of rooftops visible from the sky, it was clear the land sustained a large population, their signatures of which were plainly printed across the landscape. Soon, under the Vertlyn, the chequerboard was revealed as cultivated fields and meadows filled with varying crops and livestock, with each individual patch bustling with life.

'Would you look at that!' exclaimed Jack. 'Beautiful.'

'It looks a lot like Devon from up here, Tiea,' observed Mark. 'It's almost like we're coming home.' Mark gave Jack a wistful look.

'Well, for me, gentlemen, this *is* home,' replied Tiea, 'and I wouldn't have it any other way, despite the current threats.' Tiea looked out of the pilot window. 'Below us lies Atlantis, and the big city beside the sea is Atlanta, our capital. I've lived here all my life. My family owns the factory responsible for the manufacture of these planes. We also make a model much like the Hovertrans—vehicles which are not dissimilar to the cars of your world.'

'Rich *and* beautiful, Tiea. Well, you can't get much better than that,' Mark laughed, brightening up again.

Tiea smiled. 'Thank you for the compliment, Mark. Sadly, we used to be wealthy, but now we're suffering terribly from taxes and other financial penalties imposed upon us by His Highness. It doesn't stop there, either. He takes our workers whenever he chooses with the sole purpose of swelling his military. He forces us to produce hardware for his fighting vehicles in our factories, at usually less than cost. In addition, if we manage to create and develop new systems to improve our own products, he'll simply take them from us if he considers them to be useful. And, probably worse than actually stealing our ideas, he removes our most creative minds—our designers and craftsmen—and places them where they'll be of most benefit to him. Piece together this entire scenario and we're just about on our knees right now. We can't stop him—and we daren't protest.'

'Maybe it would do you some good to stand up to him a little,' Mark commented. 'Everyone knows, bullies respond to strength.'

Tiea forced a laugh. 'That's true, Mark; bullies usually *do* respond to strength. But, in this instance, the response of this bully is to wreak havoc. Trust me, those that have tried before simply disappear, never to be seen again. I wouldn't like to give much thought to what they actually went through. Standing up to the king achieves nothing. Effectively, it plays right into his hands. He does as he will with those who protest and simply puts his cronies in their place, effectively commandeering their assets and ridding himself of another subversive element standing against him.'

The two men listened patiently, compassion coursing through them at what Tiea—and the entire population—were forced to endure at the hands of their so-called leader.

'And so this is why you've joined the resistance,' observed Jack.

'Of course,' smiled Tiea, apparently lifted with the reminder that she was actively pursuing a way to overcome the current problems. 'It's one of the reasons, but there are many more, some of which you'll see for yourselves later.'

The shore had now been left behind and the craft was flying beside a range of hills. Flashing by to the left lay Atlanta, which was set into the hillside, bordering the ocean. The hills and city encircled a large bay with a natural rock formation forming a harbour wall across the entrance. From above, it looked much like any other city they'd flown over, the network of streets filled with houses and shops, parks, lakes and a large dockland area, all of which looked very familiar to the two men.

'It looks like a bigger version of Torquay, Jack,' Mark commented, feeling a little homesick.

'I was thinking more Portsmouth, but either way it's a bit spooky when you consider what it really is,' replied Jack.

'Probably even spookier if you dwell on *when* it is,' Mark said dryly.

Using her communicator, Tiea began speaking with Atlanta's air movement controller, indicating to the airmen they'd almost reached their destination.

Within minutes, they were flying lower and decreasing in speed, the Vertlyn subsequently banking towards an area of grass beside a Mediterranean style house, and it was clear they'd arrived. The house stood in its own grounds surrounded by six similar properties. They were built on a hilltop overlooking the city. Tiea slowed to a hover above the lawn and settled the plane onto the grass, killing the engine as it sank into its landing gear.

There was no doubt as to whether Tiea's family had indeed once been privileged. The house looked splendid from the outside, with spellbinding views from the gardens which the airmen were currently enjoying. A myriad of small white dwellings with bright orange roofs, latticed by soft yellow roadways and dotted with large ornate town houses, flowed down the hillside in all directions to the waterfront. Travelling across the bay, busy with its varied shipping, the men's eyes were drawn over the harbour wall to the endless ocean, beyond which was the bright blue backdrop of a cloudless sky, bathing in hot, bright sunlight. The warm breeze which raised white-capped waves to the far horizon rustled the leaves on the trees across the hillside and within the gardens around them.

'How do you even try to describe a place like this?' asked Jack. 'It's just breath-taking.'

'Well, it's certainly not Torquay, Jack. It's not raining for a start!'

'I know it's your home town, old boy, but you'll not endear yourself with your compatriots making comments like that,' replied Jack grinning.

Tiea shook her head smiling, pleased they were obviously impressed with her home.

At that moment, a small brown and white dog raced from the side of the house, jumping up at Tiea and spinning round with excitement as it raced around the visitors.

'I see the welcoming committee's arrived, Tiea,' said Mark, kneeling down to stroke the dog.

'It is if she's here,' smiled Tiea. 'She's Jole, my brother Kolit's dog. If she's around he won't be far away—she never leaves him. Anyway, let's go inside and you can meet everyone else, then you can get freshened up and changed into something comfortable before we go down into the city. You can't go down there wearing those uniforms, that's for sure. If you don't appear like one of us, we won't get very far,' she said, hinting at danger.

'Hang on,' Jack interrupted. 'Before we go anywhere, Tiea, is that one of the power-generating pyramids you've talked about?' He pointed towards a massive structure, standing on otherwise undeveloped ground beside a lake

'Yes, that's one of the ones built by the Ancients. It's the biggest of the lot and powers a thousand square miles of the grid on its own.'

'That's one hell of a pyramid, Tiea—it's huge! Don't tell me it's built of gold as well?' Mark asked incredulously, noticing the sun flashing off its golden surfaces.

Tiea laughed. 'Maybe gold-encrusted power pyramids would solve a lot of our problems! But sadly not! It's covered in a type of metal although, at this point in time, we're unsure what it is; we have no idea of its elements at all. What we do know, however, is that it's totally impregnable—we've so far never managed to get into it.'

Mark and Jack stood gazing at the phenomenal structure, once again completely mystified as to how something so incredible and vast could have been built during such a time, especially when similar structures—with fundamentally less capabilities—were only just being considered in the twentieth century.

Tiea also stood reflecting on the overwhelming infrastructure. 'There's something different about this pyramid,' she contemplated quietly. 'We have been able to gain access to all of the pyramids built by the Ancients—all except this one. The questions seeking to establish why that may be are endless; the answer's probably hidden within somewhere. Maybe the answer isn't meant to be found, which is why the Ancients made it inaccessible. Who knows?'

'They obviously don't want it to be discovered,' remarked Mark. 'But, having said that, it's definitely strange they'd hand you so much knowledge and technology but then opt to withhold something seemingly important.'

'I agree,' replied Tiea. 'Of course, everyone wants to know of the greatest pyramid's hidden secret—what untold story it has to tell. I personally wonder if some things are supposed to remain shrouded in mystery.'

Mark leaned over to Jack and whispered into his ear. 'She just keeps getting better and better.' Mark glanced back over to Tiea, and a light smile danced across his face, one Jack had never before seen.

'I have a question, Tiea,' Jack stated, trying his best to revert back to the matter at hand. 'If you've never been inside, how do you maintain or use it? How does it work?'

'Actually, there's no need to enter a pyramid when it's complete and the crystal's in place,' replied Tiea. 'There's never anything more to be done. Once the crystal's in the required position, it automatically starts to feed power into the grid. Pyramids have no moving parts to maintain and there are no control systems either—they just work as soon as the crystal's correctly aligned. We even seal up our own pyramids after the crystal's been installed because there's no reason to get into it again. Obviously, it also provides additional security.'

'Incredible,' muttered Jack.

'The entire system works flawlessly,' continued Tiea. 'For example, if you want to get inside when the work has been completed, you'd need to remove countless tonnes of masonry to do so. It would take a huge amount of time and, as the king ensures all the pyramids are constantly guarded, there's therefore no opportunity for any major excavation project to be implemented unnoticed. As I said flying over here, we regularly attack his materials in transit, but once the building is actually completed and sealed, there's nothing more we can do to put a spanner in the works,' Tiea explained.

'But why?' asked Jack. 'We've seen the effectiveness of your weapons. Rema caused quite a landslide using only her backpack! We've also been on the receiving end of your Hovertaks. Very nasty, actually, but they were aircraft; presumably your land-based weapons are bigger and more powerful again? No matter how much stone's involved, I can't actually see any attempts being hampered,' observed Jack.

'Unfortunately, Jack, all our weapons are ineffective against the pyramids; the power they're producing—as a side effect or part of the design, we're not really sure—actually protects them from energy weapons local to the structures. It essentially forms a shield of sorts. The energy released from our weapons dissipates on the shield and is therefore unable to penetrate through. As I said, if one wanted to get inside—not that I can see a reason for doing so—this would need to be by digging.' Tiea smiled. 'Believe me, Jack, if we could destroy them, we would.'

'The big building with all the spires and trinkets sitting beyond the pyramid over there...' Mark said, changing the subject. 'Is that something to do with the king?' Mark pointed to a majestic edifice, which succeeded in dwarfing everything around it with the exception of the great pyramid. The building was surrounded by a series of smaller units, with the reflection of various machines parked around the site seen in their mirrored walls as the sun bounced off them.

'That's the kings pretty little town house, Mark,' Tiea answered sarcastically and grinning wryly. 'As you can see, he likes to indulge in the finer things in this world, but never thinks twice about taking the hard-earned luxuries from everyday folk.' She exhaled a deeply aggravated sigh. 'But we can't stay here admiring the view all day, boys. You wanted proof of Rema's story and you won't get it from up here.' Tiea smiled and politely ushered them towards the house.

Approaching the front door, Tiea, Mark and Jack were met by a distinctive looking couple who appeared to be in late middle-age, whom Tiea subsequently introduced as her parents. Looking beyond them into the house, the airmen saw two other men standing in a light, airy room staring through a window, apparently looking out at the views. They were of a similar age and stature to themselves.

Although they had received a courteous welcome from Tiea's parents, Jack and Mark could nevertheless see they were troubled, their anxiety reflecting in the faces of the two men standing by the window. It transpired that the men were Tiea's brothers, who, when introduced to the airmen, surprised them by responding in a totally incomprehensible language.

'I'm sorry, gentlemen, but you've just run out of people who speak English,' said Tiea, smiling. 'Or actually, more to the point, my brothers aren't wearing one of these.' Lifting back her hair, Jack and Mark saw a small device fitted behind her right ear. 'In truth, not many of us here can actually *speak* your language. I certainly can't, but this little gadget makes it unnecessary. When you're wearing one, you can understand all languages and you can speak any of them. The strange thing is you don't know you're speaking a foreign tongue or listening to one either; however, it's a moot point really as you can understand everything anyway, so it doesn't matter. I can assure you that, right now, I'm speaking to you in the same language as my brothers. And when you reply, it's in my language too—or rather, that's how I hear you.'

'You know, I did wonder about that,' Mark replied. 'It didn't really make sense to me that everyone we've met up to now not only speaks English but also have all the right nuances and inflections; right down to colloquial language, it's all perfect.' Mark laughed. 'In actual fact, I said to Jack when we first saw Rema that I hoped she spoke English, and now I see it didn't matter anyway.'

'As it happens, Mark, Rema is actually one of the rare few who can actually speak your language!' laughed Tiea. 'Rema isn't a fan on gadgets and she hates relying on them, so if she can do without them, she'll do that. Personally, I can't really see the point—if you've got them, why not use them if it makes for a much easier life?' She considered her brothers for a moment. 'I suppose I should have asked my entire family to wear them, knowing they were going to meet you, but I think you'll appreciate it more now when you fit these little gems yourselves.' Tiea handed two devices to the airmen, helping to fit them correctly. She told them they'd experience slight discomfort initially, describing the sensation to be like iced water running through the left hemisphere of the brain. The grimacing men indicated the devices were initialising, and she assured them that it would soon pass. The equipment was invading their vocal and audio senses, and they were adjusting them accordingly to allow the men to instantly achieve what it would have taken them a lifetime—probably longer—to achieve without it.

'Testing, testing, one, two, three,' said Mark grinning, refusing to take the contraption seriously.

'Understood,' replied one of Tiea's brothers. 'Mark, I'm Rafh, and this is my brother Kolit. I trust you can understand me now?'

Mark's grin went lopsided, his cheeks turning slightly pale. 'Bloody hell,' he replied, somewhat dumbstruck.

'That answers *that* question, I think,' Jack commented. 'I believe you've finally fazed him!' Jack fiddled with the gadget now fixed behind his ear. 'It's very strange, I must say. It provides a very weird feeling. I suppose such a device is yet another development of your extremely gifted Ancients?'

'You probably don't need to ask, do you?' Tiea said with a smile. 'But yes, they are. They came with the time transporter—it's obviously not much use being able to travel to another place and time if you can't understand anything when you get there!'

Mark smiled warmly at Tiea. 'So, what's next on the agenda? I believe a trip into a pub in the town is in order now we're actually able to speak your language!'

'Yes we're going to town,' Tiea laughed, 'but not to enjoy ourselves. We have much more important things to do than drink ourselves into oblivion.'

'Ah, a crushing blow that, Jack,' said Mark, dramatically clutching his chest. 'And here I was, truly believing that this woman would be so easily misled. Doesn't anyone ever want to have a bit of fun around here?'

Tiea and Jack both shook their heads and smiled at each other. 'Always the joker,' quipped Jack.

Tiea advised that the plan was to disguise the two airmen as Tiea's brothers before leaving for the city. The airmen had witnessed Rema's remarkable transformation last night, and therefore weren't surprised at the prosthetics they were given. Pulling on the latex-like masks and donning the clothes borrowed from the brothers, they soon emerged as identical copies of the two Atlantien men.

'How do I look, Rafh?' asked Mark. 'Wow, I sound strange!'

'A vast improvement in appearance Kolit,' replied Jack. 'I think you should consider making it permanent. But yes, you're right—your voice still sounds a little high-pitched I'm afraid. Probably need to knock it down a few octaves to suit the new rugged look,' said Jack, grinning.

'Very amusing, ha bloody ha,' responded Mark dryly. 'I was about to say something along the same lines myself but considered it to be in rather bad taste,' he sniffed, the disdainful look not quite working on Kolit's face.

'Seriously, gentlemen,' Tiea interrupted, 'you both look and sound great. Now it's time to get on with it and put this plan to the test. Let's hope we pass the public assessment!'

The three of them bade their farewells to Tiea's brothers who handed their identity papers to the airmen, assuring them they'd now keep out of sight in the house until their return. Her parents warned them to say as little as possible when they could be overheard by strangers, believing the pitch of their voices as potentially giving them away to anyone who knew the real brothers well. Nevertheless, the general consensus was encouraging, and Tiea reassured the group that she would be there to steer them away from any potential problems, if at all possible.

Mark and Jack left the house with Tiea leading the way, and climbed into a waiting Hovertrans. The men watched as Tiea engaged the drive. The strange little vehicle rose a few inches above the ground, slowly moving away from the house. Reaching the highway, Tiea allowed the craft to glide right and precede down the hill, accelerating towards the town, a low humming sound coming from the vehicle.

'Not quite the old MG, is it, Jack,' Mark said with a smile.

'Not quite... but, like the Vertlyn, I suppose it does the same thing only goes about it differently. A shame about the steering wheel, though, and there's nothing on the floor to control it either! Actually... where are the brakes, Tiea?' asked Jack, a hint of alarm in his voice.

'No bloody brakes? Are you kidding? Oh my god, Jack! We've been sabotaged, we're done for! Goodbye, cruel world!' Mark theatrically grabbed onto the edge of his seat with both hands.

'Will you two stop mucking about? It's time to get serious now,' chided Tiea, a hint of a smile across her lips. 'All the controls are in the armrests of my seat, gentlemen, so you can calm yourselves. Panic over! I control the vehicle using buttons with my fingers—including the brakes, you'll be pleased to know.' She rolled her eyes. 'I thought twentieth-century men were supposed to be fearless and brave?' she mocked, looking directly at Mark before turning her attention back to the road.

Mark straightened his back. 'There's nobody more fearless, Tiea, let me assure you of that. We fear nothing!'

'Well, joking aside,' Tiea continued, 'I'd much rather be in this than any other vehicle. At least I know this won't go charging headlong into anything on the way. It's difficult to wreck one of these because it takes evasive action if the controller doesn't. Anyway, let's concentrate on the job in hand.' She threw the men a serious look. 'Please, I can't stress to you enough how careful you will need to be in the town. Think about everything you say and do before you say or do it, and use my brothers' names at all times.' She paused for a moment. 'If you attract attention and we're caught, I really wouldn't like to consider what could happen to my family *and* ourselves. Please try to keep that in mind.'

'I'm sorry, Tiea,' apologised Jack. 'We might like to have a bit of a joke and some banter, but we're professionals in our field—or we were back home, in the field we knew—and so I assure you that we know how to be serious when it really matters.' Jack threw Mark a warning glance, silently advising him to quit the foolishness whilst Tiea was concerned about her family.

'Thank you, Jack,' Tiea responded warmly. 'I appreciate the consideration.'

'So where are we going and what can we expect to find there?' Mark asked.

'First we're going to a prison just outside of the city centre where you'll discover one of the king's more renowned traits: he thinks it's a wonderful idea to put his suffering prisoners on show. He encourages people to visit, believing such an action to be a good deterrent—which, of course, it is. Therefore, for our purposes, it's not that risky and it's a good place to begin. I'm sure you'll be moved by what you see but don't show it—you must follow my lead at all times, no matter what I do. If anything I do seems wrong, immoral or even distasteful, I'm acting and you need to follow suit.'

Mark and Jack nodded their agreement.

'If all goes to plan there, we'll move to more sensitive areas. Obviously, these will be places people avoid if possible and where we could ultimately encounter the king's police in force. It's down to you, really: if you need to see more and are comfortable, we'll continue on until you're satisfied or until we run out of time.'

Tiea's Hovertrans passed through the suburbs, heading towards the city centre. Earlier, Tiea had made light reference to her vehicle having the inbuilt ability to avoid collisions as a standard addition to its manual controls. At the time, this point was nothing more to the men than an interesting fact, but the vehicle steering itself drew their minds sharply back to this throwaway comment, and quickly identified the disadvantage to such a mechanism. Obviously, a vehicle which could assess traffic direction and movement and sense objects could never be a drawback, but the fact that every other vehicle on the road possessed the same skill and dexterity ultimately proved to provide the men with a somewhat nerve-wracking journey.

'Look out Tiea!' exclaimed Jack.

'You'll kill us in a minute if you don't watch it!' Mark further stated.

On this occasion, a speeding Hovertrans shot from a side road, flew straight at their front end, with both vehicles effortlessly circumnavigating a potentially fatal situation.

'Calm down, boys!' Tiea said, laughing. 'There's nothing to worry about—except perhaps you making me jump with all that shouting!'

'Making *you* jump? That's good that is! I've not been so frightened since a mate of mine took me on his motorbike at a hundred miles an hour round the roads behind Moretonhampstead! And trust me, those Devon roads are torturous!'

'He's got a point you know, Tiea,' Jack said, hanging onto the edge of his seat. 'I'm not sure I can stick much more of this either. Your driving is more frightening than the entire Luftwaffe put together!'

'Men,' smiled Tiea. 'You'll soon get used to it. Anyway, I really can't see your problem—it's not possible to hit anything!'

Finally, Tiea turned into an open area near the city centre and parked the Hovertrans beside a row of similar vehicles. The two men staggered from the vehicle.

'We made it,' Jack said light-heartedly.

'And alive!' quipped Mark.

Tiea rolled her eyes. 'Men really do exaggerate.' She glanced around her quickly. 'Now remember everything I've told you.'

The men nodded, serious now.

'It might actually be a good idea to eat before we move on, if you'd like.' Tiea suggested. 'It's lunchtime now, so the taverns will be full. This is the best time to experience a little local atmosphere. I suspect you'll lose your appetites later anyway, and a drink or two will help you relax.'

'She keeps coming round to my way of thinking, Rafh,' joked Mark. 'I knew there was something about this woman I liked.'

'You never change, Kolit,' Jack remarked.

Whilst practicing their new identities, Tiea led the airmen to the city square, a large open area teeming with people and surrounded with ornate buildings. As a city, it had all the usual activities the airmen would expect. Rows of shops interspersed with public buildings and private dwellings; taverns and tables; picturesque buildings. Tiea chose one of the taverns and, ignoring the opportunity to dine in the sun, took the airmen inside.

After being outside in the glorious sunshine, the tavern was dim with its low ceilings and dark wood. But, as their eyes became accustomed to the gloom, the airmen picked a free table and waited for the tavern's staff to tend to them.

'Being here brings a whole new meaning to the term "timeless" doesn't it, Rafh?' observed Kolit. 'Looking around us, I'd say we could be in Italy or the south of France.'

'Steady on, Kolit,' whispered Tiea urgently. 'Those places don't exist yet. Please don't mention your world here again. That's the sort of comment that will succeed in attracting the kind of attention we really don't need.

Mark took heed of Tiea's warning and promptly shut his mouth. The two men were now reluctant to converse freely, instead considering carefully everything they wanted to say. However, despite their reluctance to talk amongst themselves, Mark and Jack nevertheless took the opportunity to take in their surroundings, and it was when considering their environment and the streets outside the tavern that they both felt a certain unease.

Jack's and Mark's thoughts both continued along the same vein.

It was lunch time on a beautiful summer's day in a lovely city. The air was warm with a purity bestowed by the ocean and unsullied by exhaust fumes. The shops had their doors wide open, and there was certainly no shortage of taverns and cafés. Hundreds of people milled around the square and amongst the surrounding streets—but the people looked like they carried the weight of the world on their individual shoulders.

Reflecting on this point further, Mark drew a mental comparison of his own city to this one, recalling the summer days he'd spent there. He remembered how a day like this influenced the mood of the people there; true, it was renowned as a holiday resort that could significantly lift the spirit in itself, but the atmosphere was generally happier and more relaxed than this. There were shops, parks, boats, views, eateries and the ocean. What else could one need?

Mark knew and realised that, in a city such as this—and maybe even with Tiea as a part of his life, in whatever capacity—he'd have just about everything he'd need to pass the time and enjoy his life.

Jack's thoughts were not dissimilar to Mark's, although he thought of Rema, and spending days with her in this beautiful city.

With the two men silently contemplating the city and its vast beauty, it became all too clear what was wrong: the city's people were unhappy; there was no laughter, no children playing, no dogs barking or running after balls, not even the sound of birds singing their day-song. In the tavern, conversations around them were stilted, spoken in muted tones, accompanied by furtive looks and nervous gestures. The men realised now that the same had applied in the streets—there was a general depression prevailing, maybe even verging on fear.

At that moment, a waiter arrived at their table and offered them each a menu. Tiea made a recommendation and they all placed their orders. She then ordered some wine and the waiter, shortly reappearing with a jar and four tankards, which he set down on the table.

The waiter moved on as they filled their tankards. Looking round to check no one could hear them, they quietly continued their conversation.

'Atlanta's a beautiful city, Tiea,' began Jack. 'It's a pity about the atmosphere here though… it's already giving me the creeps. What the hell's wrong with everybody? I know you're at war but, judging by what you've said, the king's winning as usual, and it's happening far away from here anyway. Surely it's not of any particular threat to these people?'

'Strange isn't it,' Tiea remarked. 'You've been here mere minutes and you have already picked up on the mood—*that* is how bad it's become.' Tiea sipped her wine, contemplated the taste for a moment, and then nodded her approval. 'To begin with, as I touched upon earlier, the people here are poor. They can barely afford the essentials, and so it puts a great deal of pressure on families. Our society has become totally elitist: if you're not one of the chosen, life's unbearable.

'Without question, the city's absolutely beautiful, but that begins and ends with the architecture and the scenery—they're about the only beauty left here now. It takes people to make a city completely beautiful and vibrant; sadly, we lack in a bustling, joyful populace. Ultimately, pleasant surroundings don't feel relevant to those suffering with hard times, and they're no help at all when you're suffering as badly as we are. In fact, it probably only highlights our distress. Generally, people are desperately trying to survive. Most of them are now hopelessly in debt, trying to provide for their families. They've only one choice left to continue and that's to increase their borrowing. As with any form of *assistance*,' Tiea said disdainfully, 'this comes from the king's bank because, quite simply, there's nowhere else to go. Of course, once you're forced to do that, he's got you: any short-term gain soon turns into a complete nightmare as he changes the original terms as and when he sees fit.'

Jack shook his head. 'He sounds like one hell of a bastard.'

Tiea nodded. 'To be in their position because of life's general circumstances would be one thing—we all experience highs and lows by default; we get through them and they build character. But in this instance, the king and his hierarchy have engineered everything. They've caused the people to fall. They've stripped everyone of everything they possibly can, and purposely driven them into destitution—at which time they call in their loans, knowing there's no chance they'll be paid, and taking all remaining assets. Effectively, they become the sole beneficiaries of what can only be described as their own rape.

'So much unhappiness just because of one individual...' Mark mused. 'I wouldn't mind blasting him off the face of the planet.'

'Of course, Kolit. Don't you think all of our people want away with this so-called leader? We don't readily embrace violence, however, but we seek an end nevertheless.' Tiea paused for a moment, gazing out of the tavern windows at the people slowly milling by, a look of sadness across her pretty face. 'When the king intercedes on those defaulted loans, in many cases, the people have no assets. In this situation, the king offers two choices: execution or a lifetime of slavery in whatever employment he deems suitable for them. Those who've avoided this so far know they'll soon succumb. In the meantime, like those who preceded them, they're still forced by their circumstances to continue to borrow yet more from the king. Effectively, they're borrowing the monies stolen from them from the thief who stole it, all the while realising that they'll end up breaking their backs in slavery.' Tiea's eyes began to shimmer as tears welled. 'What you're feeling around you is frustration and despair.'

Mark leaned across the table and patted Tiea's hand, providing a warm smile. 'If it's that bad, why aren't people rising up against the king? It sounds like there'd be no lack of support for such an endeavour if someone were to get the ball rolling. Given the circumstances, why can't your resistance do just that?'

'The king knows exactly what he's doing; his policies automatically prevent any uprisings. He controls approximately ninety per cent of all of our once-independent companies and just about everything and everybody is in hock to the king, which consequently provides him with an unbreakable stranglehold over our entire society. By attacking our financial structures and industries, he controls the majority of everything. He's successfully divided the people and he rules them with a rod of iron.' Tiea shook her head. 'It's almost impossible to rouse such a demoralised populace. Rallying them against their circumstances requires a victory of monumental proportion to break his domination.'

'You're telling us he's achieved all he has by manipulating money?' Jack asked incredulously.

'We've been assaulted in the worse possible way. We've been crushed under a mountain of debt with interest accruing daily. Outstripping our daily ability to pay it tears at the mind. That worry alone is enough to destroy all other emotion; however, even that pales into insignificance, and panic really sets in when threatened with repaying the original loan from time to time. And of course you've still got to somehow live. Believe me, Rafh, it's an insidious and heartless process.'

'It's deeply sad to hear things are as they are. This should be a happy, bustling city, Tiea. The people should be free. Surely freedom is a given concept and rightfully everyone's?' Jack asked.

'I believe there's a well-known phrase you may be familiar with,' Tiea said, addressing both men. 'The pen is mightier than the sword. Here, the sword hangs very closely behind the pen, I'm afraid. The combination is a disgustingly effective weapon. Everything you've heard so far pales beside the physical and additional mental tortures the king so willingly inflicts upon his people to back-up his fiscal policies,' she answered bleakly.

'Perfect circumstances then, I guess,' remarked Kolit sarcastically. 'I think I may have lost my appetite. In fact, in spite of the wine, I feel less relaxed now than when we arrived!'

'I'm sorry to highlight all of this doom and gloom,' Tiea said glumly, 'but I feel you should know exactly what we're dealing with it.

Owing to *circumstances*,' she said, eyeing them knowingly, 'this has also become your battle, your city, your home. These are the people you'll soon know. We have to fight this cause knowing what we would ideally want to achieve.'

'And that would be what exactly?' Jack asked.

'Quite simply, peace and tranquillity.'

Jack smiled ruefully. 'Well, you've certainly given us a lot to think about. So far, it looks as if Rema wasn't far wrong in what she said and, if it's due to get worse, I think we'll soon be backing her up.'

Their meal arrived and they watched silently as the waiter placed the dishes around the table, fussing and fretting until he was satisfied with the display.

Tiea had chosen a colourful selection of spiced meats in rice accompanied by a mixture of dark and light breads with a platter of mixed vegetables. The airmen promptly attacked the food, nodding in appreciation, finding it all very much to their liking.

'You manage to polish off a great deal of food despite losing your appetite, Kolit,' Jack said to Mark. 'Thank goodness you have or I doubt we'd be left with much!'

'Well, I wouldn't want to be rude seeing as Tiea's gone to the trouble of entertaining us. I felt I should force myself to eat a little,' he replied with a grin.

A short while later, Tiea dabbed at her mouth with a napkin and said, 'Come on, you two. Finish the wine and let's get away from here. We've plenty to see yet before we leave, and Rema wants us back before dark.'

'Hold your horses, folks,' Mark said urgently, a slight note of trepidation in his voice. 'Don't look now, but the Gestapo's arrived, I'm afraid.' From his vantage point facing the entrance, Mark observed several heavily armed men in black uniform turn in from the street, entering the tavern behind his companions. They strode in, demanding everyone have their papers ready for inspection. Jack and Mark threw Tiea worried glances as the guards passed from table to table, checking documents and slowly filtering around the room towards them.

'Fuck it,' muttered Tiea. 'Just show them my brothers' papers and don't catch their eyes.'

The tension mounted as the men completed their inspections at the preceding tables, becoming almost unbearable as they drew ever closer. With no opportunity for escape, the trio had no option but to wait for the policemen to confront them. Unarmed and poorly prepared, they were well aware that this had the potential to be a very dangerous situation. Their survival relied on Tiea's brothers' papers, their borrowed disguises and the officers accepting both without question.

They silently awaited their fate.

Finally, the police surrounded their table and the waiting was over. One of them arrogantly demanded their papers, snatching Tiea's first. He scrutinised them at length then thrust them back at her. With similar charm, he examined Rafh's documents next, furiously leafing through them, tossing them at the table when he'd finished.

Kolit wasn't so lucky.

The officer was aware of the Alrene family as they featured on the king's latest target list. Having carefully studied this list, the officer in charge knew they had been a very wealthy and influential family, and were amongst the few remaining industrialists independent of the king. The Alrenes and those like them had so far managed to fend off the king's machinations to date, collectively retaining considerable influence over society, thereby causing him intense frustration. However, feeling they were still too powerful to directly take on, he had instead opted to erode their position by more subtle means.

Just recently, the king had issued a list of all the families he was targeting, which was published and distributed amongst his special forces—a section of the police that he'd totally corrupted and in which these bullies were enlisted. The families on the list were to be investigated at every opportunity. If his police could discover a serious offence that could be held against them, it would solve another of the king's problems. Furthermore, provided it was undetectable, they could also engineer one.

Looking at Kolit Alrene's papers in front of him, this officer thought he'd now seen a slight opportunity. The offence he'd spotted was, in itself, trivial. In fact, in any other situation, he'd gain nothing by arresting him, except possibly looking stupid. However, if he could goad the man enough maybe he—or, better yet, this entire group—may commit something far more serious, subsequently greatly endearing him to the powers that be.

'Kolit Alrene?' the officer asked, sneering and puffing himself up, punching Mark's shoulder hard and staring menacingly into his face.

Mark looked up sharply, startled by the unexpected physical contact. 'Yes, I am.'

'"Yes, I am" *what*?!' thundered the officer.

'Is there a problem, Officer?' Tiea asked hurriedly.

'Shut up you slut! I don't remember asking you to speak!' the man shouted in her face, returning his attention to her brother.

'I'll ask you again. "Yes, I am" *what*?!' he screamed again, delivering another blow to Mark's same shoulder.

'Yes, *Officer*, I am Kolit Alrene,' replied Mark, so far managing to maintain a calm demeanour in spite of the provocation.

'These papers are filthy! Don't you realise it's an offence to carry illegible papers? Look at the mess they're in! I can barely make out your visual!' The officer indicated a small, relatively unnoticeable blemish on Kolit's papers which had slightly obscured the image transposed on the front page. 'So what have you got to say about it, you little prick?' he continued, attempting to goad Kolit into an altercation which could later be charged against him.

'I apologise, Officer. I hadn't realised they were so bad. I'll get them cleaned up immediately,' he promised, still showing no outward sign of resistance to the bullying man.

The officer glared at the three siblings, but so far there was no slight indication his plan was working. He'd hoped he could force them to fight back—attacking a policeman was a capital offence. But, quite clearly, this line of action seemed to be in vain. Knowing realistically he couldn't pursue it further, the officer opted to let it go, throwing the papers across the room. 'Now pick them up and look after them in future! You'll not get off so lightly next time, rich boy.' Swaggering off to the next table, the policeman left his target scrambling on the floor, gathering up the documents, his colleagues smirking at him as they followed their leader away.

Unable to resist a last effort, he delivered his final insult by stamping on Kolit's fingers and twisting his boot as he went past, him causing him to drop the papers he'd just collected.

Completing their inspection with no further incident, the troopers stared menacingly back at the three grim-faced individuals. Tiring with this eventually and deciding they'd made their point, the men turned to the door and marched back out into the street, disappearing amongst the crowds.

When they were finally out of earshot, Tiea jumped up and put her arm around the shaken airman. 'Are you okay?' she asked, hugging him tighter as he nursed his injured right hand.

'No, I'm not okay, Tiea. That little shit attacked me because these papers were smudged for fuck's sake—and for that hurt my shoulder and stamped on my fingers. I'm far from okay right now!' His voice was furiously shaking.

'That little bastard,' said Jack.

Mark felt completely humiliated, but promised himself there and then, that he would take his revenge and ensure the officer never forgot his—or rather Kolit's—face. Imagining the officer and his band of thugs through a Spitfire's gun sight, being tossed around in bloody heaps by the plane's armaments, already made him feel slightly better.

'That was bloody nasty,' Jack commented, his face depicting his mounting concern for his friend. 'Thank God you kept your temper—although I don't know how you did! When that supercilious little bastard started punching your shoulder I nearly lost control of mine!' Jack offered his friend a comforting pat on the back. 'I'm sorry you had to go through that, old boy.' He sighed and looked around him at the now-silent tavern. 'I'm really not sure we quite realised what we were taking on coming here.'

'Well, I suppose it's the kind of thing we were looking for to back-up Rema's tale, but I think next time we should bring a few reinforcements!' Mark said ruefully.

'What do you want to do now?' asked Tiea. 'Should we continue or would you rather call it a day?'

'No, I'm alright now, Tiea, just a little shaken up. Let's continue our research shall we?' He offered Tiea a reassuring smile. 'But I'll say one thing: even if the bloody navy won't join you, you can count me in if you want me.'

'And that goes for me too, Tiea,' Jack confirmed.

'I'm sure I can arrange that easily, and thank you for the offer. Let's stay here and let Mark recover whilst we finish our drinks, then we'll go to the prison I think you should see.'

The three of them sat for a time, reflecting on the unexpectedly savage turn their visit had taken, noting the furtive glances directed at them from other tables whilst they finished the wine. A little while later, Tiea settled the bill and they went back out into the square, the sun seeming cooler and the once-beautiful city seeming much less attractive to the airmen following their tavern ordeal.

Tiea guided them across the square, leading them towards a corner in the far right where a street wound down the hill towards the bay.

The time spent in the tavern had sharpened everyone's senses, and they were all now too aware that it took only one encounter to completely skew their plans. The two men now realised that Atlanta, whilst beautiful, wasn't as similar to their home towns as they'd originally thought.

As it had now materialised, Atlanta was far removed from anything they'd ever known before.

After walking a short distance, the group found themselves on a small street with a row of terraced houses on each side. Amazingly, the street led into an open area—right beside the golden pyramid.

'What a sight,' Mark said in awe. 'It's absolutely huge, Tiea! And there's not a mark on the ruddy thing, no lines of craftsmanship, no sign of construction. Surely something that large can't be made in one solid lump?'

'Buggered if I know,' replied Jack, equally uncertain. 'But it sure looks like it has been. How the hell one manages that I can't imagine.' Jack turned to Tiea. 'You told us earlier that it's producing power for this city and way beyond, so I presume that, right now, every vehicle and building we see here is using it? 'You'd never guess just by looking at it, would you? It seems strangely still somehow for something that's obviously so busy.'

'I'd definitely expect to see a lot more activity than this—which shows no indication of any energy-production whatsoever,' Mark commented. 'Anything we've got producing power makes an inordinate fuss about the whole thing. I mean, there's no smoke or steam pouring out of every orifice, no heaps of coal or ash... nothing. There aren't any lorries or cranes charging about either. Just complete stillness.'

Beyond the open ground and its dramatic view of the pyramid, the street twisted round to the left, leading the group into another built-up area. Turning the corner, the airmen saw what was clearly a prison, and assumed it to be the one Tiea wanted them to see. The street ended at the entrance to a large compound filled with a range of single-storey buildings with barred doors and windows. The compound was surrounded by high stone walls, and ringing the parapets were wicked metal spikes curving inward and sharpened at the tips. Large metal gates stood at the entrance, but these were presently standing open. A simple barrier guarded by gaolers blocked the exit in lieu of the gates, and people filed past in either direction, their documents checked by the guards as they passed through.

'I hope we don't have any trouble with the merry men at the turnstiles,' sighed Mark, rubbing his shoulder at the reminder of what could potentially befall them this time. 'They look like a bunch of mean bastards.'

'We should be fine with this lot,' Tiea responded. 'As I said, the king wants people to see his horrible little show in here, and so unless something's very amiss, they're only really here to prevent prisoners from escaping—not that there's ever much opportunity of that; the inmates are either starving, too ill to move, or lacking in the necessary body parts to enable escape,' Tiea whispered, her eyes filling with tears.

Jack and Mark passed a startled expression between themselves.

Moments later, the airmen and their guardian passed through the security check without incident. Tiea then led the men down a marked walkway, leading from the buildings near the gate into an open area behind. Here, others trod the path ahead of them, gazing at the scores of unfortunates who were in varying states of distress.

The prisoners were either in cages or strapped to implements of torture in the open. They'd been scattered around the area, with small spaces left between them, allowing spectators to enjoy the king's macabre horror show. Naked, broken, half dismembered, blind or screaming, each cage exhibited a different slant on the same disgusting theme. The horrified airmen were led on around the evil spectacle, realising that the punishments inflicted on the prisoners worsened the further the walkway led them round. Unfortunately, the prison implemented a one-way system, thereby ensuring all visitors were forced to observe every last, cruel show before being permitted to leave.

As the tour continued, the sights became ever more distressing, with the final cages containing only ragged flesh hanging from brutally disfigured bodies and dying mutants in utter despair. Finally, their ordeal terminated with a nightmare of almost unrecognisable forms, with screaming and crying echoing down the halls, sanity long since departed.

There was no hope left for these poor people.

The horrific acts, perpetrated upon souls who had undoubtedly once been normal and led perfectly common existences, affected the airmen profoundly. A deep resolve filled them, and they promised themselves and each other that this would not be permitted to continue. He who was ultimately responsible for these foul acts would have to be stopped—and if that meant risking their own lives, then so be it. Either way, they vowed, they would ensure that this world would be freed from such an abomination.

'What the hell have these people done to deserve this, Tiea?' Jack asked, his throat choked with emotion.

'They've upset the king, plain and simple. The extent of any upset is irrelevant; the fact remains that he became pissed off for some reason and they suffered as a result.' Tiea turned away from the men, dabbed at her eyes, and again turned to face them. 'There are no criminals here. All anyone has ever done is rebel in some way, and this is the result.'

'It just doesn't bear thinking about,' Mark said. 'For God's sake, Tiea, let's get out of here. I think we've all seen enough.'

'This can't be allowed to continue a moment longer,' commended Jack, anger furiously vibrating in his voice. 'You do realise we have to stop this?' he said, looking directly at Mark.

Mark nodded his acknowledgement.

'Unfortunately, we can't leave just yet,' Tiea said, causing the men's faces to drop. 'That one-way system is implemented throughout the entire prison. Unfortunately, we've only been through part of it. I'm afraid we have to complete the tour,' she said sadly.

'Please don't tell me there's more of this?' Mark asked, suddenly feeling nauseous.

'I'm afraid so. It's where they start on the prisoners, and so it's not quite as bad as what you've just seen. However, I'll need to warn you of one thing…'

The men exchanged worried glances.

'You're expected to enter into the spirit of things,' Tiea continued. 'It's completely sickening. Some enjoy it, of course, which makes the entire scenario far more disturbing. But just make sure you do as I do and you won't stand out. Trust me, gentlemen, standing out is something you really don't want to do or we'll say here longer than we planned. Much longer. Remember that as we go round.'

With the warning fixed firmly in their minds, Tiea led them down the next path which led to a large building, coming up behind other spectators who were shuffling in through the doorway. Into the next room were cells lined down each side, and the walkway ran through the centre. The cells were barred at the front and divided from each other by stone walls, forming forty separate cubicles. In every cell, the king's gaolers were providing a different show for the gratification of the spectators moving along the centre aisle, the crowd viewing everyone as they passed by.

Queuing in the aisle just before the first two cells on either side, the three comrades began their nightmare journey through the building. A nightmare of noise could be heard: the cracking of whips, the screams of the whipped, the begging of the victims and, perhaps worst of all, the spectators shouting and cajoling the tormentors into greater efforts. The deeply questionable form of entertainment ranged from extreme physical punishment through to scenes of humiliation and complete depravity, the gaolers seeming to perform to greater heights with the encouragement of the crowd. And it was then, upon considering the crowd, that the men both realised that, as per Tiea's advice, they weren't to stand out—and refusing to partake in the encouragement of abuse would be doing exactly that.

Nausea engulfed the group, sweat covered their palms, and they prayed to soon be through with this next ordeal.

Following Tiea's lead and being as reserved as they felt they could get away with, they each added their voices to the jeering, encouraging crowd as they continued the interminable shuffle through hell. Finally emerging from purgatory, the walkway delivered the group adjacent to the main gates. Their papers having been perused once again by the guards, they silently exited the prison.

Each dealt with the experience in their own way as they slowly walked away, no words passing between them until they'd reached the pyramid heading back to the square.

Mark was the first to speak. 'You know, I couldn't have been further from the truth could I? I really thought this was quite a nice place when we arrived—new and exciting, beautiful, technologically advanced, interesting and perplexing... Now I see it's actually fucking terrifying. Hell on Earth.'

'I've never seen anything like that, and I'm not keen to see anything like it ever again either. No wonder the people around here are so oppressed.' Jack was shaking with delayed shock, his eyed red from fighting back tears—tears of anger, compassion, sadness and fear. Tears for the people, and tears for his new life.

'You'll never get used to it,' remarked Tiea. 'It's something we've had to accept as it's been going on for such a long time. It is how it is now. But what really disturbs me is the increasing number of people who actually seem to enjoy it.' She shook her head sadly. 'The scum who rule us are winning in more ways than I could ever have imagined. Why is it that great power always corrupts like this?'

'It's not always the case, Tiea,' Jack comforted. 'But sadly, for a select few, power is all empowering and warps the mind.'

'Rema travelled to Rome not too long ago,' Tiea told them. 'She said those in great power were at the height of their corruption. She spoke of the so-called *games* they played, which their citizens seemed to enjoy immensely and which weren't much different to the king's own practices, by the sound of it. What a world.'

The group were deeply saddened and frustrated.

'Anyway,' Tiea said, trying to compose herself, 'it's getting late, and if you want to see more we should get on with it.'

With that the airmen stating that they'd actually seen far more than they'd ever wanted to see, the group instead continued to the square. Retracing their earlier steps, they returned to the waiting Hovertrans and climbed aboard. Moments later, with its distinctive hum, the vehicle rose above the pavement as Tiea flicked on the power unit, driving it slowly through the streets and back to her house.

With heavy hearts and more to mull over than they could easily digest the airmen had little to say throughout the journey.

Upon returning to Tiea's home and after removing their disguises, the three of them spent some time discussing the day's events with Tiea's family. Gratefully sipping a glass of wine, the post-mortem continued.

'I can't believe they attacked you, Mark—and essentially over nothing,' Kolit said, pointing out the offending smudge on his papers. 'Even they wouldn't normally do something so petty.' Kolit pondered the situation for a moment, gazing out of the window. 'Hmm. It wouldn't surprise me if there was more to it. We've had a few problems with the king's specials lately. Maybe we're being targeted.'

Tiea considered the prospect. 'It's possible, but they might just have been bored. Without question, the officer was trying to provoke Mark into something more serious, but it could've been nothing more sinister than that,' Tiea said.

'I highly doubt boredom was responsible, Tiea. We all know there's only a few of us left in business. There are only ten remaining firms in Atlanta that the king doesn't control, and we're all being harassed by him in one way or another. He's increasing the pressure on us all. Our days are numbered, I fear. And if this plan of ours doesn't work, we'll all end up being a part of His Majesty's fucking floorshow,' Rafh spat angrily.

'Then we have no option but to make sure it works,' Mark reassured the group. 'Jack and I will move Heaven and Earth to convince our people to help—you can rely on that now. We genuinely want to help, especially after today's sojourn into your friendly little town. The fact remains that, if we want to survive here, we need to ensure we win this battle.'

With Mark, Jack and Tiea exhausted following the recent events, time dripped away slowly, with Tiea becoming more and more anxious to leave by the minute. She'd spoken with Rema who'd advised that the fleet was headed for the resistance base on Kira and was expected to arrive within the hour. Rema also told her that the captain needed the two airmen to attend a meeting aboard the carrier, where their report would be crucial. She'd instructed Tiea to land on the carrier, placing the airmen where required, and reminded her time was critical.

Feeling they'd made new friends in Tiea and her family, and being a great deal wiser for it, the two men said their goodbyes and expressed their desire to meet again, but hopefully under better circumstances.

Tiea fired up the Vertlyn and they swiftly departed from Atlanta.

Sometime later, two miles from the coast, Jack spotted a group of buildings tucked away in the middle of a large forest close to the sea. The buildings stood alone, far from any other habitation. They had what appeared to be watchtowers and fencing surrounding the site. 'That place looks remote, Tiea,' he stated. 'Is it another of the king's prisons or something similar maybe?'

'Actually, it's a school,' Tiea responded. 'Ostensibly, it was built by the king to provide the best education for his hierarchy's children, which it possibly does. Essentially, the king remains unconcerned as to whether or not the education is provided; he simply insists that all his key servants send their children here. His only concern is that he's effectively got their children hostage, thereby ensuring he has yet another hold over his minions.'

'Well, hasn't he thought of everything,' Mark replied dryly. 'A more conniving, scheming bastard you'd be hard put to find anywhere else. He seems to have the whole lot covered and recovered.'

'Oh, he's all that and a whole lot more—just don't underestimate him. For one thing, he's no fool,' Tiea replied.

They flew on towards Kira, discussing their visit to Atlanta and the king's behaviour when, approximately halfway home, ten Hovertaks screamed beneath them, flying in the opposite direction. Engrossed in their conversation, the trio had failed to see them coming, and the sudden arrival of the warplanes shook them badly. Already frazzled by the day's events, they instantly assumed the worst.

Once again with no chance of defending themselves, they stared helplessly at the fighters, concern mounting rapidly that *they* were the ones being hunted.

The Hovertaks had actually flown from Chetoa, an occupied country seven hundred miles to the north of Atlantis, and were currently heading for the landing ground in Atlanta. The high command had called in all available aircraft from their surrounding territories, and the planes were responding to their orders. Although they saw the Vertlyn above, they'd no reason to suspect it was of any interest to them, therefore opting to fly by without incident.

After a few moments, the group decided that the Vertlyn appeared to be safe, and the three shaken occupants relaxed as the Hovertaks disappeared into the distance.

'I don't suppose this baby has any teeth, Tiea, just in case we meet any more of those?' asked Mark.

'I'll assume you're joking, Mark—surely you wouldn't consider taking on Hovertaks in this, even if it had weaponry would you?' Tiea threw him a concerned look. 'You might have a low opinion of the king's pilots after this morning's scenario—'

'—But I doubt they'd have much trouble sending you through those pearly gates if you tried,' Jack finished.

'I might if I had no choice, Wing Co.,' Mark replied.

'You'd have no chance, Mark. This aircraft's for pleasure only. But, thank Ra, those fellows clearly weren't interested in us. Outnumbered, outperformed and lacking weapons, I suppose we could've stuck out our tongues at them,' Tiea smiled cheerfully.

'I feel that would be a far better tactic than what I was considering! The sight of my pal in the back sticking out his tongue and flapping his hands around his ears would frighten the bravest pilot! We couldn't possibly have lost such a battle!' Mark laughed, looking out at the great blue sky.

With the danger now passed—in the short-term, at least—the group relaxed a little and allowed a calm silence to descend, allowing them to enjoy the scenery without any imminent fear for their lives.

CHAPTER ELEVEN

The fleet was steaming north-bound around Kira's rugged shoreline and, with a while to go before they expected to reach their destination, Rowsell was already planning his next move upon being safely anchored.

Turning to the Atlantien resistance leader beside him, he said, 'Rema, as soon as we've anchored the fleet at your base, I intend to convene a meeting on Victorious with all our ranking officers. I've got to tell them what's happened as soon as possible. I need to get them on-side and ensure I have their immediate support for what we're intending to do now or we simply can't move forward. I realise by then it'll be late, but I feel that could actually benefit us: as all of our officers will be away from their posts in this meeting, we'd be highly vulnerable, and so it would be preferable to speak to the men under the cover of darkness and reduce the risk as much as possible.'

'I appreciate your concern, Captain. However, I assure you the anchorage is well defended anyway. Obviously, updating your people is paramount, and must be done at the earliest opportunity. However, if it helps, we could accommodate this meeting at the base. It would be easier and much quicker to land your men on shore than to have them board the carrier from the lake anyway,' Rema replied.

'Thank you for the offered assistance, Rema. I agree that it would significantly speed up the process, but I think we need to stay on home ground, as it were—for now at least. I'm not sure it would be a wise move to expose our people to your personnel and technology until they know all the facts and have been properly prepared for such. There'll be hundreds of people attending this meeting. With that in mind, any panic or disaffection with the circumstances would be easier to control on-board the carrier. Provided we can get our message across successfully and when everyone's settled down a bit, maybe then would be a better time to introduce them to your world.'

Rema nodded. 'Of course, Captain, whatever you feel is easiest.'

'We're a superstitious lot in the navy, Rema, as I'm sure you're aware. Ghosts, monsters, pirates and the like... Well, there are endless threats to the unwary mariner when on the old briny, and so it's probably better we don't fuel their imaginations any more than we have to at this point. I'd also like to request your presence, if at all possible.'

'I understand your situation,' Rema said positively. 'Having got to know your people so well living amongst them, I forget how strange we must appear to you. Anyway, thank you for your invitation; I'd be happy to come over to you and I'll bring a colleague. I'll inform the others as soon as we arrive.'

'One more thing,' Rowsell stated. 'We'll need those airmen back here as soon as possible. I think it would be of significant benefit that we have their report before the meeting. Hopefully they'll have something useful to tell us or we're going to be in big trouble. If you could arrange for your pilot to bring them straight to Victorious when they return, I feel that would give us more time to debrief them,' Rowsell requested.

The fleet was now approaching the outer bay of the natural harbour into which Rema led them. Early evening was now approaching, but the sky remained bright with the day's sun, still high in the sky. The captain gazed at the convoy following the Plymouth in line astern, starting as he noticed the three U-boats running on the surface, bringing up the rear.

From the captain's position, he was able to see the bay which, like the beach they had previously left behind, was surrounding by steep cliffs running in a semicircle and plunging into the sea at either end. The cliffs here, however, had wrapped around the beach, enclosing the bay within its walls, leaving a gap of only approximately half a mile between them.

The sea ran right up the cliff faces, which raised sheer for approximately a thousand feet. Mid-point in the cliff on the land side of the bay was a natural fissure cutting through it, and no more than six-hundred yards across, he could see this led into a large lake behind.

Rowsell ordered his command to reduce speed to four knots and, remaining in line astern following the Plymouth, the last few ships entered the bay. Slowly, one by one, the eighteen vessels sailed across the waters, passing through the gap and into the harbour beyond.

The enclosed body of water of the harbour was pear-shaped, with the narrowest area adjacent to the entrance. A vast area spanning several miles across, the lake was surrounded by high, steep-sided, heavily forested hills. As Rema had promised, the natural feature provided an ideal anchorage for the fleet—and one which they could conceivably defend.

Moored at the far end of the lake, the captain noticed what he assumed were five Atlantien ships. With the light now failing as the sun descended in the sky, the ships were somewhat indistinct, although Rowsell considered that, judging by their overpowering design, three of them were potentially warships, the remaining two undoubtedly cargo vessels.

The captain set about dispersing his fleet within the lake. His goal was to give the warships the best defensive positions, ones from where they could both protect themselves and the remaining merchantmen. First, he positioned Victorious nearest to the entrance of the harbour, facing the furthest shore, thereby ensuring his planes had enough room to fly from the carrier if required. Next he anchored his warships in a staggered line along the middle of the lake, which enabled them to cover the entire lake and the surrounding hills with their heavy deck and anti-aircraft guns. With the merchantmen placed either side of the warships close into shore and the submarines split up amongst them, he was content they were now in a position to provide formidable resistance against any potential aggressor.

Rowsell had efficiently and safely anchored his entire fleet before darkness. Now completely closed in, the huge task was complete—a testament to his seamanship which had, once again, impressed Rema. During their journey together, she had been able to observe his easy and capable style of command, which had brought together the many varying vessels—all designed for different duties—into a cohesive force, now operating as a single unit.

'My compliments to you, Captain. You ran that entire operation like a well-oiled machine,' Rema complimented. 'You've obviously done this before.'

'Just a couple of times,' replied Rowsell with a smile, secretly pleased with himself considering how smoothly the operation had gone.

With all vessels now anchored in position, Rowsell ordered Victorious to prepare the hangar deck for the coming gathering and issued orders to every ship that all commissioned and non-commissioned officers of the convoy were required to attend. Upon completing these arrangements, Tiea and the airmen returned from Atlantis.

Rowsell watched as the small aircraft flew in over the hills behind the base. He immediately contacted the carrier and requested they accept the plane aboard. 'We'd better head over there ourselves, Rema,' the captain advised. 'There's not much time to debrief them as it is. I'll get us a boat.'

~*~*~*~

From the air, Mark and Jack could now see the fleet had been efficiently anchored in three staggered lines, the carrier located nearest to the exit of the lake. 'It looks like whoever's in charge is good at what they do,' Jack observed. 'If the harbour down there's anything to go by, I'd say we'll be part of a very professional operation.'

'Prepare yourselves,' Tiea advised. 'I assume we're to land on that large vessel there,' she said, pointing down to the phenomenal Victorious.

Mark and Jack checked their safety belts, not sure whether Tiea was capable of meticulously manoeuvring an aircraft onto a sea vessel. But within only a minute or so, Tiea had successfully landed the small aircraft onto the deck.

'Well done,' Jack complimented. 'I couldn't have done it better myself.'

'Not just a pretty face, my girl,' said Mark, grinning.

Tiea smiled. 'Thank you. Well, I must say goodbye now,' she advised as the men jumped out of their seats and onto the deck. 'I need to leave; I have things to tend to. I do hope the day wasn't too painful, although I know that's probably an understatement!'

'You're not coming with us?' Mark asked, surprised.

'I'm afraid not, Mark. I really have got things to do.' She paused for a moment. 'But I'll happily meet you for a proper drink sometime, if you'd like.'

'The sooner the better I say,' said Mark, cheering up considerably. 'When's it to be?'

'Hopefully after we've delivered our message to the king,' Tiea replied. 'I'll catch up with you in Atlanta when this ordeal's over.' She gave him a sparkling smile. 'Anyway, good luck with your meeting. Both of you.'

'And thank you for all of your assistance, Tiea,' Jack commented, stretching into the plane and taking her hand in a friendly shake. 'I'll hope to see you again.'

'That goes for me, too,' Mark continued. 'Anyway, let's hope the next time we visit your city together it won't be as stressful!' He hopped back into the plane and gave her a gentle kiss on the cheek. 'Goodbye for now, Tiea.'

Moments later, the two men heard the Vertlyn's engine begin to whir, its whine increasing. Then, with a final wave, Tiea lifted from the deck and flew out across the lake.

Shortly after Tiea's departure, Captain Rowsell and Rema arrived on Victorious and quickly made their way to the wardroom, keen to conduct the airmen's debriefing. They found the two men sitting at the wardroom table, drinking tea, eating biscuits, and chatting together.

'Good evening, gentlemen,' greeted the captain. 'I see they've looked after you okay then.'

'Good evening, Captain,' Jack replied politely. 'And good evening, Rema.' His eyes lighting up, Jack gave her an affectionate smile. Turning his attention back to the captain he said, 'We've been made to feel very welcome. Thank you, Sir.'

'Wonderful. Now, down to business,' the captain commanded. 'I've convened a meeting here later with all our ranking officers. I don't mind telling you, I'm not looking forward to it too much. I'm going to lay everything on the line, and I hope you've managed to achieve a positive result today. I'm going to need all the help I can get with this one! The meeting's due to start in two hours' time, so let's crack on shall we? The floor is yours.'

Rema and the captain took their seats at the table.

Jack was the first to speak. 'In that case, I'll get straight to the point, Captain. Let me start by saying, I'm sure you'll be very pleased to know that we haven't wasted our time at all. Now we've been to Atlantis, I'm not sure whether Rema actually understated quite how bad things really are.'

Mark guffawed slightly, clearly reiterating Jack's comments.

'There is much to tell,' Jack continued. 'I hope you'll be patient whilst I run through everything.'

Both the captain and Rema nodded, and Jack began with their story of the day's events.

Almost two hours later, Jack had spoken of all he and Mark had encountered during their trip, detailing everything from the language gadgets to the vehicles, the frightening confrontation in the tavern, the incredible, overwhelming pyramid, and the deeply disturbing prison. Now, Captain Rowsell sat seated at the table, visibly pale, his eyes wide.

'Essentially,' Jack stated, 'considering Mark and I only went on a very short trip, it remains that we've been taught a lot about society here. We certainly know the bare bones, which I hope has put your mind to rest a little—at least in the sense that we've been told the truth, as far as we can see it.'

Having listened intently to Jack's version of events, with Rema filling in relevant gaps associated with local knowledge, the captain had pieced everything together and felt easier in his mind that he'd taken the right, albeit only, decision under the circumstances. Nevertheless, he acknowledged that, if events had been regaled with even the tiniest fragment of accuracy, it remained that this world was extremely dangerous, and he had a duty to protect his men from ever experiencing any of the horrific things he'd heard of.

With time now running short, the airmen, captain and Rema left the wardroom together and moved up to the hangar deck, preparing themselves for the meeting which was about to begin.

Night had now fallen, and the last of the officers were making their way to Victorious in a stream of small launches which had been sailing across the darkening waters of the lake to the carrier for the last two hours. Now warm and still, the lake resembled a millpond, and the moon cast an eerie silver glow across the harbour as the last of the stragglers left their ships. The trees penetrating the skyline stood iron-like before the last vestiges of sunset. The ships, floating ethereal and silent at their moorings, cast reflected images in the water, the tall superstructures silhouetted against the dark forest backdrop. Galland's submarines appeared predatory in the soft moonlight, lying half submerged in the water, their long black hulls resembling hungry sharks, waiting to feed.

Dominating all was the vast carrier Victorious. A deadly machine in action, the behemoth now lay sleeping. For the men in the small boats, journeying alongside the carrier's persona was nonetheless intimidating, which was unsurprising as, from the waterline to the top of her radio masts, she towered halfway up the cliff behind her.

With some difficulty, the last contingent was lifted aboard Victorious, gravitating in groups towards the hangar deck on their way to attend the meeting. Glistening footprints clearly marked the route they were to follow, left by a few unfortunates who'd fallen into the lake whilst disembarking from their launches.

The tension mounted as the waiting extended, a buzzing of voices ebbed and flowed through the hangar as they speculated as to the nature of their predicament.

Prior to the meeting, the captain agreed with Rema that he'd outline the situation to his men and then hand over to the resistance when he'd fully explained their position. He asked Jack and Mark to remain with him, them being the only officers who'd experienced life first-hand amidst the general population. Although it had been short-lived, the captain nevertheless wanted their input in the approaching proceedings.

Rema's deputation comprised six resistance leaders, one of them being Lac Lanter who they'd nominated as their main spokesman. They'd informed the captain that Lanter was their chief tactician and was highly regarded by them all. He was also the prime director behind the mission which had brought them all to this time from 1940.

At last, all the officers had arrived and Rowsell called the meeting to order. A deathly silence descended as the confused men prayed they'd now get answers to the questions they had been asking for two days. A few of them, ever optimistic, even hoped the answers would be palatable.

The captain began by introducing the resistance to his officers and explaining that their presence would become clear a few minutes into the briefing. He asked them all to be patient until he and Lanter had finished speaking, pointing out that there was much to cover, and so it was therefore more than likely that answers would appear naturally during the course of the talk. Assuring them they'd be given every opportunity to speak at the end, he launched into the briefing, calling upon the airmen to recount their visit around the middle of his lecture. He ended by summing up all the facts and offering them his conclusions.

After speaking, the captain then handed over the meeting to Lanter, who promptly presented a history of the resistance and the reasons they expected the fleet to ally itself with them. Between all of them, they'd left no doubt in the officers' minds concerning the situation they had needed to address.

Having delivered his speech, Lanter sat back with the others, awaiting the barrage of questions which they'd naturally assumed would overwhelm them at this point. Unexpectedly, a long silence ensued as the shaken and confused officers grappled with the ramifications of the situation.

Eventually, a young cockney NCO decided to air his views on the subject. 'Cor blimey! Yer all knows how to spin a good yarn don't yer? But you proper done me fucking head in with that one though, and aint that the truth!' He hesitated momentarily but, demonstrating the spirit Rowsell had hoped the meeting would inspire, he continued. 'Still, now we're here, lads, let's tell his old kingship where he gets the fuck off and show the bugger he can't carry on like that no more.'

Laughter emanated throughout the vast deck.

The captain felt encouraged by how the meeting was now progressing, and he continued to provide his men with the opportunity to ask questions.

The comments and questions continued, the mood of the gathering swinging to and fro—anger at having been kidnapped, frustration at being unable to return, annoyance the resistance seemed to consider the whole situation unavoidable, and genuine sorrow at the loss of their families and friends they had been forced to leave behind. Nevertheless, surfacing was a hardening desire to support the underdog, whilst slowly accepting the inevitability of the situation and the realisation they'd never return to their own time.

Towards the end of the meeting, each officer began to envisage his future prospects in this place, dealing with the facts as presented in their own manner.

All of the men, without exception, were trained fighting men with combat experience. As a result, most saw an opportunity to continue the job they'd initially been trained for.

There was considerable support offered by the resistance to the men in the form of financial benefits. The resistance had been generous in their terms. Lanter outlined their basic package, and further detailed exactly what they could expect to receive—both in property and position—should the king be defeated, as the captain originally suspected, whereupon more dissenters swiftly reappraised their situation.

Finally, the collective opinion—whatever the individual reasons behind it—was found to be in favour of supporting the resistance in their struggle. Together, it was decided that they'd reached their decision, and they were all aware they'd live or die by it.

From now, there was no going back.

Rema and her colleagues were delighted with the outcome. At last, they had a real opportunity to take their war direct to the king. Thanks to their new allies, they were finally a force for him to reckon with, and they fully intended that his reckoning would be very painful for him.

In conclusion, the captain dealt with the immediate practical issues raised by their decision, issuing orders to his officers. Their first duty was to inform the ranks of the situation, and he assured them none would be forced to join the battle against their will. Any person declining would be detained on Kira until such a time that the captain or his senior officers decided it was safe for them to leave; he'd not risk the enemy capturing any of his people. The captain subsequently arranged a Council of War to be conducted with the Atlantiens and his top-ranking commanders for midday, which was to be held at their base.

Thanking all present, Rowsell called an end to the proceedings.

'Well, I'd say that was a good outcome for our cause, Rema,' Mark said, forcing his way through the milling throng of servicemen around him to reach her. 'Nothing like the seventh cavalry galloping over the hill to raise the spirits, old girl.'

'You're right there. The meeting really couldn't have gone better for us, could it? It was all I'd prayed for, and now we've every reason to fight on.'

'Definitely,' continued Mark. 'And trust me, after the day I've had, I can't wait to get to grips with the bastards!'

'Me too,' said Rema, her eyes sparkling. 'It's payback time. I've lost many dear friends to our rotten king and his henchmen.' Rema glanced away. 'Anyway, enough of that for today. About your accommodation: can I offer yourself and Jack a place to stay at our base? You're part of our team now!'

'That would be fantastic,' Mark said cheerfully.

'That sounds great,' Jack said, appearing through the crowds.

'Bloody typical,' complained Mark, feigning displeasure. 'Just as I was discussing sleeping arrangements with this beautiful creature, you have to turn up!'

'Well, at least she doesn't have to make arrangements with the oil rag now the mechanic's arrived,' retorted Jack with a grin.

'Now now, calm yourselves,' said Rema playfully. 'It's been a long day. Let's head back to the base. And how about we go with the use of these…' She said, holding up three anti-gravity packs.

'Yes!' exclaimed Mark excitedly, thrusting his fist into the air, a huge smile across his face. 'What's the use of living in a world as technologically advanced as this one if we can't enjoy the perks?'

The air was crisp, the gentle breeze brushing across the group's faces as they sailed through the silent darkness. The night-sky was black, the only light provided by the moon and a scattering of brightly shining stars.

'It's breath-taking up here, Rema,' Jack remarked wistfully. 'What an incredible sight. And the silence is profound. I've never heard such a hush.'

'I suppose not, Jack, but this is nothing unusual for me. But, I do so love being up here; it's a great way of appreciating the view,' replied Rema.

'Well, the beauty of it all's somewhat lost on me,' said Mark. 'Not that I want to put a dampener on your idealistic moment here, but the last time I saw someone gadding about in the sky near to a submarine, they came to a very sticky end—and we're getting a bit close to one right now.' Mark looked nervous as he eyed the under-water vessel suspiciously. 'Don't you think perhaps we should change course a little?'

Rema considered the situation. 'I'd say it's better to be safe than sorry. Turn into the shore and we'll steer away from all the ships. About the last thing we need is to be shot down by our own side!'

Following the water's edge, they soon arrived over Rema's base.

'Mark, we'll land over there on the sand beside that jetty,' Rema said.

Descending gracefully, they touched down on the shore, deactivating their backpacks as they landed.

The airmen looked around, but apart from the decrepit old jetty, there was nothing else to be seen, with the forest leading right up to the water's edge. There was no sign of the large facility that Rema had mentioned, and although she'd said it was underground, they'd expected to see some evidence of it—if it was indeed here and as large as she'd indicated.

Jack idly wondered if Rema's base was on one of their ships that stood anchored off the shore opposite, but since none were of any great size and they were clearly not underground, he quickly disregarded the thought.

Mark was clearly thinking along the same lines, but had not given it too much thought. 'Which of those boats do you use as your base then?' he asked.

'None of them, Mark; the base is underground, as I said. Follow me and you'll see.'

Turning towards the forest, Rema led the men into the trees. Immediately, the ground rose steeply, and they scrambled up the hillside. They'd climbed a few hundred yards when Rema stopped before an impressive tree, which stood towering above them. The trunk itself was large enough in girth to accommodate a small truck; Jack considered it similar to the giant redwood tree native to the Americas. Rema placed her hand against the trunk and, to the amazement of Mark and Jack, rotated a small section of bark. Then, with a light push, a door opened into the base of the tree, bright light pouring out from the interior.

Quickly looking around them, Rema stepped through the doorway, leading the way into a chamber with steps leading down to a passageway, cutting into the hillside. As the airmen had observed before, the walls, floor and ceiling were smooth as glass.

'The passage at the bottom of the steps leads into the complex we discovered two years ago,' Rema explained as she walked through the pristine corridor. 'We've since utilised it as our headquarters, amongst other things. Considering the last time you came with me into a place built by the Ancients, I'll warn you before we go in this time: you'll see strange things you won't understand in there, but don't let it worry you. Simply ask if anything shocks you.'

From the base of the steps, the curving, well-lit passage extended to a door at the end which, when Rema pushed it open, revealed a vast chamber, buried deep under the hill.

'Oh shit,' said Mark, his jaw visibly dropping. 'You weren't kidding were you, Rema? Judging by this lot, I'd say there will be a great deal we won't understand!'

'It's so vast in here!' Jack commented. 'I can't see any end to it.'

'It can be quite disorientating at first,' Rema smiled.

'It's absolutely incredible, Rema,' gasped Jack.

'Stunning, isn't it? What you're seeing is a large-scale manifestation of a completely different technology. As unbelievable as it appears, in reality, everything you see in front of you is either a tool manufactured by the Ancients or the results of the Ancients' using them. To me, this all appears normal now—I'm used to it already, but I admit it's taken some time to reach that point.'

The chamber was truly magnificent. Its floor area covered one square mile and was two hundred feet high from floor to ceiling. Perfectly square with perpendicular walls and a flat ceiling, it clearly wasn't a natural formation either. The vast space the Ancients had constructed was a feat of engineering spanning way beyond the airmen's comprehension. Lacking any supporting framework to hold up the roof and the massive weight of the hill above, they didn't need to be engineers to know that it was an impossible space to create—but here it was anyway.

The whole area was bathed in a soft light, which seemingly emanated from the atmosphere; there were no apparent light sources anywhere, yet the chamber was subtly lit up.

Filling the entire space were a variety of machines and structures, the functions of which the airmen couldn't even guess at. And in one corner stood a large pyramid which, at its apex, was just below the roofline.

Although well past midnight, many people still worked at the machines. Others moved across the area, busily dealing with the items they'd manufactured. Sealed crates and boxes were tidily stacked in all directions, presumably ready to ship out later. Although the airmen obviously had no idea what they were producing, it was clear this was a factory of some kind which, even to the uninitiated, appeared to be running very smoothly.

'What are you making here, Rema?' Jack asked.

'We produce a variety of military and other hardware here, ranging from the backpack/weapon units which brought us here from the carrier, communication equipment, mobile power transmitters, vehicles and spare parts, right down to clothing and footwear. We produce enough from here to satisfy all our requirements for such things, along with some to spare. Anything we produce over and above we give to assist our allies,' Rema explained.

'I'm almost afraid to ask, but is the full extent of your operation within this chamber or is there more?' asked Mark.

Rema quietly laughed. 'A whole lot more actually, Mark. Beyond the factory we've a research unit, administration offices and living accommodation. There's also another chamber like this, a little smaller though, which we use to house our aircraft and to repair any damaged equipment. In fact, the rest is all pretty much what you'd expect in the case of any large commercial operation in 1940—except, of course, for B Wing, our research unit, which we'll keep well away from for now. Anyway, it's much too late to think about going there and I reckon we've all been through enough today, so I'll not subject you to any further revelations,' she said somewhat mysteriously.

Mark and Jack exchanged nervous glances.

'Talking about being tired...' Mark said, continuing on with their conversation. 'What about those sleeping arrangements you were going to arrange for us, Rema? Fascinating though this is, it's looking like we have another busy schedule planned for the day, and I think we all need some rest.'

Rema cut across the corner of the main chamber and led them through to a stairwell. Selecting one of the two staircases rising up from it, she ascended to the next level.

The next area, unlike the first chamber with its factory operations and packing lines, was completely luxurious. The staircase rose into a large carpeted entrance hall with a striking ornamental stone archway across the room opposite them. Through the arch, the men could see a wide carpeted corridor beyond, inset with many doorways. Both in the hall and the corridor beyond, wall-mounted globes emitted a warm, soft light.

Within the hall, the walls were covered with murals, all painted directly onto their surfaces, illustrating widely varying scenes in strikingly bold colours. Brightly dressed people walked city streets under azure blue skies, watched the world go by as they sat outside taverns, eating and drinking wine. Without question, the detailed design of the mural and the general surrounding architecture was crisp, professional and unflawed—far outshining anything Jack or Mark had ever seen in 1940. Looking closer still, Jack could see hunting scenes, battle scenes and seascapes, all of which leapt out at them in an ocean of colour and intricacy. The variety was endless. The murals covered the entire ceiling, with every last inch looking like it had been given just as much attention as the previous.

The hall was clearly a recreation area, with groups of comfortable padded chairs located around the space, with ornate light-wood tables. Across the entire far wall of the room was a serving counter faced with carved timber panelling and a seamless, polished stone top. Shelving laden with glass bottles and golden drinking vessels stood behind the counter, and another arch led into a kitchen beside them. In front of the counter, a line of wooden stools stood awaiting the next occupants but, at this early hour of the morning, no other souls stirred.

'We'll scrap the sleep plan for now, Jack,' laughed Mark, 'we've just found another local! That's two in one day, more or less. And, even better, I shouldn't think we'll be assaulted!'

'I reckon it'll still be here later, Mark,' Jack remarked, patting his friend on the back. 'Come on, we haven't slept for bloody hours, and I for one need to recharge after that lot today—yesterday, rather.

'Probably best, I suppose,' Mark grumbled. 'Lead on, McDuffie. Into the arms of Morpheus we'll go at last, but I shall sleep the sounder knowing this watering hole's waiting for us—and it'll be your round by the way, Jack!'

Rema continued to lead them on and, once reaching her destination, turned to face them. 'You can have the second and third rooms on the right, just through the arch.' She pointed across the room. 'You take the first one, Mark. You'll find everything you need in your rooms, including a change of clothes for later. Sleep well, and I'll meet you both here at eleven for a late breakfast.'

The two men wished Rema goodnight and left together to find their rooms.

~*~*~*~

A short time later, Jack stretched out on the large bed and looked around him. Feeling slightly better after having just washed and shaved, he took a moment to reflect on all that had happened the past two days, and quite how odd all of it really was. It had only been forty-eight hours ago when his life had been normal.

Then there was the thought of Patricia who had turned out to be Rema. Without question, he'd become even more attracted to her over the last two days and, to some degree, she had proven to be a cushioning blow to him: he had not been forced to leave behind everything, as Mark and the thousands of navy men had done; here, he had someone whom he had liked very much back home, in 1940. And he was glad she was here. Her presence seemed to compensate a little for the things he'd lost, although it was still incredibly difficult to believe that he'd never see his family and friends again.

Quite possibly the worst thought was thinking of all of his loved ones who would undoubtedly forever question what had happened to him, and who would never stop hoping for his safe return. The thought was heart-breaking.

Still dwelling on these thoughts, he pulled the warm duvet up to his chin and turned off the light. As he drifted off to sleep, he heard a soft knocking on the bedroom door. Flicking the light back on and assuming it would be Mark, he stayed in bed and called, 'Come in, old boy.'

The door was pushed ajar and, to his surprise, he heard Rema's soft voice. 'Are you decent, Jack? May I come in?'

'Well, I'm in bed, but if that doesn't bother you please do,' he answered.

Rema opened the door and stepped into the room. She'd changed her clothes and was now wearing a short black skirt and a simple white blouse. Around her waist she wore a thin leather belt with a pretty silver buckle, plain leather sandals on her feet, and a braided silver necklace around her neck. She'd left her long silver hair loose, which now spilled halfway down her back and sensually covered her breasts. Framing her face, her hair accentuated her large ice-blue eyes, pert nose, and full lips. She'd completed the effect with light musky perfume and a hint of make-up.

Jack noticed she was carrying a bottle and two golden goblets. If her intention had been to gain his full attention, she'd succeeded beyond her wildest dreams.

'Wow, Rema, you look absolutely fantastic! What can I do for you?' he asked with a slight smile.

'I know it's late—well, early—but I needed to see you alone. I don't know when there'll be another chance.' She pointed to the edge of the bed. 'May I?

'Of course.'

She took a seat next to him. 'Soon our campaign begins, and who knows how that'll affect us. And to reiterate Mark's earlier sentiments, shouldn't we enjoy life whilst it's here? We don't know what awaits us in the future.'

'Well certainly, Rema, but I'm not sure I follow,' Jack responded, slightly unsure.

'This isn't easy for a lady,' she smiled coyly. 'But let me just say, it's obvious we're attracted to each other—we have been since we met back in 1940. So why don't we just enjoy ourselves now, Jack Bannerman?'

Jack's face broke out into a delighted smile. 'I can think of nobody else I'd rather enjoy my time with,' he said pleasantly. 'And you know, suddenly I don't feel tired anyway!'

'I've brought a bottle. Let's share it and get to know each other better. Hopefully, if Tiea informs me correctly, it's the same stuff you had in Atlanta that you liked.'

'Thank you, Rema, that sounds perfect. Would you hand me that robe over there and I'll join you.'

Once decent, Rema handed Jack one of the goblets. As their eyes met, a passion flickered between them and, without any words, their mutual desire, which had already been burning brightly, flamed more vibrantly.

Reluctantly breaking the eye contact between them, Rema filled the goblets and crossed the room to sit in a high-backed, two-seater chair opposite the bed, placing the bottle down on the table which stood before it, motioning for Jack to join her.

Time ticked away as the pair relaxed, talking and drinking. They discussed their younger days, and it transpired that she had come from a farming family like Jack, and so they spent some time comparing their experiences of a childhood spent on a farm. Notwithstanding the vast span of time that stood between them, they found they shared memories and a sense of familiarity, which ultimately brought them closer together.

Like Jack, Rema understood the land and was a farmer at heart, both points becoming clearer to him as she discussed in-depth the finer points of the occupation, which greatly impressed him. He waxed lyrical over her knowledge of things agricultural, going so far over the top with his praise that, laughing, she gently reached over and pulled him towards her. Lightly brushing her lips across his cheek, she gazed once more into his eyes.

Experiencing a sudden surge of desire far stronger than anything he'd ever felt before, he was incapable of controlling it. Placing his hand at the back of her head, he pulled her towards him, crushing her lips to his mouth. She instantly responded, kissing him passionately and rolling onto her side, pressing her body firmly against his. Passing her hand into his robe, she explored his body, moving ever lower. Surrendering to their mutual desire, he responded, sliding his hand into her blouse and caressing her pert breasts. Her nipples quickly hardened under his touch, and with one hand raking his back, she clumsily pulled away her skirt and top with the other.

Rema's lithe, tanned body swam into his vision. Now partly revealed with pure white underwear covering her most intimate areas, her silver hair danced teasingly, obscuring and then revealing the fullness of her breasts, her passionate embrace enticingly exposing her rising lust for him.

Jack pulled away, his desires continuing to increase, his passion exploding when he looked at her startlingly beautiful face. Her mouth set slightly open, eyes smouldering and her body glistening invitingly, his defences were all but conquered.

And now his lust rivalled hers.

Rising swiftly, he pulled her with him and, hugging her tightly to his body, carried her to the bed, throwing her onto her back and shedding his robe. Grasping her remaining garments, he stripped the white lace away. Then climbing over her, he kissed her savagely.

As they kissed, she lightly grasped him and guided him inside her, and together they made love with complete abandonment. Their lovemaking explored many avenues, driving each other on until, virtually exhausted, they surrendered to the ultimate climax.

Afterwards, lying back, pressed tightly together, they basked contentedly in the afterglow, softly caressing and now kissing gently as they drifted into a deep and contented sleep.

CHAPTER TWELVE

The king sat in his office, staring unseeingly at the wall in front of his desk. His commanders had just departed, and he was now reflecting on their previous conversation.

He knew he'd been unreasonable throughout, but justified his actions by reminding himself that there was very little point in being the king if one couldn't be unreasonable whenever it suited. He therefore decided that he'd conducted the meeting in an exemplary manner, and continued on with his thoughts.

He'd now need to respond quickly, as he really wanted to be far from his palace as soon as possible. He knew he must prioritise carefully, deciding what he really needed to take with him to Rammath, and then instruct his minions accordingly. Although he fully expected the chiefs of staff to work miracles, even he couldn't expect them to perform if he didn't provide them with any indication of his expectations. Taking stock of the situation, he made notes prior to committing his orders to paper for his chiefs' attention.

He had to take his administrators from the palace, as they were charged with handling all of his personal wealth; 'totally indispensable', he wrote. His guardsmen and their equipment had to be assigned to look after his safety; 'of tantamount importance', he noted. And his wives must be permitted, complete with their entourage, as must his closest friends; 'possibly questionable but whatever', was inked on the page.

In addition, he considered it to be essential that he evacuate his appointed hierarchy who, next to himself, were the most influential of all the citizens in the realm. Naturally, this contingent would only include those he could trust completely. These people formed his government, carrying out the day-to-day politics of his empire. Controlling the civilian issues of commerce, law-making, policing, taxation, medicine, science, religion, records and the like, they were also responsible for implementing such infrastructures in new territories, when his conquering armies had moved on. They were the eyes, ears and hands of the king. Although completely answerable to him in every instance, in reality, he only included himself in the major decision-making processes. He found the affairs of state, in the main, to be repetitive and completely boring. Frankly, such affairs were a waste of his time and fundamentally got in the way of the real business—enjoying himself, ruling, and illustrating his power at any opportunity—and so he kept his involvement in day-to-day affairs to a minimum.

Although the bulk of the servants were spread across his kingdom, a great many were still based in the capital. Doubtlessly, they would come up with the preposterous notion that he should remove their families and friends from danger too. 'No chance whatsoever,' he scrawled angrily. In addition to the government were the underlings, most of whom they would need in their turn and were also housed in Atlanta.

In spite of his weeding, the overall numbers requiring evacuation were becoming prodigious. 'Ra almighty! What do these people expect of me?' he muttered to himself, calling for assistance from the sun god and feeling completely hard done by. Nevertheless, he understood that he couldn't govern alone; they were paramount to his operation of maintaining the society he'd created.

Now, with the most important concerns addressed, the remaining issue for the king was his treasures here in the city. Although he possessed the equivalent in Rammath, that was quite beside the point. However, no matter how hard he thought, the king couldn't realistically see any way of removing many of his jewels and gold from Atlanta in short order. Without question, the realisation hurt him deeply, and he continued to feel like this whole situation was proving to be completely unfair to him.

He again strayed from the task at hand. 'I'm surrounded with incompetence,' he muttered. 'How could those military imbeciles failed to have seen this coming? To have left their king in such tantamount danger is monumentally stupid!' He threw his pen down onto the desk in frustration.

The king, now having completely exonerated himself with this magisterial appraisal of his commander's capabilities and his perfectly understandable inability to have prevented the overall situation, now returned to planning his withdrawal from the front line. Essentially, the one and only saving grace from which he could take a little comfort was the fact that he'd always been incredibly attentive when it came to paperwork: he had decreed all records must be completed in triplicate, and had further insisted each copy to be distributed to three different locations, one of which was Rammath.

His realm had become so large, and the issues involved in administrating it had grown to be so convoluted that, without these records, it would ultimately have been ungovernable. The king, despite having countless faults, was at least a master in the art of self-preservation. He constantly ensured exit strategies were permanently in place—and in as many directions as possible. Realising that, should he have to flee his present location for any reason, he would need to have all his records intact and available somewhere else in order to continue his beneficial rule with minimum disruption.

Everything needed to be maintained, or who knew what kind of chaos could erupt! The peasants and their debts would slip through the net; they would escape unharmed from their crimes; his wealth would suffer. And he couldn't allow any of that to happen—not ever.

He brightened up as he reviewed his notes, acknowledging the possibility of an additional bonus to be gained: some of his more irritating companions could be conveniently forgotten at this juncture. Of course, there were a couple of his wives and a select few members of his parliament—all of whom insisted continuously on disagreeing with him. And what was more, their disgraceful lack of support could be punished further still if the resistance were to capture them—a thought which lifted his spirits further still.

Pleased with himself that he'd ensured a means of escaping whilst maintaining high rule, he called out to his secretary and dictated the letter in which he issued his orders to the chiefs of staff, detailing his requirements for the evacuation to Rammath. Once written and signed, he assigned the task of the delivery to the poor woman, who would undoubtedly receive the furious response of each of the chiefs.

Next, the king communicated with all of his top civil servants and the heads of the various government departments, ordering them to prepare themselves and their staff to leave Atlanta the very next day. Ensuring the real reason for their sudden departure was kept confidential in order to avoid a panic, he instead stated that their presence in Rammath was essential for the final phase of the war against Mu.

Finally, he informed his guard's commanding officer and his personal household secretary of his plans. Leaving them the same instructions as the civil servants, he left his office and headed for the nearest palace bar with the full intention of getting 'royally drunk', as he so often did.

Arriving at Maltor's headquarters, without delay, the three chiefs implemented the reinforcement of Atlantis as instructed by the king, ordering home a substantial number of their troops and equipment from the battlefields of Mu. Having discussed the logistics at some length with their respective field commanders, the general consensus of opinion led them to believe that they could expect two hundred aircraft in Atlantis in three days' time, later followed by fifty thousand men, all of whom must only carry personal equipment.

Accompanying their troopships would be fifteen warships, the whole arriving en masse in seven days. The bulk of the army's heavy equipment would arrive six days later. In total, a period of thirteen days would be needed in order to complete the entire operation. Content that this was practically the best they could do, their period of maximum exposure was now limited to only three days until all the aircraft arrived.

Leaving their field commanders enough ordnance to continue on with the battles in Mu, and accepting that this would, in reality, now become a holding exercise for them for the foreseeable future, they were happy that they'd ensured both fronts were covered—provided, of course, they were granted the necessary time to complete the exercise.

'Oh great,' said Cesa Neda when he'd digested the contents of the king's letter, which had been delivered in triplicate to the three commanders a few moments before. 'And just how many people are we talking about here and where do we get the figure from, I wonder? It's all very well for him to command that we transport this and that to Rammath immediately, but didn't he consider that numbers would be useful?'

'Infuriating,' Maltor agreed. 'However, looking at these orders, we'll have no choice but to ship them out and, even though we don't know how many people they'll turn out to be, it's bloody obvious it'll be more than our aircraft here could cope with.'

'Then I'm guessing that ultimately means *my* ships—and I can't spare any! For Ra's sake, we're going to be attacked by a predominately seaborne force and now we've no ships to repulse them with!' Neda's face began to turn a furious shade of red.

'Back off, Cesa,' commanded Maltor, 'you'll do yourself no good ranting about the situation. I agree that the position he's put us in with these orders hasn't helped us much. Undoubtedly, with demands like these, he's played into our enemies' hands and weakened us further still, which I didn't think was possible!'

'Do we have to put up with this forever,' asked Aharmer, clearly at the end of his patience with the king's selfish demands. 'Perhaps this is the time to do something about him.'

'Meaning what?' Maltor probed.

'Meaning, what would we do if his blasted Argotak developed a malfunction of some kind—maybe inadvertently flew over Kira and landed in the middle of the resistance forces? We couldn't help that, could we?'

'Sol, think before you speak,' Maltor said, though nonetheless enjoying the vision that sprung to his mind. 'The king, however obstructive and objectionable you personally believe him to be, is still our leader. Agreed, a fair proportion of the population are disenchanted with him, but he still enjoys reasonable support. Disposing of him is not the complete answer anyway—his chosen government would remain. Undeniably, they share his views and ideals, and would simply continue to follow the same path.' Maltor looked at the two men. 'If you wanted to rid us of him—and I say *if* in a hypothetical sense—then you would need to have an overall plan which not only removes his royal pain in the arse, but also his government. In that case, you would need to have a suitable alternative ready to replace the entire system quickly, or the result would be total anarchy.'

'Hmm,' considered Neda. 'It makes for a very interesting hypothetical scenario.' He smiled to himself.

'If you're serious, Sol, and if you really did want to overthrow or assassinate him—or anything else, for that matter—I would want to see your plan. Hypothetically, of course. It would need to offer a workable method of governing the empire and provide a cohesive and, more importantly, improved system than that which currently exists or, quite simply, there would never be any point.'

'Well...' delved Neda. 'Did you have anything in mind?'

Sol looked from Maltor to Neda, considering whether he should expand, or whether doing so could ultimately prove to be the end of his life—or, worse still, a lifetime of torture. Undoubtedly, he trusted his two colleagues more than anyone else, but the fact remained, one could never be certain where one's ultimate loyalty lay. What if one—or both—were to report to the king his terrible musings?

'You look doubtful,' Maltor stated. 'I hope you know you can trust us?'

Sol nodded, still unsure.

'Well, do you really want to get involved with the affairs of state? Remember, we're speaking theoretically...' Maltor continued.

Sol remained tight-lipped. 'It was just a thought; a moment of frustration, nothing more.' he lied.

'Okay, Sol,' replied Maltor. 'But remember, the bottom line is this: we're soldiers; we fight wars, we don't do politics. And to be fair, the king allows us to pursue our chosen profession for which we're amply rewarded. I'm not saying that the time won't come that we may want to come together and discuss a plan like this in more depth, but considering the current circumstance, I feel now isn't the best time. We need to remain focused on the task at hand. As much as I wish we could, we can't ignore the immediate threat, and so we need to maintain concentration.'

'Of course, Rak,' replied Sol. 'I'm just frustrated and concerned. If we're defeated here—and the fact remains that we may well be—we're faced with a long, hard fight to regain our former glory—if we ever do. Without question, the shock of such a defeat would have a serious effect on the morale of our troops. I'm sure I don't need to point out to either of you—or indeed anyone else—that the ramifications of losing our homeland are endless.'

'Well, as it stands now, we're here, alive, and preparing to fight,' Maltor stated enthusiastically. 'We haven't even been attacked yet, Sol, let alone beaten. The enemy faces the problem of attacking a defended island: we have thousands of men here. Admittedly, they aren't all front-line, but they're well equipped. And we have our shore defences in place all around the island, all of which are fully manned with experienced, formidable soldiers. Furthermore, we've many aircraft and heavy land-fighting vehicles stationed across the island. Neda still has some ships available, even when allowing for the fact he must send the bulk of them away with the king's retinue. Remember,' Maltor continued, 'five of those are of the Altha variety: The Vale of Entatra and her sisters are akin to a veritable army in themselves. I'm damned if I'd want to face those bloody things but they'll have to'

Sol sighed, knowing Maltor spoke wisely, but nevertheless feeling his fears were justified.

'It isn't like you to seem beaten before you even start, Aharmer. Of course, I acknowledge that we're not in the best position, but it's far from hopeless, man.'

Sol nodded. 'You're right, Rak, let's get on with it. I'll get over this, I'm sure,' he replied, his quick mind already turning back to the job at hand.

The three chiefs set about their preparations and were soon well on the way with their mission.

Aharmer formulated his plans to utilise his air force, initially reluctantly focusing on the king's requirements. The flight to Rammath would have to cross a dead spot in the grid, which was indeed considered to be the cause of their problems in other areas. At least he had the advantage of the king's largess when it applied solely to him. At huge expense, the king had fitted his personal aircraft with its own pyramid-crystal generator. His engineers had suspended it in a gimbaling framework, which ensured the unit remained perfectly aligned irrespective of any change in direction or the angle the aircraft took. All his escorts would need the power produced by this generator to cross the dead area on the way to Rammath. Being the only aircraft in existence with such a facility, Aharmer had already contemplated asking the king to let the air arm use it to bring back some of his machines from Mu. Unfortunately, however, he knew the answer without asking, and considered it wasn't worth the effort. Instead, he decided to send an additional flight of Hovertaks to accompany the king, thereby reinforcing his existing personal escorts on the flight to Rammath, which would then be required to move on.

At present, most of his fighters were concentrated within the main airfield near Atlanta. He intended to redistribute them to the coastal landing fields around the island, thereby providing each field with a greater ratio of firepower, leaving a slightly greater number to defend the capital. Each field was only a few minutes' flying time away from the next, which would allow them to reinforce each other quickly in the event of an attack on an individual airfield. It also provided a general spread of air cover around the coastline, subsequently enabling him to at least offer some form of immediate resistance at any point that the enemy chose to invade the island.

Without question, Aharmer had to acknowledge the fact that the enemy might choose to attack on several fronts, in which case he also had that possibility covered. Should they decide to concentrate their attack in one place, there should be enough warning to move some reinforcements over to cover it; however, it remained that this was not such a good scenario, but lacking any intelligence concerning their intentions, it was nevertheless considered to be the best option to be feasibly employed.

In all probability, he considered, the enemy would use a series of air strikes, initially prior to any major invasion in the hope of eliminating his air defences. His planned defence would reduce the risk of large concentrations of his aircraft being destroyed on the ground in the event of a surprise attack, and would give him the ability to counter their strikes wherever they attacked him. Generally, they were all reasonably content with his preparations.

Maltor, on the other hand, had his own problems to contend with in the defence of Atlantis. Having insufficient troops to efficiently cover the entire island, it was vital that he selected the right strategy.

Unfortunately for him, there was no moving all his forces around at hundreds of miles an hour. Instead, he had to correctly place his men where they'd be most needed—and he had to get it right. Having no idea where the attacks would take place provided no assistance; in fact, about the only good thing he could see at the moment was the fact that, once the king had left, at least he then wouldn't need to worry about him as well.

In the end, Maltor decided that, in his enemy's position, he would attack Atlanta: vast factories were located both within and around the city, which constituted the bulk of the king's manufacturing capabilities—and therein lay his weakness. Even if they didn't totally succeed overall, the resistance nevertheless had the potential to cause serious damage, consequently depriving the king of their output, which would be a critical disaster he would struggle to overcome.

In addition, there were other vulnerabilities to consider. The island of Atlantis had various major cities—areas which were principally involved in commerce, housing the Atlantien financial institutions and related businesses. Their local industries produced and supplied the domestic needs of the nation, manufacturing clothing, furniture and the like. Using the River Rapalla as their highway—on the banks of which were two neighbouring cities, Sindrel and Lestapart—activity was busy and flourishing. However, although undeniably important to the economy, Maltor nevertheless did not consider them to be prime military targets: both cities at least had the protection of several pulse beam units, all of which were stationed on the cities' outer borders, and which Maltor decided would remain in place.

But then there was the consideration of the city of Enebal, which stood at the north of the island. Next to Atlanta itself, it had the largest port and the greatest concentration of heavy industry, and therefore had the most significant military importance. The rest of the island was predominantly dedicated to agriculture, and the towns and villages served such activities with just a sprinkling of light industry operating within them.

Enebal was vulnerable, and was arguably amongst the most important areas of Atlantis. It needed protection.

Following his instincts, he decided to move the larger part of his force close to Atlanta, which would leave Enebal's medium garrison to defend the city. He'd beef-up his coastal pulse batteries by allocating two Hovertancs to each unit, thereby doubling the firepower in every location. He would keep his crack regiment, the 57th Archers, in reserve and accordingly locate them nearer to the small town of Entatra, which was pretty much dead-centre of the island. The relatively small and highly mobile force was equipped with the necessary flying transport, enabling them to move themselves and their equipment from Entatra, ensuring they could reach any point on the island within only two hours. This subsequently allowed Maltor the option to reinforce any weak areas developing as the invasion progressed.

With his planning complete, Maltor considered that, under the circumstances, he could feel reasonably confident.

Cesa Neda, having subsequently received the head count he needed and being somewhat surprised at the king's efficiency, had allocated four large troopships escorted by four warships to transport the king's retinue from Atlanta. He'd instructed the port authorities to ready the docks to receive his troopships and to clear the area of all other activities, thereby placing priority upon the king's people. He needed to ensure they were taken away as quickly as possible, and anticipated the whole operation would be achieved in an eight-hour period.

The troopships were already in the harbour and would move to the dockside during the night in readiness of receiving passengers. Two of his allocated warships were in port, whilst the other two were currently patrolling within five hours' sailing time of Atlanta. Under their new orders, they'd join his fleet in the harbour before daylight.

He now had five large warships, two small beam weapon ships, and a handful of small armed patrol boats, all of which would be available as his contribution to his comrades' defences. However, the warships would take approximately twenty hours to return to Atlantis due to currently being positioned far out at sea. Considering the time it would take the warships to arrive, he'd instructed them to return to the port in Atlanta and would advise them of any changes en route. As they were currently unavailable, he would need to redirect them later should anything develop in the meantime, thereby leaving his options open.

The three men, now with their planning virtually completed, discussed their individual strategies. Agreeing with each other's arrangements so far, they were prepared to put them in place.

Maltor had one final point to agree with his colleagues. 'Much as I hate the idea, gentlemen, we'd better decide what to do about Amis and his project. Cesa, under the circumstances, I think we should load him, his team and their blasted machine, though regrettably, onto one of your ships. Maybe then they could set up in the base at Rammath and we could take it from there. If the unthinkable happens here, we really will need something powerful in our arsenal. In any case, I don't think we dare risk the enemy getting their hands on him or his research.'

'I'll take them with the others, Rak,' Cesa confirmed. We really can't let him fall prey to the resistance—although it's possible he might hinder them more than he helps them!'

'Then we're agreed,' said Aharmer.

With the men able to do little more until their audience with the king later, they confirmed they'd meet at the palace just before eight, retiring to gain what little rest was left available before the meeting was due to take place.

CHAPTER THIRTEEN

Jack and Rema woke just before eleven. Exchanging morning greetings and still sleepy, they smiled at each other and lightly embraced. Realising they'd only time for a quick cuddle, they quickly arose from their bed. He, missing no opportunity to gaze at Rema as they both washed and dressed, experienced a manifestation of his pleasure at the sight, much to her amusement.

'Clearly you weren't satisfied earlier, Jack,' she giggled.

'Of course I was,' he smiled, 'but one simply can't get enough of a good thing!'

'I don't think I'd better meet Mark at breakfast dressed like this,' she remarked, looking down at last night's outfit of seduction. 'I'm going back to my room to change. I'll meet you both in the hall shortly.' Rema brushed a light kiss across Jack's cheek and silently left the room.

Ready to face another day, Jack freshened up and walked to the hall, a smile on his face despite the past days' events. Unlike the early hours of this morning, the hall was now bustling full of people.

Jack spotted Mark in middle of the large dining hall. Sitting at a table, he was in deep conversation with an olive-skinned young man, obviously of Atlantien origin. He was of a medium build with a strikingly handsome face, thick black hair spilled over his shoulders, and wore what was obviously an airman's uniform.

Jack walked over to the table.

'Morning, Jack,' Mark smiled. 'Meet Cal, he's a Hovertak pilot. Cal, meet Jack, he's the novice in our team—shows some promise but a long way to go yet, I'm afraid.'

Jack smiled and shook Cal's hands. 'And I see you've met the prankster of our little duo, otherwise known as Mark the tale-weaver,' Jack laughed. 'I'm pleased to meet you, Cal.'

'Well, sit down then, old boy, grab a beer and join in. There's a good opportunity for you to learn something here,' said Mark with a grin.

'Beer at eleven in the morning?' Jack laughed, dismissing the idea with a wave of his hand. He pulled out a chair and joined the others at the table, whilst Mark filled a glass with the barley alcohol from a stone jar on the table.

'You have to have a beer,' Mark said, placing the glass on the table. 'A fine brew this, Jack. Not quite the beer we're used to, but pleasant enough. Cal informs me that it's quite strong though—a little goes a long way,' warned Mark.

With Jack comfortably settled, the conversation resumed. Jack learned that Cal had once been a flight leader in the king's Air Arm, holding a rank more or less equivalent to Mark's, but he'd become increasingly unhappy with the duties imposed upon him whilst flying for the king.

Cal had said, 'Murdering enemy soldiers with a pulse beam weapon seated in an invulnerable Hovertak above them was disgusting enough, especially when you consider they were, in the main, still fighting with bows, arrows, swords and spears. When the king thought it would be a wonderful idea to further demoralise his foes by actively seeking out and reducing their undefended settlements and families to atoms via the same method, it became too much to bear.'

Cal, accompanied by his entire flight, had defected to the resistance along with their machines, and they had been fighting for them ever since. They'd been in constant action for the last two years and had become greatly feared by the king's men wherever they appeared. Sadly, their numbers had reduced during this time, and there were now only four remaining.

Cal went on to talk about his life in general and his time spent in the king's service. He briefly outlined what appealed to him about his society, and what didn't. Without question, Cal had some amusing anecdotes involving himself and his comrades, and a multitude of other individuals.

Mark and Jack listened attentively as Cal told his tale, noting a comprehensive description of life as it existed in this time. Spoken by an officer and an airman with similar experiences to their own in many cases, they found it easy to empathise with him. In a relatively short conversation, they had been able to acquire a general overall flavour of the times, which had added considerably to their experiences of yesterday.

More importantly, Cal was in a unique position in that he could provide further insight into their foe than the majority of the resistance. In actual fact, as the conversation flowed, both men were becoming increasingly uncomfortable. Cal explained in more detail the military infrastructure as it currently existed. They already knew the king's forces comprised an army, air force and navy, but nevertheless had no idea of the strength these collectively represented.

Jack and Mark's knowledge expanded greatly when, using Cal's rough calculations, they realised that, taking into consideration all three of the king's services, they were facing a total over of more than two million fighting men—not to mention their equipment or allied personnel.

'Fuck me,' exclaimed Mark. 'In that case, I'd best find another cartridge for my pistol from somewhere.'

'Doesn't look too promising, does it?' Jack observed dejectedly.

And it was then that Rema joined them at the table. 'What's up, boys? You look like you've seen a ghost,' she said cheerfully.

'Hi, Rema,' Jack replied with a light smile. 'Well, Cal here was just giving us an idea of the king's strength. After what he's told us, it seems to us that we'll all *be* bloody ghosts before long I'm afraid!'

'If it wasn't for Rema we already would be, old boy, so let's just look on our remaining time as a bonus!' Mark quipped

'Good point, Mark. However, I still recognise the odds are definitely stacked against our favour.'

'Let's eat,' Rema suggested. 'We can discuss this further over lunch before we go to the meeting.'

Strangely, the conversation hadn't affected the men's appetites, and they retired to the bar to order food as Rema suggested, returning to the table and continuing the discussion.

'How far did you get with it all then, Cal?' Rema enquired.

'I've outlined the current state of the war and spoken a little regarding the role I've played in it. I covered a little of our history and provided a short overview of our society. We also spoke regarding general air tactics. When you arrived, we'd just totalled the likely numbers facing us at the moment,' said Cal.

'Do you mind if I take over for a while?' Rema asked.

'My pleasure,' answered Cal, eyeing up the food which had just arrived.

'Actually, I think I'll eat first, if nobody objects,' Rema decided.

They started on their meal, Mark attacking the food on his plate with his usually great gusto.

'I suggest you stop when you reach wood,' Jack said to him, grinning at his friend.

'I'll try to remember that,' he mumbled in response through a mouth full of food.

'Ra, I was ready for that! Something's made me quite hungry,' Rema said when she'd finished, looking slyly at Jack.

'I expect it was the sight of old dobbin over there shovelling in his oats,' Jack replied, blissfully unaware of the trap he'd just fallen into.

'Did you say *oats*, Wing Co.? That's an appropriate word in present company, I reckon,' Mark announced triumphantly, sniffing loudly as he looked from Jack to Rema and back again.

Blushing furiously, Rema wondered just how thick the walls really were between Jack's room and his. Not wishing to approach such a matter, she hurriedly moved on, smarting at Mark's innuendo.

'Let's get back to business then shall we?' Rema said sharply, secretly deciding she'd be very careful if she tried any verbal sparring with Mark.

'So now you're aware of the approximate size of the king's forces; obviously, you're not too pleased with the scenario. Of course, I agree with the notion that, should you be expected to face them all at once, the situation would be hopelessly dire. However, you aren't—and it's as simple as that. The armies are spread quite thinly across the world, with no really significant concentrations located anywhere, with the exception of Mu. He's got more than half his strength involved over there, but he can't move them all out to deal with us anyway. If he did, the Mu army would simply follow his retreat and reoccupy their lands—and they wouldn't stop at the borders either. The further he was to pull back, the more of his previous conquests they'd take. There's no doubt that, should they advance through their neighbours' lands, there'd be no shortage of volunteers desperate to exact revenge on the king.' Rema looked at each of the men. 'Their forces will swell dramatically, and the further they come, the stronger they'll be.

'At the very least, I'd guess that he's committed to holding his positions and has been forced to accept that he can only afford to remove some of his forces; too many and he'll be defeated in Mu with the resultant decline of his territories elsewhere.

'At the present time, more than half of his remaining armies are involved in policing the lands he's already conquered, and he can't reposition them for the same reasons.'

'So, if what you're telling us is correct,' began Mark, 'we're not facing a couple of million in forces, but probably around...' He started to count on his fingers. 'Only around a quarter of a million? I feel completely secure now.' He rolled his eyes sarcastically.

'I know it looks hopeless on the face of it. I honestly understand that. However, we actually estimate the strength he could commit to fighting us as being nearer to one hundred thousand. Add to your force three warships, thirty aircraft and four thousand well-equipped troops, complete with their own boats, and our odds increase. Then consider that, if we can take Atlantis itself, we'd be able to rely on at least another hundred thousand people—all of whom would be ready and willing to join us—which, in reality, will undoubtedly turn out to be a somewhat conservative estimate.' Rema replied.

Mark considered what Rema had said. 'Okay, maybe I was wrong. I apologise, Rema. But I just need to be sure that we have at least a partly feasible plan. I don't want us—or *any* of your people—fighting a battle we have zero chance of winning. Lives would be lost for nothing.'

'I have to say, doubling our strength and halving the opposition does improve our odds somewhat,' said Jack, 'but I think the fact remains that we're still significantly outnumbered. Is there anything else going in our favour?'

'Quite a lot, actually,' Rema responded. 'For a start, not all of the king's available forces are currently located in Atlantis. We know from our intelligence that he's already in the process of moving a large force back as quickly as possible, but it will take approximately two weeks for the operation to be completed—and that's if it all goes smoothly. At present, he has an estimated fifty thousand troops, one hundred aircraft, five large warships, and a collection of smaller boats, all of which are currently available to defend the island. In addition, of course, Atlantis is heavily defended with fixed installations of pulse beam weapons, which are scattered around the coast and the major cities. They have a large complement of heavy ground attack vehicles, and we estimate around ten thousand civil policemen, who they could call in to assist. Formidable still, granted; however, they're as weak as they'll ever be right now.' Rema spoke with confidence and authority. 'On the other hand, we have only two days at most before their air reinforcements arrive.'

'So if we were to attack immediately, we'd then be down to a ratio of ten to one against in men, give or take a little, but the fact remains that their weapons probably vastly exceed ours in number. They still have all the advantages, plus it's an island which makes it an even more complex proposition for attack. With that said, I'm not sure how you feel we can succeed...' Jack looked deeply concerned.

'Of course, I agree that we can't guarantee victory against such odds. It's possible, I suppose, but we have no intention of asking you to try in any case. What I can tell you, however, is that we're able to further savagely reduce their capabilities. I'm sure you'll find it much easier than you believe now when the time comes. Unfortunately, I can't tell you our in-depth plan, simply because if anyone within the king's army were to get wind of our intentions, they could, to a large degree, implement a counteraction,' she told them mysteriously.

'The plot thickens…' Mark said, rising from the table. 'Well, that meeting's due to begin.' He turned to Cal, who had been sitting quietly contemplating the debate between the three. 'It was good to meet you, Cal, and thank you for filling us in a little more. We'll probably need a get together with your boys and ours when we know what we're about. I'll see you then, if not before.'

Leaving the hall, the group parted company with Cal, and the three of them headed off to the Council of War.

CHAPTER FOURTEEN

The Atlantien military chiefs were back in the king's private office at the palace. Arriving at precisely eight in the morning as he'd commanded, he'd called them in at nine forty-five. They'd just finished advising him of their plans and were currently awaiting his reply, unsettled as much by another long wait as the general situation.

Finally he spoke. 'I've carefully considered your proposals, and I'm generally happy with your preparations in all areas except one. You will increase the number of Hovertaks accompanying my flight to Rammath. I won't risk my life by being as lightly defended as you are currently proposing. You'll send two flights to protect me, which is altogether more appropriate. Furthermore, all of those aircraft will remain in Rammath to bolster my defences there,' said the king.

Two flights—each comprising twelve aircraft—coupled with the king's own flight, which he always had in attendance when travelling by air, meant that thirty-six aircraft were allocated to his journey. Taking into consideration the fact that he was not expected to be flying near any danger en route, Sol Aharmer considered sacrificing an entire flight was already overkill in the extreme. He'd thought the king would be perfectly content with that. He'd also assumed the king would allocate his personal aircraft with its on-board generator to bring his Hovertaks back over the dead area after he'd finished with them. Given the flight time, it was expected that they'd have been back to Atlantis within a day, and he'd doubted the enemy would attack quite that quickly.

Pulling hard on his chin with a thumb and forefinger and clenching his teeth together, Aharmer fought to keep control of his temper. He was about to lose the benefit of the original flight, plus twelve more. Furthermore, what he hadn't anticipated was the fact that now they weren't going to return either.

'As you command, your Highness,' Aharmer replied in a strangled voice.

'Excellent,' said the king, acknowledging Aharmer's distinct discomfort. 'In that case, I will depart in one hour's time. My officials have virtually completed their preparations in the city and, once ready, will arrive at the docks around lunch time. They promise to be aboard your ships, all loaded and ready to go, before midnight. You will set sail as soon as the last person is aboard. I expect you to drive those ships to their maximum—I need those people in Rammath urgently.'

The king then dismissed his commanders who returned to their respective headquarters to put their defences in place.

The king left his office to supervise the loading of his most valuable treasures. He had earlier commandeered three Argotaks from a civil carrier in Atlanta, which he now completely filled to bursting point. The craft were freight carriers used by the Atlantiens, either in their designated role or in a modified version as passenger or troop transport. Large ungainly aircraft, they nevertheless had an enormous capacity in either format, and were surprisingly fast in-flight, falling only a little short of the Hovertak's abilities.

Even though he'd grossly overloaded the giant aircraft, the king had so far barely scratched the surface. Regretfully, he had to accept this was the best he could do, given the fact he was keener than ever to depart this morning.

The king's personal aircraft was a sumptuously modified Argotak, and stood ready for his departure in the grounds of the palace. Leading his entourage on, they boarded his plane in readiness for the journey—minus, of course, two of his wives, both of whom disfavoured he'd sent on a last-minute errand.

Minutes later, flying over the palace in a barrage of whirring sounds, his escort of Hovertaks appeared. Engaging their hover mode, they awaited his presence in the sky. With their protectors suspended above, the four Argotaks rose from the ground, and the journey began.

Gazing down, the king watched as his palace slowly disappeared. From his vantage point he was able to see his two wives returning from their mission, staring up and desperately waving at his receding aircraft. He smiled victoriously.

The ground shook around the palace as the aircraft accelerated away. Leaving Atlanta for the safety of Rammath six hours beyond the horizon, his Majesty wondered darkly if he'd ever return.

Far below, and hearing the whining of multiple aero engines passing over his headquarters, Aharmer looked up from his desk and gazed out through the large floor-to-ceiling window in the west wall of his office. On any other day, the view would have enormously lifted his spirits, the beauty of Atlanta providing the most incredible and inspiring of backdrops. This morning, however, told a different story; the view was irrelevant as he watched the armada of aircraft flashing away across the hilltops.

Aharmer smashed his fist down onto the desk top. Too angry to care who heard, he shouted at the retreating planes, 'You cowardly bastard! Run whilst you still can!'

Undoubtedly infuriated by the king's selfish decisions and the situation in which he had subsequently put his people, the three chiefs of staff had nevertheless been reasonably satisfied with the defences they'd put in place. Furthermore, Aharmer and his colleagues had considered other options and, wishing to be sure they'd selected the best available, they spent time looking at alternatives.

Taking the line of attack being the best form of defence, they agreed that, given more ordnance, it would have been the best strategy. It infuriated them that the king's unwarranted drain on their limited resources was the deciding factor in abandoning this idea; however, should they be reinforced in time, they'd throw everything at the resistance on Kira and their losses would no longer be an issue.

For now, however, owing to the king's actions, Aharmer was committed to sit and wait, worrying over the strength—or lack thereof—of their defences. The sight of his king running away, taking with him an inordinate number of their aircraft and knowing a repeat performance was coming when their ships left later, was more than Aharmer could stomach. Punching his desk again for good measure, he strode out of the room, deciding to check his remaining aircraft had now been deployed in accordance with his orders.

Having slept only a few hours, Captain Rowsell's leading officers were congregated back on Victorious, and Rowsell was speaking.

'I'm pleased to tell you the crew of Victorious has reacted favourably. They'll fight with us, and so far I've no indication that anyone here intends to rebel. Have any of you had problems with your commands?'

'I can't be entirely sure of the position of Erwin Gould, Captain of the U82,' answered Galland. 'He hasn't disagreed with us, but he wasn't happy with my decision to join forces. I so far haven't had the opportunity to consult with him in-depth and so I still have some doubt; otherwise, all my men are behind us. Before we embark on any campaign, however, I'll ensure we have his unqualified support or we will otherwise leave him behind.'

Brigadier Henry Forsyth of the British army was the next to comment. 'My troops and I are ready to follow the man in the moon, Captain Rowsell, just as long as we can get off your damn ships. Most of us get seasick in a bath, and we'll willingly fight to put our feet on solid ground again. Essentially, we're all with you and, like me, no one can see any real alternative anyway, so no problems from our end.'

The remaining officers, now having had their say, all appeared keen to get started on the new mission. In the end, it transpired only ninety men had elected to leave their posts, all of whom stemmed from the ranks and were content to stay on Kira working for the resistance in a supporting role.

'Well, that's that, gentlemen,' said Rowsell. 'Strange though it may be, we're now fighting for the resistance movement of Atlantis.

'Having overcome the first hurdles, we'll now prepare our forces for immediate action. I want us to ensure we are armed and ready, and see no reason to delay this—irrespective of our Council of War later. The Chief Engineer of Victorious will now liaise directly with the resistance people and tend to the details. Lanter told me last night they've some new technology of their own to add to our equipment, and so it would seem he's the man for the job.

'Furthermore,' Rowsell continued, 'Lanter also offered us a tour of the base prior to this afternoon's council. It's considered that this will give you all the opportunity to familiarise yourselves with our new employers, which will be no bad thing. He's due to collect us in a few minutes' time. I advise that you use the time wisely to become accustomed to your new environment. If all goes well, we hope to remain as civilians for a long time.

'You are dismissed, gentlemen.'

Later on that afternoon, after having shown the new troops around the base, Lanter headed to the appointed Council of War meeting. Lanter was accompanied by his military and scientific deputation, and were closely followed by Rema and the two airmen.

Once introductions had been completed, Lanter began. 'Firstly I'd like to take this opportunity to formally welcome you here, and I do appreciate how peculiar the circumstances under which we've met really are. In spite of this, so far, in principal, we've managed to reach a mutually acceptable agreement. Speaking for all of us here, we're delighted you've joined us and that we have achieved this so swiftly. As I'm sure all of you are aware, timing is of the essence. With that said, we're immensely grateful that you were able to make a decision of such magnitude without interminable delay.

'Firstly, as I think you're all aware from earlier conversations, the military leaders of the opposition have apparently seen no reason to heavily defend their homeland. Considering no possibility of attack there, they've committed the bulk of their armies to the conquest of other lands. Having been highly successful in this action, their armies have now moved on far from home. Accordingly, they're now very weak in Atlantis, with their main strength currently located thousands of miles away.

Lanter continued. 'Undoubtedly, this presents a unique opportunity for us, but we must take a hold of such as quickly as possible. Therefore, the first joint action we propose is to invade the island of Atlantis itself—a task which is to be carried out immediately. We have a window of approximately two days before our enemy starts to significantly reinforce his position. They're amassing their resources in the Kingdom of Mu, ready to send back to Atlantis, and they've already dispatched a large force of warplanes.

'You may be surprised at our wish to engage the king in a major conflict so soon, and I'm sure you'll also consider the timeframe improbable, apparently leaving no time to prepare the logistics, let alone a campaign. Please bear with me; we've already carefully planned this attack and we have some remarkable new weaponry to assist us. I'll put it all to you now—and trust you'll agree—that it's not as impossible as it may appear. Our informants on Atlantis know the king's defence strategy and have passed it on to us here. We know exactly where his forces are positioned and their relative strength. Our own forces are ready to leave immediately—and so are yours if you accept that everything you need is already aboard your ships. Your ships, of course, have just arrived halfway through a tour of duty, and will therefore require little action to re-supply them now. We will, however, be required to modify some of your equipment and transfer some of ours to your ships, but we've enough people and machinery. With your help, gentlemen, we should have no problem achieving our objective within the timeframe available.'

The conference continued as, together, they refined Lanter's existing plan. Eventually content with the overall strategy, it was agreed that the new phase of war be opened more or less in-line with his original intentions.

Leaving Kira before midnight, the attack on Atlantis would begin.

The meeting was concluded, and all left to make their respective preparations for the imminent battle.

Once the meeting had drawn to a close, Rema asked Jack and Mark to remain with her to assist her in the science wing. Their roles in the coming action required no further preparation, as it had already been decided that Jack and Mark were to sail on Victorious together. Rema would stay with the resistance during the action liaising, as and when required, with the allies. The airmen would fly with the navy, joining their pilots in combat, and partaking in their final briefings en route. With this plan of action decided upon, the men were free until they sailed from Kira.

With the group of men dispersed, Mark, Jack and Rema began to head to the science wing. This area of the base was now completely quiet and still, with the troops busy implementing the next stage of their plans. Their footsteps echoed down the long corridors, the men still unsure why they were needed.

Mark broke the silence. 'Are we allowed to know what you need us for, Rema, or is this some secret operation?' Mark smiled, his curiosity again winning over his patience.

Rema smiled. 'You're not a fan of secrets, are you, Mark?'

'Nope. So, care to divulge?'

'Very well,' she nodded. 'You may remember in our first meeting that I briefly mentioned three scientists, all defected to us, one who was a spy? You met them all today at the Council of War. Freyr, who was sitting on my left, is the spy. I didn't go into much detail before, but I think it's now important you fully understand the situation. Bear with me if I repeat anything you already know.'

'Although a scientist herself, Freyr is also an agent of the king, employed by his military in the position of a mole. Whilst working on Amis's transporter, she came to establish that two of her fellow scientists were about to defect, which she promptly reported to her employers. They decided to use this to their advantage and so, rather than arresting the scientists involved, they charged Freyr with convincing her colleagues that she shared their views and to instigate herself within our ranks by defecting with them. As I'm sure you've gathered by now, the king is always seeking to gain a foothold amongst us, and this was an opportunity they couldn't resist. We, of course, have our own spies in the king's camp and so, before she even arrived, we were well aware of her true identity.

'Forewarned, we've been playing a dangerous game with her ever since. We've so far managed to keep her away from any really sensitive information, but have managed to have her feed completely false data back to the king regarding the matter transporter. Fortunately for us, this has delayed Amis in his research to some degree. Sending him out on the wrong track has been a major factor in his failures to date. The downside, however, is that she's made them aware of the size of our operation here, which is something they'd not fully appreciated before. It was a difficult decision to allow her to come here but, on balance, we're happy we've gained the advantage thus far.'

'In my opinion, you've all taken a considerable gamble,' remarked Jack. 'Still, it seems it was worth it, judging from what you say. I understand your logic to a point, but why on earth did you allow her into our meeting today? She's bound to inform the king's men of our plans. If they believe what she tells them, they'll move everything they've got to Atlanta to meet our attack now. How the hell can that possibly help us?'

'That's exactly what we want her to do, Jack, and it's the main reason Lac couldn't reveal the true nature of our new weapons at the meeting. It's vital she passes on the content of the meeting and, although they'll realise we have something, they won't know what, and so that in itself doesn't really matter. Actually confusing them is part of our plan. With that said, however, this is the last contact she'll be permitted to make with them of her own volition—they'll find out soon enough what it is we've got when we attack them. By then, it'll be too late.'

Mark whistled. 'Well, I'm damned if I know, Rema, but I reckon you must enjoy stirring up hornets' nests.'

'Believe me, Mark, everything's fine and you'll see why later. Can we leave it now for the moment? I've asked Freyr to meet us in B Wing in an hour. I want to give her plenty of time to talk with her chiefs first before she comes.

'One thing you should bear in mind is that it's very possible I'll need to detain her, but there are a number of things I wish to investigate with her before we call in our security to take her away. In that instance, I may need your help with that one, which is partly why I've asked you to come. However, there's also another reason for your being with me, as there's something else I want to show you. This part you'll enjoy—it's all weapons-related!'

'Sounds intriguing,' said Mark. 'Details would be good, though!'

'I wouldn't expect anything less from you, Mark,' she smiled. 'The transporter, which we've discussed at some length, is not the only Ancients' artefact we've found here. There are others which you'll see for yourselves; however, when the transporter failed, an extraordinary effect was triggered, which affected the rest of them. Every other artefact has since become operational. As the transporter died, the remaining machines turned themselves on.

'Before then, despite all our efforts, we had been unable to even guess at their purpose. To be honest, we now have tools we didn't even know were useful at all. Even more amazing, the aliens left instructions for each machine—all of which became apparent as they became operational. We now know what they all do and how to use them all.

'Either through accident or design—though almost certainly the latter—we've gained a further significant portion of the Ancients' technology. Using this in conjunction with your help, our ability to wage war on the king has increased beyond our wildest dreams. I'm sure you'll agree when you see exactly what I'm talking about.'

'Hmm,' considered Mark. 'It certainly sounds like you could have something useful here, Rema. But I must say, in my experience, machinery—or anything remotely useful—has a habit of giving up the ghost at the most inconvenient of times. I therefore wouldn't put too much emphasis on these new gadgets of yours—whatever they may be.'

'You have a flair for looking on the bright side, Mark,' Rema chided. 'Of course, I'm not in a position to be able to guarantee they won't fail, but we frequently use machines to fight our battles alongside us. In this instance, however, these artefacts have no moving parts, thereby eliminating any potential problems stemming from that direction; therefore, practically, they're likely to be more reliable.'

'And if they *were* to fail?' Jack probed. 'What then? Would your teams be able to fix these artefacts?'

'If the Ancients don't want us to use their technology we can't; we can only employ it if they show us how to, or if they otherwise leave strong clues for us to unravel in time. In this case, the artefacts were seemingly handed to us on a plate. For whatever reason, it seems to me that the Ancients want us to use these tools. I don't think they intend for them to let us down. Call it blind faith if you like, but I'm confident,' reassured Rema.

At this point, the three comrades had reached their destination. Rema led them into the reception of B Wing where they awaited the arrival of Lara Freyr.

B Wing was undoubtedly a high-security area. The doors were made from steel and were guarded with security agents. The men, adorned in blue overalls, granted access to only certain personnel, engaging the opening of the door with a silver disc, which was passed in front of a small computer screen and bleeped to confirm disc verification.

'Quite clearly a restricted area,' observed Jack.

'Extremely, Jack. As I said, this is where most of the Ancients' artefacts are sited. In addition, we also have research projects of our own being carried out in there. We're very protective of this place; it is the single most important facility we have, and so it's absolutely vital its security remains uncompromised, as you'll soon appreciate.'

Jack nodded but looked somewhat concerned. 'You know, Rema, the issue of this Freyr woman worries me a little. I know you've assured us that you've got it covered, but are you completely sure she knows nothing about your new-found capabilities?'

'Absolutely,' Rema responded confidently. 'Most of the artefacts have only been available to us for the last two days and, during that time, we've kept her away from here, giving her a task in another location. Having said that, we were also very lucky with the one machine that did come to life a few weeks ago: in that instance, only two of our scientists were present at the time, both of whom are completely trustworthy, I assure you. Like the rest, it came with instructions, as it were, and so they ensured they shut it down immediately and consulted with Lac.

'Currently, there are only half a dozen of us who know about it and, until the attack commences, as we've agreed, only Captain Rowsell will be included. Its influence, greater than all the rest, will break Atlantis tomorrow, which is the main reason for us believing our limited forces will prevail against them—and why you're here to help us.

'I assure you, Freyr knows nothing of this machine, or the rest of them. Regarding the artefacts, we've let her see only what we wanted her to ever since she arrived. She's in for a shock later when we go inside, though—and that's the main reason I want to meet her here. She's a good scientist with a brilliant mind, and I'm hoping seeing what's happening in there might draw her out.

'As I'm sure you'd expect,' Rema continued, 'we've been monitoring everything she does. Lately, though, we've been convinced she may be having second thoughts about working against us. The reports she's sent to the chiefs recently haven't completely stacked up. With that in mind, she also has talents that we would really benefit from. I'm almost sure she wants to join us, and we need a double agent badly ourselves. I intend to confront her but, at the same time, offer her a get-out clause which she might choose to take. But, on that front, I suppose we'll have to wait and see what transpires.'

Just then, as Rema concluded, Lara Freyr arrived in the foyer. Spotting Rema and the men, she walked over and joined them. 'Hi, Rema,' she said, and nodded to the airmen. 'You wanted to see me?'

'Yes, Lara, I did, but first we need to go to the transporter, there's something there I want to discuss with you. My friends here will be tagging along.'

Clearly suspecting nothing, Lara nodded and stepped aside, allowing Rema to lead the way. Rema used her disc to gain access, and they filed through into B Wing.

Expecting something momentous, Jack and Mark were somewhat disappointed. They'd entered another room, slightly larger than the foyer. Within it was a security station where several armed guards occupied the space behind a set of iron bars which formed a wall across half the room in front of them. Rema spoke to a guard and, silently, a section of the barrier slid aside, allowing them all to pass through it. Seeing no other exit, the airmen exchanged puzzled glances. They'd watched others entering as they'd done but, aside from the guards, there was no one else in the room.

'Okay, Rema, I give up. I've clearly failed the intelligence test,' said Mark. 'Where's everyone gone?'

'You'll love the next bit, Mark,' Rema smiled. 'I think it's right up your street. Just follow me and enjoy the journey!'

Intrigued by Rema's rather ambiguous answer, Mark looked around again but was unable to see how any of them could embark on a *journey* taking more than three or four steps in any direction. Undeterred by this, he said, 'Hang on then, I'll get my hat and coat.'

Laughing, Rema walked straight through the wall in front of her and disappeared.

CHAPTER FIFTEEN

Two hours into his flight, the king and his party were happily engaged in their favourite pastime. Having been drinking heavily since they left Atlanta, they were all now far from sober. Naked couples writhed on the cabin floor, engaged in every conceivable sexual deviation: men on men, women with women, all outnumbering the traditional man and woman partnership.

Seated, the king himself had a naked woman held face down across his lap and was contentedly beating her bare behind with a large wooden paddle. The spectacle had attracted a group of his wives and friends, all who found her kicking and screaming added hugely to their general appreciation of this impromptu orgy.

Five and a half hours into the flight, they reluctantly abandoned their activities and prepared for their arrival at Rammath.

The king adorned himself in a suit of soft black leather, tailored somewhat ineffectually to hide his gross paunch. He pulled on long black boots and placed a red bandanna around his neck. Completing the effect, he hung a harness of leather straps across one shoulder and around his waist, and attached to it his ceremonial sword in its scabbard. Happy he now looked suitably menacing, he was ready to leave his aircraft when they arrived.

The king's hefty entourage promptly followed suit, retrieving their strewn clothing and, with the obvious exception, all seated themselves comfortably. They were looking forward to the next round of excesses the king had arranged for them to celebrate his presence in Rammath.

With the present excesses over for now, the king's thoughts returned back to the treasures he'd left in Atlanta. He decided he'd time to send the transport back when they'd unloaded, with orders to refill them and return immediately. This meant sending his precious aircraft to provide the power they'd need, which was, of course, the one thing that did concern him. However, his greed overcame his worries, and he left the cabin to action his new instructions. In the cockpit, he issued his orders to the pilots and contacted his officials at the palace to prepare the next cargo prior for their arrival. Issuing orders to the flight leader of the Hovertaks, he commanded that half his force be sent back to escort them.

Six hours into the flight, the king's armada swept over the massive river Tyrad, which ran through the endless desert for a thousand miles to the sea beyond. Ten minutes later, the citizens of Rammath were treated to the sight of their king and his escorts landing in a welter of sound and swirling sand on the desert floor just outside of the city walls.

Columns of troops stood to attention each side of the roadway leading to the city gates, and a group of trumpeters lined the walls above them, ready to welcome His Majesty.

The king, with his favourite wife Alana on his arm, and his entourage following a respectful distance behind them, strode from the plane and walked up the road towards the gates. A joyous fanfare greeted the party when they entered the city, and excited crowds cheered and waved enthusiastically as the king and his cohorts slowly made their way towards the palace, winding through the hot dusty streets of his second city.

If there was anything guaranteed to please the king, it was a grand entrance. Even he could find no fault with the arrangements his officials had made with this one. However, it was a good mile from the city gates to the palace, and although the servants walked with them, holding large sunshades above their heads, the late afternoon heat was nevertheless unbearable. He resolved in future to insist on some form of majestic transport; walking amongst his adoring subjects like the conquering hero was okay, but after a gruelling journey, he felt other plans would need to be made in the future.

Rammath was once the capital city of the Incha nation. In his inimitable style, the king could see absolutely no reason for the existence of the Inchas. With this opinion in mind, he had subsequently declared war on the nation, and proceeded to virtually annihilate their culture in a bloody campaign lasting several months.

Their country comprising mainly of desert was not particularly extensive, nor was it of much practical use to the king. Nevertheless, he acknowledged that its location created the ideal stepping stone to begin the much greater task of conquering Mu, which perfectly suited his military commanders. The capital he inherited—then only a small walled town comprising mainly of huts—was far from any conceivable danger, which therefore made the location even more appealing. 'And in any case,' he'd said to Alana during that time, 'with a bit of work, I could make it quite nice.'

Having committed himself with that earth-shattering observation, he appointed an army of engineers, architects and master craftsmen to direct a multitude of enslaved labour. Collectively, they levelled the existing edifice to the ground, designing and building a magnificent city, rivalled only by Atlanta itself. The project had taken ten years to complete, had virtually bankrupted his entire kingdom, and critically slowed his military programme owing to a fundamental lack of funding. Nevertheless, Rammath ultimately ended up meeting the king's requirements, and was suitably 'nice'.

'I'm tired and I need a bath,' Alana said to her husband. 'Must we always walk on these occasions? Especially in Rammath, my Lord, this heat is insufferable.'

'Our subjects need to see us now and again. It gives them confidence to have us amongst them. We drive them hard, and it's only right we should reward them with our presence at times. It inspires them and could lift them to achieve more,' replied the king, taking a political viewpoint and ignoring the fact that he was actually in total agreement with her. 'Everyone loves a pageant, and occasions like this are a perfect opportunity, my dear.'

Eventually, the party reached the palace. Upon entering the grounds, the crowds lost sight of the king and his entourage, and waved their farewells as the high gates closed behind them.

Shortly after, the sound of the king's aircraft lifting into the sky reverberated through the streets. Another return journey for the pilots, and the king would have more of his desired possessions.

~*~*~*~

In Atlanta, the three service chiefs were in a dilemma. Having spoken with their agent on Kira who'd been present at their enemy's Council of War, the commanders were analysing the contents of her report. Currently, they were struggling with the resistance's plan for the invasion of their island. This they were expecting, of course; however, they couldn't come to terms with their proposed tactics.

'What the hell are they playing at now?' demanded Maltor. 'I don't like this at all. The resistance may be many things, but foolish isn't one of them. I'd love them to come at us as they plan; on the face of it, they'll annihilate themselves. But then there is the consideration that maybe they know of our agent and are therefore feeding us crap, hoping we'll move our defences and then attack us elsewhere. That poses one scenario. Or maybe they really can interfere with our defences in some way, which makes them feel their plans are achievable.' Maltor silently considered the situation, his mind rushing down each of the possible avenues, none of them making much sense—and none of them providing any degree of reassurance. 'Either way,' he continued, 'we've a big problem.'

Aharmer looked concerned. 'Okay, but I'm sure the resistance don't know about Freyr. How could they? We've had no sign that they even suspect her. If they knew, of course they would feed us false information but they'd hardly need to set up a meeting of that magnitude just to achieve that. If they've cottoned on and they still let her in, it really makes no sense at all. In addition, the planning of a major action takes weeks—they couldn't attack somewhere else just like that. If they're coming tomorrow, they're coming here. No doubt about it. If that's the case, however, they seem very sure of themselves, and don't seem overly fazed over how strong we are.'

Maltor nodded in agreement. 'Absolutely. That's certainly how it seems.'

'I'm pretty sure they're not lying when they say they've got something significant we don't know about, Rak, and the only difference I can see now in contrast to before is their new allies. Maybe it's *they* who have the secret weapons to which Freyr refers. Granted, they themselves aren't secret, but we know absolutely nothing about the weapons they're carrying! Perhaps the resistance know something they use is capable of negating our forces. Their allies haven't been here long enough to fully understand our weaponry—they probably don't even realise themselves they've got it.'

'Hmm, that does make sense,' answered Maltor. 'We're all terrified of our plans falling into the wrong hands, especially when a new weapon's involved and security's absolutely vital. I think you might be right and they were being naturally cautious. If they're so sure their allies' weapons can overrun us and their allies don't know that, there's still no reason to tell them until the last minute either. If it is indeed their weapons the resistance are relying on, they'll be carrying them anyway, and there's therefore no need to risk discussing it. It would appear that they know we'd be able to counter their efforts if we knew, which is why they're remaining so secretive. That in itself tells me that they're going to attack us here, exactly as proposed, and they definitely have something nasty in store for us—but what that is, and just what we're supposed to do about it, only Ra knows.'

'Simple,' Neda said confidently. 'Atlanta is clearly their target and, unless you've forgotten, we also have our own well-kept secret. Without doubt, now's the time to employ it.'

Maltor and Aharmer nodded enthusiastically but remained serious.

The decision made, they revised their original plans, moving every available resource to Atlanta, and continuing to agonise over what they might face when the invasion began.

CHAPTER SIXTEEN

The stunned silence continued to rest heavily inside the room.

After several moments, Mark spoke. 'This place is beginning to get to me a bit now. People don't just walk through walls where I come from, you know. When are they going to learn to behave in a civilised manner and use an ordinary bloody door like the rest of us?'

'Hmm,' Jack mused. 'I wish she'd warn us about things like that. It's just as well we don't have weak hearts or we'd be sampling their surgical skills right now.'

Freyr smiled and walked ahead of the two airmen. 'Come on, chaps, Rema's waiting. I'll go through next.'

Shrugging their shoulders, the two men walked forward confidently, and were stunned when they both bounced off the wall and thudded sharply to the floor. Gazing up at the guards who were now in fits of laughter, it was clear they'd just been duped.

'Sorry, gents,' said one of them, holding his sides. 'I must have turned it off... accidentally, of course!'

'We're surrounded by comedians,' Mark grumbled.

'Had to be done, I'm afraid,' replied one of the guards, choking back laughter. 'It's a little initiation ceremony—everyone gets the same treatment the first time. It won't happen again.' The guard smirked, stifling his laughter.

'Well, I doubt I'll see the funny side next time,' Jack replied, not wishing to admit he'd not found it particularly funny this time either.

The guards motioned for the airmen to continue. Gingerly approaching the wall, they tested it with their hands, which duly disappeared. Glancing at each other, Mark and Jack carefully walked through the wall to find Rema and Freyr standing on the other side.

And then, with no warning given, everything went wrong.

A tight, vice-like grip constricted their skulls, and rational thinking was no longer an option. They'd arrived in a vast open space which was impossibly small, standing on a solid floor, into which they sank. Looking up into a spinning black hole with blinding pulsating light shooting erratically, they narrowed their eyes against the stygian darkness. Inverted in the arctic heat, they now rose into the solid liquid around their feet. In utter silence, their eardrums vibrated with an unbearable cacophony. Feeling the exuberance of youth and the crushing debilitation of old age, and with every sense in a complete state of disorientation and confusion, they felt completely out of control and were subject to a rollercoaster of feelings of panic and perfect peace.

They were experiencing birth and death simultaneously when Rema's voice broke through the barrage of disjointed sensations and, with that, their equilibrium was instantly restored and the pressure flicked off.

'Jack, Mark, listen to me: what you've experienced only happens the first time you enter here. What you're feeling now will pass. We're inside one of the ancients' artefacts—or machines, if you prefer. Initially, it requires that you be identified, and so it reads your mind, completely disorientating your normal senses. Just give it a minute and you'll be okay, you'll see.'

Badly shaken by their surreal experience, the men looked dazedly around them. They were standing beside the wall through which they'd entered on a high platform. Below them stretched a large chamber and several crystal structures of varying sizes had been placed, seemingly randomly, across the floor.

'Why didn't you warn us like you promised, Rema? That really scared the crap out of me!' exclaimed Mark, still struggling to recover.

'I'm sorry, Mark, but I just couldn't do that in this instance. We used to but found if we tried to prepare people, their minds would automatically resist the machine's probing.' She looked at the men sympathetically, and offered a warm smile. 'Resisting the machine would only result in more pain... I didn't want that for you.' Her eyes rested on Jack.

Jack returned Rema's warm gaze with fury and anger. 'And are there any more fucking initiation ceremonies to go through, Rema, or can't you tell us that either?'

'That's pretty much it,' Rema smiled, 'although I suppose it would be relevant to mention that we're no longer on earth. And by the way, the wall trick also reduces the time you're probed. If you're still slightly humiliated when you arrive here, the mind seems to accept the intrusion more easily. We used to make first-timers strip off before entering, which actually seemed to work well.'

'And I thought you lot were just having a laugh,' Mark said sardonically. 'Still, upon reflection, I probably prefer what you do now.'

'Look, Rema, I'm sorry for the frustration, but it's very unpleasant,' Jack apologised. 'I don't really know what to ask first after that; the obvious thing is what's happening down there, I suppose. Actually, I think I'm more intrigued to learn why you said we're not on earth anymore! Let's start with that one shall we?'

'As good a place as any', Rema replied, 'but, there's no point in Lara getting involved with it—let me finish with her first if that's okay. We have to be down there, though.'

He nodded in agreement.

'However,' Rema continued, 'I'm not quite sure how to approach this with you chaps, but suffice to say, when you're in here you don't have to do much walking if you don't want to. With that in mind, I suggest you prepare yourselves for more of the Ancients' technology; now the machine recognises you, it'll do it for you.'

'Oh God, now what?' Jack groaned

'Don't worry, it's quite fun, actually,' she reassured. 'We're going to that large crystal structure behind the partition over in the far corner. Just think that's where you want to go and you'll see what happens.'

Standing beside the large crystal structure with Rema and Freyr, the airmen scratched their heads, looking confused once again they were nonplussed by everything they hadn't seen getting there. Having done as Rema had asked, they seemed to have just arrived without any effort. Their last memory was looking at where they were now standing from across the other side of the floor.

'Boo!' Jack heard Mark's voice come from behind him and almost jumped out of his skin.

'What the hell do you think you're doing, you idiot! You scared the life out of me!'

'Appreciating the Ancients' technology, old chap.' The voice now came from directly above him.

Looking up, Jack saw Mark with his feet planted firmly on the ceiling, hanging upside-down above his head. Rema and Freyr were in fits of laughter as they watched Mark's antics.

'Trust you to turn the whole bloody thing into a circus, Mark,' Jack grumbled. He turned to Rema. 'You really should know better than to bring a clown like him into a place like this.'

'Relax, man!' Mark complained. 'Have a go! I could play for hours and not get bored with this!'

'Yes, lighten up, Jack. You really were more fun back in your own time,' Rema quipped. 'And I'll say one thing, Mark: it really doesn't take you long to catch on, does it?'

Jack glared at Rema, a little stung by her remark. 'Well, it's just a safety concern, that's all,' he mumbled.

With Mark's feet now back on the ground next to Jack, the airmen took a few moments to look around, and now saw the people they'd seen entering B Wing busying themselves around the crystal formations.

'What are those lumps of rock everyone's so involved with, Rema?' Mark asked. 'They're very pretty but they surely can't be the machines you've been cracking on about?'

'That's exactly what they are, actually. Now you've seen them—and actually experienced a little of what they can do—are you any happier about it all?'

Mark laughed. 'In truth, I'm not sure I know what to make of any of this—especially the feelings—but I'm not surprised you've had problems using them: in my view, a machine should have levers, dials, switches—something. Machines this size should make a comforting racket to let you know they're working; you know, a smell of hot oil or warm electrics. They should, at the very least, have a seat to give one a clue as to where to operate them from. An irregular glass-looking thing, lacking levers and on-off switches... it's not a proper machine!'

Rema grinned at Mark's opinion of the most advanced technology ever seen. 'Not overly impressed as yet then, Mark?'

He laughed. 'Well, quite honestly, Rema, never has my flabber been so gasted! Everything you tell us or show us around here leaves me feeling like kindergarten material. Of course I'm impressed–especially after gadding about on the ceiling!'

The group laughed.

'But if you're really asking me whether I'm happier to do battle now that I've seen what's supporting us,' he continued, 'then I'm still uncertain. You've promised these machines here will make us virtually invincible, but now that I've seen them it's actually harder to lay my life on the line, relying on these things to protect it. They're totally alien, Rema—there's absolutely nothing about them I can relate to at all. And, considering the fact that your people don't understand how these things work really disturbs me more than what they look like!'

'Very true,' Jack commented. 'I'm happy to accept you can use these machines, Rema, because quite clearly you can and we've had first-hand knowledge of it. And I'm sure a lot of men who'll be fighting tomorrow don't know the ins and outs of their equipment either; so long as it works, so what? The difference, however, is that there is always someone who *does* know and who *is* able to make necessary repairs, but in this instance, you don't—and, quite frankly, that scares me.'

'I'll be shitting a brick!' Mark injected.

'You say this one here has stopped working,' Jack continued, 'and that's fair enough, I suppose. Soon, however, we're expected to face hopeless odds of survivability, which are ultimately dependent on the assistance of these things. What if the rest fail and there's nobody able to fix them?'

'But then again,' Mark said, 'what other options do we have? Rema assures us they've all been serviced by the last owners, and I guess that's the best we're going to get. And, honestly, I'm bored with the whole subject. So why don't we just get on with the only thing we know we can do around here and blast the buggers out of the sky!'

'Well,' sighed Jack reluctantly, 'if you're going up, dear boy, I suppose someone had better be there to look after you.'

'Absolutely!' agreed Mark.

The two men shook hands and gave each other a pat on the back.

'Rema what's happened?' Freyr's excited and unrestrained voice echoed. 'The last time I was here nothing was working, and now it seems that, apart from the transporter, everything is!'

'A lot's happened here in your absence, albeit only a few days,' Rema replied nonchalantly. 'However. I haven't brought you here to discuss the machines—this is a personal matter concerning your future within the resistance or otherwise.'

'Or otherwise...?' Freyr's face lost its colour and she looked at Rema wide-eyed.

Rema nodded and continued. 'We know you're working for the king's military, Lara, so there's no use in you denying it. Our own Intelligence made us aware of that before you arrived. And now, well, the time has come to confront you, and I feel this is the best place to do it—not least because it's totally secure. You know you can't contact anyone from in here. You also know you can't get out past the guards should I order them to stop you and, at the moment, your presence here raises no questions.'

Lara straightened her back and applied a stone, unfazed expression.

'If we hadn't known about you, Lara, you could have done untold damage to us. But, thankfully, we knew all along, which allowed us to use your treachery to our advantage. Nevertheless, we've badly compromised our own position here by taking you in. I can tell you we've denied you access to truly sensitive material no matter what you think, but clearly we couldn't keep you away from everything or you'd have been no use to us anyway. Now, for the sake of the planet, we have to stop Amis in succeeding and delivering to the king the means to destroy our world.'

Jack and Mark watched on as this confrontation—although undoubtedly a calm one—unfolded before their eyes.

'She's good,' Mark whispered to Jack, looking at Rema.

'Very,' Jack agreed.

'Foiling Amis's plan is of paramount importance to us no matter what the cost,' Rema continued. 'Your being here has given us the opportunity to feed false information back to Amis, which has aided this so far. We've been damaged by you but, in a way, you're a gift from the Gods. And without question, one thing's for sure—that I think they've damaged themselves far more by sending you away.'

Lara stood composed and undeterred, but curiosity and questions swam in her eyes.

'As a spy, Lara, you're questionable, but the fact remains that no one can fault you as a scientist. You were very close to solving the riddle of the artefact you and Amis were working on; actually, having said that, you probably realised you were far from enabling it to successfully transport matter. Regardless, by our own estimations, you were only days away from learning how your machine produced the antimatter that destroyed Rak Maltor's island. I'm sure you're aware: Amis has been headed in that direction ever since, and intends to reproduce the effect as a weapon.' Rema paused for a moment to allow the potential of this plan to sink in. 'Depending on your reaction now, I may have a suggestion for you.'

Lara looked quickly to Rema and around the room.

'If you decide to take me up on what I propose, this needs to be done before I have you arrested: an arrest would indicate to everyone that we've got a problem with you—and, for what I've got in mind, that simply wouldn't be acceptable.'

Lara stood in silence, weighing up the situation. After a few moments, she released a long sigh. 'In truth, I wondered when you'd face me with this, Rema—and, of course, I don't deny it. I've been used by everyone, it seems, but you've indicated another reason for bringing me here.' Lara looked at Rema, wondering when the answers to her questions would come. And, as much as this hadn't been in the plan, she knew and understood her cover was blown—not only recently but from the very beginning! In such a situation, there was only one way this could be handled: every woman for herself. 'Obviously, you want to change the way things stand or you wouldn't have confronted me in this way. So what do you need me to do?'

'What you've been sending Maltor recently is clearly wrong,' Rema responded, 'and you obviously know that. You've been accurate on occasions, of course, but you didn't tell them there are other artefacts hidden here. You gave them an indication of our numbers on Kira, but understated them by fifty per cent. Furthermore, in many areas, your reports were vague and misleading, but there was no reason they should be. So why, Lara? You could've given them more accurate data but you chose not to. You haven't even told them our transporter has failed or that its last act brought our new allies to us.'

'Before I came here, I was obviously working for the military,' Lara said, 'but primarily for selfish reasons. As you say, I'm a scientist and, as such, of course I've boundless curiosity. They offered me the opportunity to work with Amis and to be involved with the most exciting project of our time; albeit their reasons were underhanded, but at the time I considered I couldn't have been in a better place to indulge my passion. All they wanted was an independent view of progress, and so I became part of the biggest project on earth, funded by the greatest wealth imaginable. I think even you might understand the attractions. I desperately wanted to unravel the secrets of the Ancients' technology—it borders on obsession for me. In truth, I wasn't even aware you were involved in a similar project until I joined Amis, but from the little information he had regarding your research, it soon became obvious to me that you were ahead of us. With that in mind, when given the chance to come here, of course I jumped at it—stupidly, on reflection, when you consider the terms I accepted. But I suppose my selfish passion blinded me.' Lara sighed and looked saddened momentarily. 'I wasn't in place here long before I realised just how corrupt our leaders are and how dangerously cruel their regime is. You've opened my eyes to many things since I've been here; you've made me see what's really happening around me. For the first time, I see there are more important issues to be considered. I truly believe you're the only hope now, and I wish I'd handled things differently.'

Rema nodded in acknowledgment of Lara's shame.

'Just for the record, however, I would like to tell you that you underestimated me in one sense. I'd been privately researching a theory of my own when I was with Amis. You said we were far from achieving our goal, and I agree the others certainly were—but I wasn't. I was nearer to the answer than you've obviously thought. My previous research told me much of the information you were giving me here was wrong. I realised then that you probably knew the truth, although I obviously hoped that wasn't the case. Nevertheless, I understood the information I was sending to Amis was, in all likelihood, false and misleading—but I still sent it, Rema—please think about that. I didn't want Amis to implement his terrible plan, but I know I could have handled this differently. I know I should have come to you sooner, to tell you the truth and ask to be a part of your team.'

'That's for sure, Lara,' Rema replied. 'And I realise that your previous actions do support what you say, and so I'm prepared to give you the benefit of the doubt. Although I must say that I'm very impressed that you've acquired further knowledge yourself through your research. Clearly I wasn't as aware of the full situation as I'd initially thought.'

'Oh, what a tangled web you lot weave,' said Mark sarcastically. 'I reckon this cloak and dagger stuff's likely to drop one in hot water!'

'Well, in a convoluted way, Mark, you're probably right, only sometimes there's no other choice,' stated Rema grimly. Turning to Lara she said, 'What I propose now is that we continue on in the same vein.'

Mark looked at Jack, and shrugged his shoulders. 'Some people just don't take warnings, do they?'

'I truly want to help, Rema,' replied Lara, undoubtedly relieved to know her knowledge had saved her. 'What do you want me to do?'

'I want you to go back and re-join Amis.'

Lara paled and fear shadowed her face. 'Do you think they'll just accept me without question now?' Her voice trembled. 'I'll do it, of course, Rema—but how do you intend to achieve it?'

'I suggest you contact Maltor now, Lara. Tell him you've been compromised and are about to be arrested, then we'll create a believable scenario that allows you to escape. Your talents really are outstanding, Lara, and providing your story stacks up, the chiefs will send you straight back to Amis. I can't imagine they'll put you anywhere else, simply because they're going to need anyone with your talents to progress with Amis's research.'

Lara nodded reluctantly.

'When you get back with Amis, your objective is to try to confuse his research as much as possible. I think we both know what you can do in that direction is limited, but you'll be able to tell us when he's on the point of a breakthrough. Remember: should he succeed, there's no defence against such a weapon—it'll be all over and there'll be nothing more anyone can do about it. At least buy us as much time as possible, Lara, but you must tell us before it runs out. Obviously, the more time we get to regroup after the Atlantis campaign the better—getting to Amis after this will undoubtedly be a major exercise. And you should know this, Lara: they're moving Amis's entire project to Rammath as we speak: they've loaded everything aboard a ship in Atlanta and he's on his way, and so there's already little time to lose.'

'I'll give it my best, Rema,' Lara replied confidently. 'I won't let you down.'

'I hope so, Lara, for everyone's sake. Lanter's men are waiting for you back in B Wing. Please leave now, and they'll escort you to him and he'll take it from there. Good luck and may Ra go with you. It'll be some time before we meet again, I think.'

With that, Lara left the group, instantly appearing on the platform, and with a wave she faced the wall and walked away.

'Well that's that then, Rema,' Jack said. 'I hope she's able to do it. I wouldn't want her job, make no mistake!'

'I'm sure not even she wanted the job, Jack,' Rema smiled, 'but at least it went the way I needed it to—and I'm glad you were here with me.' She smiled at Jack, their eyes locking.

'Stop that, you two!' groaned Mark. 'Don't you go all lovey-dovey on me now, it's totally inappropriate—this is a serious business, you know!'

'Sorry Mark,' said Rema, stifling a giggle. 'I can't help being distracted sometimes by your lovely friend!'

'Anyway, back to business,' Rema said, straightening herself and trying not to look at Jack. 'Now Lara's gone, I'll give you a quick rundown on this place, and then I'll explain what these machines will do to mess up Maltor and his cronies—maybe then you'll cheer up a bit! I want you to see as much as I'm permitted to show you before we invade—in spite of what you think. It'll burden you with more information, but there's so little time I've really no choice.'

A worried glance passed between Jack and Mark, the two airmen knowing already that, when Rema decided to make revelations, in some way or another, that always spelled bad news for them!

'I told you we aren't on Earth but, to all intents and purposes, it doesn't really matter because we've no way out other than the portal we used. Obviously, we can pass back through the portal whenever we choose, but this takes us back to our world anyway. To explore what's outside of here—considering what we know currently—is impossible. As far as we're aware, there isn't a way.

'The blunt truth is we're nowhere. It's an anomaly existing independently of the normal space-time continuum. Whatever happens in the universe—even if it ceased to exist—we wouldn't be affected here. No doubt, this place and the machines together form part of the Ancients' grand design—a subject I've no intention of exploring now, you'll be happy to know! Suffice to say, despite the two centuries' research we've carried out, we so far haven't got anywhere with it yet. Essentially, this provides a classic example of their supernatural technology, for it not only serves us, but the inhabitants of other worlds use it concurrently. We've never met them, and I suspect we never will in here—but that's not its purpose.

'Practically, it has to sustain different coexisting life forms, and adapt the environment accordingly. If you breathe nitrogen, have eyes destroyed by light, have sixteen legs, no arms and communicate by thought only, your life expectancy in our environment could be somewhat limited.'

'Hmm,' pondered Mark. 'And to which of our venerable neighbours are you referring, Rema?'

'Don't worry, I was merely illustrating a point, Mark,' Rema smiled. 'However, if such a life form existed, then this place would adapt and sustain it. There will be many different life forms in here now; we exist in parallel. We simultaneously utilise the same equipment, which adapts itself to suit each of our practical requirements, and we're thereby provided with environments that individually sustain us—and all at the same time. And it is for this reason that you are probed when you first enter: so as to keep you alive, it must adapt everything to suit you, but it firstly needs to ascertain the life form with which it is dealing. Once this is done, it stores your individual signature, carrying out the process automatically as you pass through the portal on subsequent visits.'

Mark and Jack looked unconvinced and puzzled.

'I'm simply telling you exactly what the Ancients told us, backed up by the experiences we sometimes have when using the machines,' Rema said, attempting to reassure the men. 'I realise it doesn't make any difference to what we're doing now—I'm only telling you this to make you appreciate just how advanced their technology is. I understand that you're worried because you're going to become reliant on it soon, but I was hoping you'd realise just what's backing you up when you're in danger; unfortunately, however, it seems I've not succeeded, have I? I understand that, to you, it's completely illogical and therefore difficult to comprehend. What you don't understand yet is the limitations imposed by applying human logic when evaluating the Ancients' handiwork.

'Nevertheless, I suppose this really isn't the time for a deep discussion regarding how the Ancients' technology does or doesn't work: you've experienced it, you see some of it here and, when we leave, I'll show you something else. But, for now, let's leave the transporter and move on. We'll move over to the crystal on the left and I'll begin a tour of the equipment.'

The group moved across to a huge crystal formation that stood just beyond the low partition surrounding the transporter. Rema pointed at a small, flat shelf cut into the face of the otherwise irregular crystalline structure, directing them to stand before it.

Once the two men stood in place, Rema began. 'Imagine that you're suddenly surrounded by a flight of hostile Hovertaks. You'll be in-range of their weapons in two seconds, flying at three hundred feet, alone and out of ammunition. Your engine's running rough and you're quickly losing power. In such a situation, you can't shoot at them, you can't out-fly them, and you're too low to dive away. So, what do you do next?'

'That's easy, Rema—die,' Mark replied cheerfully.

'Undoubtedly,' she smiled. 'But place your hand on the middle of the shelf, Mark, and think about that exact scenario. You'll feel a slightly strange sensation, but it's nothing to worry about.'

Tentatively, Mark extended his arm and laid his hand flat on the shelf. Watching curiously, Jack watched as Mark instantly assumed a dreamlike posture, his eyes unfocused but seemingly listening. After a short period, he removed his hand from the shelf and grinned widely. 'Intelligent machine, Rema! It's perfectly clear now what I'm to do! Can't imagine how I missed it, old girl.'

Jack looked at Mark confused. 'Care to elaborate?'

'Obviously, I activated my plane's shield and they were buggered! Their bloody purple balls just bounced off it, as I popped and sputtered on whistling Rule Britannia and smoking a fag.'

'The important point here is that you survived odds of twelve to one when, to all intents and purposes, you were completely helpless,' Rema said delightedly.

'Absolutely, old girl, worked like a charm it did. Although I do see one tiny weenie insignificant little snag with it,' replied Mark.

'And what's that?' asked Rema, smiling in anticipation.

'We don't have those shields on Spitfires—or anything else, for that matter. Your machine bloody well cheated.'

'Ah but it didn't, you see. Now you've got them on all your war machines, thanks to this heap of rock, as you first called it!' Rema said triumphantly, watching the look on the airmen's faces as the truth dawned on them.

'Hang on a minute, Rema, are you serious? My God, that changes everything,' said Jack excitedly. 'We really are invincible then!'

'Unfortunately, Jack, that's not quite correct. In a concentrated attack, the shields can only provide temporary cover and they're only effective against energy weapons. The power to the shields is depleted every time they're struck by a beam weapon and, although they recharge rapidly from the grid, if they're struck repeatedly with no time to recover, eventually they'll fail. And furthermore, they give no protection from missiles, such as bullets, spears, arrows and the like. With that in mind, it is still possible that you could die.

Somewhat crestfallen by this, Jack replied: 'Okay, perhaps we're not invincible, but we're a damn sight better off than we were before. Our enemies don't have guns like ours—they rely on energy weapons, so these shields are still a massive boost. Even if they have their limitations, I still reckon they've more than evened the odds against us now. And, if the king's forces are reduced to using bows and arrows and the like, they'll struggle a bit with them against our fighting machines!'

'And that's exactly what it may come down to, Jack. Finally, they're going to get an overdose of their own medicine—and I hope they choke on it!' Rema said with a dark smile.

'Well,' said Mark, 'I, for one, never doubted such a giant amongst machinery could do anything less than perform miracles! You've only got to look at its sleek lines and perfect paint job to see that!' he continued, backtracking slightly. 'And you know what, Rema? I'd quite like to know a little more about all these thoroughbreds if at all possible!'

'I thought you were bored with details, Mark? And I might remind you: you referred to them as "lumps of rock" just ten minutes ago!'

Mark smiled sheepishly. 'Who me, old girl? No, you must be mistaken!'

'Yeah right,' she laughed. 'But let's continue.' She walked over to a very large machine. 'This engine here is the brain, if you like. It's the command unit and supervises the actions of the others; although they can function independently, this unit links them together. If we'd had the use of it before, I feel things would've been so much easier. Nevertheless, it was a real breakthrough when it activated a few weeks ago. You've felt its power, Mark: you gave it a problem which, on the face of it, would only have one answer—but it gave you an alternative. It was much the same with us, only our problem was incomparably more complex. We asked it how we could defeat the king, and restore the world with order and balance. Without question, we had no faith in finding an answer; the king's forces were going to attack us here sooner rather than later, and we couldn't have resisted them. Our last act would have been to destroy everything on Kira to prevent it falling into his hands. Without Kira, we would've been so weakened as to be virtually ineffective elsewhere.' A wave of sadness clouded Rema's eyes, but she took control of her emotions and continued with her story. 'When the king had conquered Mu, as he must, he would've concentrated on what was left of us and that would have been the end of the resistance—assuming, of course, he hadn't already destroyed everything with his new weapon. However, all that being said, we now have a workable solution in the form of tools we didn't possess; as you said, Mark, it cheats.'

'Indeed it does,' commented Mark, 'but it's fine at doing so!'

Rema nodded. 'Thanks to this machine, we now have a whole raft of new tools. You've seen just one of them but there are many more.'

Rema directed her attention to across the other side of the room. 'The four devices standing over there manufacture and distribute the equipment designed by the command unit. From the left, the first three carry out the manufacturing, whilst the largest on the end transports the finished products to the destination at which they're required. The three in the middle of the floor are satellites of the command unit; they're additional processors it uses when multitasking. The two on the far left operate and maintain the many facets of this anomaly, which is essentially what's happening in here at the moment. Sounds quite straightforward when it's put like that, doesn't it?' Rema asked.

'If you happen to be an Ancient, I'm sure it is,' muttered Jack.

'Well, either way, I won't bore you with any more long-winded elaborations for today,' she said.

'What about the remaining devices near the platform?' Mark asked.

'I'm afraid that, at this point, I can't tell you what they do; their purpose is still a secret. All I can say for now is that they'll throw the opposition into a blind panic when we use them.

'Anyway, let's get back to the things I can tell you about. Regarding the shields, they're more suited to you. All your heavy equipment is now fitted with them, but most of ours aren't. We can't use them effectively because the energy they produce interferes with our propulsion and weapon systems. Actually, even if our engines weren't affected, we couldn't fire through them. Nevertheless, we've fitted them to our ships, but it seems that they can only use them when stationary and, of course, they can't use their weapons. But, on the more optimistic side, at least they're protected after a fashion.

'In addition, we can also shield the base here on Kira if necessary, which we can defend thanks to the weapons your captain is kindly donating to us. It's more important than ever that we protect ourselves properly now. We're fitting anti-gravity units to all the planes so that you won't need runways anymore; for the attack on Atlantis, this will add fifty more fighters to your air force as it will more than double your carrier's capacity to launch and retrieve its aircraft.

'Fantastic,' Jack smiled.

'The additional fighters are a bit of a bonus, of course,' Rema continued. 'Having the anti-gravity devices and the resulting capacity gained on Victorious means you can utilise the cargo of new Spitfires you're carrying immediately after they've been reassembled. You've now got a small transporter system on Victorious. Using that, you can instantaneously move your troops and equipment from the ships to the shore, which then applies, of course, in reverse. This system has no frills, as such, but has a range of only five miles; nevertheless, you won't need landing craft any more for one thing, which, in itself, eliminates one of the most hazardous concerns of establishing our beach head in Atlanta.

'Furthermore, your planes and ships now have the same navigation system that was utilised in Tiea's Vertlyn which, as you now know, pinpoints your position wherever you are on the planet.'

'That's great—I love that thing!' said Mark enthusiastically.

'And that's about it,' Rema concluded. 'The rest is up to us.'

'Well, that's a hell of a lot more than we had yesterday, Rema,' said Mark. 'It won't be easy but at least we've got a fighting chance now, which we didn't have before.'

'Indeed. The odds may be stacked against us, but we have some very advanced tools at our disposal—and, of course, the greatest motivation. Anyway, I think that's about it in here. Let's get back and get ready for the off,' Rema finished.

Instantly standing on the platform, they glanced back at the incredible crystals, then turned and walked through to B Wing.

As promised, Rema took the men to the area behind the wing, which should have contained the structure housing the ancients' artefacts they'd just left. The airmen, although having been pre-warned, were nevertheless suitably impressed when they encountered a suite of offices, full to bursting with people from the resistance, all preparing for the upcoming invasion.

To prove the point—and relying on a well-proven measurement system—Mark returned to B Wing. He paced the distance from the portal through the security room and foyer, and then strode back to the other side, counting the paces as he went. Jack and Rema watched as he stopped halfway through the offices and pushed against the wall in front of him with both hands. Scratching his head, he then turned to his friends. 'By my reckoning, I'm now opposite the portal. They've either turned it off or it's not here; either way, this isn't where we've just been.' Mark eyed Rema curiously. 'That doesn't exactly prove *the anomaly* isn't on earth, Rema, though I admit it sure isn't where it should be—that I do grant you!'

'Hmm,' contemplated Jack. 'I don't understand the Ancients' technology, but having the use of it is all that really matters at this point, eh, Mark?'

Since the arrival of the forces from 1940—and the assumption that they'd join them—the base on Kira had been a hive of activity, and the resistance had been busily preparing themselves and their equipment for the attack on Atlantis they'd predicted would soon follow. Having already amassed everything required for the venture, they now only awaited confirmation from Rowsell's forces: the moment the captain left the meeting with Lanter, confirming his force would attack Atlantis, the resistance embarked on the final phase.

The resistance ordered Larn Rolac, their top engineer, complete with a hand-picked team of resistance fighters, to group at Victorious. Rolac and his colleagues, joining Chief Engineer David Duke and his team, all set about preparing the fleet for the invasion.

Notwithstanding the activities of the Joint Commanders, at grass-root level, things had progressed with surprising speed: Rolac and Duke had instantly taken to each other, both clearly sharing a passion for all things mechanical, and they quickly established a rapport. This had developed into a mutual admiration within the first half hour. Somewhat amusing to behold, it nevertheless had greatly assisted the task at hand, and a firm friendship between the men had been established, which would last from then onwards.

Duke commanded the tankers to refuel the fleet and then despatched an army of mechanics and assistants to every ship due to sail. Throughout the fleet, they assembled, readied, dispatched and received the various weapons stowed away on-board the merchantmen. Whilst Duke was involved with these duties, Rolac and his people brought aboard the new transporter, and carried out its assembly on the port side of the flight deck towards the bow.

Now, having completed his arrangements for the time being, Duke joined Rolac beside his weird machine. 'Well, Larn, I'm glad the captain warned me you'd come bearing strange gifts. He also ordered me to do my best to comply with all your wishes, but I'm afraid I'll have to ask you to remove this thing. It's right in the way of my aircraft, amongst other things. Just what the hell is it supposed to be anyway?'

'It's a transporter, and it's just one of the many new machines Lanter discussed with your captain after last night's big meeting. I think you're in for a few surprises today, David.' Subsequently, he went on to explain the functions and operation of the transporter. Realising how this would transform his entire concept of logistics, it had the chief beside himself with excitement. Having swamped Rolac with questions and finally grasping the general principal of the machine, Duke shook his head in wonder. 'So, if I aim the beam using this one and lengthen or shorten it with that one, encircle the target using this and press that, I've dematerialised everything within it at that point,' said Duke, indicating the arrangement of the machines controls, 'then what happens?'

'Something you really don't want to happen, actually,' Rolac said, laughing. 'If you'd pressed that last one, it would've dematerialised everything held within the beam, right enough, but that means literally *everything*, David. So, before you do, you must engage this one, which effectively slides the beam under your target as well, wrapping it up, for want of a better description. It'd be slightly embarrassing delivering your troops into battle standing on half a ship as well—especially when it then fell over because the water drained away! But, apart from that, you've got it so far. Now you can relocate the beam to wherever you want, using these dials which pinpoint the relative positions on the grid map displayed on the screen. Then push the green button, which reconstitutes the target at the location you've chosen.' He indicated the remaining controls.

'That's absolutely incredible,' replied Duke in wonder. 'So now we use it to transport everything around the fleet this afternoon, then stow it away until we need it again, I presume?' replied Duke, never doubting it would work but nevertheless still worried about the obstruction it caused on his flight deck.

'We do have to, but then again we don't,' said Rolac, grinning as he qualified his cryptic answer. 'We'll use it now to shift everything we need, as you say, but it's not in the way because you don't need the runway anymore.'

'Larn, it's a bloody aircraft carrier! Without a runway it's a monumental waste of fine steel—unless you want a giant battering ram, I suppose. What good is this ship if we can't use our planes?'

Deciding this was as good a time as any, as Rolac listed all the additional equipment the resistance was supplying. However, his briefing—apart from many practical queries—begged the obvious final question from Duke, speaking as an engineer. 'There's no doubt all this strange equipment will make us pretty bloody powerful, possibly almost invincible,' considered Duke, 'but is it reliable, Larn? I don't understand how it works at all, and I notice even you struggle a bit with some of it, but our lives do depend on this, you know. Having been around this kind of technology all your life, what's your gut feeling?'

'I'm quite happy with it all, David,' Rolac reassured his friend. 'So far, the Ancients' technology has never let us down—as long as they've left specific instructions on how to use it! Any problems we've had with it in the past have arisen as a result of tinkering in the dark, as it were.

But, all of these machines, we've got operating procedures explicitly set out for us. I've no reservations whatsoever, David—we can totally rely on them all, I assure you.'

Content with Rolac's answer, Duke now focused on the logistics with the resistance officer. Following their superiors' orders, they used the transporter in earnest, shuffling men and machinery around the fleet. Eventually, they had assigned everything to where their bosses had stipulated so that the invasion could begin.

Initially, the allied crews were stunned to see things rapidly appearing and disappearing around them as the Chief Engineers supplied the fleet, completing the task in hours rather than days, as they'd normally expect. On the ships and the shore, the allies and the resistance worked together directed by their officers' commands. As fast as they assembled or gathered together the equipment they'd ordered, it was snatched away to its final destination.

'Well, that thing certainly saved us some time with that exercise! If everything else works as well as your transporter, Larn, we'll nail them to the wall,' said Duke with a smile.

Elsewhere, demonstrations were being conducted throughout the fleet. The resistance personnel were training their allies in the use of their equipment, and likewise, the resistance was being trained by its allies.

Two Hovertaks, complete with their pilots, were transported aboard Victorious from their base beside the lake. The navy pilots gathered round them, receiving a crash course on the machines and the tactics they generally employed. Having concluded the lecture on the Hovertak, a Seafire—complete with all the new technology—was transported to the scene. Immediately, the allied pilots swarmed over it, eager to see the alien additions made to this once-standard fighter. When briefed, they remained undaunted by the effect these devices would have when actually flying the modified Seafire; every pilot wanted to be the first to try them out. Flight Sergeant James Roberts pulled rank and climbed into the cockpit.

'Remember what I told you, Flight Sergeant: when you want to fly this plane normally, you must reduce the lift when increasing your forward speed concurrently. If you don't, you'll tear the wings off. Don't forget: in your aircraft, one force fights the other, and you have to balance it out physically, so be very careful the first time you do it.

'On the other hand, we don't have quite the same problem with the Hovertaks. As I previously mentioned, the anti-gravity unit is required at all times to ensure flight owing to their aerodynamics. But, they're designed that way and automatically adjust the forces themselves. Unfortunately, however, without completely redesigning everything, we can't do that with your aircraft, and so this is very much left to your own skill, I'm afraid. Your Seafire's wings are too long, and their internal structure isn't designed to resist the strain they'll encounter if you miscalculate. When your forward speed gives you sufficient lift, turn the unit right off because, clearly, you won't need it anymore,' Flight Leader Cal Verta reminded him.

Nodding, Roberts started his engine allowing it to warm up. Now, with its engine running smoothly in idle, Roberts engaged one new device, and the Seafire lifted vertically into the sky. The mechanics had fitted the dial control operating the unit to the top of the throttle lever. As Roberts pushed the throttle forward, he spun the dial backwards, his thumb reducing the lift from the anti-gravity unit. Attaining sufficient momentum for his wings to support the aircraft, Roberts, as instructed, turned the dial fully back, which subsequently switched it off. Now flying normally, he completed a circuit of the lake, reversing the procedure as he approached Victorious.

The pilots on the carrier watched in fascination as the Seafire—complete with its Merlin engine ticking over at about five hundred feet—hung stationary above them. The plane sank slowly to the deck beside them, and Roberts climbed from the cockpit as the Merlin sputtered to silence.

'Well, gents, that worked a treat,' said Roberts, looking smug. 'We'll have no trouble adapting to that one—it couldn't be simpler!'

'My God, Larn,' exclaimed Duke, 'I've seen some crazy things here today but, make no mistake, for me, that seemed the strangest of the lot so far.'

As the Seafire roared low over the base, sharply banking around for its return trip over the lake, Rema Mark and Jack had emerged into the factory area, returning from B Wing. The giant space was now completely open on the side overlooking the lake, which afforded them a view of the frantic activities in progress.

'It's like Piccadilly Circus out there! You'd be forgiven for thinking something's about to happen looking at that lot,' said Mark. 'But, before we go into that, what happened to half the hillside which must've been piled up on top of this area last night?'

'That's easily explained,' said Rema brightly. 'You saw what happened to the rock face that I opened with my hand lance when you first got here. Well, this works on the same principal—only bigger. You didn't think we got everything here in through the tree surely?'

'Of course not,' said Mark sharply, unwilling to admit that, in the absence of any other entrance he had seen last night, that's just what he had thought. 'And anyway, even if I had, you defy logic everywhere else so why not here as well?'

'Hey, you two, look at that!' cried Jack, distracted by a Seafire carrying out a manoeuvre over Victorious never considered by its original designers. Following the line of Jack's pointing finger, the group watched the conclusion of James Robert's maiden flight in his modified aircraft. A sight slightly overshadowed by the sudden disappearance of several hundred resistance troops stood by the lakeside in front of the factory, who'd also been watching it.

Mark looked at Jack and raised an eyebrow. 'I know, don't ask,' he said.

'Philistines,' said Rema, showing off her post-history knowledge.

'That reminds me—we'd better think about boarding the carrier ourselves soon or they might leave without us,' said Jack, as the men reappeared on the deck of the nearest troopship.

As he was speaking, two Hovertaks materialised where the troops had been, and the two pilots climbed to the ground. One was Cal, who walked over to the trio when he saw them standing by the entrance. 'Hello, people, I'm glad I've caught you,' he said warmly. 'I was thinking I might struggle to find you with all this going on. Anyway, I've a present for you two gentlemen; come outside and I'll show you.'

Whilst walking from the factory, Jack and Mark saw another large structure built into the adjacent hillside, which also stood open. Inside, it housed a substantial contingent of Hovertaks, with two brand new Spitfires parked regally in the foreground.

'Now *that*'s what I call a machine—and you really can smell the new paint!' Mark said with delight, running his hands over the fuselage of the craft nearest him.

'Just off the production line. Well, straight out of crates anyway,' said Cal with a smile. 'This is your surprise, gentlemen, compliments of Captain Rowsell. They're fuelled, armed and fitted with the anti-gravity, shielding and navigation equipment.'

Mark and Jack were delighted, excitedly walking around their new craft and keen to try them out. Cal showed the airmen the workings of each of the gadgets, and suggested they carry out a trial flight to ensure they were fully aware how to utilise the controls. Offered the opportunity, Mark and Jack agreed to join Cal and his comrades in a demonstration show.

'It looks like we'll be off pretty shortly then, Rema,' said Jack. 'When we're done I think we'd better go to the carrier. What's your plan?'

'I'm staying here until the Hovertaks leave, and then I'm flying with them. If you're not coming back here, I figure the next time I'll see you will be in the sky over Atlantis. So, until then, good luck to you both—and let's hope it'll all work out for us.' She moved closer to Jack and delicately placed her hands around his neck.

'You're a dark horse—you never mentioned you were a pilot,' said Mark, having little regard for the affectionate embrace.

'Okay, Rema,' smiled Jack, passion flaming in his eyes. 'I suppose I'd better get going. But promise me you'll take care until we see each other again. I couldn't bear to lose you now, you know.' He ran his thumb down her face, concern frowning his forehead, and then placed a warm kiss on her lips.

Moments later, Rema watched as her friends climbed up into their new planes, running up the engines, and taxied out onto the narrow beach.

Suddenly, a red flare shot into the sky above Victorious, signalling the start of the exercise. Cal waved to the airmen, and the two Hovertaks lifted from the beach then accelerated away, almost brushing the trees on the hilltop as they disappeared behind it.

'Right, Mark, time we joined them,' called Jack on the r/t. 'Let's get going and see how we get on with the gadgetry.'

'Could be interesting. Still, it'll be good to get up again. Seems like centuries since we were last there, Wing Co.,' Mark replied, grinning at Jack from his cockpit.

'Quite,' said Jack, laughing at his colleague's joke.

Applying a few more revs to the Merlins, ensuring they didn't stall, the pilots hesitantly engaged the anti-gravity units and the planes lifted from the beach.

'Fuck a duck!' Mark whispered to himself as his Spitfire effortlessly gained height. Looking at Jack keeping pace beside him, he raised his thumb, an action he realised with a start he shouldn't be able to perform at this juncture—he usually didn't have a hand spare during take-off.

Looking down on the fleet below them, the two men saw the ships were now surrounded with a green corona, which slightly distorted their profiles but otherwise left them quite visible.

'Let's go, Mark, and don't forget to use your shield. Cal and his mate are around somewhere—we don't want any accidents.'

Following Cal's instructions, the pilots accelerated their engines, reducing the effect of the anti-gravity unit commensurately, and were soon flying steadily. Mark moved in behind Jack, and they pulled up sharply together.

~*~*~*~

On Victorious, Captain Rowsell watched from the flight deck accompanied by Duke and Rolac. The Captain had organised this demonstration primarily to illustrate the new equipment, and Rolac had convinced his two allies that the best place to observe this would be out in the open. They watched the Hovertaks disappear over the hills, and the captain wondered briefly why Rolac chose this particular moment to 'attend to some urgent last-minute preparations.' Rolac walked away, heading back inside the carrier as the Spitfires followed the Hovertaks into the sky.

The two Spitfires were flying one slightly behind the other at about five thousand feet, now circling the lake, and the two Hovertaks screamed in low across the bay to attack the anchored fleet.

'There they are, Mark,' Jack announced. 'Four o'clock low, coming in over the bay, headed for the gap in the cliff.'

'We'll get in behind them as they pass the carrier, Jack. I'll take the one on the left.'

Meanwhile, Cal manoeuvred his Hovertak. 'Close up, Abdua,' he directed his wingman. 'We'll split when we enter the lake. You take the ships to the right and I'll take the left. We'll bank around above the base and attack the warships along the centre of the lake together. Remember: watch those Spitfires at six o'clock high—looks like they've spotted us.'

Cal and his comrade approached the gap in the cliff. Wingtip to wingtip, they flashed into the inner lake, banking sharply left and right as they exited the opening. Purple balls of energy flashed from the noses of the Hovertaks as they attacked the merchantmen and submarines moored either side of the lake.

Jack and Mark were now right behind their respective quarry, and Mark's thumb automatically went for his gun button as Cal's Hovertak entered his gun sight.

'Hey, you guys, don't forget this is just a demo will you?' Cal said with concern, his urgent call reaching Mark's ears over the r/t.

Going slightly cold, Mark realised that was precisely what he had done. Looking through the arc of his propeller past Cal's fighter, he saw the deadly rain of energy balls from Cal's weapon were absorbed and dissipated by the shields surrounding the ships: although he'd hit every one along the line, they remained undamaged.

From his viewpoint, Mark found it difficult to see individuals on-board the ships, travelling as he was at around three hundred miles an hour. However, the glimpses indicated that their nerves were not quite as intact as their ships. Clearly, a few had thrown themselves into the water, screaming, causing him to break out in laughter.

Reaching the end of the lake, the four aircraft executed a tight inward turn, the Spitfires continuing to pursue the Hovertaks. Coming together, they roared and whined back along the centre of the lake. Cal and his wingman flew lower, firing liberal doses of their purple projectiles onto each warship as they passed, which culminated in a spectacular light show as the Hovertaks pasted the huge carrier at the end of their run.

Rowsell, lifting himself back to his feet from his prone position of hugging the deck, turned to a white-faced Duke, who was also shakily rising beside him. 'Whose bloody stupid idea was that, I wonder?' complained Duke.

With some relief, the men watched the aircraft soar up and disappear over the cliff, noticing as they did an amused Rolac grinning down from the bridge above. The captain scowled up at him.

'Now it's your turn to complete the exercise,' called Cal to Jack and Mark, who were still flying right behind him. 'Are you going to make it easy for us?'

'Not on your nelly, mate! If you want us, you've got to get us!' Mark called back, looking forward to the competition with the Hovertaks. 'Whatever happens, just remember you're dead anyway—we had you before you fired a shot when you first arrived!'

Cal signalled to his wingman, and the two fighters broke right and left again, and banked sharply back over the fleet, with Mark and Jack glued to their tails. Levelling out, the Hovertaks instantly slowed and shot straight up as the king's pilot had done over the beach. The two Spitfires flew straight under them. Although they realised what had happened and respectively stood the Spitfires on their wingtips, trying to outturn their adversaries, it was too late: Cal and his wingman emulated the manoeuvre and almost simultaneously fired at their targets.

Jack and Mark felt a tingling sensation and were momentarily blinded by a flash of white light that sizzled and wriggled across the boundaries of their shields.

'Bugger, I forgot you could do that! Oh sod it!' shouted Mark, highly annoyed at being duped so easily by Cal, who had now effectively shot him down.

'Well, I suppose that's the point of the exercise, Mark. Perhaps we'll be ready for it next time—when it counts. Looks like we're in the chair though when we meet these blokes for a beer,' Jack said, equally chagrined.

The four aircraft flew close together after their rather brief encounter. Jack and Mark waved to a grinning Cal and his wingman, and they split apart again. The Hovertaks headed back to base to re-join their unit, whilst Mark and Jack flew to Victorious, seeking permission to land. With permission received, they lowered their Spitfires onto the flight deck, guided in by a crewman waving his signal wands.

'You know I'm still smarting over that. We've seen them do it before, and yet still we fell for it,' Mark said as he joined Jack on the deck.

'Bloody nuisance! What with the whole navy looking on, we looked like a pair of amateurs! Best we tell them it was just part of the demo,' replied Jack with a sigh.

'Well, it's a bad start but, that aside, if it weren't for the shields, we'd be history,' said Mark.

'Ah, now you've hit the nail right on the head haven't you? I reckon those Hovertaks could have easily destroyed us all with their weapons, but we're all still here—not a ruffled feather amongst us,' observed Jack, absorbing the lesson.

'I suggest you don't adopt the feather approach with the jolly jack tars, Jack. You might end up in the water too,' Mark said, laughing out loud at the idea.

Captain Rowsell joined the airmen beside their planes and they exchanged salutes. 'That was one hell of a show, gentlemen. It frightened the bloody life out of us down here! Still, we don't have time for any training, as such, so it's a good thing it was dramatic; at least our crews know what to expect now. And they'll be more inclined to trust the shields after that little demonstration.'

'I assume by that comment, Captain, that we're going to fight, which means you're now satisfied with all the equipment? Hopefully this includes the big secret as well? Jack asked, hoping to draw more information from the captain.

'Wing Commander, you know I can't elaborate on that one just yet; you'll find out all you need to know within the next few hours anyway.' And, with that cryptic statement, Captain Rowsell left the flight deck and returned to his bridge.

CHAPTER SEVENTEEN

The king turned as the palace gates closed behind them. 'Well, that's that over with for a while, thank Ra,' he said with a sigh of relief. 'A little rest and we can enjoy the pleasures of our new palace, Alana.'

'Yes, my Lord. We don't spend enough time here. Apart from the heat it's a beautiful place. I'm glad we've come,' she replied.

The king reflected that she actually had no idea how glad he was himself to have escaped Atlanta, thinking it could very well get much too heated there as well.

The king's party had just reached the entrance to his palace when they heard the approaching aircraft. Drawn to watch the show, they all stopped and gazed as the planes flew over them.

Looking at the aircraft, the king thought it unlikely the puny resistance could actually inflict any real damage upon him, irrespective of their new allies. The sight immediately restored his faith in his invulnerability. How could he doubt it, especially considering these aircraft were only a tiny part of his vast force? It hadn't occurred to him his soaring confidence was due mainly to his present location rather than his warplanes: being far from immediate danger, he would soon forget his recent panic. And, in anticipation of the pleasures he had arranged for himself and which awaited him tomorrow, the sweat-beaded forehead, the racing heart and the mental images of his own demise were quickly forgotten.

Fussing around the king and his party, the servants efficiently attended to their every whim. Having been provided with refreshments adhering to all of their needs, his guests retired to their sumptuous accommodation, happy to accept the king's suggestion of rest and noting his instructions for tomorrows' entertainments. The king then left to occupy his own quarters in the south wing, taking his wives and servants with him.

Just for a moment, he regretted building such a huge palace. Walking through room after room, all laden with exquisite furnishings and glittering with golden ornaments, he felt momentarily tired at the sight. Even the carpets—inches deep—failed to ease his aching feet after traipsing through forty large vestibules. But finally, they arrived, and leaving his retinue in the care of the servants, he climbed the stairs to his private apartments, taking only Alana with him.

The king's apartments occupied an eighth of the palace, within which he'd bestowed every conceivable luxury. Being the richest man alive, it would be something of an undertaking to describe quite how extreme the accommodation really was; suffice to say, in design and accoutrements, he had ensured nothing but excellence to its ultimate limit.

The king and Alana had gone straight to his bedroom, stopping only to lift a large jar and two golden goblets from the wine cellar on the way through. Dropping onto the bed, they lay together drinking and staring dreamily through the window.

Night fell quickly onto the desert sands, the oppressive heat dissipating only slightly as the sun retreated. The couple watched as the sky turned purple, catching the last gasp from the setting sun, melting to deep indigo, speeding to ebony. Full and dark yellow, the huge moon rose behind the rolling dunes of the desert, its light uncertain through the hanging mists, ghostly gossamer diffusing the horizon.

Slipping to the floor, Alana lit candles placed in sconces around the walls before lighting the fire in the large, open fireplace opposite the bed. The darkness surrounding the palace hardened, becoming solid in the shadows, as their room lightened and became fluid.

Soft wavering candles and the deep flaring of the log fire combined to awaken sliding, shifting images. Wraiths danced amongst the huge timbers supporting the high vaulted ceiling, writhing across the walls and floor. Shimmering light bounced from the gold and silver ornaments, and then reflected in the window and crystal chandelier. The logs whistled and sang in the grate.

Alana placed her goblet on the intricately carved stone mantelshelf above the fire, reached around and loosened the fastenings of her dress.

She twitched her body and it slipped from her shoulders, falling to the deep red carpet around her feet. Stepping from the dress, she slowly removed her underclothing and stood naked before the fire. Then, lifting her goblet from the shelf, she tilted her head and drank deeply, heightening her desires with the strong, smooth, dark red Atlantien wine. She caused a rivulet to tumble from the side of her mouth, and it coursed down her neck, running between her breasts into her deep shadowed cleavage. Dripping below like droplets of blood, the wine trickled down across her belly, mingling with her triangle of coarse black hair. Slowly decreasing, it ran on between her legs, further moistening her intimate places. Gravity pulled the wine on, leaving no time to linger, and two tiny veins slid over her brown inner thighs, ever reducing until they expired finally at her knees.

The king lay on his bed, propped by a mountain of soft cushions. His attention was focused completely on Alana's supple brown curving body, silhouetted by the roaring fire behind her. The firelight cast a huge shadow, pooling her nakedness in black relief across the room, painting the wall and ceiling with dancing, inviting images. He'd been contentedly enjoying the show, but desire flared as he watched the wine caress her form.

Rising from the bed and tossing off his clothing as he went, the king approached Alana. 'Alana,' he said, 'One day I'll tire of you because you're a whore but you're a beautiful one. We've been together for years and done this so many times, yet it seems I'm still not bored with you. Keep this up, Alana, and there may be many more.'

'I will, my king,' she purred.

The king knelt down and griped her haunches. Using his tongue, he removed the traces of wine from her body. Reversing the direction, he started at her knees and, unaffected by gravity, he lingered wherever he wished, journeying slowly up her body until he eventually reached her mouth. Kissing passionately, they fell to the floor. Past masters in the art of lovemaking, they repeatedly drove each other to the pinnacles of pleasure, climaxing together when the fire had died to a smouldering red glow.

It was long into the night when the couple finally sated, sat watching the embers, drinking wine with the candles sputtering and slowly dying around them.

A chill crept across the room, breaking the spell. Alana suddenly shivered and the king, with his arm about her soft waist, lifted her and led her to their bed. They lay pressed together beneath the blankets, comforted by the warmth of their bodies. Alana reflected as she rested beside him. This cruel, heartless man—her husband and her king— occasionally still surprised her. Sighing deeply, she smiled.

Their eyes turned back to the huge window. A carpet of stars filled the night sky, millions of bright diamonds resting against a jet-black backdrop, the moon bathing the scenery with a hard, white luminescence. Contentedly watching the tranquillity, the slumbering city and spectral white desert faded away as the couple drifted into a deep and untroubled sleep.

CHAPTER EIGHTEEN

Myriddian Amis still couldn't quite believe his luck. Unexpectedly, early yesterday morning, he had been released from the holding cell into which Maltor had so callously thrown him. He'd endured two horrible days of uncertainty, two days of pacing his tiny cell with no contact from anyone apart from his gaolers. He'd almost lost his sanity trapped in there—a state of mind which was admirably assisted by a certain sadistic gaoler who, although remaining silent at all times, insisted on raising his eyes to heaven and drawing his finger across his throat. This he did at every opportunity, and especially when Myriddian pleaded with him for any information he could give regarding his fate.

If he ever regained his former stature, he'd make sure the bastard paid for that, he promised himself. And it wouldn't be a finger he drew across that miserable little sod's throat either.

Still, be that as it may, he was free now and leaning on the deck railings of one of the king's ships, now heading for Rammath.

Upon release, Maltor had ordered Myriddian to relocate the project in Atlanta. He was to gather his transporter team, together with all their relevant equipment, and get the whole outfit to the docks immediately. Not wishing to incur Maltor's wrath again, he'd moved heaven and earth to achieve the chief's wishes. With all his people and gear loaded on-board by mid-afternoon, they'd sailed at midnight.

Looking out over the deck, Atlantis had disappeared over the horizon two hours ago, and now all Myriddian could see was the convoy around him and a restless empty ocean under a watery moon.

Judging by the mass exodus he'd witnessed yesterday—notably one which seemed to involve anybody who was anybody in Atlanta along with all their staff—the powers that be must be seriously worried about something; he didn't believe for a moment that it had much to do with the Mu justification given out by the king either. The fact that Maltor had completely about faced with his project and released him with orders to concentrate on producing the bomb without delay didn't bode well either. There was no doubt in his mind that all of this was related to the resistance and the strange navy which they seemed to have brought here.

'Can't sleep, Myriddian?' asked a soft voice.

Turning his gaze from the sea, Myriddian saw Jalat Youl approaching him, one of the many wives of the king's finance minister.

'Hello, Jalat,' he smiled wearily. 'No, I can't, and by the looks of it neither can you.'

'I'm surprised any of us can. I'm worried to death. What in Ra's going on? I'm confused, Myriddian. The king has taken virtually the entire government out of Atlanta, and there was so little warning. He took Kolp and Farna with him on the plane to Rammath, and the rest of us were ordered to follow in these ships. But they wouldn't let us get the children. When I refused to go without them I was practically arrested by the police and thrown on-board anyway. Then they locked us all in our cabin until the ship sailed. I can't believe Kolp has let this happen.' Her voice waivered tearfully.

'I wish I could tell you more than what you already know, Jalat, but I'm afraid I have no idea what's happening. I've never seen anything like this before. One thing's for sure, though: nobody else had much of a choice either. I saw people being dragged literally kicking and screaming from their houses. The police are taking such a hard line; there must be something seriously amiss this time.'

'It's getting cold out here, Myriddian,' Jalat replied, shivering slightly. 'They say the bar's open all night so I think I'll go in there. You coming?'

Nodding his head, Myriddian followed.

They found a secluded area in the bar, which was surprisingly busy considering the hour, and resumed their conversation in well-padded chairs with a good supply of strong ale.

Taking a sip of his ale, Myriddian considered Jalet, and wondered if she might know more than she realised; after all, as one of Kolp Youl's wives, she might have come to acquire information without realising it— information which, to her, might have seemed worthless but might actually have been the missing piece of the puzzle. 'Hasn't Kolp mentioned anything unusual recently, Jalat?' Myriddian began. 'Was he worried about anything you know of or did he say something before he left with the king that could help to explain what all of this is about?'

'No, nothing,' Jalet sighed. 'Up until a couple of days ago, everything was running as normal. He was worrying but only about the usual things, like funding. Incidentally, you didn't help him much with that either—it's costing a fortune repairing the damage caused by that tidal wave. But why the king didn't seem to be more upset at the time confused him. He was even more surprised when, after the event, His Majesty demanded more money for your project.'

'He'd probably understand better if the king told him why, Jalat, but that's the trouble with the man isn't it? His reasons for dragging us all over to Rammath are a joke. Not even he would disrupt everything so completely over some matter in Mu. Kolp's well up there though; he must know the real reasons surely?'

'He hasn't been permitted an audience with the king for the last two days, Myriddian. Mind you, nor has anyone else, as far as I can see. He seems to have been totally involved with Maltor and his colleagues; I suppose that's slightly unusual, now I think about it.'

'And his entertainment staff, I believe,' Myriddian scoffed. 'At least he can always find the time for a bit of relaxation whilst the rest of us are left to sweat bullets!'

'Yes, as ever,' Jalet smiled sarcastically, sipping her drink. 'But surely if something was really wrong he'd have concentrated more on the problem, wouldn't he? But then again, why couldn't we wait for the children? When we asked Kolp, he just told me not to worry about them, that they'd be brought to Rammath later. As if that's going to ease any mother's mind!' Jalet's voice quavered, and she took a moment to compose herself. 'He didn't seem too worried about them, Myriddian. In fact, it seemed that the most important thing for him was that we leave Atlanta without delay. And in doing that, we've abandoned our children.'

It was becoming clear to Myriddian—considering the woman's watery eyes and her deflated demeanour—that she wasn't really going to tell him anything more than what he already knew, and that it was unlikely—in her present state of mind, at least—that she'd contribute anything more of value this morning. 'I'm sorry, Jalat,' he began compassionately, 'I don't know what to say, but I think there's going to be trouble in Atlanta or there wouldn't be such a flap. I've no idea what's coming,' he lied, 'but your kids' school's a long way from there. Maybe they'll tell us what's happening soon, but there's nothing you can do for now, in any case.' He gently took her hand and held it in his own. 'I'm sure they'll be fine. Now, why don't you try and get some rest?'

'You're probably right, Myriddian,' she smiled weakly. 'I'm sorry I bothered you with my worries. I think rest's a good idea.' And, after downing her drink, she left Myriddian and headed for her quarters.

Breathing a sigh of relief at managing to get rid of the emotional woman, Myriddian spotted one of his colleagues, Joel Barr, drinking alone at the counter. As Jalet disappeared out of sight, he moved towards Joel.

'Why, friend,' he said, patting Joel on the back. 'You look quite miserable and definitely a little worse for wear. Come and join me—I'll buy you drink.'

'Oh, hi, Myriddian,' Joel greeted Amis. 'Thanks. I'll have a large one.'

'That confirms it, son: you look decidedly pissed off. What's up?'

'What *isn't* would probably be an easier question to answer, Myriddian. It's bloody obvious what's about to happen if you know about the resistance and their new pals at Kira. I wish to Ra I'd had nothing to do with any of this. I was quite content with my lot before you involved me in the transporter experiments.'

'Were you, Joel?' Amis asked sarcastically, raising an eyebrow and calling Joel's comment into question. 'I'm not entirely sure that's true. If memory serves me correctly, you actually seemed very content when you considered the prospect of immeasurably increasing your own wealth. I also recall that, at the time, you pushed hard to involve yourself in the project.'

'Have it your way, Myriddian,' Joel sighed, exasperated. 'I'm not looking for an argument, but neither of us has any reason to think kindly of that machine now it's all but ruined us. How are we to give the king what you've promised, eh? None of us—and that includes *you*—know how the fucking thing was set up when it destroyed the island. The whole project scares me shitless—and it should do! For Ra's sake, we accidentally transported a stone no bigger than a thumbnail. Didn't you realise, Myriddian, the anti-matter it produced would've had the same mass? Doesn't that worry you? I mean, it destroyed the whole fucking island and it caused more damage than a full-scale hurricane to everything within a hundred miles! Consider this, Myriddian—and think very carefully about it my dear friend: what if you'd placed the emendator under the Hovertak and that had gone instead at the same settings?'

In spite of his cool exterior, Myriddian's palms were sweating and his pulse was rapidly increasing. Up until this point in time, he'd gratefully noted that this scenario had gone by unrecognised—but Barr was now that one exception. Again, his spine tingled.

But of course, Barr was right: four tons of anti-matter released into the world definitely wasn't going to improve things, and catastrophic would be the outcome, to put it mildly. Once more, Myriddian's head spun with the dreadful consequences that would inevitably have followed. He'd considered them at the time and they'd haunted him ever since. Due to this, he was now terrified of the machine—and he was also terrified of the king and his chief's actions if he refused to continue with it. No matter how much he wanted to push the situation to the back of his head, Barr's words forced him to consider whether his salvation might eventually lie with the resistance: if they could defeat the king, surely they'd scrap his project—wouldn't they?

The snag there, of course, was that they'd hardly be likely to show him much mercy: his past behaviour had put him squarely in their sights—and that was long before he'd become involved with this. Secretly, he wholeheartedly agreed with all his colleague's sentiments, especially as it seemed he'd be damned whatever choice he made.

'I'd appreciate it if you'd keep that small thought to yourself, Joel,' responded Myriddian, clearly irritated. 'In case you hadn't realised, the only thing keeping us alive at the moment is the king's desire for this weapon. Believe me, I had no choice in the matter. If you kick up a fuss about this now and he listens, we're both finished. There's no doubt we were very lucky this time, but in future, we must endeavour to avoid this.'

'"Endeavour to avoid"? And what the fuck do you mean by that, you fool?' Joel spat angrily. 'You really think that's sufficient? Let's endeavour to avoid reducing our planet to ashes, shall we? Of course, if we can't, at least we've endeavoured so that's all right, isn't it? Myriddian, don't you understand? *We*'re the greatest danger to the world. We need to stop messing around with that thing! We can't figure it out! For Ra's sake, man, can't you just stop worrying about yourself for a moment and think about what you're doing for once in your life? The stakes are too high this time! Accept it: we're swimming through treacle. We're never going to control that hideous machine. I'm not going on with this, Amis, and if you intend to, I'm going to stop you. Ra, help me: I'll kill you myself if you won't back down.'

Although Barr's words were slurred, Amis recognised they were full of conviction and his eyes flashed determination. Concern swirled in the pit of his stomach but, adopting his steadfast, cool exterior, Amis replied tersely, 'Shut up, Joel, and stop making a fool of yourself. Come on now, let's get you out of here before you get into real trouble. You're drunk, man. I'll walk you back to your cabin and we'll discuss this tomorrow.' Hauling him to his feet, Amis led him from the bar and out onto the deck.

Emerging from the bar opposite the stern, Amis steered them behind a large capstan standing before the stern railings. The moon disappeared behind a bank of high level cloud and the darkness around them thickened. Checking the area was deserted and the capstan concealed them, Amis pulled a knife from his jacket. Stabbing Barr once through the heart, he tossed his body through the railings and into the ocean below.

'Fuck you, Joel. You'll not threaten me again now will you, my dear friend?' Leaving swiftly, he made his way back to his cabin.

CHAPTER NINETEEN

'**W**ell that didn't take too long then, Jack, did it? We had the chance to retire there for a minute and we've blown it. Buggered if I know why we never learn. It's a shame you didn't fool our venerable skipper into revealing his secret, though; it's really bugging me.' Mark let out a long, exasperated sigh.

'Well I tried, didn't I, old boy?' replied Jack. And yes, we're committed again right enough—and pretty soon, by the looks of it. The trouble with our captain is that he doesn't say enough sometimes. However, I think what he did say seemed encouraging.'

'Well, it wasn't discouraging, I suppose. But anyway, we can't stand here all night admiring the scenery Wing Co. Let's grab a cuppa before we seek out our Fleet Air Arm buddies. It'll give us a chance to get our story straight.'

'Seems sound to me, Mark. And we're all scheduled to meet on the hangar deck in about forty minutes anyway; I could use one before we get involved in a major planning session.'

The main fleet was scheduled to leave Kira at eleven, with the submarines departing the lake two hours earlier. With the resistance insisting that the king's navy represented the greatest threat to their plans, Galland and his men were being dispatched in the hope they'd destroy them before the main fleet arrived off Atlantis.

Rowsell's forces comprised his four warships, supplemented by three beam weapon boats from the resistance. He had one hundred fighter aircraft, thirty torpedo bombers, and thirty Hovertaks providing air cover. His ground forces consisted of eight thousand soldiers, all of whom would travel in four troopships: two of his own and two supplied by the resistance. Supporting them, he was taking two cargo vessels containing fifty battle tanks, sixty-five four-inch field guns, additional small arms, bombs, supporting equipment and ammunition plus the hospital ship. The tankers and three cargo ships, surplus to his present requirements, would remain at Kira.

The overall plan was to locate and sink the king's beam weapon carriers as a priority, and then concentrate all their resources simultaneously in a massive assault on Atlanta itself. Provided Galland was successful, they'd calculated the opposing forces to be forty thousand troops, one hundred fighter aircraft, two medium-sized warships and ten patrol boats. In addition, the enemy would field approximately thirty fixed-shore defence batteries and would have an additional forty mobile beam weapon units in the frontline. Courtesy of the Ancients, the additions to their regular armaments—which they'd installed this afternoon—would go a long way to redressing the imbalance.

But the odds remained stacked against them, although the captain was confident those odds would be reversed, provided the untested weapon performed as promised.

The voyage from Kira would take ten hours, putting them off Atlanta at nine the following morning. That left them thirteen hours from now to brief their forces, prepare their weapons and snatch a few hours' rest before they commenced the attack.

On-board U35, Galland was in deep discussion with his two captains. He'd resolved his differences with Erwin Gould, and together with Hans Moulder, they were planning their solitary mission.

'The onus is on us to prepare the way for the main attack. This is our prime directive. When we succeed, we'll take up a supporting role as required within the main fleet. In truth, we're not much use strategically after we've completed our mission, simply because our weapons aren't particularly suited for an assault against land-based forces. Nevertheless, they'll doubtless find us a task somewhere.

'I've every confidence we'll achieve our principal directive with ease this time; we're a remarkably different force than we were. The new technology we've been given has capabilities way beyond anything we've ever experienced before. And, thanks to the navigation system we're now using, we actually not only know precisely where we are at all times, but we also know where our enemies are too. And, better yet, ours is apparently unique in that respect. The resistance has told us the enemy uses a similar system insomuch as it tells them where they are and with how to get to their chosen destination, but they can't read our signature from the grid as we can theirs, and so they'll have no idea we're gunning for them. With this in mind, we have a significant advantage, and we must bear this in mind at all times.

'Moving on, we've all seen what the new shielding device can do. Without this magnificent piece of equipment, I doubt any of us would still be afloat after that demonstration. They say it's vulnerable, but in the unlikely event we're attacked ourselves, we'd be unlucky if we couldn't submerge before it failed. Another thing in our favour is the fact they don't have submarines here; they've never seen one, let alone fought one! They're completely unprepared, and if they spot us, they'll have no idea what they're looking at. They may well see our torpedoes streaking towards them, but I very much doubt they'll even take evasive action; once again, they've no idea what's coming.'

'You paint a pretty picture, Commander, and I can't fault what you're saying,' Moulder responded. 'But consider for a moment a couple of points: firstly, do you have any idea how fast the enemy ships are? And, more importantly, as we're never going anywhere in the submarines again, how much use are these marvellous devices anyway?'

'I appreciate your concern,' Galland replied, somewhat irritated, 'and I'll respond to your first point. Of course, our diesels and the batteries powering our electric motors have now been removed, but—'

'Well, forgive me for appearing stupid, Kurt,' Moulder interrupted, 'but I personally think they're both quite important points—particularly as you seem to think we're about to leave at any moment!'

'He's got a point there, you know,' said Gould.

'Gentlemen, please let me finish!' Galland said sternly. 'You know perfectly well the resistance engineers are adapting our electric motors to draw their power from the grid. They're similar to the engines in use here and can be modified to suit and, so I'm told, considerably enhanced relatively easily. With that taken into consideration, it seems you have both forgotten that they knew we were coming and had everything they needed already to hand. In spite of your doubts, I'm assured they've virtually completed these modifications, and considering the time they've taken, I personally think it's very impressive. In actual fact, I'm pretty impressed with the preparations they've carried out in *all* areas before we arrived.

'That aside, however, we've considerably lightened our boats by removing the heavy diesels and batteries along with the fuel oil. I'm assured that, when the motors are adapted, we can expect to achieve sixty knots submerged and, depending on the sea state, it should be possible to exceed that on the surface. That alters things a bit for us, doesn't it? We no longer have to rely on stealth alone; in fact, as the ships we're likely to encounter sail at a maximum of fifty knots in calm waters, we're now considerably faster than they are, which makes a welcome change. That alone makes our boats even more useful now. With the exception of the destroyers and the resistance's three small beam boats, we've nothing else at sea with any chance of keeping up with them.'

'Did you say sixty knots, Kurt?' Gould whistled. 'My God, that's ten times faster underwater than the poor old tubs were designed for! Can they cope with that?'

'It's true we can't risk any great depth at that speed, but otherwise, I think they'll hold. Obviously, the deeper we go, the greater the pressure from the water above. Combine that with the vastly increased momentum, and it's probable the hulls wouldn't hold. However, at the moment, the enemy hasn't anything to attack us with when we're submerged, and so there's no reason to run very deep anyway. And, of course, we're not committed to sail that fast if we don't want to.'

'I might point out, Kurt, that our new top speed is possibly faster than our torpedoes. If the boats don't fall apart and we fire them off at that speed, we'll end up running into them ourselves! I consider that would make us something rather *less* than invincible at that point!' Moulder said light heartedly.

'You're still not having it, are you, Hans?' Galland shook his head in frustration. 'You know very well: all the torpedoes we're carrying have been enhanced in the same way.'

'Well, I for one am reserving my judgement at the moment,' Moulder responded. 'However, it would seem to be the case that, if everything works as you expect, we could be in the happy position of operating the only war machines which are untouchable here at present.'

'Providing we don't run into anything or each other, we are indeed in that enviable position,' replied Galland, 'and it would certainly be good for you to take that on-board. Without question, whilst the prospect of colliding is apparent, that seems less likely now we've the added advantages of powerful underwater lights and the viewing device in the control room. Depending on how clear the water is around us, submerged, we will be able to see where we're going and the immediate area surrounding the boat. Added to everything else, we no longer need to refuel and we're also each carrying sixty torpedoes owing to the room we've gained for storing additional armaments—and, of course, our English allies who've supplied the best part of them. Each of our submarines is now significantly more powerful than a battleship, which might shake our enemies up a bit, don't you think?' Galland smiled optimistically.

'Let's put it this way, Kurt,' Gould replied. 'I think, at sea, we might just have become the top dogs in the ninth century BC. And I love the idea—I mean, who wouldn't? For one thing, we won't need to skulk about at the bottom of the sea, dreading being depth-charged when it's all gone wrong anymore—an experience I for one won't miss at all!'

'Nor I, Erwin, but shouldn't that be the eleventh century BC?' Moulder responded.

Right, gentlemen, I'll leave you with that thought,' Galland smiled. 'Now it's time to return to your boats. The resistance will run through our new equipment and we'll sail immediately following their brief. Provided they maintain the present course and speed, in four hours' time, the enemy warships will be one hundred and twenty miles off Kira on their way to Atlantis—let's make sure we're there to greet them.'

Aboard Victorious, Captain Rowsell briefed his pilots in the short time available before he'd be committed to the task of delivering the fleet to Atlantis.

'Fifty miles from Atlanta, we'll launch every aircraft we've got. The Swordfish and the Seafires will be armed with bombs and the remaining fighters will provide air cover. The resistance will add their Hovertaks rendezvousing with you above the fleet as you form up. You'll be given targets of opportunity in and around the city, but clearly you'll concentrate on the military defences first. I'll leave you to decide the most appropriate targets with Mr Lanter, who'll join you soon to give you the coordinates and refine the general tactics you've to employ.' Rowsell lit a cigar and inhaled long and hard. 'I know some of you here believe we're in possession of a highly classified weapon, and I can indeed confirm this fact. Unfortunately, however, I'm presently unable to reveal what that weapon is, although I can tell you that, if it works—and I'm assured there's no reason it won't—the resistance you'll encounter will be minimal. Nevertheless, should you meet stiff opposition, in addition to your existing weapons, you all have the new enhancements at your disposal. But I warn you, gentlemen: if you're faced with serious protracted opposition, the weapon will have failed, and in such an event, it is paramount you prepare yourselves to fight with what you've got and to base your decisions on that.'

The scores of men aboard Victorious murmured amongst themselves, some optimistic whilst others were unnerved by a lack of detail and such a cloak-and-dagger attack.

'Have faith in us and each other, gentlemen. I wish you all the very best of luck, and ask that you all utilise your training and experience to your greatest ability.' And after saluting his men, the captain left the hangar deck.

'You know, Jack, our poor captain's confused,' said Mark with a light smile at his lips. 'First he tells us everything's hunky dory and it's going to be a walk in the park, and then he changes his mind, agrees with my thoughts, and says that there might not be a happy ending and we're probably all going to die!'

'You're just miffed he won't share his secret with you, Mark,' Jack laughed. 'Anyway, he didn't say anything about dying—he simply said we need to be prepared.'

'Oh, and now who's miffed, I wonder?' sniffed Mark.

'Well, alright; I'm not happy about not knowing the full details either. If one knows one's got a struggle on one's hands, that's one thing and one can deal with it but, like you, I find the uncertainty of this situation a little frustrating.'

'Agreed, Wing Co. Still, it's not so bad for us: at least we outnumber their air force. The army's got a real problem, though, and that's a fact! The whole thing revolves around us being more capable than we appear, I'm afraid.'

Throughout the deck, the airmen were engaged in conversation as they waited for Lanter to arrive. Only a very few had seen the enemy, and these were at a premium at present. The survivors from the action above Kira were besieged by groups of their comrades. Eager to speak with them but uncertain of their reception, they'd left the RAF officers alone up to now.

'They're a bit standoffish this lot, Jack, but they seem keen enough to have a go,' Mark observed.

'Well, you know how it is, Mark: when new boys arrive, it's always a bit tense at first. Still, maybe we'd better make the effort to get to know them; we'll be working in their team very shortly.'

As they were speaking, Lanter, accompanied by one of his Hovertak pilots, entered the hangar. He introduced the man as Abdua Lorht, who had coincidently served as Cal Verta's wingman in the demonstration over the lake. Calling over the allied pilots to join them, he unrolled a survey map highlighting the layout of Atlanta city and the surrounding area. Pinning this to a board, he was ready to start planning the actual attack with the assembled pilots.

'Good evening, gentlemen,' he said. 'Gather round please and we'll discuss your side of the invasion tomorrow. You've already been given the timing by the captain, I believe, so that part's already been decided and allows us an hour to take out the shore defences before the fleet arrives in range of the city.

'Unfortunately, as for the rest of it, we've no choice but to prepare two completely different strategies to follow in the attack. However we choose to deal with this, we must have the ability to switch from one to the other instantly depending upon the resistance we encounter when we arrive over the city. Before we get going, I'm prepared to give you a little more background information, which I'm sure you all understand is necessary.'

Lanter looked upon the sea of faces before clearing his voice and continuing. 'You're all aware we have a device that we expect to make our task relatively simple. And I think you're also aware of the fact that, should the enemy discover what this is, even at this late hour, they could dramatically reduce its effectiveness. So, for all our sakes, I still cannot reveal the fundamentals. However, what I can say is this: when we use it, it'll virtually eliminate the enemy's weapon systems.'

A gasp and excited comments arose from the audience.

'Settle down, gentlemen, and let me continue,' Lanter commanded over the wave of commotion. 'Essentially, the weapon we're discussing is unproven. Irrespectively, however, we see no real reason to suspect it'll fail; nevertheless, as trained and experienced leaders, we have to acknowledge all possibilities—and of failure, there is a chance, albeit a slim one. We've not tested our weapon simply because, by its very nature, that would reveal its capabilities to the enemy, which is what we're seeking to avoid at this point in time.

'The fact remains, gentlemen, that we're not one hundred per cent sure of the outcome, which is precisely why we must plan in a contingency, hence the two strategies. But before we move on to the invasion itself, we have an immediate threat to deal with approaching from the sea.

'Currently, the enemy has five extremely powerful beam weapon carriers heading back to Atlanta. We hope Commander Galland and his submarines will deal with them for us, but there's an outside chance that he may not or otherwise that their attempts will prove unsuccessful. If they get through, they have the power to counter our secret weapon; whilst it is true to state that the enemy doesn't realise this, that's beside the point—they just have to be in the vicinity. However, Commander Galland does have major advantages now. His submarines are far from what they were and, in reality, it's very unlikely he'll fail. However, should failure become our reality, we'll have to carry out an attack ourselves—and should this become necessary, we'll need to attempt this well out at sea. If we sink them within a hundred miles of Atlantis, I'm afraid it wouldn't guarantee they couldn't still affect us. You'll have to trust me when I tell you that their wrecks could still prove to be a major problem. If this is absolutely necessary, it will be well before our attack on Atlanta itself, which would mean the overall timing wouldn't be affected. After we've resolved the main action together, we would then need to devise a suitable strategy here; then, should the need arise, we'd be ready for implementation.

'Firstly, then, I'll give you a brief overview of the two scenarios I see facing us when we invade, and then together we'll plan the best way to respond either way. In any event, we'll form up over the fleet, as planned, and subsequently proceed directly to the city. The Hovertaks will provide high cover to the Swordfish torpedo bombers so as to protect them from enemy aircraft. There are two reasons for this: firstly, your bombers are very slow, and secondly, the Hovertaks are unshielded. Accordingly, in the first wave, we'll want to attack the shore batteries and their Hovertaks using the Spitfires and Seafires in an attempt to clear the decks before they arrive. In this first wave, all the fighters will protect the Seafires who've adopted the role of fighter bombers until they've released their bombs. At that point, all of you can then seek targets of opportunity, concentrating on those areas that remain the most active. By the time the others arrive, you'll have mopped up a considerable proportion of their defences—or so it is hoped.

'Your Swordfish are carrying eighty per cent of the bombs on this mission, and I intend to use their payload exclusively to attack the enemy's army and their equipment, which clearly presents the greatest threat to us later. When they arrive, you'll all protect them, allowing them to press home their attack; with this in mind, remember you must conserve some ammunition for this purpose. When the bombers have completed their mission, those with ammunition left are required to stay with them and cover them as they return to the carrier, whilst the rest of you should get back as quickly as possible. The Hovertaks don't need to refuel or rearm, and so they'll remain over the city, covering your retreat and continuing the fight. The carrier will accept you when you return, where you'll refuel and rearm, at which point we'll return and follow more or less the same strategy. Whatever has happened at that time, the ships will be in range of the city and will add their guns to the attack.'

An undoubtedly sombre atmosphere had descended across the deck, with the faces of all pilots either grey with worry and anxiety or simply deflated with pessimism.

Lanter looked at the many men, and recognised faith was quickly depleting. 'Importantly, gentlemen, this scenario assumes the weapon has failed. Of course, it would be one Hades of a fight but, because of our shields, we can still win. Remember that.'

Lanter smiled as his men pulled their shoulders back and stood more upright, clearly listening to his message and readying themselves to fight the battle.

'Your secondary aim throughout, men, is to leave intact as many of Atlanta's facilities as possible. We'll need them later to take our campaign beyond Atlantis. Having said that, I realise that—particularly when you're under pressure in combat—the last thing you'll want to worry about is infrastructure. My message is simple, gents: don't destroy anything for the sake of it—that's all I'm asking. Essentially, however, the damage will have to be what it'll be to complete the invasion successfully. This is only the secondary objective.

'Now I'll move on and we'll consider what I'm actually expecting. There'll still be some resistance, I'm afraid; it's unavoidable. However, it's conceivable that the initial attack will defeat it. Possibly, that could be achieved even before the bombers and their escorts arrive. If this is the case, the whole theme changes, and we will then need to take prisoners and occupy the island. Nevertheless, we shouldn't need to smash everything up to achieve this.

'You can take heart for now because we're expecting to have more difficulty after the event. Clearing up the remainder of the king's forces and preventing him from reoccupying his homeland will be an undertaking greater than the invasion itself, believe me. After the invasion, the enemy will know how to counter our main weapon—and it won't be nearly so useful. I'm sorry to belabour the point, gentlemen, but if we retain as much of the infrastructure as possible at this point, we'll be massively stronger anyway because we'll have more to adopt. The greater the number of Hovertaks and the like we can produce, the less we will have to rely on anything else.

'Well, that's about it, in a nutshell. Let's now flesh out the bones together and get ourselves prepared.'

An hour into the pilot's briefing on-board Victorious, the modifications to the submarines were complete. They'd tested the new equipment, which seemed to perform to the resistance engineers' satisfaction and, keeping a small team of these people on each boat as a precaution, Galland was ready to put to sea.

Standing in the sail of U35, he looked around him at the furious activity still continuing unabated as the final preparations progressed. Sailors swarmed over the fourteen vessels, which were due to sail themselves in just two hours' time. They were surrounded by a multitude of smaller craft of all sizes, and still he witnessed the strange appearances and disappearances of men and equipment which had so fascinated him earlier.

In the fading light, oily smoke drifted from the ships' funnels, mixing with the light mist rising from the lake. Around them, the heady cocktail ever deepened the increasing darkness the approaching night promised. Galland could feel the anticipation in the air, and the shouting of sailors frantically preparing their ships echoed through the surrounding hills.

'We begin to look the part now, don't we, Joseph?' he asked his first officer who accompanied him in the conning tower. 'Let's hope we can act as well when it comes to it. This'd be a big operation under normal circumstances, but when you consider the number of unknown factors involved in this one... Well, quite frankly, it scares the crap out of me. The propensity of strangers with strange weapons working together for the first time boggles the mind. Personally, I'm glad we're off doing our own thing—at least we've only ourselves to worry about.' He glanced over at the many men, all shouting their chaotic requests and questions. 'I only hope our commanders manage to sort this lot out. I don't envy them in their task. Anyway, it's high time we left, Joseph. Even if these motors of ours perform as we're promised, we're still cutting it a little fine. I want us to intercept them—not have to chase them all over the bloody ocean! It's possible they'll have aircraft on patrol so when we leave the harbour we'll submerge and hope we can stay down until we get there. But if it hampers our progress, we'll have to abandon the idea and risk it.'

Back at base, Rema was standing with Cal Verta besides the Hovertaks, which were parked in the hangar beneath the hill adjacent to the factory. With the portal still open, they watched as the three submarines slipped their moorings, sliding peacefully across the lake, heading for the exit. They formed up in-line astern just before they passed Victorious. Slowly, they entered the narrow chasm between the cliffs, emerging into the outer bay a few minutes later. Two hundred yards across it, they applied half revolutions to their modified motors, appearing to all interested in their departure to have been kicked by a giant's foot. The U-boats' sterns dug deep into the water as the bows rose up on the waves created by their rapidly increasing momentum. The three submarines shot across the bay like startled greyhounds, disappearing in sheets of spray out into the ocean beyond.

Rema and Cal were mightily impressed, despite not being entirely sure how a submarine putting to sea should appear. The sailors watched from their ships on the lake and, despite having seen it many times before, nevertheless gazed open-mouthed in stunned disbelief.

Seaman George Jones, in spite of this dramatic sight, stood casually smoking a cigarette beside the rear gun turret of the Plymouth. 'Fuck me,' he exclaimed at the three submarines' spectacular exit. 'I'm glad the scary bastard things aint after us no more—look at the buggers shiftin'!'

Captain Bartlett watched the submarines departing from the other side of the turret, and smiled wryly upon overhearing George's comment, knowing he probably couldn't have put it much better himself.

'At last it begins, Cal,' said Rema wistfully.

'Not before time, Rema. Maybe it's the beginning of the end. It's the first time we've had a chance like this, but tomorrow will tell, of course. Let's hope it's the end of the beginning and we deliver a punch that rocks them to the core—and hopefully one they'll never recover from.'

'I pray to Ra you're right, Cal. It's a sound plan on the face of it, but if it goes wrong...' She shook her head. 'In that case, we've nothing in reserve, and that isn't exactly very comforting. To be honest, I don't much like the waiting; it gives me too much time to think about it all. Unfortunately, there's nothing left to do now except sit and worry until we fly off tomorrow. I'll feel differently then I'm sure.' Rema sighed contently. 'Imagine how good it'll feel when we join forces and become part of a major invasion! We'll be the pursuers this time, rather than the hunted—that'll make a pleasant change, I'm sure!'

'Quite,' responded Cal. 'I've been thinking about that myself, but I'm afraid I'm still concerned. We're so reliant on these people, aren't we? There's no doubt they can fly—we've already seen that over Kira—and their machines proved to be up to the job too. You say you want be part of their aerial fleet and soon you will be, but efficient aircraft in large numbers isn't always everything, you know.' He looked at the Hovertaks and back to Rema. 'The hands on the controls within those aircraft will determine how effective they really are. Okay, granted, numbers should help, but it's the minds controlling those hands, isn't it? And that's my worry.'

Rema nodded her head, acknowledging that Cal had a point.

'Unless you're a natural killer—which, let's face it, not many of us are,' continued Cal, 'you've got to have motivation to make you kill. It's one thing being forced to defend yourself, which might mean you've no choice, but it's quite another to become the aggressor and cold bloodedly set out to do it. And therein lies the problem: will they do what they need to do when the time comes? And what's to motivate them, Rema? What's going to drive them to do it for us, I ask you? We're asking a lot of them—and the fact remains, they've really had no time to prepare themselves for this.'

'You make a good point, Cal,' Rema replied with a light smile. 'But my faith rests on one belief, and that is, like us, they're warriors: it's what they do, what they're trained for. And remember: it was their decision to fight with us; they've accepted this is their world now and appear not to be overly impressed with the way its run either. I really believe they'll do it—and I think you can rely on that. I'm putting my life on it, and I'm not worried about their conviction, and neither should you be. They're good men and, in spite of your worries, I'm happy to fight with them.' She gave Cal a warm, confident smile. 'Anyway, it's too late to worry about it now—we fly at eight tomorrow morning. We're ready and the fleet will soon be gone. We've done all we can, Cal, so let's have a drink and get some much-needed rest.'

CHAPTER TWENTY

The Vale of Entatra, with her four sister beam weapon ships, was flying at fifty knots. Considering she was twice the size of an English battleship, it was an impressive sight to behold. The five huge boats were heading for the port of Atlanta, having been called back by their chief, Cesa Neda. Sea Master Toloy Lafteg was in overall command, and he lay back in his comfortable reclining sea chair, which was bolted to the floor of the armoured control pod, high up in the ship's superstructure.

The powerful vessels carried twelve beam weapons apiece located in six swivelling turrets, much akin to Rowsell's war ships. The weapons had an effective range of over twenty miles, and could reduce a large building to rubble with one easy bolt of energy from a single weapon. They required only five crew members to operate each ship owing to the fact that they were fitted with a machine in the control pod which operated every mechanical function on the entire vessel; however, as a contingency, ten crew were aboard each vessel. Taking the information from an array of sensors positioned around the ship, the machine used its artificial intelligence to apply the optimum reactions from the boats' systems to satisfy the commands of its human masters. Sea Master Lafteg, sitting comfortably in his seat, had only to voice his orders and the ship's brain carried them out at the speed of light. So far, this remarkable system had never failed him. Moreover, in terms of gunnery, the machine was awesome, calculating range, trajectory, deflection and number of given targets in a micro second. It was capable of hitting twelve different targets at varying distances and elevations simultaneously. As yet, Lafteg had not known it to miss anything he'd ordered it to attack; obliterating each target with the first salvo, he'd rarely needed another. Indeed, he'd found it more usual that, should there be more than twelve targets in the vicinity, the remainder surrendered remarkably quickly.

Sailing swiftly over a calm sea in the intermittent moonlight with his brutal leviathan beneath him, Lafteg was, as usual, feeling God-like. Neda had ordered him back to assist with the defences, but he was presently at a loss to understand why the man had seemed so concerned. Personally, he was hoping they would attack; nothing would give him more pleasure than squashing the puny resistance. The impudence of these people was beyond belief: they possessed a few small beam ships supported by a handful of stolen Hovertaks. Without question, the size of their army was a standing joke, and he was therefore confident his ships would swat them away like flies. In his opinion, the truth was that he'd easily manage with the Vale of Entatra alone—and it therefore came as something of a surprise to the pompous sea master when this fantasy was rudely interrupted.

The two sister ships sailing on his port side erupted and sank almost instantly in a welter of twisted metal, smoke and fire. Their forward momentum, aided by the enormous weight of the ships still being driven flat-out by their powerful engines, had caused them to be pushed remorselessly beneath the water as their bows vaporised. The wave created by their unexpected demise crashed over Lafteg's ship, obscuring his vision as it thumped across the windshields of the pod. As the water was cleared by the shield wipers, an even greater surprise lay in store for him: the other two ships of his fleet, which had been sailing to starboard, disappeared in much the same manner.

'Help!' he screamed at his inanimate subordinate, leaping from his chair in panic. His terror increased markedly when he realised the beam weapon turrets of his ship were swinging wildly, unable to locate a target. Desperately scanning an apparently empty ocean, he noticed five silver trails streaking through the water—heading directly towards his ship. And, whilst he had no idea what they represented, he recognised that they must clearly be significant. And, having expected his ship's brain to take evasive action against the obvious threat, it hadn't even occurred to him to intervene.

Seconds later, a shard of shattered windshield embedded itself in his temple. His final moments witnessed sheets of fire engulfing the ship, his eardrums bursting in the massive explosion. Although he could never have known the systems he trusted were incapable of recognising the unrecognisable, and were therefore incapable of dealing with such an unlikely situation, relying on these systems—which had notably proved invincible to date—had ultimately cost him his life.

'All surface!' ordered Galland on-board U35. 'We'll search for survivors before we leave the area.' High on adrenaline, he was delighted with the outcome of their attack—but, typically, would not add further to his enemies' suffering.

Since leaving Kira, Galland and his small fleet had made unbelievable progress courtesy of their modified engines. They'd found sixty knots submerged had been easily achieved, leaving them stunned by their boat's enhanced performance. Guided by the alien navigation system, they'd tracked the progress of the enemy ships since leaving the island. They'd positioned themselves ahead of their course twenty minutes earlier and, through their periscopes, the captains had watched the enemy approaching. They'd been forewarned by Lanter about the size of the enemy boats and the speed at which they were travelling, but to observe this was still unnerving—and even more so for the crew who, for the first time in action, could also see what was happening displayed on the screen in the control room.

Blissfully unaware of the danger awaiting them, the enemy formation had ploughed on, presenting to Galland and his fleet a relatively exposed, vulnerable target. The three submarines had placed themselves in-line abreast, facing the enemy. Moulder, aboard U79, had fired a spread of twelve torpedoes at the two ships on the left of the formation, whilst Gould, aboard U82, had fired the same pattern at the two on the right. Meanwhile, Galland had chosen to dispatch five torpedoes at the central ship. They'd planned the ambush with deadly precision, proving once again to excel at their chosen profession.

They'd swept away the opposition in a matter of minutes. Only one torpedo had failed to connect—and not a single shot had come their way.

Obeying their commander, the submarines rose from the depths and their crews searched in vain for survivors. Apart from miscellaneous wreckage littering the sea, there was no sign of life. Abandoning the fruitless pursuit, Galland radioed to Rowsell on Victorious, who was now well under way himself. Galland was momentarily surprised to receive the captain's congratulations before he ordered him to return to join the fleet: having watched the enemy ships disappear from his own navigation system, he was already well aware of the outcome.

Sailing from the scene, impressions of the nightmare they'd delivered invaded all their thoughts, causing the usual post-action soul-searching amongst a number of the crew. Putting the moral issues aside once again, Galland thought their role in the coming events would be even more significant following this victory, at least until the enemy was able to devise counter measures against them—and to do so effectively. No doubt they would eventually find some way to defend themselves but, until such time, the damage the U-boats would cause the enemy would be out of all proportion to their number.

CHAPTER TWENTY-ONE

Dawn was breaking, and the allied fleet was half way to their rendezvous when Lanter, who was working on the bridge of Victorious, became aware of a major problem. Looking worriedly at the lightening sky, he turned to Rowsell. 'Captain, I think we're about to be attacked. There's a large concentration of aircraft headed directly for us.' He'd been monitoring the navigation system and had observed the signature of the aircraft appearing on the map, which were now tracking quickly towards them.

'Judging by their numbers, they must have come from Mu. It would seem they've retrieved them before we'd anticipated, Captain, and now it unfortunately looks like they're using them to attack us.'

'How much time have we got, Lac?' asked the captain, concern creasing his forehead.

'If they continue on the same course, an hour at the most—and then they'll be right above us,' replied Lanter.

The enemy had strategically placed several large warships at intervals across the dead spot in the ocean between Mu and Atlantis. Feeding the power from their on-board generators directly into the grid, three hundred aircraft had been permitted to fly straight through in one huge formation. Although the chiefs had originally declined to risk this method, Sol Aharmer had persuaded his colleagues to try under the circumstances. Apart from a few heart-stopping moments for the pilots when the power fluctuated between the vessels, they'd made it through, which had enabled the chiefs to gain the use of the fighters to repel the imminent invasion. This welcome addition had now left all of them feeling considerably more confident.

'In that case, Lac,' Rowsell continued, 'I intend to scramble our fighters immediately; We can't risk them being caught on the deck when they arrive. I assume now wouldn't be the time to activate our secret weapon, in spite of this unexpected intrusion?'

'That's a tough question, Captain. Personally, I'd rather see whether the shields will suffice on their own without bringing out the big guns too early. It would undoubtedly prejudice our chances in Atlanta if we do. Damn the king's chiefs—we really could've done without this.'

'I won't argue with you there, Lac, but we've got to deal with it now, I'm afraid. I don't suppose they'll just fly over and give us a merry wave, will they?'

'Most unlikely, Captain!' Lanter smiled wryly. 'But we'd better reserve judgement until the battle starts. If we're being decimated, we've no choice but to expose our hand, don't you agree?'

'Completely, Lac. Now, let's get our planes in the air—at least we can't lose this one, whatever happens.'

Without delay, the captain scrambled the fighters. Their pilots, tousled and sleepy, struggling into flying gear, poured from their quarters, assembled beside the aircraft, shivering in the early chill.

'I wouldn't have signed on for this had they told me I'd have to go off at some ungodly hour, fighting the horrible foe without my eggs and bacon, Wing Co.!' Mark complained over his shoulder as he climbed into his Spitfire.

'Oh, I don't know Mark, nothing like a spin in the early sunshine to start the day, you know. Anyway, you were the one spouting off about bashing up his nibs earlier—now's your chance to put your money where you keep your mouth!'

'Well, that's as may be, but I'm a little short of brass at the moment and it's still disgustingly early,' Mark replied.

'Good morning, gentlemen,' Rowsell greeted his pilots. 'Unfortunately, there has been a change in our somewhat well-formulated plans. I'm sorry to say there's been a hitch, with the enemy now appearing to be one step ahead of us. Their aircraft are approaching as I speak, and will arrive in approximately forty minutes. I can tell you now: it's a large force. What I can't tell you is how large, but it's certain they significantly outnumber us. You'll be reliant on your shields in the first instance. You must remember their limitations—you can only sustain five direct hits before they diminish. Or, to put it another way, after each strike, it takes at least three minutes for the shields to recover their full strength. If you're suffering badly up there, we'll activate the secret weapon—but it's important you are all aware that doing so really is a last resort. With that in mind, assume we won't and put up the best show you can. When you're in the air, you'll see the enemy on your navigation system, but remember that the system can't tell you how high they are. That being the case, I suggest you use your vertical lift to attain as much height as possible before flying normally.' Rowsell looked from one pilot to the next. 'Good luck and good shooting. Remember: when they're in range of our guns, we'll also be firing, so don't get in our way. Your shields won't protect you from us.'

As they prepared to leave, the noise on the flight deck became unbearable. One hundred Merlins sputtered and barked into life, backfiring and running rough. As they warmed up, the armada lifted up into the watery sky. Captain Rowsell watched as they left, silently praying they'd all return, but knowing this was most unlikely. And then, with a small shrug, he left the deck and walked back to the bridge.

'How did they know where to find us, Lac?' Rowsell demanded when back on the bridge, frustrated his men were out to defend an attack without warning. 'We've seen no reconnaissance aircraft or shipping in the area. I thought they didn't have the capability to plot our position?'

'I'm afraid it's probably my fault, Sir. I arranged for Lara Freyr to steal one of our Hovertaks and escape as we left Kira. She was told to fly straight to the military airfield in Atlanta and report directly to the Chiefs of Staff. I've given her a sound cover story, and the fact she'd brought a much-needed Hovertak and important information with her should support it fully. I instructed her to tell them the fleet had left Kira and was making for Atlanta. Of course, at the time, I hadn't expected them to have these reinforcements available. Going on the information I had, I considered it to be a small risk; after all, if they'd had the resources, they'd have attacked us on Kira when they first discovered what we were going to do. Clearly, at that time, they intended to await us because, lacking additional forces, they'd no choice.' Lanter sighed deeply. 'I suspect what's happened, Captain, is that she's done as I requested, and because they've significantly increased their air force, it's changed their mind-set. They now obviously intend to wipe us out long before we can threaten them in Atlanta—and, from their perspective, why wouldn't they?'

Rowsell groaned and wiped his sleeve across his forehead. 'You possibly made a mistake, Lac, but we'd have had to face these aircraft sometime. As long as the shields are effective, maybe it's actually better out here. It's going to be crowded enough anyway around the city, and the damage that lot would cause falling from the sky would just add to the carnage.' He gazed out into the sky, contemplating the fate of his men. 'But, with that said, however, if it helps, Lac, I fully support your actions regarding Freyr anyway. Nevertheless, I still wonder how they found us so easily.'

'I don't think they've necessarily found us exactly,' Lanter replied. 'They knew we were coming, and there's not too many ways to approach Atlantis from Kira. And why would we take a circuitous route? From up there, they can see seventy miles in any direction on a clear morning like this. Taking a rough course, they'd easily find us then simply by looking. I actually think their present heading is purely coincidental.'

'Just our luck,' muttered Rowsell. 'Still, it is what it is. Let's cook the bastards.'

Up in the sky, the pilots got their first glimpse of the enemy.

'Oh my god! There's swarms of them!' exclaimed Jack as he saw the approaching Hovertaks appearing over the horizon.

'Marvellous,' laughed Mark.

'Oh fuck!' said Flight Sergeant Roberts, ignoring radio protocol. 'This is going to be interesting.'

'There they are, right on our present course.' Tult Taypor was in overall command of the king's Hovertaks. Having located the enemy, he marshalled his forces for the attack. 'If that's all of them, this should be easy. Pity we've lost the element of surprise, though. No matter, let's split them up. Adopt formation pattern ten and get in behind your flight leaders. And don't forget: we've been warned to expect problems with these invaders. That haze around those aircraft might well be one of them. Be cautious when you engage them, at least initially.'

The king's army began to shift position. Battle was imminent.

~*~*~*~

'This is it, chaps,' called Roberts, who'd taken overall command of this mission. 'Looks like they're splitting up already. Form squadrons behind your appointed leaders and we'll counter it.'

In their recent planning session, they'd nominated various pilots as flight leaders in order of experience. The nature of air warfare dictated that, although working as a team overall, they'd usually be flying in separate units. How big or small would be dependent on the circumstances facing them. Each pilot had established a pecking order right down to a pair, such as attacker and wingman. The ten most experienced pilots, with Roberts still leading, pulled their planes out of the pack and headed for the separate formations confronting them. Establishing who would attack which formation confronting them on the way, they ensured each had the required number of aircraft accompanying them. Without doubt, it would have been easier for them if the enemy hadn't split so many ways, but it was a credit to the airmanship of the allied pilots that they achieved it swiftly.

In ten opposing formations, the air forces met in a welter of bullets and bolts of purple energy. The orderly appearance disintegrated as the sky filled with hundreds of swirling, climbing, diving, twisting aircraft, their engines screaming and protesting. Pushing their machines to the limits and beyond, the pilots began to fight for their lives. In seconds, falling, burning, mutilated men and machines rained from the gigantic battle like autumn leaves, disappearing into the uncaring ocean below.

'Watch your tail, Wing Co.!' cried Mark as he fought off one of the Hovertaks pursuing Jack's Spitfire. He'd seen Jack's plane take three strikes already from the Hovertak he'd selected, and was relieved to see it blown apart in front of him as he hit it just behind the cockpit. Nevertheless, his friend was still beset by two more but, thanks to his assistance, was now able to evade them.

'Oh fuck, the bloody things!' Mark shouted when a sizzling bolt of energy spread across his shields, experiencing the now all too familiar tingling sensation that accompanied it.

'Thanks, old chap,' called Jack. 'You helped a lot there, but you'd better watch your own tail now.'

Mark smiled wryly as he saw he was now in trouble himself. Two Hovertaks suddenly appeared right behind him, the pilot of one appearing to be well-skilled with his energy weapon. His shield dimmed as he threw the Spitfire around the sky, frustrated at every turn by the nimble Hovertak's continuous sniping. Unable to shake off his pursuers using the tactics he knew, he decided to use one of their own against them. Ignoring the warnings he'd previously been given, he twisted sharply back on the throttle and engaged his anti-gravity system. The alarming flexing of the wings and the audible scream of tortured metal rising above the general cacophony told him he may have pushed his luck too far this time. The starboard wing tore off, spinning wildly away from his Spitfire, and the remains of his aircraft shook uncontrollably.

Now he knew for sure: his luck was running out.

Whatever he'd done purposely, he'd also unknowingly managed to switch off the anti-gravity system as his thumb involuntarily spun back the control. Adding to his troubles, his shield flicked off and the dismembered plane spun down towards the sea.

'Oh no, not him! Please, God, not him!' cried Jack, his eyes misting. An energy bolt struck him and he lost sight of his friend's death spiral. Reluctantly, he was once more committed to defending himself.

Beside himself at the loss of his friend, Jack flew like a man possessed. And, for the first time in his life, he knew the meaning of true hatred.

Killing three Hovertaks in as many minutes, he mentally spat on their graves. Fury dictated he expended prodigious amounts of ammunition on each kill. Not content with shooting them down, he literally tore them to pieces. Anger subsiding, he returned to the carrier to refuel and rearm, his heart hanging heavy inside him as he reluctantly departed the fight.

Meanwhile, Roberts looped at the top of a climb, setting up to swoop down and attack the aircraft below him. From above, he found himself looking down on the whole affair. He watched, fascinated, as the opposing air forces struggled to gain superiority. Generally, the Hovertaks were showing their lack of experience, making the same mistakes as the group he'd fought over Kira. These were costing them dear as his comrades—who were showing no mercy—regularly knocked them down.

The battle was escalating on the sea far below him. He watched several Hovertaks attacking the fleet. With the exception of the resistance vessels, Rowsell's ships were putting up an impressive barrage in their defence. He also noted they were gaining a few successes. Nevertheless, he felt for the men of Atlantis, trapped in their boats, forced to sit and take it, their shields in place, unable to use their weapons and unable to move.

One thing was clear, however: the enemy pilots didn't lack courage and were fighting like demons. Now, the only thing standing between them and success was the shields, which were glowing bright green around all the ships and most of the aircraft. The more hits the shields deflected, the brighter they grew, some fading suddenly as their power was exhausted. He was afraid that, once the enemy pilots realised this and concentrated on the clear machines, they would have the advantage in terms of number, which would ultimately result in a greater likelihood for the battle tide to turn. Praying the enemy would remain oblivious to the shields' downfall, he focused in on two Hovertaks, which were now chasing a Seafire, its shield looking a little clear round the edges. He poured a stream of bullets into the rear of one of the Hovertaks. He watched as the second Hovertak flicked onto one wing and screamed away, diving as he left, its pilot undoubtedly deterred after seeing his comrade blown to pieces.

Roberts remained in defence of his unshielded comrade until he saw the green haze returning.

On-board Victorious, Cal's wingman, Abdua Lorht, was acting as a lookout for the captain and Lanter. This duty had brought him close to his bright red Hovertak on the flight deck of Victorious, his eyes glued to the battle above, although he remained not entirely convinced he should've been left out, particularly as they'd gone to the trouble of distinguishing all the resistance aircraft with the bright new livery; nevertheless, as the battle developed, he saw the sense in his role. The captain had impressed on him the importance of noting the number of allied planes the king's men shot down, further qualifying the statement by telling him that, if fifteen allied aircraft were destroyed, they would need to radically change the strategy. Unbeknownst to him, the captain and Lanter had agreed to sacrifice only fifteen aircraft before they activated their secret weapon.

They were now ten minutes into the fight, and Abdua had counted only four allied planes lost at present. He'd tried to count the falling Hovertaks—although this was easier said than done in the chaos of gunfire and flashing purple explosions and raining shrapnel—but he predicted the figure to be around fifty. Also distracted by his audio senses, he soon realised the incredible noise of this battle was not restricted to the aircraft alone; in fact, just about every gun was in action around the fleet and the combined racket made any degree of concentration almost impossible. Coupled with this, he also noted his new allies seemed to have a propensity for blasting off with the ships steam whistles and klaxons at every opportunity. He could only think this extra racket was somewhat unnecessary given they were totally lost in the existing cacophony.

Suddenly, his heart lurched as he watched a Spitfire heroically defending a beleaguered colleague, whilst being chased by two Hovertaks. He neglected his duties completely when he saw it attempting one of his own manoeuvres. Instantly recognising the tactic, he dreaded the outcome. Sturdy as the Spitfire was, he knew it wasn't designed to cope with the stresses the sudden conflict of inertias would inflict upon it. Worse than that, it suddenly occurred to him that there were very few pilots so far familiar with this Hovertak antic—and only one he considered wild enough to actually attempt it during such a ferocious battle. His heart sank a little deeper as he watched, knowing but nevertheless hoping Mark, a man he very much liked and respected, wasn't in the pilot's seat.

Just then, without warning and just as he'd feared, the aircraft twisted and tore apart under the strain. The manoeuvre had succeeded insomuch as the Hovertaks flew straight under the doomed plane—but that was as far as it went. As the shattered remains spun towards the sea, Lorht willed the pilot to escape from the wreckage, hoping desperately he'd see the strange conglomeration of fabric and rope spread out above a tumbling body.

As he wished for a miracle, twelve Hovertaks attacked the carrier simultaneously. For the first time, he felt the heat of their weapons penetrate the shielding, which turned a sickly light green. The last two bolts went straight through and blew two smoking holes in the flight deck, one either side of his Hovertak. The shockwave knocked him from his feet and rendered him unconscious. Although the shield around the carrier was infinitely more robust than those on the aircraft, it was unable to withstand this massive onslaught.

'Captain, we'll not survive another attack of that magnitude,' called second officer Peter Turnbull, 'at least not until the shield's recovered a bit.'

'I'm afraid you're right, Peter,' replied the captain. Turning to Lanter he said, 'Lac, we'd better decide now what we're going to do or we could lose Victorious.'

'Captain, I have to say, this isn't going as well down here as I'd expected. The shields are good but they're not good enough to save our ships when they're being overwhelmed like this. The aircraft are faring better, but they can keep out of the way whilst they wait for their shields to recharge, and they have their comrades to cover them. Either way, they've already devised a strategy ensuring that's working well for them at present. The problem down here is that we can't avoid trouble like they can up there. Without our shields, we're sitting ducks in these ships.' Lanter sighed and rubbed at his temple. 'I know what you're asking, Captain, but if we use the weapon now, we won't stand a chance in Atlanta. If we show our hand now, by the time we reach them, they'll be able to counter it; not altogether admittedly, but what we're seeing now convinces me it'll be enough to beat us. I'm sorry, Captain, but the choice is this: we'll use it to escape this attack if it's your wish to do so, but if we do, we must abandon the planned invasion.'

Captain Rowsell nodded in acknowledgement of Lanter's recommendation.

'The only other option,' Lanter continued, 'is to use our aircraft to protect the ships until our shields recover. I realise that makes them more vulnerable as they'll have to abandon their current ideas and stay close to us instead... but it's an option.'

'I hear what you say, Lac. We'll try the fighters for a short time, as you suggest, but I'll not have them destroyed. If we allow that to happen, we won't be able to continue, and we'll have sacrificed them for nothing,' Rowsell stated.

Roberts had decided to implement the captain's orders by using half his aircraft to cover the ships, leaving the rest to further protect the defenders. As the shields depleted on the aircraft around the fleet, they switched places with their comrades. Having more flexibility, the high-cover aircraft were keeping their shields more or less intact; continuously, they reversed their roles as required. This simple concept by Roberts was proving to work remarkably well so far: his improvised strategy was not only ensuring the enemy was kept away from the boats, but they were also continuing to whittle them down, their own losses remaining insignificant.

Refuelled and rearmed, Jack re-joined the group of fighters covering the ships. He found himself flying next to Roberts as he entered the formation.

'We're holding them at the moment, James, but there's another lot about to hit the Arcadier,' Jack called to him.

'There's a surprise. Unfortunately, they've switched tactics as well—there's also a bunch heading towards Victorious. Take half of my fighters with you, Wing Commander, and cover the cruiser; I'll watch the carrier with the others.'

Dropping his port wing, Jack peeled his Spitfire away from Roberts. Calling ten of the team with him, he banked around towards the cruiser. The enemy was countering Robert's strategy by changing their own: now, they concentrated on the ships but had allocated a proportion of their number to protect them as they did so; this had reduced the ability of the allied pilots to conserve their shields as they were now all equally committed at both altitudes.

Looking around him, Jack could see most of the shields were looking decidedly wan.

Back on the bridge of Victorious, Turnbull turned to the captain. 'They're catching on, Sir. That little trick isn't working so well anymore. We're going to suffer pretty shortly, I reckon. I can't see many planes properly shielded now either, can you?'

'No, Peter, I can't but they've given ours a chance to recover. We'll call them off and they can go back to doing it how they were. It'll give us a better chance to use our weapons anyway with our own boys out of the way. Now they've bought us the time let's use it and concentrate on shooting down more Hovertaks for them. You never know—changing tactics again might throw them off a bit too.'

Waiting to depart, Jack breathed a sigh of relief as the new orders from Victorious came over the r/t. 'Thank God for that,' he whispered. Now released from the task of defending the fleet, he and Roberts lifted their squadrons, joining the secondary battle being waged above them.

As the captain had hoped, the unexpected appearance of twenty additional aircraft thrown against them confused the enemy. Better than he could have expected, it caused the demise of yet another fifteen Hovertaks, all of which had been busy with their own private battles and hadn't seen the reinforcements coming in. He'd also been proven correct in terms of his gunnery: between them, the fleet had knocked down five more enemy fighters in the determined attacks they made against the Arcadia and Victorious.

'By my reckoning,' said Lanter, 'we've destroyed over half of the enemy's aircraft already, Captain. The tide seems to be flowing with us at the moment. I think we may just get out of this if the trend continues.'

'I'm not so sure, Lac,' replied the captain, clearly concerned. 'Our fighters will be getting low on fuel, and a lot of them must be just about out of ammunition. They'll have to come in soon and replenish both. That'll only leave the few who've already been here on their own up there. The Hovertaks are constantly replenishing their fuel and ammunition from the grid, today such a scenario becomes an enormous advantage. Unlike here, in our world, we all share the same disadvantages. As we leave to rearm and refuel, so do our enemies. Granted, it's not necessarily commensurately, but more or less. Unfortunately, that can't be the case now, can it? As we leave for supplies, they'll obviously stay fighting, automatically becoming ever stronger as we grow ever weaker. We'll either have to wait and see what happens or we do something about it beforehand.'

'How much longer do you feel we can continue at this level?' Lanter asked.

'Mere minutes, Lac,' he responded. 'It can't go on much longer than that, I'm afraid. There's no doubt in my mind now; we're going to lose this one—and it's completely down to your peculiar power source which, ironically, has also preserved us up to now. Our pilots have fought like heroes, they couldn't have done better, but without fuel or ammunition, there's nothing more the aircraft can do. That then rather leaves it up to us down here—and we know we can't do it for long without them.'

'And just how long does it take to refuel and rearm a plane anyway?' Lanter asked. 'Surely it can't be that involved?'

'You're missing the point, Lac. It's really not about how long it takes to attend to one aircraft, is it? We've got that down to twelve minutes, which is pretty good going, and we can attend to twenty planes at once, which is also not unreasonable. But remember, Lac: we'll have at least seventy planes coming in within minutes of each other. We'd have to get them down, refuelled, armed and away again. We could probably turn twenty planes around in under twenty minutes. Assuming we actually manage to get the first twenty airborne again, we'll then have to resupply another batch, but the original twenty will have expended everything once more and be returning.'

'I see,' sighed Lanter, pessimism now creeping into his voice.

'Of course, in reality,' the captain continued, 'they'll have been wiped out long before—as I'm sure we will be too because we now know we can't stand the onslaught we'll undoubtedly be getting for that long, and we also have no aircraft defending us. The point is, we'll never again have more than twenty aircraft flying at once. We're buggered unless the enemy leaves us alone or we can defeat them with such a paltry number. And, although I'm sorry to say it, under the circumstances, that seems extremely unlikely.'

Bitterly disappointed but now fully appreciating their predicament, Lanter said, 'Alright, it appears we've no choice then. When the bulk of our planes disengage, we'll use the weapon—at least we'll destroy this lot, which I suppose is something. When we're done, we'll return to Kira and prepare to defend it—and may Ra help us after that. It looks very much like it's all over, Captain.'

With defeat in their eyes, they gazed across the flight deck of Victorious to the ships beyond, captured by the demonic abstract hung before them. Smoke and flames belched from the ocean. Showering brass cartridges flashed, reflecting sunlight as they skittered across dark steel decks, spat out by manic anti-aircraft guns. Demented aircraft whirled, glowing flack bursting amongst them, energy bolts and tracer darting between them, tearing at the blue backdrop.

Hanging surreal in the sky, a theatre audience of escaping pilots sat apparently unsupported in their seats, watching the performance and a flaming Hovertak disappearing behind Arcadia. It appeared far from over as they sadly watched thirty of their aircraft peeling away from the battle, banking towards the carrier.

'That's as far as we go, Captain,' Lanter said sadly, a dark expression painting his face as he reached for his communicator. 'It ends here. Your men deserved better from us.'

Grabbing desperately, it dropped from his hand as he was startled by thirty bright red Hovertaks passing the bridge at four hundred miles an hour, no more than thirty feet from where they stood. They screamed above the flight deck and blasted away at the enemy fighters, oppressing the fleet as they went by.

'Good God, Lac! Where the hell did they come from? This looks a little like the miracle I wasn't expecting! You might have told me help was on its way, man!'

'This isn't my doing, Captain, but Ra indeed appears to be with us! Let's hope they can make the difference now they're here.'

As they gazed in disbelief at the unexpected reinforcements, they heard petty officer Peirce's voice. 'I think that's just added another to our force, Captain.'

Looking to where he pointed, they saw Lorht's Hovertak rising from the deck, the pilot grinning happily back from the cockpit as he accelerated away to join his companions. One minute out from the carrier, he downed an enemy Hovertak which had sought to ambush Cal Verta, recognising instantly his oppressed aircraft by the markings his friend had applied recently to its fuelsage. Impressed with the way their new allies marked the victories they'd scored on their fighters, Verta had added a twist of his own; personally, Abdua found the twenty naked ladies with crosses through them slightly distasteful.

The resistance and their allies could now converse machine to machine, having adapted their respective systems to complement each other in all cases.

The new arrivals heard Jack's voice in their headset communicators. 'About bloody time! Would you lot be so kind as to assist us up here and stop mucking about with the captain's playmates? It's us that need the help right now!'

'Sorry, Air Marshall, we'll be right there,' answered Rema cheekily. In an almost vertical climb, she soared up to join the struggle above, followed by the rest of her flight.

And then another voice sounded through Jack's earpiece. 'I'll be right with you too, Mr Churchill.'

Jack's heart raced, his mouth open in shock, his eyes full of hope and excitement.

'Well, you'd better hurry up then, Mark, or there'll be nothing left for you to do up here!' said Tiea, flying resistance Hovertak Seven.

'Suits me fine, old girl,' he replied happily, as he rose through the carrier's shield in another new Spitfire, drawn from its reserves.

Jack barely registered the enemy Hovertak he had just targeted exploding before him as his eyes misted over with tears of relief. 'Mark... You gave me a bloody heart attack! Good to have you back, old boy!'

CHAPTER TWENTY-TWO

The three Atlantien commanders were gathered in the control dome of the airfield in Atlanta, listening in on the on-going battle. Delighted with the ability to reinforce themselves with three hundred additional aircraft, they'd instantly committed them all against the resistance and their allies, who were sailing in to attack them. Considering the immense firepower of the Hovertaks, they'd reasonably expected to annihilate the enemy and prevent any more trouble from that direction, once and for all. Like three excited children, they'd settled down to enjoy the show they'd put on. But shortly after, they resembled three worried old men.

'We're being slaughtered and I don't understand it! Taypor told us we outnumbered them at least three to one, but now he's pleading with us to pull him out. I can't believe he's lost two hundred aircraft already and, to top it all, the bloody resistance have now thrown in their own Hovertaks against him!' stormed Maltor.

'Like it or not, Rak, he's right. We've got to get them out of there—and fast. If we don't, we'll end up losing the whole fucking lot! I'll call them off now; it's suicidal to leave it any longer.' He banged his fist down on the table, anger coursing through every vein in his body.

Aharmer continued, frowning deeply. 'About all they've achieved out there is exposing the secret weapon we've been worrying about, and proving conclusively we can't deal with it. Those peculiar shields our pilots keep shouting about are the reason we're being decimated. When they get back, we'll need to study their visuals in the debriefing. Between us all, we've got to come up with something clever we can do about it in future—or there simply won't be one.'

'We've got about four hours, Sol,' Neda replied condescendingly. 'So we're going to have to be very quick! And I'd say it actually needs to be brilliant if we're to stand any chance whatsoever.'

When Aharmer ordered his Hovertaks back to Atlanta, he demanded Taypor to do so immediately.

'You can expect all seventy Hovertaks back over Atlanta within the next hour, Sir,' Tult replied.

Furious he'd lost thirty more aircraft in the brief time it had taken them to take a decision, Aharmer returned to the subject of the invasion, which they'd now failed to prevent. 'And where the Hades is Lafteg Cesa? He's long overdue—by an hour at least! I can't understand why he's not contacted us. Or perhaps more to the point: why haven't you raised him?'

'We've been trying to raise him for hours, Sol, but there's still no response. The last contact we had from him was when his ships passed north of Kira. He called in then for permission to attack it, actually,' replied Neda.

'Typical,' Maltor complained. 'At what point do you consider we should start to worry then? Keeping silent isn't exactly one of Lafteg's attributes. He should have contacted us by now and he hasn't, and I'm beginning to wonder if the resistance might be involved here as well.'

'It's just not possible they've destroyed them, Rak. There's got to be some other explanation,' Neda said, the tremor in his voice unmistakable.

'The Vale of Entatra and her type are, by far, the most powerful weapon carriers we produce. We know just how deadly they are. We helped to design the bloody things—they're virtually invincible! And this time, there were five of them sailing together.' Maltor considered his colleagues. 'If you choose to ignore the facts, then so be it, but let me tell you: it's not possible to defeat three hundred Hovertaks with only one hundred similar aircraft, but they just have. If we don't hear anything from Lafteg very shortly, I think we can safely assume the worst. And I'm sure I don't need to remind you both that, without Lafteg and his ships to support us, our position here becomes even more tenuous.'

'I think it would be wise to send a couple of Hovertaks to search for them, Rak,' said Aharmer. 'I'll order Taypor to send two from his flight. Maybe they'll clear up the mystery for us.' He contacted Taypor once again, ordered him to search for the Vale and her sisters, and gave him their last known position. 'I don't believe this, I honestly don't. This invasion's already turned into a complete nightmare. They've just destroyed two hundred and thirty aircraft and probably five of our most powerful ships,' ranted Aharmer.

'Ra only knows what they'll do when they get here then,' complained Neda.

'It's looking very bad, I agree, and I understand now why the cocky bastards think they can drive us out of Atlantis. But they've not finished us yet—not by a long way, Cesa,' replied Maltor. 'We've lost the first battle, but in doing so we've forced them to show us everything they've got. And they'll be pissed right off they've done it before they intended to. I suggest we be patient and see what our men bring back. They've downed some so I know we'll find a weakness somewhere.

'Quite,' Aharmer responded. 'In spite of all the new technology, they're obviously not totally invulnerable. What we've got to do in the time remaining is find out how our men secured these victories and duplicate their actions. Undoubtedly, they'll press on with the invasion now, but we've still got a few hours to play with before they can possibly get here.'

Maltor nodded. 'I'm confident this won't be a total defeat—at least not yet. We've flushed out their secret weapon, and I'm sure we'll find the answer to it. One thing's for certain, though: if they'd arrived here first, it could've been absolutely disastrous.'

'We've done it, Captain, they're leaving,' said Lanter, eagerly scanning the skies above the carrier.

'It looks like we have, Lac, and right in the nick of time. Those pilots will never know how close they came to foiling our plans and, of course, dying in the process. It was all much too close for comfort. It was all over—there wasn't even time left for the shouting when your aircraft arrived. But why did they come if you didn't call them in?'

'I really don't know, Captain. I suggest we ask Rema; no doubt she figured in it somewhere,' answered Lanter. 'Speaking of which, can we get her Hovertaks aboard now they're here?'

'I don't think so, Lac. We could probably take on a few but there's definitely not room for them all.'

After some discussion, they decided that Rema, Tiea and Cal, accompanied by Abdua, who was based on the carrier anyway, would be taken aboard, with the rest sent back to Kira. A more acceptable alternative than hovering above the fleet for the next four hours, they would return to meet the original schedule. Issuing their orders to the aircraft in flight, they relaxed: the invasion could now continue as first conceived, and they were delighted with the unexpected turn of events.

'What the hell happened, Mark,' called Jack as he ran across the flight deck to Mark, who was climbing down from his Spitfire. 'I thought you were gone—toast, buddy.'

'I'd rather not comment on that, old boy, if you don't mind,' replied Mark.

'Well, I saw you try that stunt,' Abdua commented. 'Why didn't you believe us when we told you your planes couldn't do it?'

'Oh God, bugger my luck. In all that bedlam I'm surprised anyone noticed, let alone someone who knew what he was looking at!' replied Mark sheepishly. 'Okay, so I tried to confuse them by stopping and letting them pass, but to be fair, I'd really nowhere else to go. My shield was almost gone and they were all over me. Quite honestly, I thought I'd little to lose at the time.'

'Well, if it's any consolation, Mark, I was tempted myself once or twice today. When what you know just isn't working it's hard to resist something new.' Jack shook his head. 'But, I know few of us would just go ahead and sod the consequences. Still, whatever's happened, I'm just glad you're still here.'

'Me too, Wing Co.,' smiled Mark.

'But how did you escape anyway? I didn't see your chute, and the last I saw of what was left of your kite, it was hammering downwards in several pieces!'

'Well, I couldn't open the canopy and jump because the damn thing was gyrating about so violently it kept throwing me back in the seat. But somehow, it occurred to me to try the anti-gravity thingy, and I discovered it was switched off. I spun up the power and the blessed thing only worked, which was quite remarkable. What was left of my poor old kite slowed to a halt just above the water and bobbed about a bit in the air. Admittedly, it was upside down, but I wasn't complaining, and then it wasn't long before the rescue boats from Victorious found me. Think you might say I'm one lucky bastard,' he laughed.

'You really are something else, Mark, make no mistake,' Jack said laughing. 'Oh and here come Rema, Cal and Tier. By the looks of it, they're the last ones to return.'

The three men watched as the Hovertaks lined up above the crowded flight deck and descended slowly, sandwiching themselves into the last available space. The distinctive high-pitched whine reduced to a murmur as the engines slowly wound down and the aircraft rested firmly on the deck.

Jack rushed over to Rema's Hovertak, first embracing her as she set foot on the deck and then kissing her passionately. Only slightly hindered by her helmet and headset, she eagerly responded.

'Thank you, Rema,' Jack said as they moved apart. 'You made all the difference turning up like that—and what's more, you probably saved all our lives as well. It was a brave thing to do, but it worked, thank God.'

Tiea approached Mark as Rema and Jack stood hand in hand. 'I don't suppose there's a space in your air force for me by any chance? I like the look of your debriefing methods, I must say!'

'I'm afraid it's obligatory, old girl; customary after every successful battle it is! Fancy trying it?' he replied outrageously.

Laughing, Tiea replied, 'Perhaps not right now, thank you, Mark, but maybe I could be persuaded later. Given the right surroundings and all that, who knows what might happen?' She gave him a teasing smile as her cheeks flushed a rosy pink.

'Well I for one am more than happy in my own air force thank you,' said Cal with a laugh.

The group broke out into laughter. Their relief that the first battle had been successful and was now over was tangible, and they were all pleased to be back on the ground, all of them safe.

In the wake of the battle, the fleet reorganised to continue the invasion. Having rescued the survivors and any flotsam they considered useful for spare parts, the fleet moved on. On Victorious, they concentrated their efforts on resupplying their aircraft as they sailed towards Atlantis.

On the bridge, the captain and Lanter were in deep discussion. 'We suffered unbelievably lightly, Lac, considering what they sent against us,' the captain began. 'We lost only two pilots, seven aircraft and had a couple of holes punched in the flight deck of Victorious. There was no significant damage inflicted upon the remainder of our fleet, and no other lives were lost on our side. The enemy, on the other hand, lost over two hundred aircraft—and we've retrieved one hundred and forty seven of their pilots, who now, of course, won't be flying against us anymore. By any standard, it was a resounding victory, which must, by now, be worrying the crap out of the powers that be in Atlanta.'

'I trust they're tearing their hair out, Captain, and it's not before time,' Lanter observed. 'It'll make a change for them to not be crowing after a battle. Nevertheless, having to fight them here may not have helped overall. The pilots are now tired and they're bound to be stressed—neither of which will make the next phase any easier for them, you know. For now, though, their heroic efforts have preserved the status quo. Our main weapon hasn't been compromised, and we're still virtually guaranteed to win the day in the end. And I suppose you're right in what you said earlier; there'll be less damage to the city caused by falling Hovertaks now.'

'It was an unfortunate episode in some ways, but we've learnt a lot from it. One thing being we so nearly lost everything in spite of the shields. Mercifully, we didn't thanks to our combined air forces. We know something else as well now: although our aircraft are a match for the Hovertak initially, in a long battle, we can't support them adequately—not from a carrier, at least. When this little show's over, I think the sooner they revert to a supporting role, the better.'

'Which is the plan anyway, Captain. When we take Atlantis, we'll have all the manufacturing capabilities we need. We can then produce as

many Hovertaks as we want—and any other weapons, for that matter—
and we'll have a pool of people itching to use them. In truth, at that
point, we'll only require your men and machines for very specific duties,
which, of course, is a subject we've touched upon already. When we've
consolidated our position, all your resources will be employed in a
supporting role. We know they're irreplaceable, and so it's vital we
preserve everything we have for as long as possible.'

The captain nodded. 'I'm as confident as you that we'll overcome
the first hurdle. But you'll need to move quickly when we've taken the
island: your king won't sit back and leave us alone to consolidate at
leisure, I'm sure of that, and in the meantime we'll still be very exposed.'

'Indeed he won't, but he'll need time to regroup as well, although I
agree that time will be of the essence. However, our new order has been
intricately planned, and so there's no reason to believe it won't function
swiftly. Once we've unseated the present incumbents, the transition will
be relatively seamless.'

'Quite so,' responded the captain.

'Although our aim is ultimately true democracy, we've structured a
system to serve in the interim,' Lanter continued. 'There will be freedom
of choice but, in the meantime, the people we've appointed will govern
Atlantis.

'As you're aware, on the war front, we'll be running that side of
things, which means, Captain, that we have the best leaders available for
that purpose also, don't you think? Concerning the fighting men under
us, we've recruited a significant number of the king's officers already
here on the island. They will subsequently bring like-minded troops with
them. The same applies within the civil police force.'

'I can't say that last bit fills me with confidence, Lac,' the captain
responded, concern apparent in his voice. 'If the whole thing relies on
servicemen who've been working for the king, I can see problems
arising.'

'Where their loyalties lie is an understandable concern, Captain, but
in any case, we're far from totally dependent upon them. We have our
own forces which we're currently using, and globally have a vast, though
passive, support. As I've already indicated, when we occupy Atlantis, we

expect a large number of volunteers—who will undoubtedly be willing but, of course, largely untrained. We need good people to redress this quickly, and that's how we view the officers and troops joining us here initially.'

'That still doesn't alter the fact that, from a military perspective, at least in the short-term, we're on a sticky wicket in Atlantis, Lac.'

'In the short-term, yes, I have to agree it's a possibility,' Lanter confirmed, 'but it's not as bad as you might think. We're not intending to wage a global campaign immediately. Until we're completely ready, the task is only to defend Atlantis itself. You'll need to remain in the front line, but only until we sort out a training programme for our forces which will allow them to replace you. The mechanics of the government and industry are a factor, but neither of these considerations will directly affect our defences. What's more, we'll still have the weapon which will continue to protect us all to a degree. In reality, once we control the island, it becomes reasonably effective again, simply because the king will need his ships to counter it. Commander Galland has just proved he's the answer to them but, Galland aside, we also know how vulnerable ships are to attack from the air—especially by shielded aircraft.'

Rowsell nodded his head.

'The fact remains, Captain, that when we've pulled this off, they'll have an impossible task in terms of reoccupying their homeland. I don't think they're capable of achieving such an undertaking with the means at their disposal as things stand at the moment.'

The captain took a moment to consider all Lanter had said, and finally nodded his head. 'Okay, Lac, I suppose I'm slightly happier with everything now, but we've wrapped around to the wild card again. Not having the means at their disposal will probably result in them developing something new,' he mused darkly, 'and we can be pretty sure what that something will be.'

'Unfortunately, Sir, it's almost inevitable and, as you say, that's the stumbling block in the whole affair. We've no defence against an antimatter weapon other than to destroy the facilities they're using for its development. Clearly, at the same time, we must also ensure we destroy any plans and remove the people working on them. If we leave anything behind they can revive, the problem will re-emerge. Later on, however,' Lanter continued, 'once we've taken the island, we'll need to deal with this threat immediately. We can't afford to delay, and we mustn't fail either or everything we've done so far will count for nothing. If we succeed, then what we face is a protracted war of attrition and it'll be a titanic struggle, I'm sure. But without question, Ra willing, we'll eventually prevail,' he predicted.

'Well, if we get that far, I'm sure you're right—providing you're offering something better and you stick to your principles along the way. In such a scenario, I can't see you doing anything other than getting stronger all the time.' Rowsell eyed Lanter questioningly. 'But another thing, Lac, leaving aside the military and global issues for a moment, what *are* you offering the people on Atlantis?'

'In a nutshell, Captain, freedom to control their own destiny with minimum interference from the state.'

'Only Utopia then, Lac?' Rowsell smiled. 'I can't see them going for that, you know!'

'Sarcasm, Captain?' Lanter grinned. 'I'm sure support from the populace will be very strong once the king's out of the equation. Our goal is to reverse the king's policies and re-establish the old order. We'll set free all those imprisoned unfairly by the king and provide help and support for all of them and their families. The issues of destitution and poverty will be speedily addressed.'

'Not an easy task, you know, Lac,' Rowsell observed.

'Of course not, but necessary, nevertheless,' Lanter countered. 'Although circumstances dictate we service our war machine, where possible, output will be switched to provide a better standard of living for the general population. Almost without exception, the independent manufacturers support us, whereas those who don't will be given payment in full for their facilities before we replace them. We'll return the businesses the king stole to their original owners, removing his puppets in the process. The debts fraudulently imposed upon the general population will be forgiven, and any monies due will be returned to them through the king's bank, which we'll subsequently continue to operate ourselves with more acceptable terms. As soon as it's practical, our society will revert to a free and fair electoral process, and the systems of justice will be completely overhauled. I don't expect it to be without its problems, of course, but we've been planning the occupation for years. Now we're ready to take it on.'

'It sounds very like you're aiming at a government for the people by the people, Lac—and God help you with that one.'

'You continue to be rather negative, I feel, Captain—but time will tell I suppose. In spite of your views, I think you'll soon find we've a plan to achieve it. After all, we've enjoyed it once and we shall enjoy it again.'

'It's not that I'm negative, Lac,' smiled Rowsell, 'rather, realistic. They're noble goals, and I'd love nothing more than to see them achieved. But I'll just wait and see.'

'We're comfortable with our plans to govern Atlantis. We were uncomfortable with the plans we had to conquer it. The truth was, we simply didn't have the military might to successfully invade in the first place, which is something of a disadvantage, wouldn't you agree?' Lanter smiled light heartedly. 'Covertly, we've been invading it for years, of course, which is why we're confident of the infrastructures we propose being acceptable, and also why we have the people in place ready to take them over. To be honest, it's a slow, frustrating and rather obtuse approach which doesn't begin to compare with what we're doing now. But, the fact remains that the events of the past few weeks have provided the complete solution. Without question, the presence of you and your men here is what we needed to complete the jigsaw.'

'Politics, politics, politics, Lac,' Rowsell laughed as he dismissively waved away Lanter's views. 'And no matter how hard I try, I just can't seem to become that enthusiastic, I'm afraid. However, speaking as an irregular shaped object forming a small part of the picture, I've a battle to fight for you. And, taking account of our coordinates, I'm getting very close to launching it.'

As things currently stood, the fleet was an hour from the rendezvous point. Galland had contacted Victorious, confirming he was on schedule, and the Hovertaks on Kira were preparing to depart once again. The aircraft on the carrier were ready for action, and the pilots sat in the ready room, speculating upon the reception they could expect above Atlanta. Spirits were high following their recent victory, and they were confident in their shields now they'd established a tactic to support them.

On the troopships, the soldiers also yearned for the opportunity to show their mettle. They'd not appreciated cowering under the shielding whilst being bombarded by the king's planes; only the lucky few allied soldiers who'd supplemented the ships' guns with suitable weapons of their own had been in action, with the rest left to observe and pray.

CHAPTER TWENTY-THREE

'We've got the answer we needed,' Neda said. 'All we have to do now is concentrate enough firepower on those shields and they'll fail. The visuals prove beyond doubt we can overcome them if we adopt this strategy, so providing that's what we do, we won't be beaten again. The trick, of course, is how best to achieve it.'

As Maltor had suspected, when they'd debriefed their pilots and studied the visuals they'd brought with them, a pattern had emerged. Having finished with their pilots, they'd dismissed them and were now alone in the debriefing room, putting the final touches to their defence, bolstered by the discoveries they'd made.

'Thank Ra we attacked them when we did—this proves it was well worth the sacrifice. They'll be highly disappointed now when we pound them into oblivion. We'll be rid of the whole bunch of them, and we can get back to our missions elsewhere,' Aharmer cried triumphantly.

'I agree, it's certainly looking considerably better, but as Cesa says, we've still got to do it somehow. I think you may be a little premature in assuming it's going to be that easy. They're bound to hurt us badly in the process anyway if you think it through. Take, for example, the scenario in the air,' Maltor speculated. 'The air force has no choice but to allocate at least two aircraft to attacking each one of theirs to guarantee the firepower required to break their shielding. It's difficult to be certain, but I'm thinking that will give them slightly better odds when you compare the number of aircraft we each have available.

'What's more, we know our shore batteries have an effective range of four miles, but we don't know the range of the weapons their ships carry. If we have to pull back because their range exceeds ours, that's another advantage they'll have. If it turns out they have these advantages, it's probable they'll reduce our air force and shore defences fairly rapidly. Nevertheless, we can reasonably expect to reduce their air force dramatically in the same period; at that point, we'll probably remain more or less equal. At some point, though, they've got to put their army ashore; they can't achieve everything from the sea and their airpower will be savagely reduced.

'And of course, in our favour, we have forty thousand troops armed to the teeth and waiting to repel them. Unless they've shielded each soldier—which seems unlikely—we'll clear them faster than they can bring them in.'

Neda looked unconvinced. 'The fact remains, if we'd had the Vale and her fleet here, we wouldn't be faced with any potential losses, they'd never even pass go. Sadly, that's not the case.'

'A fact which obviously didn't escape their notice, Cesa,' continued Maltor, 'but we know they're not coming now. The flotsam our pilots found was in approximately the right location, which can only mean one thing. I know it rankles but you'd better get over it. It'll be expensive but, one way or another, we'll defeat their army today—and the majority of their air force as the icing on the cake. However, I'm expecting their ships and possibly a few aircraft will escape. I doubt we'll finish this completely here. But no matter. When our reinforcements arrive, we'll attack their cursed island and drive the remains of them out of there.'

Aharmer continued. 'The resistance has forced the issue this time, though naturally, of course, this isn't the route we'd have chosen. Regardless, their actions have placed them within our focus, and, as you say, Rak, we won't back off again until they're history. I'm sure when this is over the king will command us to do it anyway—which, looking on the bright side, makes it a whole lot easier than before when he was refusing to listen.'

'It does indeed, and they'll rue the day they started this. But the bastards have already given us a beating, which I don't appreciate, especially not when it involved sinking our capital ships and costing us an unacceptable number of Hovertaks. And what's worse is that we've clearly more to lose before this is over.' Anger flamed in Maltor's eyes as he spoke. 'Without doubt, those who perish here today will be the lucky ones. In future, I intend to kill every remaining resistance member or sympathiser as slowly and agonisingly as possible. Never again will anyone dare to challenge us like this—that's a promise, and I'll it carry out without mercy.'

'You'll have to join the queue, Rak, but we'd better deal with one thing at a time. Right now, I'd like us to speak further with Lara. Thanks to her, we're in a much better position than we would have been otherwise. Arguably, it's still not particularly enviable, but without her information, we'd have been caught napping. She was on Kira right up until the last minute—and it's possible she knows more yet,' Neda speculated. 'She might well have seen or heard something useful and not even realised it.'

With the three in agreement, they sent for Lara.

She was nervous as the chiefs' aide led her to the trio, having by now convinced herself they'd rejected her story. Abandoned in a bleak little room for over two hours, the uncertainty had played hell with her emotions. When she'd arrived in Atlanta, the deception she'd planned with Lanter had gotten off to a good start. The guards, who surrounded the Hovertak when she'd landed, were led by an officer who'd worked at Amis's research laboratory at the time she was there. The man recognised her, which had helped enormously, and as she'd requested, immediately took her to meet with the chiefs.

During their meeting, she was confident they'd accepted everything she'd told them. Indeed, regarding her escape in the Hovertak, they'd become quite complimentary, recognising that the resistance had lost a valuable asset. Furthermore, they had also recovered one of their stolen aircraft. But they'd become somewhat agitated when she'd told them the allied fleet were at sea and heading to invade them, and were due to arrive off Atlanta in a few hours' time.

Having delivered this valuable information, the chiefs cut the meeting short. Leaving hurriedly, they'd ordered her to stay put until they could resume the discussion. Since then, she'd been left alone with her thoughts.

'Firstly, we wish to compliment you on your escape, Lara. The information you've brought to us has proved invaluable,' Maltor commended as she entered the control room. 'Thanks to your information, we located their fleet well out at sea and, as you've said, it's beyond doubt they were intending to attack us today. It also appears the shielding you'd heard them discussing does exist, although not in the form you'd imagined, and so were right about that too. Fortunately—but at great cost, I'm afraid—we've now discovered what they meant when referring to *shielding*. In the light of which, I'd like to establish whether you've seen or heard anything else which might also be as significant. For instance, did you see the green haze surrounding their ships as you left, or did anyone pass comment on anything as remarkable?'

'No, Chief Maltor, I didn't. That's the shielding I heard Lanter referring to? I told you before what I thought at the time. I assumed he meant increasing their armour in some way. Does this green haze have the same effect?'

'Similar, Lara, but I'm asking the questions and I don't want to stray from the point. Please, let's go through once again what you heard in the factory, and this time include every detail—even if it makes no apparent sense,' Maltor commanded.

'As you wish, Chief Maltor,' Lara replied. 'I'll do my very best. As I said before, I overheard Lanter speaking with Rema Sark as they passed close to my hiding place. As I waited for the opportunity to steal a Hovertak, they were checking the aircraft together and discussing the invasion. He was talking to her about shielding their allies' war machines, and I remember now I heard him say it wasn't possible to do the same for their troops. He also mentioned they'd have a major problem if you discovered their weakness, but thought it unlikely you'd work it out in the heat of the battle. He also felt that, if you did, it would probably be too late to review your tactics quickly enough to change anything anyway.'

'He wasn't far wrong in that either, the smug bastard,' Maltor spat. 'Even though, thanks to you, we were prepared for something, we couldn't do anything about it, of course.'

'Luckily, it only took losing two hundred Hovertaks to find out,' Aharmer whispered to Neda sarcastically.

Lara continued. 'There are a few things they said which I haven't mentioned, but they were moving away and I only caught snatches of their conversation. However, if we reconsider this verbatim, it may mean something to you.

'Lanter said, "Due to the nature of the weapon, we must call off the invasion if…" at which point they both turned and walked away along the next line of aircraft. But I heard him mention "beam weapon carriers" followed shortly by "not much chance of failure" and, a little while later, "provided they're nowhere near Atlanta, essentially, I expect this battle to be very short indeed". He could still have been pursuing the same subject, I suppose, but I can't guarantee it; obviously I missed a large part of the conversation, and the remainder was so disjointed it made little sense, but I simply couldn't get closer without risking my position.' Lara paused, considering the situation.

'One thing I did hear more clearly,' she continued, 'was Sark commenting that "the mopping up undoubtedly raises more problems for us than the invasion", which seemed to be a strange thing to say. He responded by emphasising that the king's men would be demoralised by their weapons being "negated"—although I'm not certain on that point—and that there would apparently be little resistance following the event. It was then that they were called away. Obviously, there is a lack of clarity considering what I could and could not make out, but I would say, without question, they're confident.'

'It might have been helpful if you'd tried to remember snippets of conversation at the time, Lara,' Aharmer said coldly.

'I'm sorry, Chief Aharmer,' she replied, 'but at our last meeting, you didn't give me much time to gather my thoughts.'

'It all sounds rather ominous, if you ask me, Lara. However, are there any other items you noticed that could possibly give us a lead? Is there anything new or peculiar at the base perhaps, or on any of the ships?' Maltor pressed.

'I saw nothing untoward in the base, but there's one possibility,' she further commented. 'As I flew here, I passed the enemy ships approximately three miles out from Kira. I caught a glimpse of a machine on the allies' flagship which hadn't been there before. It didn't look anything like the other machines that surrounded it, and it definitely wasn't there when they arrived. But, aside from that, I don't think I can tell you anything more that I haven't already.'

'One crucial point to query, Lara, going back to Lanter's words, is whether he made reference to weapons plural or weapon singular... Think carefully before you respond.'

'He said "weapon", singular, Chief Maltor; there's no doubt in my mind.'

'Thank you, Lara,' replied Maltor. 'Now should you remember anything else of importance, please ask my aide to bring you straight to us; you may interrupt us at any time. In the meantime, we must get back to the work at hand.'

Leaving her alone once more, the chiefs relocated to the control dome at the airfield from where they'd previously decided to direct their forces.

'Maybe we should have questioned her in more detail, Rak,' commented Aharmer when they'd settled in. 'Although I suppose the bulk of what she told us then only makes sense now we know what their shielding comprises. But I'm still concerned.'

'The fact remains that, on the face of it, they're hopelessly outnumbered. What's more, they obviously realise their shields are fallible, yet they continue to come against us. Reason would dictate they're all going to die here—and either they've completely lost their senses or, as we suspect, we're missed something vital, and it's actually *us* in that terrible predicament. Nevertheless, it's essential—critical, in fact—that we are as prepared as possible. I suppose we've done enough—although I suppose we could have done more. But, it's too late to change anything now, so we'll stand or fall with what we've got.'

Maltor's colleagues nodded bleakly.

'And as I said, preparation is key here. With that in mind, if the resistance is prepared to face what would appear to be impossible odds— and if we are beaten—then winning would never have been possible, but we'll know we did everything we could. If they've a weapon we can't defeat, we'll lose—but in such an instance, it may not be impossible to save ourselves. Therefore, I suggest we plan our own evacuation in the short time we have remaining.'

The two men seemed to look optimistic immediately, and nodded in agreement.

'I'm in favour of devising such a plan,' Aharmer replied.

'Good,' Maltor responded. 'Our Vertlyn is ready, Rak, as always. Are we not to escape in that if it comes down to it?' Neda asked.

'Possibly, Cesa, but it's a weapon of sorts; we've modified it hugely and provided it with armament. All the warnings we've received point to negating our weapons. Does that mean just the weapon systems or, if they're mounted on a machine, is that included as well? It's just possible, and if that's so, it won't work period, which means we'll be stuck here if that's all we're relying on,' Maltor replied.

'That applies to just about every other vehicle we pick as well, Rak, unless you intend to sail away in a private yacht,' Aharmer retorted.

'I hope it doesn't come down to that, Sol. If the Vale wasn't able to resist them, it'd be a very poor choice.' Maltor contemplated quietly for a moment. 'No, what I'm considering is the king's Argotak. It's parked with the others under the palace—loading his bloody treasure at the moment, as it happens—which makes it readily available. We'll make sure it doesn't leave until we see what develops. There are two good reasons in my mind why it may be our answer: firstly, it's clearly not a weapon, and so it's conceivable it could remain unaffected; and secondly, it can fly across the dead zone straight to Rammath.'

'You seem to be forgetting, Rak, that the dead zone's no longer a problem. Our ships are covering it with their on-board generators. I take the point regarding the weapon, but the Vertlyn could fly there just as easily now,' Aharmer reminded him.

'But are you sure about that, Sol?' Maltor countered. 'We haven't heard anything from them, like our beam weapon carriers before. I'd rather not risk it after that. Essentially, we have to consider the worst case scenario; whilst I hope it's not going to be necessary, we still need to give ourselves every opportunity to escape if it comes down to it. I suggest that, should it become apparent at any point that we're going to lose, we grab Lara, board the king's plane, and try to reach Rammath. We can then regroup our forces from there.'

'If the resistance don't kill us, the king definitely will, Rak. You do realise this, don't you?' Neda asked. 'We should send his aircraft away now before they're caught up in all this and find another solution. If he finds out we held them here when we could have got them out, Ra knows what he'll do.'

'Well then he mustn't find out. Now, get one of your tame air arm fitters out there, Sol; he'll find a problem with the plane if we ask him to—one requiring immediate attention. That'll explain any delay and we'll flesh out the tale later if we need to.'

'Sounds good to me, Rak—but why do we need Lara now?' Aharmer asked.

'You're not thinking this through, Sol. She was involved with my friend Amis who, I might add, thought the world of her abilities. If the resistance really have come up with a rake of super weapons, we need some of our own pretty damn quickly. I think she's the one we need to help Amis resolve his problems with the antimatter project. In the absence of our own super weapon development programme—which we don't have because, up until now, we haven't needed it—it's actually the only thing we can develop in the immediate future. Nevertheless, it's awesomely powerful and is the obvious place to direct all our resources anyway, don't you agree?'

'Without question, a powerful new weapon which our enemy can't resist will be urgently required if we lose Atlantis. If that happens, using the ones we've got, we're obviously buggered in every other direction.'

'I hope you're right about where we should be directing all our resources, Rak. The weapon you're talking about is highly dangerous; naturally, that would be absolutely wonderful—provided you're sure it will only affect our enemies. The fact remains however, that although it's potentially all powerful, it's also potentially very unstable. It could easily damage a lot more than just them if you intend to use it—like us, for instance.'

'Rather than be beaten by this rabble, I'm prepared to risk that, aren't you?' Maltor replied savagely. 'Anyway, this is a discussion for the future. Right now, I'm duty-bound to inform the king of everything that's occurred this morning—and what we're doing about it. It's still very early in Rammath, but he'll have to get up for this one.'

As he'd suspected, when Maltor contacted Rammath, the king was nowhere to be seen. Upon experiencing the usual trouble when encouraging anyone to disturb him, he resorted to threats. After considerable delays and obstructions, which had notably raised his temper to boiling point, he finally spoke with an equally bad tempered king, who he'd aroused from his bed. Never the best company in the mornings, His Majesty was excelling himself with his vile temper from the outset of their conversation.

'How dare you disturb me at five in the morning, Maltor! You'd better have a very good reason for this,' he ranted. Before Maltor could reply, the king continued. 'What the Hades is this? There's a message here from my pilot stating his on-board generator wasn't required as the grid provided sufficient power without it. Why did you not tell me we could fly direct to Atlanta using any of our aircraft? There was no need to send my Argotak back with the other transports, and you must have known that when I informed you of my intentions! If I'd known this I'd never have sent it back! What's more, he also tells me now it's stuck there with a mechanical problem. Should anything happen to my aircraft, Maltor, I'll be holding you personally responsible!'

'Your Majesty, firstly please accept my grovelling apologies,' Maltor began. 'We're beset here at the moment, which is occupying all our attention. In theory, you'd have got your transports and fighters through without it, but we're only relying on a temporary set-up using our ships to feed the grid. It's possible this method could fail, and so I considered it a risk we shouldn't take. I'm sorry that I didn't inform you of this, but it's a small matter compared with our problems here.'

'*I'll* decide what should and shouldn't be considered a small matter, Maltor,' the king bellowed, 'especially when it concerns my property! You seem to forget with whom you're dealing, man. You're getting way above your station adopting that attitude with me. I demand your immediate apology!'

'For Ra's sake! Shut up, man! And for just once in your life, listen!' Maltor groaned without restraint before continuing. 'We're in terrible danger here, and we demand your cooperation—not a shitload of unhelpful ranting. If you won't discuss sensibly our position here and support us, you can stick your jobs up your arse and we'll join the resistance ourselves!' Already on the edge, Maltor had now completely lost his temper.

'Oh my Ra, you've gone and done it now, Rak,' whispered Aharmer, his head in his hands. No one had ever spoken to the king in that kind of manner, and Maltor's colleagues now dreaded the consequences, particularly as Maltor had indicated their consensus. The fact they did was probably beside the point, but they nevertheless wished the man had been a little more circumspect.

Immediately, fire spread through the king's veins. His emotions in turmoil, he couldn't speak. He struggled to take in breaths and fought back the desire to smash the communicator into his desk. With enormous effort, he forced his emotions back under control. A brooding calm descended.

Realising the situation in Atlanta must be dire for Maltor to speak to him in this manner, he suspected it would become pretty serious for him in the longer term—and the notification of such he was grateful for. Under the circumstances, this presented him with a dilemma. On the one hand, whilst he barely considered Maltor's threat to join the resistance, knowing they'd be the last people on earth who'd want him, on the other hand, he could end up starting his own movement—and possibly taking the other chiefs with him—the damage of which could be enormous. Unfortunately, with the situation as it was, there was no one left in Atlanta with the power to arrest him and prevent it, which further limited his options.

Nevertheless, the king realised that, if he allowed Maltor get away with this, he'd lose face with them all. More importantly, his power over them would be badly compromised. He'd lost his temper, of course, but he'd nevertheless commanded his own king—the most powerful being, the ruler of the highest stature—to shut up. Any insult directed against him constituted a capital offence, in the king's opinion. Normally, he'd execute any man foolhardy enough to deliver one without hesitation. But these weren't normal times, and Maltor also wasn't just any man. The king came around once again to the crux of it all, acknowledging and understanding that he couldn't do without him—or the other chiefs, for that matter. At least not yet.

In the end, the king, whilst bitterly regretting allowing these men to become so powerful in their own right, decided that any actions taken immediately would probably be a mistake, and so postponing any decisions in this arena would be wise. With this in mind, he carefully delivered his reply. 'Maltor, I'm prepared to forget what you've just said. I must assume the situation is graver than we could have conceived and, owing to that, I'll accept your apology this time, but take heed of my warning, Maltor: if you *ever* speak to me like that again, I promise you: you will be executed, irrespective of the circumstances. Whether you like it or not, I am your king, and I demand your unquestioning loyalty and respect at all times.'

'Your Majesty, I offer to you my full apologies and assure you I am your loyal servant as ever. But, as you will appreciate, the fate of our island hangs in the balance which, in my defence, has clearly affected my judgement,' Maltor replied penitently.

In his mind, of course, Maltor was certain this would not end the matter, even if the king was prepared to, which was nevertheless unlikely.

Putting his future relationship with the king to one side, he went on to explain their precarious position which, although deeply upsetting to His Majesty, didn't surprise him unduly. Forewarning him of the potential outcome of this invasion, his uncanny instincts had already removed him from danger, but Maltor had now confirmed his worst fears.

Approving the defences his chiefs had put in place, he then insisted they evacuate to Rammath, preferably sooner rather than later should the situation become hopeless, offering them his Argotak for the purpose he thought would be prudent; since it was apparently unable to leave immediately anyway owing to the repairs it required, the king had lost nothing by attempting to appease Maltor. However, he was blissfully unaware that, by commanding they evacuate the treasure transports concurrently, he had negated his largess towards them somewhat in the minds of his Chiefs of Staff.

CHAPTER TWENTY-FOUR

'**O**h dear, looks like there's a storm brewing over Atlanta, Wing Co.,' Mark said with a light whistle. 'Maybe we should wait until those black clouds disappear; I'd rather not get too soggy.' Mark flew to take up his position in the attack formation as he referred to the clouds of Hovertaks already occupying the skies above the city.

'Don't forget your umbrella then,' replied Jack, who was also eyeing up the opposition. Looking closer to home, he saw all the bombers rising from the carrier's deck. The fighter bombers' sleek lines—although interrupted by the bulbous bombs, hanging beneath them—appeared a more serious adversary than the open cockpit biplanes, disregarding the fact their bomb load was actually considerably lighter. Considering what they faced, and even allowing for their shielding, flying these archaic looking aircraft, in Jack's mind, was possibly not the best position to be in right now.

Reflected sun flashes striking from a contingent of aircraft far beneath, swiftly approaching the fleet, attracted his attention. Startled, he recognised them as Hovertaks. Automatically, he banked his Spitfire towards the perceived enemy. He relaxed when he saw their red livery, realising the aircraft had returned from Kira. The scene spread out beneath him was again surreal. With some difficulty he suppressed the desire to dismiss it all as a bad dream. He was, by no means, alone in this; the combination of alien geography and technology he found so difficult to accept played on everyone's minds.

'Colourful little bunch, we are, Wing Co.,' commented Mark. 'Slightly unusual to look at, though. No matter, a fight's still a fight, I suppose—and no doubt we'll all pull together when the time comes.'

The respective flight commanders were busy marshalling their aircraft. Jack was in overall command and directly leading the fighters whilst Rema controlled the resistance Hovertaks. Flight Sergeant Roberts commanded the fighter bombers, and Flight Sergeant Evans was responsible for the Swordfish. Everything that could fly was now airborne and all were, hopefully, in capable hands. When the leaders had assembled their respective formations, they left en masse towards the city. The fast flying fighters and fighter bombers soon left the slower Swordfish and their Hovertak escorts far behind.

~*~*~*~

On-board Victorious, Captain Rowsell was speaking with Galland over the r/t.

'Commander, you will take your force and attack the enemy patrol boats. As you'll notice on your screen, they've moved them out of the harbour. It would appear they're fanned across the entrance, approximately two miles out. It's just possible the two largest ones may present a specific problem to us; it's therefore vital you destroy those first if at all possible.'

'Understood, Captain.'

'Go in and plough the field for us, Commander. When you've wiped them out, withdraw and report back. However, if any of them retreat into the harbour, don't follow them—we'll deal with them later. Inside, you risk being damaged by our own air forces. Remember: your shields won't protect you from them.'

'Yes, Captain,' Galland replied.

'Furthermore, since you can't realistically attack anything on shore,' Rowsell continued, 'you've completed your mission when you've destroyed those boats or they've entered the harbour. I won't expose you to unnecessary danger, and we'll call upon your services again when the main show's over. If, however, the invasion fails, it's likely you'll be on your own. Since you're quicker than anything else on and the only things which can travel under the water, you'll almost certainly escape. In that event, you've no choice but to look after yourselves. There will be no resistance left to support worth mentioning, and the few remaining on Kira will destroy everything there immediately upon knowing it's all over.'

'As you command, Captain,' Galland confirmed. 'We'll leave immediately, but I'm confident we'll all come through this. I believe, as our allies have indicated, the weapons we carry will ensure the best result from this invasion.'

'Good luck, Commander,' Rowsell said finally, before ending communication. Turning to Lanter he asked, 'So do we have progress?'

'The first wave is successfully away, Captain,' Lanter replied as he watched the retreating aircraft grow small in the distance, followed by Galland's submarines, which disappeared beneath the waves. 'The fighter bombers and their escorts will attack in approximately ten minutes and, from then on, we must keep the enemy under constant pressure.'

'We'd better get away ourselves then, Lac. By the time we arrive, there should be little left they can do—and then it's up to us to finish the job,' replied the captain.

The sea churned around the sterns of the ships. Slowly, they increased speed towards the hazy island lying on the horizon. As with the aircraft before them, a mixture of cultures and machinery, all drawn from different points in history, had been thrown together, seemingly by the will of one small group of humans.

A small group they undoubtedly were but, in turn, they were mutely guided by an all-powerful race from beyond the stars.

It was the influence of this race, who, circumnavigating all the laws of nature as Rowsell understood them to be, had left him directing a battle he knew, in reality, couldn't possibly exist. They'd also left him with the annoying fact that the one law this race so far hadn't interfered with was that between failure and death: this remained exactly as he'd always understood it.

Struggling with these confusing concepts—all of which were currently testing his sanity to the limits—the captain fervently hoped he'd perform adequately under these inexplicable conditions.

The captain turned to Lanter. 'We'll give your king the one minute we need to establish our targets, as we agreed with our men. But that's all he gets—then it must go off, Lac. You're sure you're absolutely ready at your end?'

'We're ready and waiting, Captain,' Lanter responded.

'Good. At the moment we've approximately two minutes left to abort the mission,' Rowsell clarified.

Lanter nodded. 'From the second they attack our aircraft, they've precisely one minute to destroy us all and, if they can't do that—which they won't, of course—it's all over for them. From then on, I trust it'll go exactly as we've planned.'

Above the ocean, Jack led from the front, opting for his preferred position which also gave him an uninterrupted view of the target as they approached it. He was somewhat puzzled by the enemy's intentions regarding their Hovertaks: they hovered above the city, seemingly reluctant to engage with his force.

How different this situation was now compared with the last time he'd flown here. The irony was not lost on Jack who remembered being a passenger in a private plane, but who was now an invader controlling something infinitely more sinister.

'Tourists to tyrant bashers in one easy lesson, Wing Co.; that's us you know.'

Jack heard a familiar voice in his ear.

'Why the lazy sods won't come and get us surprises me,' Mark continued. 'I personally think it's quite rude they've not said a polite hello by now. We would have done in their position!'

'Now you've said it, Mark,' Jack said, adrenaline evident in his voice. 'It looks like they've decided to do just that.' He took a deep breath. 'Watch out, everyone, they've woken up. Fighters, close up on the bombers and keep those bastards away from them. Remember, we've only to hold them off for one minute, so we're told. If that's the case, there's no excuse to lose a single one of them! Stay with them until their bombs are away, and then we're free to roam until the others arrive.'

'Fighter bombers, we'll follow the plan as agreed,' called Roberts. 'To confirm, we'll identify the optimum targets by the firepower they're throwing and attack the heaviest concentrations. When your bombs are gone, split into pairs and strafe anything belonging to their military.

Check your shields are working—I reckon we're going to need them. And don't forget to save some ammo for when the Swordfish arrived.'

'You won't need shields, Flight Sergeant,' Mark called. 'I'm here to protect you now. Put on your cossie and relax in the sunshine. I guarantee you'll not even get a scratch.' He pulled his Spitfire close above Roberts's heavily laden Seafire.

Jack grinned and shook his head.

'The moment of truth approaches, Rak, but they don't look particularly daunting now they're here, do they?' Aharmer said, as he watched the enemy approaching.

'Quite ordinary, in fact, if you ignore what they look like' Maltor replied. 'Under normal circumstances, I don't think this attack would worry me unduly. Judging from the visuals, though, they're obviously shielded. In actual fact, it looks even stranger when you see the effect in front of you. Still, leaving them alone until they're in range of our ground defences will considerably help the Hovertaks. You'd think between the two of them they'd easily repel the bastards.'

'The ships are moving in.' Neda was observing the enemy fleet through a handheld viewer. 'And there's another wave of even more peculiar looking aircraft escorted by Hovertaks behind this lot.'

'Well, we can't wait for them, too. Just before the leading planes cross the harbour wall, we'll throw everything at them. When we've knocked this lot out, our Hovertaks can take the rest over the sea—including those bloody ships, if they can get at them,' replied Maltor. 'Sol, have they brought the Argotaks into the tunnels under the palace yet? You'd better make sure they're safe before this all kicks off.'

'Don't worry, Rak,' Aharmer reassured. 'I've already dealt with that one.'

Jack, responsible for escorting the bombers, watched as the Hovertaks gained the advantage by forming up above his aircraft and preparing themselves to swoop down on top of them all. 'God, I hate this role,' Jack muttered to himself. 'You're always on the back foot: you can't leave them, so you're never in the right place to defend them properly either.'

And it was at this point that his forces were half a mile from the city limits—and Hell smashed into them.

The severity of the defence they encountered momentarily stunned them all. Every beam weapon on- and offshore fired simultaneously from below. The Hovertaks dropped on them, adding a colossal barrage from above. Caught in the middle, every aircraft was savagely pounded by the furious onslaught.

'Holy crap,' cried Mark as balls of energy slithered across his shields. Already half-blinded by the dazzling radiance which filled the air around him, he was now furious. 'You nasty bastards,' he shouted, pulling his Spitfire up to meet the Hovertaks falling down from above.

As Jack rose to engage, he realised the paradox: above him were a flight of Hovertaks, swinging down towards him, obviously considering him their prey and, with his shield fading, his life now totally depended on the shiny stones. He dreaded a voice in his ear fulfilling his prophecy.

Roberts shouted through his earpiece, his craft banking towards the docks. 'Eleven and twelve groups: stay with me. The heaviest fire is coming from the docks—we'll bomb that. Nine and ten groups: bomb the batteries around that pyramid. Seven and eight groups: bomb the airfield. We'll leave the rest for the next wave. When we're done, we'll all concentrate on those bloody Hovertaks.'

'I'm hit,' yelled Chris Ford, pilot of a Seafire in eleven group. It promptly exploded in a burst of purple and red; the colours of horror and death for the alliance; success and avail for the enemy. The explosion subsequently engulfed the Spitfire of Robin Courts.

~*~*~*~

When the enemy crossed the harbour wall, the fury of the first salvo had even surprised the chiefs. The aircraft all but disappeared when the converging balls of energy merged into a wall of palpitating deep purple light around them. Nevertheless, the chiefs were somewhat disappointed when they all came through the wall of death—but they'd noted the shields around them all glowed brightly.

Now looking from the control dome at the falling planes, the chiefs began to relax.

'I don't believe it! They *are* relying on their shields, the fools!' Aharmer laughed delightedly. 'Look at that! We've got two of them already!'

'I think this could be over already,' grinned Maltor sardonically. 'We're hitting them time and again. Look, the shields are fading around all of them now.'

Mark found himself temporarily unopposed. Having shot down one of the two Hovertaks that had been chasing persistently, he tried to keep their comrades away from Roberts and his group. The other shied away. Using the respite, he looked around and his heart sank; his own shield was dimming, and he saw most of the others were too. Although they'd shot down several Hovertaks between them, the number was nowhere near enough; they hadn't even scratched the ground defences—and it was obvious they couldn't sustain much more of this.

Wincing as he watched a Seafire explode and the wreckage slam into a Spitfire, he began to question the wisdom behind this venture.

Selecting a pair of Hovertaks he spotted lining up behind Roberts, he banked towards them and levelled out. He decided to chance a crossing burst, which he hoped might get them both in one pass. He was applying pressure to his gun button when they literally fell from the sky, disappearing into the harbour below him in clouds of spray.

'Fuck me! What happened there?' he cried in amazement.

Meanwhile, Jack realised he faced certain death—but refused to accept it without a fight. He dragged his plane onto the port wing and screamed away from the mass of Hovertaks facing him. Corkscrewing back, he shot straight up and looped right over, bringing two of his enemies into his gun sight.

This dramatic flying, had there not been quite so many Hovertaks in the vicinity, would probably have saved him. Now, two more energy bolts scrabbled across his shield, and it promptly flicked off.

Jack looked behind him: five Hovertaks remained glued to his tail. Looking forward, the two out in front remained in his sights. 'I'll bloody well take you with me then!' he yelled, firing a burst, only to witness it soaring through empty air. Blinking twice, he still couldn't see the aircraft he'd fired at. And upon twisting round, he saw only empty sky behind him.

And it was then that he heard Mark shouting delightedly over the r/t. 'Ha ha! You lose, you bastards! We've got you now! Goodbye, our noble king—you're history! You're banished!

As his ears filled with the excited chatter swamping the airwaves, Jack finally realised what was happening. The words he feared never came, and his appreciation of the shiny stones soared.

'Fucking Hades, what've they done now?' Maltor screamed, slamming his white fist into the table and turning deathly pale. 'What the Ra's happened to our Hovertaks? Why have the batteries stopped firing? Pull up, pull up, why don't you! What's the bloody matter with you all? You're going to die, for fuck sakes!' His eyes grew wide and bloodshot, and despair slowly crept across his face. 'Oh my Ra, we're losing all of them!'

Barring only two, the Hovertaks' propulsion systems had shut down simultaneously; their anti-gravity units failed, and without them, their short stubby wings provided insufficient lift. Lacking the ability to glide, they flew like stones. Their once-proud pilots—now best described as panic-filled passengers—were trapped in dying four-ton aircraft. They fought slack controls, cursed their dead escape system, screamed at the aircraft, cursed the king, called for their mothers—but ultimately faced the inevitable.

Diving Hovertaks extended their flight directly into the ground. Climbing, they stalled and fell backwards. In-level flight plummeted directly south. Whatever their attitude or altitude, the end result was always the same. All but the two still powered ceased to fly and hit the ground within seconds of each other.

Equally helplessly, the chiefs stood riveted, spectators forced to endure the multiple scenes of destruction as their falling planes erupted across their own city, devastating everything in their path.

His comrades were dumbstruck, offering no answers to Maltor's helpless demands; staring open-mouthed at the spectacle, they'd none to give anyway. One fell right in front of their control tower, causing them to jump backwards in alarm as the black falling mass shot past their viewpoint. It thumped into the ground, shaking the tower to its foundations, before spreading its dismembered frame halfway across the airfield.

Horrified, the three men realised the only things capable of fully resisting the invaders now were the two large patrol boats and the 57th archers—and their entire complement of weapons seemed to be functioning normally. The remaining patrol boats were firing sporadically, and directly above the 57th the two Hovertaks flew, so far remaining airborne. However, as these last Hovertaks moved away from the Archers to defend them, they both tumbled from the sky, sharing the same fate as their comrades.

'Call up our batteries director, Sol! The archers are still firing, so what's wrong with the rest of them? Those batteries are just about all we've got left above ground to fight back with!' shouted Maltor.

Aharmer crossed quickly to the communications console, which he found to be dead. He also realised there were no lights working in the room and the cooling fans had ceased. 'It's dead, Rak. We can't talk to anyone on this, and nothing else appears to be working in here either.' Panic filled his voice, and Maltor looked on helplessly.

But, before Maltor could reply—bark more orders, continue on his path of denial—eleven and twelve groups reached the docks, their shields recovering and easily repelling the few bolts that hit them.

Totally unable to influence anything, terror gripped the chiefs. The fighter bombers screamed down, levelling out and flying low across the waterfront. They watched as two black objects dropped from beneath each aircraft and, in a line, they soared straight up into the sky above the docks.

Lobbing their bombs into an undefended target was an easy task for the allies; the entire area disappeared in clouds of smoke and towering flames.

Used to deadly but somewhat less noisy weapons, the chiefs were taken completely by surprise with the thunderous sound instantly following the scene they'd witnessed. The visual effects of the high explosives had left them unmoved, but they were ill prepared for the colossal assault on their eardrums. This proved to be too much for the already unnerved chiefs, who threw themselves to the floor, flinging their arms over their heads. From there, they didn't see groups nine and ten attack the batteries positioned near the pyramid. But they'd already come to understand the meaning of the noise it created, falling back down before they'd half raised themselves from the floor.

They'd finally regained their feet when Roberts redirected groups seven and eight from the airfield to attack the 57th archers. Unaware this had probably saved their lives, they caught the tail end of the action. With a number of fighters strafing the enemy ahead, they delivered their bombs, obliterating the archers' position, the beam weapons ceasing and the invaders continuing on.

'They've taken out the archers!' screamed Neda. 'That now only leaves my patrol boats.'

The chiefs turned their attention to the action at sea, noticing as they did so that they could clearly see the enemy fleet without the aid of viewers; they were much closer now—and presumably would soon add to the general carnage.

What they didn't see were the silver trails, running like express trains, straight at their two largest ships; what they *did* see was both of them reduced to fiery wreckage, which turned turtle and sank quickly under their shocked gaze.

'It's time to get the Hades out of here!' cried Maltor. 'We'll collect Lara and get to the tunnels—assuming we can through this mess!'

Having just completed a pass across the area of activity behind the palace walls, Jack looked down at the scene below. He'd been hammering away at the only functioning unit left on the shore. Along with six other Spitfires, they'd been using their machine guns to clear the way for Roberts's bomber groups. He'd seen troops dive for cover as his bullets tore through them, and he'd grimly noted there were many who couldn't. Now, he watched as the following bombers completed the job. Judging by the devastation they delivered, it was unlikely there were many left at all now to bother them further.

With all their bombs gone, the invaders switched to attacking anything military moving around the city, as per their orders. This proved rather difficult with a lack of movement eerily descending upon the capital. They instead contented themselves with blasting away at stationary military vehicles as an alternative, and attacking the odd flurry of running troops, apparently trying to escape the fight.

'Wing Commander Bannerman, report your status,' the captain called over the r/t.

'It's gone a little flat around here, Captain. There's not much left for us to shoot at now; there's nothing *at all* left shooting at us. We've lost only two aircraft. All theirs simply fell from the sky, and all their remaining weapons appear to have packed up. I suppose this indicates you've kept your promise to us—but what do you want us to do now?'

'We were expecting this, Wing Commander, but it's likely this situation is only temporary; they'll soon work out what we've done, and we're expecting them to regain the use of their remaining weapons shortly, so don't get too complacent. In the meantime, decide who has sufficient ammunition to cover the next wave, and the rest can return to rearm.'

'As you wish, Captain,' Jack replied. 'But can you first tell us what the hell you've done here? Whatever your secret weapon is, it worked like a dream—and more or less in the time you promised too!'

Lanter had been as good as his word; only ten minutes had passed since the start of this battle, and it seemed to be over. In spite of the captain's warning, he couldn't see how the enemy could retrieve the situation.

'We've promised Rema that honour, since it was she who worked all of this out. Call her when you've sorted your aircraft, Wing Commander,' answered the captain.

It later transpired that, in the excitement, not many had been particularly conservative with their ammunition. It became clear that only Jack, Mark and Flight Sergeant Roberts were the only ones realistically worth leaving on-station, and having ordered the rest back to Victorious, Jack took his small force to join the next wave approaching the city.

'Well, I suppose one could say it's rather appropriate, Wing Co.,' said Mark as they flew back, 'that an impossible battle should have an improbable ending.'

'I suppose, Mark, but the captain says it isn't over yet—although it looks rather like it at the moment. Anyway, we're coming up on the others; we'd better see where they want us in the pack.' And with that, Jack called Rema.

'Come up here and slot in with us,' said Rema, who'd chosen to position her Hovertaks in three staggered lines above the Swordfish, putting herself in the lead. She rearranged her immediate formation, and Jack slid his Spitfire into the space they'd provided beside Rema. Mark joined Tiea, and Roberts ended up flying alongside Cal.

'Don't scratch my new paint with that rickety old contraption please, Mark!' Tiea teased.

'Rickety old contraption?' exclaimed Mark. 'I'll have you know this fine aircraft is ten thousand years newer than the thing you're struggling along in, old girl!'

'It didn't take them long did it?' Jack said smiling as his colleague returned to his secondary position of serial flirter. 'Now we've got a few minutes, Rema,' Jack said, directing his attention to his own love interest, 'can you put us out of our misery? Tell us what happened.'

'It was simple, really, Jack: we turned off the pyramid in Atlanta,' she replied airily. 'No power means nothing works. As I say, very simple. Actually, we've disabled the entire output of the Ancients' pyramids, right across the world. This is probably pissing off the king big time right now, on top of all of this.'

'Bloody clever, Rema. No wonder it all came to a grinding halt! But I must say, I was expecting something rather more dramatic than that! I mean, not that it wasn't dramatic, of course—the effects were mind blowing,' stuttered Jack, becoming flustered. 'But it's not really a secret weapon, is it?'

'Isn't it? How much more effective a weapon do you need, Jack?' Rema smiled. 'I suppose you'd be happier with a sky full of spaceships flown by the Ancients?'

'Well no, not really. I suppose it doesn't matter what was done—the point is, we achieved our objective.'

'The king was in his counting house looking from the tower, everything was rosy then Rema pulled the power,' Mark sang happily, grinning at Tiea from his cockpit.

'Thanks for that, Shakespeare, but I think I understand the implications of it all,' said Jack. 'But if there's no power for their machines, why are you still up here? Why did some of their weapons still work? And how come you think they'll continue this battle now? And I thought you couldn't interfere with the pyramids anyway?'

'Whoa, hang on! One question at a time please, Jack!' Rema said. 'At the moment, we're using power that's being supplied from the pyramid on Kira—the one in the factory. The power it's providing is on a different frequency, and we've adapted all the machines we're using— including yours, where it applies—to function with either. Obviously, the king's forces didn't have that opportunity, which is why we remain operational and they don't.'

'Ahh,' replied Jack.

'Although we can now turn off the power in the pyramids the Ancients built, we can't do anything about the king's portable generators—or the pyramids he's built himself, for that matter. The 57th archers are based on Atlantis, and there's no doubt it was them who kept up the defence when the rest failed. They're a crack regiment, used only to operate in real trouble spots or to open up new territories. They've portable generators as standard in all their equipment. As the pyramid in Atlanta shut down, their systems would automatically switch to their own source.

'What's more, most of the larger warships are also fitted with generators, as they often operate beyond the reach of the powered areas of the grid. Some of them are so powerful they can service many other ships at the same time; put a few of them together and they aren't far off a pyramid in themselves.'

'Which is why Lanter was so worried about those beam weapon ships, of course,' observed Mark.

'Absolutely,' Rema confirmed. 'If they'd been here, turning off the power from the pyramid wouldn't have made much difference locally. And even if we'd managed to sink them here, it wouldn't necessarily have shut down their generators; they'd work just as well under the sea, providing they weren't damaged.

'Oh shit!' interrupted Cal. 'I think we'd better continue this later; they've found something from somewhere by the looks of it.'

As they'd been speaking, the aircraft had come within range of the island, and the enemy had partly regrouped. Using a contingent of Hovertancs and having reactivated the remaining shore batteries, all drawing power from portable generators, a barrage of energy bolts was being projected their way.

'It's bad, but nowhere near as bad as last time, Cal,' observed Jack. 'And the really good news is there're no Hovertaks at all. Let us handle this, Rema—at least unless we get into real trouble. They'll have difficulty hitting a moving target enough times to penetrate our shields from the ground. If you stay out of range, you can still get in quickly enough to help if you need to.'

'Sorry, Jack, but we've all waited far too long for this—we're coming and you won't stop us,' she replied, a smile clear in her voice.

'Okay... It's your show, Rema,' said Jack. 'Okay, Evans, how do you want to do it?'

'It looks like there are three main areas still pretty active, Sir,' Evans began. 'If it's alright with you, we'll split into three groups and take them on first. Hopefully, we'll not need all our bombs. Those with any remaining can regroup and have a go at those guys skulking around that bloody great palace.'

'Okay, let's do it,' Jack confirmed. 'Are you ready, Rema?'

'More than ready, Jack, more than,' she replied.

Evans appointed his bomb leaders and, as the purple rain descended around them, they split up.

As the chiefs turned to leave, the lights and fans flicked on in the control room, and all their communication systems were restored. When disaster struck, their beam batteries director, also based at the airfield, had instantly realised the power was the problem. He'd quickly rigged a small generator to restore his beam weapons around the field; this was now producing enough power to service the airfield and most of the waterfront.

As soon as they'd installed the crystals, he'd also ordered his men to move the two giant Hovertrans away from the airfield. These machines had recently been delivered from the local factory. He'd ordered them to be hidden within the vast underground tunnel system the Ancients had created. These workings riddled the city and ran beneath the hills surrounding Atlanta. A tunnel linking to the catacombs passed beneath the airfield, and these monsters were now within it and well on their way.

The vehicles had originally been produced for the campaign in Mu, and had been concealed at the airfield, awaiting dispatch. They were generator carriers, and the generators they bore were designed to sustain the power requirements of a sizeable army operating outside the grids powered areas. The resistance were unaware of their existence, and it was lucky for them they weren't operational when they'd attacked: had they been, the invasion could well have ended then and there. Nevertheless, after the thirty minutes it required for the installed crystals to energise, they'd feed the grid—and the king's army would have all the power they could possibly use.

Seeing the communications were now once again fully functional, Maltor had called up his batteries director and had learned what he'd done; this put a different light on the whole matter—and the chiefs decided to delay their evacuation.

'The man's a genius, Rak,' commented Neda. 'But how did he work out the problem and respond so quickly with all this going on?'

'He's a frontline soldier and an accomplished engineer, Cesa. He's well used to making decisions in the heat of battle,' Maltor replied.

'Well, he made us look bad. All we were doing was crawling about on the floor,' Aharmer grumbled.

'The less said about that the better, Sol,' Maltor chastised. 'We've had it too easy for too long, I think. Nevertheless, it galled me thinking all we could do was run away.'

'At least it's worth sticking around now for a bit. Perhaps we might even be useful,' Neda replied.

'To be honest, I'm disgusted and no little disturbed. We used to insist on attending every battle and liked nothing more than being in the frontline—but Lanter's little trick today has shown how the years have changed us,' Maltor reflected. 'But I suppose, to be fair, the shock of their hideous weapons might account for some of our reactions.'

'Here they come again, gentlemen—and they've got the Hovertaks with them this time. Oh and which they stole from us in the first place, I might add. I'm getting really pissed off with these bastards! They're rubbing our noses in it now!' Aharmer said angrily.

'We're not going to stop them either at the moment,' observed Maltor. 'Our problem right now is the lack of aircraft. I think we need to pull everything we can back from the mainland. How many can you draw from Southolira, Sol? It's the nearest place we've got any operational, and also from there they could be with us in around three hours.'

'Lack of aircraft is something of an understatement, Rak. But, we are where we are, I suppose. We've already taken most of them from Southolira, but they could send the rest—although that would of course leave them with nothing. And there's another issue to consider: the pilots they've got left over there are inexperienced; we took the best they had last time. I'm not sure they'd be any good against this lot—even if they weren't shielded,' Aharmer replied.

'Oh, Hades! Look at them all—and there's a pack headed this way now. There's cowardice and there's prudence, Rak. If we stay here much longer we're going to die for sure sitting up in this forsaken tower. And what use will that be to us or our men?' Neda said urgently.

Chief Maltor had seen the onset of the next attack, and the others turned to watch. The remaining beam weapons poured a carpet of energy projectiles around the massed aircraft, which was seemingly undeterred as the last attack broke into three groups.

'They're going for the docks, the palace and us, by the looks of it— and we're not making much impression on them either, as I feared.' Maltor, unusually calm, watched the scene unfold before making his decision. 'Men, we're achieving nothing here. It's time to go. We'll get down to the tunnels and reorganise our troops. They'll have plenty to fight back with shortly—maybe then it'll be our turn to be full of surprises.'

'Bloody Hades, Mark! I thought Lanter told you not to break anything unnecessarily!' Tiea cried as she viewed the devastation passing beneath her Hovertak. Turning to attack the airfield, they'd passed through the main barrage without loss. As they approached, the energy balls directed their way had lessened considerably. The shore defences now concentrated their fire on the other two bomber groups.

In this brief interlude, Tiea had become aware of the waterfront ablaze. Around the palace where manicured grounds once existed, now appeared tended to by a berserk ploughman. The golden pyramid was covered by thick, rolling black smoke, and throughout the city fires blazed and buildings hung in ruins.

The sight of her people running from their attack—and, more especially, the ones ignoring it, desperately scrabbling amidst the ruins in search of their loved ones—tore at her heart. Of the enemy she saw little sign, with the exception of the few straggler Hovertancs and beam batteries still in action.

'It wasn't all us,' answered Mark. 'The Hovertaks caused more damage than we did, Tiea. Hundreds fell all over the city. We attacked the docks and the areas around the palace, which were teeming with the king's men. Apart from those areas and strafing at some heavy vehicles positioned around the outskirts on the hilltops, we pretty much left the city alone.'

'I wish there was another way to do this,' Tiea sighed sadly. 'We're killing innocent people along with our enemy. Now when it comes, it'll be a bitter sweet victory.'

'It always is, Tiea, and there's nothing on earth—or elsewhere—that can change that,' he replied compassionately.

'Cut the philosophy, you two, and attack those bloody beam batteries for us,' yelled Evans over the r/t, interrupting the melancholy mood. 'Our old string bags are getting a bashing down here.'

Their sightseeing had been cut short by the airfield defences, which had opened up all around the airfield, and once more they flew against determined resistance.

Mark flipped his Spitfire over and side-slipped down beside the bombers, the Hovertaks following his lead. Completing the roll beneath the Swordfish, they streaked towards the batteries surrounding the airfield. Fanning out and attacking the individual sites, they cleared the way as Evans had ordered, minus two Hovertaks vaporised in the process, one with twenty naked women emblazoned across its fuelsage.

With the mission complete, the bombers headed back to Victorious accompanied by the three allied fighters. The remaining Hovertaks prowled over the city but found little left to attack.

'There's something very wrong here, Captain,' said Lanter. 'Take a look at this screen.'

The captain strode across the bridge and considered the navigation screen with Lanter, which showed both large and small concentrations of vehicles moving across the city.

'There are two things disturbing about this,' Lanter continued. 'Firstly, our pilots report nothing much is moving within the city, let alone the military. In fact, they can't find much of that ilk stationary anymore either—so what on earth are we seeing here? Secondly, in order to operate that amount of vehicles would require considerable power. When their beam weapons were operational, they alone should have used all the power from any portable generators we expected them to have available. But I noticed this apparent redeployment occurring in the final minutes of our last attack—when all their shore defences were in action.'

'What exactly are you saying, Lac? Since our pilots are right above the city and they can't see anything like this, clearly there's something wrong with the equipment? I'm not entirely with you here,' replied the captain.

'Unfortunately, I don't think there is,' Lac responded. 'Initially, I assumed there was a fault also, but I've since checked it out and everything's fine. What we're seeing is actually hugely significant and explains why there are so few of their troops about. They were obviously worried enough about our secret weapons to keep them well concealed, at least until they could see just what we had in store for them. They only needed their air arm and the shore defences in the first instance; provided their troops were readily to hand, it would be a sensible move—very sensible in the light of this, in fact, and it could have been completely devastating because they are here and in huge numbers, and that's what we're looking at.'

The captain's face visibly discoloured as he realised the battle was far from over.

'There've been rumours and legends abounding regarding a massive system of earthworks beneath Atlanta ever since I can remember,' Lac reflected. 'I honestly thought that's what they were, up to now— rumours. Looking at this, however, it seems clear to me they do exist and, what's more, they're large enough to conceal around forty thousand men and all their equipment—all of whom are undoubtedly eagerly waiting for us to set foot on the island. Worse than that, Captain, they seem to have massively more power available than we thought to consider.'

'If they really are underground, it certainly explains the lack of troops, Lac,' the captain responded, gathering his composure. 'I'd assumed up to now you were quite wrong in your assessment of their defences; I thought it relatively impossible for that number of troops and equipment to be concealed within the city. And in the light of such, I'd intended to launch our ground forces as soon as Atlanta came in range of the transporter.'

'Well, if it weren't for this information, Captain, that would have been the obvious next move,' replied Lanter. 'However, we've got to go in sometime. What we need to establish is the best way of turning the ambush they're clearly preparing to our advantage. With that in mind, if you consider the screen, you'll see most of the activity is converging on two locations—which coincidently correspond with the large clearings you can see from here on the bridge. If you look towards the pyramid, you'll see what I'm talking about. They're situated to the east and west of the city highways, right where they enter the foothills.'

The captain looked out, then at the screen, considering each of the locations highlighted by Lanter. He nodded his head in understanding.

'The king has always vetoed their development, and some time ago he declared them public parks for the enjoyment of all his subjects,' Lanter advised. 'It's beginning to make sense now. Normally, he couldn't give a toss about his subjects, and I'd always considered it uncharacteristic to provide them with his valuable real estate for their pleasure. Of course, I see it now: the parks are disguising the portals that lead beneath the city,' exclaimed Lanter, who was clearly way ahead of the puzzled captain.

'I'm sorry to appear stupid, Lac, but I've no idea what you're talking about,' he said honestly, rubbing his frowned forehead. 'They look remarkably like parks to me, right down to the ducks on the lakes.'

'It's not you who's stupid, Captain, it's me. I can't believe I've missed this for all these years.' Lanter shook his head, frustrated at missing something which now seemed so obvious. 'For Ra's sake, we've got portals at the base on Kira for a start, so they're scarcely unknown to me. That alone should've alerted me to these sites long before this. Yet again, it's taken technology supplied by the Ancients to save us from another complete disaster—especially as I really should have seen it myself on this occasion. Irrespectively, however, it's not too late—but we've been very lucky, Captain.'

'So what else can you tell me, Lac?' the captain queried.

'Well, whatever's under the city—assuming those parks are, in fact, portals—it's clear now it was built by the Ancients, as the legends suggest. This almost certainly means it's huge, and also that, in all likelihood, it had many different purposes, one of which would have been to defend the area, no doubt, and at least I see the logic behind that one now.'

The captain, still clearly confused, waiting for Lanter to explain, before saying, 'Care to elaborate on that further, Lac?'

'Sorry, Captain. Once the shore defences have been overcome, the obvious place for anyone attacking this area from the sea is through the natural harbour. And the obvious routes into the city from there are the two largest highways, which pass just outside of those parks. Of course, I don't know how it was laid out when the Ancients were here, but I'm betting that it was quite similar. Now if you look closely at the pattern emerging here on our screen, they're also moving some troops under the wasteland that sits between the highways about four hundred yards inland from the docks. It's the large clearing behind the burning warehouses and again, in the past, he's stopped any plans to develop it. They're gambling on us taking the obvious route, of course—but then, why wouldn't we? It's exactly what we would have done. Bearing that in mind, so far as we could see, there was no local resistance left. We'd have thought our initial attack had cleared the area and would be pushing on into the city with all possible speed to protect the beachhead we'd just established.'

'And as we passed over the wasteland and on between the two parks, they'd spring the trap,' said the captain, now understanding the enemy's intentions. 'And then we'd be caught from both sides, as well as from behind.'

'That seems to be the way of it,' Lanter acknowledged. 'They'd wipe us out. Only your tanks are shielded, and the aircraft couldn't operate effectively because they'd be likely to hurt us more than the enemy in such a confined space. This also applies to the ships' gunners, who could hardly be expected to put down a barrage accurate enough to miss us without pre-sighting their guns.'

'You know, Lac, it sounds good but I'm not so sure now. I see the sense in it right enough, but I think it could only apply if they were above ground. From down there, they couldn't possibly get enough troops out at any one time to really threaten us, could they? Which, now I come to think about it, would seem to apply anyway—even if we didn't know about this. I suppose they could have done some degree of damage in the first instance, allowing for the element of surprise, but I do think we would have easily contained them after that. Of course, it's easier now we know where they're coming from. We can pick them off one by one as they come out. I agree it looks like a trap, but how on earth do they expect to spring it? They'd need hundreds of doorways—or *portals* as you call them—and even then they couldn't do it.'

'I'm sorry, Captain, I should have explained more clearly what I meant by the term *portal*; it's a doorway, if you like, not several. You've actually seen one on Kira though you probably didn't realise it. The last time we opened it was in the middle of the night after our first meeting on Victorious, and then it remained open the entire time you were there. We opened the entire hillside to enter our factory and the installation beside it—and they're going to do exactly the same with the parks and the wasteland.'

'Oh my... so it does make perfect sense. That possibility hadn't even crossed my mind,' gasped the captain.

'The fact remains, Captain, that if we'd done what they expect us to—which, as I say, we would have done, I'm sure—we would have been faced with fifteen thousand fully equipped troops on either side, with ten thousand more behind us, and all without any warning. Allowing that the portals take roughly ten seconds to open, our life expectancy would've been about fifteen seconds at that point—if that. Shielding or no shielding.'

Subsequently convinced of their enemy's intentions, the captain decided to abandon their original invasion plan; they realised that to continue with it now would be suicidal. Having no viable alternative readily to hand, they rapidly convened an urgent meeting on-board Victorious between all the field commanders. There, they restructured various details in consideration of the enemy trap.

In the meantime, their aircraft had all landed aboard Victorious, minus the Hovertaks, which currently hung above the fleet. The resistance they'd expected from the city had failed to materialise, leaving them nothing to do there. Effectively, the invasion had now stalled, and they desperately needed to resume it and retain the initiative.

'What do you think they're waiting for, Rak?' Aharmer asked. 'They've destroyed everything we've got on the surface around the harbour, and obviously we've no Hovertaks left. They've no idea what's waiting for them down here, so apparently we've very few troops either. I'd have thought they'd have already landed.'

When the chiefs left the airfield, they'd taken Lara with them and entered the tunnels through the portal their batteries director had opened for the generator carriers. Using a small Hovertrans, they'd quickly circumnavigated the maze of tunnels. Arriving at the command centre they'd set up many years ago in the corner of a large rectangular cavern under the Golden pyramid, they'd left Lara in the company of their subordinates, who were working behind the partitioned area from which the chiefs were directing the defences. From this inner sanctum, they could view any area of the city using the multiple screens it contained, and accordingly communicate with all their forces—both in Atlanta and beyond.

'I'm not sure, Sol, but perhaps we've made it look too easy and it's made them more cautious,' replied Maltor. 'I'll send twelve Hovertancs out through the portal inside our storage facility at West Way; that'll bring them out just above West Park, and from there they can spread out and bombard the ships. Who knows, they may even get lucky. But whether they do or don't is irrelevant: what I'm intending to do is wake up the bastards and focus their attention on attacking the city—in precisely the location we want them. I'll continue to replace the Hovertancs as necessary, indicating to our enemy we've a strong position there. I want them to believe this is the area they've to concentrate on and draw them up between east and west parks. I also need to make the landing easy for them—well, relatively, at least. The quicker we can get them here the better. With nothing much to support the Hovertancs, it's likely to prove to be expensive, and the longer they're exposed, the worse it'll get. As I only intend to support them lightly with our troops, it's going to be expensive there too. That said, it makes sense overall for us to do this: if it were me, I'd dispense with landing craft and go straight for the docks with the troopships considering the light resistance. They'll save the time and effort involved with a seaborne invasion from small boats. If they do it—and I hope they will—our losses will reduce accordingly.'

'I think they'll go for it, Rak,' Neda commented. 'They don't realise we've something more powerful than small generators and, assuming us to be struggling with power, they're not expecting a profusion of heavy weapons. Putting up just enough resistance to draw them in will appear to them to be our best shot anyway.'

'Well, I like the sound of that,' commented Aharmer, looking visibly more optimistic. 'And if we're careful, we'll get them up between the parks relatively quickly.'

'Let's get on with it then, it'll stir them up if nothing else and let's hope they take the bait' said Maltor, grabbing a communicator and issuing the necessary commands.

'It'll be interesting to see what happens now,' Neda further stated. 'Whilst we're waiting, I'll bring you up-to-date with the progress I've made whilst you two were reorganising our men. Firstly, I've moved the Argotaks from the palace; they're now parked behind portal twenty, as you suggested Rak, and I've had Lara taken aboard the king's aircraft in case we need to leave in a hurry.'

'Where, unlike us, she can wait in absolute luxury until this is resolved one way or the other,' Aharmer interrupted wryly.

'That's more than likely, Sol, but as I was saying... Secondly, I've established that the power holds now from Southolira to here. The pyramid we built there and the generators we're using have bridged the gap caused by the disabling of Atlanta's pyramid. You can have your Hovertaks now, Rak—if you still want them, that is. They can send sixty over, but I really don't think they'll make much of a difference.'

'They might, but I think we'll hedge our bets. Get them to fly within half an hour of Atlanta and they can hover there until we either call them in or send them back. I agree if we bring them in now they'll be decimated, but if our plan works we can use them to clear away the survivors. What other news did you gather, Cesa?' Maltor asked.

'It's all bad, I'm sorry to say. I've discovered our dear friends have disabled all of the Ancients' pyramids right across the world. This, as you can imagine, is causing absolute havoc just about everywhere, but especially in Mu where we're suffering a massive defeat already, judging by the reports that are coming from there. Swords, spears, bows, arrows and the like have suddenly become far more effective against us; deadly, actually, when they're being used against troops whose sophisticated weapons are now useless. I've no doubt some of our men could revert to these primitive tools themselves and retaliate but, of course, they don't actually have any. And unfortunately, it's looking like they're not that proficient at running either.' Neda paused, considering all he had learnt and their current position. 'We're being slaughtered, gentlemen. In its own way, the situation there is far worse than here, and it seemed, until I spoke with them, that they were dying in unacceptable numbers, simply hoping the power would return on its own.' Bitterness was apparent in his voice.

'The bloody resistance! The bastards and their cursed trickery!' Maltor cursed. 'I'd no idea things had come to this everywhere else. But surely they've got generators over there they can use? They must be able to retrieve the situation to a degree, Cesa? What the Hades are they playing at?'

'I've been trying to reorganise them, Rak, but it's extremely difficult. Yes, they've got generators, but they're in such a panic they're simply succeeding in doing nothing but overloading them. However, I think I've got the message through to them now. I've ordered them to stop trying to use all their weapons at once and to instead adopt a strategic withdrawal from now on—one which only employs enough weapons to hold back the pressure and which their generators can cope with. I've ordered them to establish two lines of defence: a front line facing the enemy and one further behind. They are to withdraw southwards by alternating the lines until they gain power from our pyramid in Alonat. If they can withdraw in this fashion for two hundred miles, they'll be fully functional again—naturally assuming by then they've anything left to function with. I hope I've achieved what I think I have or it's a strong possibility they might not.

'The trouble is, even talking to them is nigh on impossible; the communications keep failing. But, if the communications are failing, it probably means everything else over there is failing at the same time. I don't need to remind you of the falling Hovertak scenario, but I'm sure you're getting the picture. I pray to Ra they've got the message.'

Maltor's face had turned red with anger and frustration. 'Well, that settles it,' he stormed. 'We've got to get out of here the moment we see the outcome—one way or another. We'll go where we can think straight and take command of the situation as a whole. If we don't regroup and take a stand somewhere, we're going to lose the entire Empire rather quickly. Ra only knows what we've lost already but, by the sounds of it, yet again, we've little time left to come up with the answer. But, before I do anything else, I'll speak with our high commander in Mu if I can get through: we must be certain he's following your orders, Cesa. I can't believe he fucked up so badly and didn't see it for himself.'

'Steady, Rak,' Neda comforted, trying to maintain some calm. 'He was caught out just like the rest of us. The resistance knew exactly what to expect when they disabled the pyramids, and clearly briefed the Mu armies accordingly. Our need to mass the bulk of our forces in one area ready for the final push this autumn has played right into their hands. It's simply ensured our enemies gain the maximum advantages all round. Effectively, our perfectly reasonable strategy presented them with ninety per cent of our troops and equipment based in Mu, all on a plate for good measure. As soon as the resistance disabled the power, a vast army appeared—seemingly out of nowhere—and attacked them right where they thought they were invincible. This alone would've been disturbing enough, but as they tried to defend themselves, their weapons failed. It's not that surprising it totally threw them.'

'Not surprising at all, Cesa,' Aharmer agreed. 'And let's face it: they've manipulated us here too. We've brought almost every active unit we've got in Atlantis to defend this city, and by doing so may well have provided them with yet another grim harvest.'

'Their planning is faultless, and doubtless they'll have exploited the dismal situation they've created to the full,' said Maltor ruefully. 'And if they keep sending these bastards against us, our bloody weapons are inferior anyway—irrespective of the power issues. Somehow, we have to stop *them*, which could prove to be difficult because it's looking like they're already the stronger adversary.

'Nevertheless, now's our chance. Something's happening out there at last—look at the screens. It would appear their troopships are heading for the harbour, so they're not going for the landing craft option, which is a good start. It also looks like the warships are about to bombard us, which is obviously not so good but inevitable, and their aircraft are flying again. This is it, my friends; the waiting's over. They're coming in.'

The three men monitored the screens around them, calmly assessing the invaders' movements, preparing to entrap them. The antagonists were entering the ring—and the brutality would doubtless resume within seconds.

The enemy warships positioned themselves across the sea outside the harbour walls, gun turrets swinging slowly round, bringing their weapons to bear on the city. Anchor chains rattling, their thrashing propellers stilled to silence. Six deadly new islands broadside on to Atlanta rocked gently as the blue, white-capped waves ran uncaringly beneath them, sparkling in the hot sunshine. The troopships steamed across the harbour, churning the calm surface as they headed towards the shattered docklands, the aircraft growling and whining above them.

To counter them, two thousand of the king's troops swarmed throughout the vast city streets towards the harbour. A black river flowed down the hillside, spreading out and disappearing from sight; the troops surrounding the docklands.

Flames belched from the warships' guns, and purple energy bolts flew from the projectors of the resistance vessels. Thunder roared across the city, and the islands were obscured by smoke from burnt cordite. The Hovertancs above West Park responded, pouring a constant stream of heavy energy bolts towards the invaders positions. The troops surrounding the docks added a lighter hailstorm of their own: every deck gun on the ships crossing the harbour erupted, raking the enemy shore positions with a murderous fire. The aircraft swooped down, adding their weight to the rising battle.

'The shields over the ships appear far stronger than those covering the aircraft,' Maltor observed. 'If we really wanted to stop them, we'll need more than we're throwing at them at the moment. It would seem there's little wrong with their less exotic weaponry either. Unfortunately, it looks to be as efficient as ours in its way—although a whole lot noisier.'

'So it would appear,' answered Neda, 'but if those gunners on the warships are trying to hit our Hovertancs, they're falling a bit short at the moment. Blasting away at West Park isn't going to bother them very much.'

'Unlike those bloody aircraft. Ra, I wish we still had our Hovertaks to keep them busy!' Aharmer said in frustration. 'Talking of Hovertaks, there's something we really should have noticed before: look at the screen on the left—the one showing the harbour area. There's a Hovertak in flames diving into the sea.'

'I see it, Sol, but unfortunately l see the pilot's got out anyway. So what's your point?' Maltor replied nastily.

'It's not shielded, Rak, and neither are any of the other Hovertaks up there, if you notice. Take a look at the resistance's beam weapon carriers—they're being pounded in a big way by our Hovertancs; in fact, they're looking decidedly battered already.'

'Well, I'm damned! So they are! But they're doing something about it now. They're shielding them; look, I can see the haze spreading over them. Why didn't they do it before we damaged them like that?' Maltor wondered. 'And when you think about it, all but two of the aircraft we shot down in the air attacks here today were Hovertaks, which indicates they weren't shielded. And if they weren't and these aren't, it can only mean they can't shield them for some reason.'

'I was right all along then,' Aharmer exclaimed excitedly. 'It's these strangers who're the secret weapons, as it were, and it's looking like only they can use them. Although I'm not sure how much it helps at the moment!'

'Hopefully, it'll be a very moot point shortly, but to go back to the ships, it appears they're using the shields with no problem, Sol—even if their Hovertaks can't. They obviously can adopt something. On the other hand, we're not getting through to them anymore and they've stopped firing back for some reason. I think I see it now: they can't fire through them either since they use the same weapons. Effectively, they're useless when they're shielded! They're out of it already!'

They watched as the battle developed around the harbour. The allies had docked their ships and were unloading their men and equipment. Under constant fire, they suffered casualties, but under the protection of the warships and the aircraft above them, these had been kept to acceptable levels so far.

Having first unloaded the tanks—which had the benefit of shielding—they moved them out from the docks to confront the defending troops. Placing a contingent of heavily armed men beneath the shielding umbrella around each tank, the combination of men and machinery slowly pushed the king's soldiers back towards the city. They inflicted catastrophic damage upon the beleaguered defenders whilst preventing them from disrupting the lengthy process of disembarkation. This strategy had resulted in a highly successful landing operation all round, leaving them with a strong foothold and minimum losses.

A successful partnership between the pilots and ships gunners had kept the chiefs busy with their Hovertancs; they destroyed them almost as quickly as the chiefs could replace them.

'Thank Ra for that! They've finally got everyone ashore,' Maltor said sarcastically. 'Perhaps now we can get on with it. At the moment we're losing men for nothing, and we don't have an endless supply of Hovertancs!'

'Even if we did, the men are becoming very reluctant to use them,' stated Aharmer.

'I don't say I blame them, Sol; it's suicidal out there and we'll soon need more troops to replace our losses. But if this deception's to work, we must fight every inch of the way. With nothing serious to pursue they might well disperse throughout the city—and then we'll have lost the opportunity to finish this quickly. We'll put out another thousand against them and pray that's the last sacrifice we'll have to make,' growled Maltor.

'It's a disgusting sight, Rak, and a lot to ask of them; they need better tools out there. Our men are fighting well but their weapons aren't up to it—we've never faced this dilemma before. There are only twenty soldiers around each of those lumbering monsters, and they're not even hiding behind them. Protected by their shields they're practically *strolling* right up to our men. They couldn't miss if they tried! They're literally tearing our soldiers apart with their Ra forsaken weapons!' cried Neda.

'The situation is about as difficult as it gets,' Maltor stated grimly. 'If we put a stop to this and bring our troops out in strength, we risk losing this battle; they could still beat us. I'm not sure they would now we've got our power back, but the point is they could. Even if we finally prevail, our losses could well be even worse than they're going to be now. Much as I hate to see this too, we must nevertheless stick by our decision.'

'Rak's right, Cesa,' commented Aharmer. 'The ultimate way of destroying this lot is to trap them between the parks. And I also think that, by adopting such an approach, we'll lose fewer numbers at the end. I have to say, though, I don't envy them out there at the moment; those machines they're using are lethal in themselves! What they don't blast to a million pieces they crush underneath them. You'll notice they don't go round the buildings our men are using for cover either; they just barge straight through them. And what's more,' Aharmer continued, 'like with their aircraft, when our men do make inroads on the shields, they simply replace them with another.' He took a moment to consider the situation, before continuing. 'Until we can use our heaviest weapons against them, they're unstoppable.'

Maltor looked at Aharmer sadly, defeat slowly edging its ways into his eyes. 'That may well be,' he said quietly. 'But we've enough weapons to deal with them a hundred times over, and they're ready and waiting.' He began to recover his composure and, standing upright and deciding to be more optimistic, he said, 'When we open the portals, they'll be hit by thirty five thousand light- and one hundred heavy-beam weapons simultaneously. They'll vaporise instantly! When we've removed their ground forces, we'll turn on their aircraft and ships: we'll show them which of the contestants is unstoppable around here!'

Under a cloudless blue sky, bathed in brilliant sunshine, the battle flowed on. Relentlessly, the allies pushed the king's men ever further back into the city. Unable to shield all their troops, their losses mounted as the king's army quickly switched their attention to the unprotected elements of the invading forces. The advance slowed to a crawl, but their unexpected success had nevertheless caused the chiefs to commit still more of their men to the fight on the surface.

Now, the king's troops were fast retreating towards their fixed positions on the high ground above the two parks.

Under extreme pressure from the ships' guns, aircraft, artillery and ground forces, the king's defenders melted away. His troops fled up the hillside with the allies now in hot pursuit.

'We've got them! Open the portals!' screamed Maltor.

With the exception of the artillery and the ships, every other piece of allied equipment and all their ground troops were now situated above the wasteland and between the East and West parks. The chiefs watched in delight as the entire enemy air force were now apparently supporting their ground forces in the frenzied attack, with even the strange twin-winged open-cockpit aircraft arriving at the battle.

'This is a real bonus, Rak. They've brought over the majority of their aircraft for the taking as well1 Ra is obviously smiling on us at last!' said Aharmer confidently.

The ground melted away, and the king's vast army was revealed. Maltor panicked. In a flash, a premonition had struck him—and he knew.

'Close the fu...' His voice died with the order incomplete as reality set in.

The portals opened fully and a green haze engulfed East Park. Fifteen thousand troops waiting there lifted their weapons to fire—and disappeared.

The shock of their comrades' untimely departure, as seen by the king's men in West Park and the wastelands beyond, caused them all to hesitate; they stood like open-mouthed statues, their weapons half-raised. Having earlier ranged their guns on West Park, the ships and artillery delivered a crushing barrage on top of the stunned soldiers. Commensurately, the aircraft rained bombs and unmercifully strafed them whilst the ground forces concentrated all their fire on the wasteland contingent behind them. Three minutes later, the green haze returned and the remaining troops in West Park also disappeared.

Completely shattered, the troops in the wastelands surrendered immediately, throwing down their weapons, milling dazedly with hands held skyward.

CHAPTER TWENTY-FIVE

'**S**till, at least it's a nice day for a dip, Wing Co., assuming you can swim, I suppose,' said Mark, banking his Spitfire round and engaging the hovering device to watch the events unfolding five miles out to sea.

'There'll be a lot who can't when it comes down to it, the poor bastards,' replied Jack, joining Mark and hovering beside him.

'I might remind you: they're same poor bastards who were prepared to wipe us all out two minutes ago, Wing Commander,' said Tiea, hanging in the sky with the other Hovertaks five hundred yards away. 'And the same poor bastards who've already killed an untold number of our comrades here today and elsewhere in the past. I hope the fucking lot drown, to be honest—and good riddance I say!'

'My kinda girl,' Mark laughed.

'Calm down, Tiea, we're supposed to be the good guys, remember? Not all of those people we've transported to the sea are bad,' said Rema.

'I suppose,' responded Tiea calmly. 'But if you play for the bad team, you reap what they sow.'

The chiefs were speechless, and Maltor sat with his head in his hands. Too late, he'd realised the significance of the pointless attacks by the ships and artillery on the apparently empty West Park. Too late, he'd realised why the resistance's beam weapon ships allowed themselves to be blasted by his Hovertancs; they'd only shielded themselves after they'd established their target—West Park.

Whilst Maltor and Neda sat like zombies, Aharmer was the first to recover. 'Oh fucking, fucking Hades! We're farting in a thunderstorm now! There's another impossible weapon they've decided to foist upon us—and this one's completely fucked us up!' yelled Aharmer.

'Very insightful,' Maltor said grimly.

Aharmer's shoulders slumped. 'I'll close the portals then; we don't want them chasing us around these endless tunnels. I'll send our Hovertaks back to Southolira; I figure we probably don't need them now. I think it would be best to destroy all the records in this control room. Then I think we'd better leave.' Aharmer attended to his self-appointed duties, his anger building once more.

Maltor's mind was processing thoughts at a crazy pace. The implications of this battle for him personally were horrendous, and he considered it best to keep his last-minute realisations to himself, choosing not to admit he'd missed something which he clearly shouldn't have done.

Neda shuffled around the control room looking through confidential files.

Recovering slowly, Maltor and Neda became anxious to leave, Aharmer compulsively insisting they destroy everything important before doing so.

Finally, the chiefs left, heading for their hovertrans, feeling the heat of the timed energy explosive Aharmer had left igniting as they disappeared into the maze of tunnels. His detonation had indeed destroyed the records, and with them the control room, bringing down half the roof over the entire space in which it stood, wiping out their administrators and blocking the only direct tunnel leading to portal twenty from their present location.

'For fuck sakes, Sol, you were only supposed to prevent the resistance from acquiring the data we left in the bloody control room!' said Maltor, fuming as he turned the Hovertrans around and faced a pile of debris blocking the way. 'It'll take days to clear up this mess! We're left with no alternative but to take the long route now!'

'Yes, well done, Sol, you've just won the idiot of the day award. As if we didn't have enough trouble already without your incompetence adding to it,' Neda said angrily.

'Perhaps if you two had helped a bit instead of trying to hurry me up all the fucking time this wouldn't have happened. But oh no, you preferred to leave without destroying anything in your rush to escape!' Aharmer retorted.

As Maltor drove the hovertrans along the circuitous route to reach portal twenty and make their escape, they argued and bickered; the infighting and confusion between them a testament to just how great a victory the resistance had won.

'The ramifications of this defeat will reverberate around the entire world forever more,' Aharmer observed. 'If we can't get our act together, in all probability, the fucking resistance will establish their precious new order—which naturally excludes us and everything we've achieved.'

A short while later, having convinced Rema to allow them to temporarily ignore protocol and go in search for Tiea's family, feared dead, Jack and Mark protectively followed Tiea's hovertak as they made their nerve-wracked journey in search of her loved ones.

'Oh my Ra, they're all dead, I know they are,' Tiea exclaimed upon seeing her ruined family home. 'Look at it, there's nothing left!'

Hovering low above the shattered remains of Tiea's home, the three friends gazed sadly down. The once beautiful house now had been reduced to a nightmare of broken blackened stumps, and was a parody of its former self.

'We can just about get these planes down in the far corner, Tiea,' Mark said quietly. 'Let's land and see if there's anything we can do.'

Suddenly, two vicious pulsating balls of purple light exploded across the shields of Mark's Spitfire, three hit Jack's, and the tail section of Tiea's Hovertak vaporised, thumping to the ground.

'Holy shit!' yelled Mark, dipping the nose, gunning the Merlin and slackening the hover system all at once. As he gained speed, the Spitfire flew once again. Sustaining two further strikes, his shield turned an angry green. Twisting back over the house, he saw Jack behind him, and below them a contingent of black uniformed police standing beside a dark blue Hovertanc, barely concealed behind a copse of trees on the opposite side of the road.

In the failing light of the rapidly approaching night, and fixing their attention on the ruined home, they'd missed the obvious: two more menacing machines slowly grinding up the hill, destroying houses in their wake. Black uniformed figures swarmed around them.

'I think Tiea may be okay,' Jack reassured. 'We weren't that high, and her Hovertak looks more or less intact. But there's too many down there for us to handle.'

'Never say die except when it applies to these twats, Jack,' Mark growled. Kicking black garbed twisted bodies into bloody heaps with his machine guns, he effectively took out the stationary Hovertanc, killing the crew.

Pushed to the limit by their pilots, the Spitfires whittled away the king's policemen coming up the hill, but they couldn't stop the heavily armoured Hovertancs. Valiantly using all their skills, their heroic efforts finally proved to be vain: ammunition exhausted, the airmen watched helplessly as the king's police headed towards Tiea's Hovertak.

'Need a little help, Wing Commander?' Roberts's voice asked casually as his squadron of adapted Seafire fighter bombers ripped along the avenue, destroying the two Hovertancs with their bombs. 'There's a little group from the army just about to arrive too. You really shouldn't keep all the fun to yourself!'

'Roberts? Good man! Where did you come from?' Jack replied gratefully, noticing the tanks and troops turning up the hill from the city centre.

'I'm going in!' called Mark.

'Okay, Mark, I'll join you. Please cover us until the army arrive, Flight Sergeant. There's still a few police about down there.'

Dropping side by side, they landed in the wasted garden as close to Tiea as possible. The two airmen leapt from their cockpits and ran across to her Hovertak, which was lying on its side with one wing bent against the control pod. Jumping onto the wrecked airplane Mark peered under the twisted wing through the shattered screen.

'Tiea, are you okay?' he called urgently, seeing her lying inert in her seat.

'Better than I should be, I suppose,' she replied. 'But I can't get out; the bloody wing's jamming the door.'

'No problem, old girl,' Mark reassured. 'The king's men are dead and we'll have you out in a jiffy.'

'You haven't seen them—my family, I mean? Is there any sign of them, Mark?'

'Take it easy, Tiea, we'll get you out first.'

'Please look for my family. I'm fine here. Just look for them.'

Reluctantly, Mark nodded his head. 'Okay, Jack will help Tiea— and the soldiers, when they arrive. I'll go and look.' And with that, he began venturing towards the ruins of the house. As he put one foot in front of the other, nerves and hope pumping throughout his body, he glanced across Atlanta to the harbour and the sea beyond. It struck him that he now stood in roughly the same spot as he had when he and Jack had first stepped out of Tiea's Vertlyn on their last visit. He was stunned by the havoc the relatively short battle had created; little now looked as he'd remembered.

Atlanta now resembled just about any city he'd seen mercilessly pounded by high explosives and the like; decades to make it, seconds to break it.

Turning back to the job in hand, he saw something he'd missed which instantly ignited a glimmer of hope: there was a small void created by the bridging of many substantial roof timbers under the nearest heap of masonry. Peering in, his heart lurched; he could just make out two bodies, and nearby was Jole, Kolit's little dog. The terrified animal was shaking and pathetically licking at the legs of one of the bodies.

In spite of the noise around him, Mark could now hear Jole whining.

'Kolit, Raff, can you hear me? Are you okay?' he called, shouting through the small crack. After getting no response, he shouted, 'Hang on, I'll get some help!' He turned and ran to where Jack and the soldiers stood by Tiea's hovertak.

Noticing his friend approaching, Jack called, 'Did you find anything, Mark?'

'Yes, there are two people trapped under the rubble; I'm assuming they're Tiea's brothers, because Kolit's dog's in there, too. It's getting pretty dark and it's hard to see under there. But we'll have to be very careful getting them out.'

Jack nodded. 'Of course. First let's get Tiea out and then we'll deal with it.'

They all leapt up onto the craft, wrenching at the buckled wing alongside them. Suddenly, it tore loose and clanged to the ground, taking Mark with it. Flinging open the door, Tiea jumped down and rushed over to him.

'Have you found them, Mark? Are they alright? Are they hurt? Where are they? I must go!' she pressed.

'I don't know for sure if they're your brothers, Tiea. There are two people trapped in there, but I can't see how badly they're hurt,' he replied compassionately.

'And my parents?' Tiea continued, her eyes shining as tears of frustration and fear crept in.

'I realise how difficult this is for you, Tiea,' Mark said quietly, taking her into his arms. 'But we need to do things one step at a time, calmly. If we rush in and panic, who knows how wrong this could go. Now, I'm here for you.' He stroked her hair as she sobbed into his chest. 'Let's get your brothers out, and then we'll search for your parents.'

'Using the transporter was an inspiration, Captain,' said Lanter. 'We'll be forever grateful to your chief engineer for that one.'

'Indeed, our Mr Duke possesses a devious mind—and one which has successfully solved many problems at once, as it's turned out. Mind you, it could still have gone horribly wrong; I hope we'll never have to take risks like that again. Normally, I prefer not to employ the all-or-nothing approach if I can avoid it,' replied Rowsell.

The captain and Lanter were drinking together in the captain's cabin on-board Victorious. In the end, the invasion of Atlanta had gone much better than even they'd anticipated and, with the mopping up operations well organised and the night approaching, it was time to celebrate.

'Quite so. The plans we had were completely inappropriate for the enemy's reactions as it turned out, weren't they? As you know, I'd anticipated an easy victory in Atlanta, then a tedious and potentially dangerous campaign to reoccupy the island,' Lanter replied. 'What I hadn't expected was such a ferocious battle, not to mention the end result of dumping our enemies in the sea! It just goes to show: you can never take anything for granted. I'd honestly expected this to pan out quite differently.'

'It will certainly make our lives easier from now on though, Lac. When we've finished hauling the buggers out and incarcerated them all, I don't think there'll be much more to worry about regarding the king's men on Atlantis.'

As Captain Rowsell and Lanter were discussing the day's events and planning the immediate future, James Roberts had returned to Victorious. Sitting on the wing of his Seafire and leaning back against the fuselage, he was speaking with Abdua Lorht. From this vantage point, they had a ringside view of the activities on-going at sea and across the city.

'I'm sorry we lost Cal today, Abdua,' Roberts said. 'I know you sometimes flew as his wingman.'

'Just about always, James,' replied Lorht sadly. 'I'm really going to miss him. He was a dear friend; we've had some good times together, in spite of it all. I was in the group who deserted with him years ago, and there were only four of us left out of that lot—until today, of course. And I'm also sorry to hear of your losses, James.'

Roberts offered a sad smile. 'Thank you, but it goes with the territory, I'm afraid. We all know the risks. But, when you consider the fights we've had today and what we took on-board, I'm surprised any of us are still here. I thought the battle first thing this morning was as bad as it gets—I've never seen so many enemy fighters in the air at one time. I was wrong, though: when we first flew into Atlanta and its defences opened up on us, I had a very close call myself.'

'I don't think you were alone in that, judging by what I've heard since. But, we've seen some pretty amazing things today!' Lorht smiled.

'Indeed—especially the grand finale!'

'I love it when a plan comes together—even though I'd no idea there was one at the time,' Lorht laughed. 'One minute we were faced with an army infinitely larger than ours, all extremely pissed off with us, and five minutes later, three-quarters of them were floundering around in the sea five miles away and the rest had surrendered! I suppose we shouldn't have doubted the powers that be, really—but even so, when those portals opened, revealing tens of thousands of angry men standing there, all with their weapons swinging our way, I didn't expect to survive, let alone beat them off!'

'It's true, the day just got better and better for us,' Roberts mused. 'Such a pity we can't borrow you lot and your weird equipment to sort our world out after this is over! There's a few nasty bastards back there I'd like to deal with in the same way, make no mistake!'

'I'll bet—and if the opportunity ever arises you can count me in. I've quite enjoyed being part of a winning team for a change. Still, I suppose we've plenty to do here for a while. We've conquered this city for sure—maybe the whole island—but it might take a little bit longer to rid the whole world of its pests.'

'Of course, Abdua,' Roberts agreed. 'It's going to take quite a while to sort things out properly around this city, I reckon—never mind anywhere else. They haven't even got all of the king's men out of the sea yet! On top of which, they are still a few staunches, fighting here and there about the place, as we can see from here.'

'You've got to hand it to them, I suppose, but some people just don't know when to quit do they? And look at those troopships over there, James! We haven't fished half of them out yet by the looks of it, but if many more climb aboard those boats, they'll all go sailing back in again, taking our ships with them!' Lorht observed.

'Bloody hell, you're not kidding, are you? Assuming they don't sink first, what on earth are they going to do with them all? That's a heck of a lot of prisoners to deal with in one go.'

Watching the rescue operations in progress, they also noticed some activity around the transporter further down the flight deck. A beam of energy shot from the machine, aimed at one of the overloaded ships, whereupon the enemy troops, lined up on her decks, disappeared, the ship visibly rising several feet.

'See, Abdua, ask and it will be given unto you today it seems! We now know how they intend to deal with that part of it then!' Roberts laughed, shaking his head. 'What a world this is.'

CHAPTER TWENTY-SIX

'**O**ne piece at a time, gentlemen. Take it slowly and don't pull anything away that doesn't want to come out easily. Grab some of that loose timber lying around and we'll use it to prop things up as we go. Now let's get on with it.' Jack took the role of leading the rescue operation for Tiea's family, knowing Mark, though capable, was much too concerned for Tiea to think straight.

Slowly, the group uncovered the space protected by the roof timbers: thirty-five determined people working closely together moved tons of stubborn debris, one piece at a time, as Jack had ordered. Half an hour into the excavations, they released their first survivor; trembling, thickly caked in grey dust with a blood-streaked nose. Little Jole sidled into Tiea's waiting arms. Her tears tracked through the dust on Jole's fur as she held the frightened animal to her chest, noticing gratefully that the little dog's wounds appeared to be superficial.

'Hey, mind where you're putting that thing will you,' came a befuddled cry twenty minutes later, and Tiea beamed. 'What the fuck's happened? Where am I? Help!' And Tiea laughed out loud with mounting relief.

As the team had removed the rubble from above their prison, the air had become sweeter, rousing Kolit from his unconscious state. Gradually awakening, he'd felt a sharp pain as a piece of broken floor joist disturbed by a prop inserted by the rescuers above him dropped between his legs. Jolted to full awareness, he'd complained, become disorientated, tried to rise, couldn't, panicked, and was now vociferously requesting assistance—all of which was fully understandable under his unenviable circumstances, but which nevertheless caused him confusion as to why his sister obviously found it all so amusing.

'Is Raff close by, Kolit?' Tiea asked, once again serious, her face clouding with doubt and worry. 'Is he okay?'

'I can't see him,' Kolit replied, his voice quavering.

The rescuers struggled on, encouraged by the knowledge that at least one person under them was still living, their efforts slowly uncovering Raff and gradually easing the weight pressing in on Kolit. Fifteen minutes later, they gently lifted the injured men to safety. And it was then that an overstressed rafter suddenly snapped, causing the rubble to collapse completely, flattening the buckled remains of the ruins.

Tiea rushed to Kolit and knelt beside him, preceded by Jole who frantically licked her injured owner, staring wide-eyed into his face. Gently, his hand found his desperate little dog, and slowly he rubbed her ears, smiling weakly up at his sister, who gazed worriedly down at them.

'Look, little brother, she's happy now she's got you back—and so are we—but we need to find out if you're hurt before you try to move. We have people tending to Raff at the moment, and they'll come to you soon. But where are Mum and Dad? Are they inside?'

'No, thank Ra. We persuaded them to go to the country just before this all happened. They're staying with Rema's folks for now.'

Tiea threw her head back and gazed up at the sky. 'Oh thank Ra and the Ancients. Thank everyone they're alright!' Tears streamed down her cheeks. Her family were all fine.

'That turned out a whole lot better than we thought it would before we started out here, Jack,' said Mark, 'but I reckon it's just as well Tiea insisted she came over when she did. However I suppose we'd better start wrapping this lot up, there's little more we can do here now.'

Mark nodded. 'If we leave when Raff and Kolit are safely away, we can take Tiea with us—if she wants to come, that is. Doubtless we're all so deep in the crap now a few minutes more won't make much difference.'

'Yes, I heard our radios,' Jack said, shrugging his shoulders. 'But we had more important things to tend to.

Within minutes, an evacuation team called in by the soldiers had arrived and settled Raff and Kolit into their transport. Tiea thanked them all gratefully and gave a final kiss to her brothers. With a clashing of gears, the ambulance ground back down the hill, followed by the army rescuers.

'Oh, Mark, what a day, but I'm so happy everyone's alright—even this shambles doesn't bother me anymore. Mind you, I am bothered about riding in that thing,' she said, pointing to his Spitfire. 'Are you sure it's a good idea?'

'Positively the best idea I've ever had, old girl! And as I keep telling you: this is a very fine aeroplane, is this.'

'If you say so, Mark, but just how do you propose we do it?'

'I'll climb in and then you sit on my lap,' he laughed, a glint in his eye. 'It's a bit tight, I agree, and we can't shut the canopy—but its plenty warm enough and we won't be in the air for more than five minutes.'

After some shuffling about, Tiea and Mark were ready to depart. Jack climbed into his plane, shaking his head and grinning. Banging and smoking, the Merlins fired up. A couple more small complaints from both engines, and then they purred smoothly.

'Fucking Hades, Mark, I thought you said this was a fine aeroplane! Didn't I hear you say exactly that no more than a minute ago?' Tiea shouted above the noise.

'Character, old girl, character. My plane's got bags of it! You're just jealous the whining old crates you fly don't have any! Now, tickets please!' he called out, lifting the Spitfire into the air using the anti-gravity device, then gunning the Merlin and accelerating after Jack towards the harbour. Banking sharply to the left, he stood the Spitfire on its port wing, flipping back level when the brightly lit airfield came in-sight through the arc of the prop over Tiea's right shoulder. As Jack's fighter swam into vision, silhouetted against the day-bright moon, he dropped in behind him and a voice from the control dome came from their radios, giving them directions to land at the field.

And it was then that Jack groaned, knowing his friend better than anyone else in the world, he feared Mark may have a plan. 'Don't do it, Mark!' he radioed. 'I warn you, just don't, okay?'

'Sorry, Wing Co., you're breaking up a bit! I can't hear! Tally ho!'

'Hold tight, old girl! Got to be done, I'm afraid, new airfield and all that,' Mark said cheerfully. 'Might as well be hung for a sheep as a lamb, you know!' And with that, he pointed the Spitfire directly at the control tower, pushing the throttle to the limit. Passing above it at three hundred and fifty miles an hour, the Merlin screamed, clearing the dome by no more than a few feet. Mark rolled the Spitfire right over three times as he soared back into the sky.

'Oh, God,' Jack sighed.

'You idiot!' Tiea screamed. 'You nearly dumped me on those bloody factory roofs back there! Let me out of this thing!' Happiness and laughter lit up her eyes. 'I mean, let me out of this wonderful, marvellous, super, exceptional aeroplane. You've proved your point, Mark. Now can we please go home?'

By now, Jack had landed his Spitfire beside a row of hangars to the right of the control tower where they'd been directed prior to Mark's air display. As he watched Mark and Tiea finally complying with instructions, Jack was trying to pacify the enraged resistance air controller on his radio. Having no success in that direction, he was delighted to see Rema emerge from the end hangar and run towards him. Abandoning the controller to his spluttering, he leapt down and ran to meet her.

'Oh, Jack, I don't believe it! We've actually done it! We've actually taken Atlantis!' she cried, leaping into his outstretched arms. Kissing passionately, they heard Mark and Tiea land behind them and the sharp ticking of an overheated engine cooling to silence.

'I think I'm ready to join up now, Mark,' whispered Tiea in the silence, nodding her head at Rema and Jack.

'Right time, right place, eh?' he asked, twisting her round and kissing her full on the lips.

In the meantime, Captain Rowsell and Lanter had returned to the bridge of Victorious. It was fast approaching midnight, and now there were a whole new set of problems to deal with.

Their land forces had virtually eliminated the small pockets of resistance left in action within the city, but now the enormous task of completely restructuring Atlantis itself faced them, on top of which there were the immediate problems of dealing with the wounded, the tens of thousands of prisoners they'd captured, and the general devastation that had been inflicted upon the civilian population of the capital. And added to this already chaotic mix, they were perplexed as to the location of the chiefs.

Lanter's face was rosy with frustration. 'I know that we need to find the chiefs,' he began, trying to control the exhaustion in his voice. 'But Lara calling us to say they're at portal twenty really means nothing to me. In reality, knowing their location is completely useless if we don't know where that location is! It's like trying to look up a word in the dictionary you don't know how to spell!'

'Quite so,' agreed Rowsell. 'Up until a few hours ago, I didn't even know what a portal was! But still, at least we know they're still here, Lac, which is a start, I suppose. As soon as they use those planes, we'll see them drawing power on our screen and then we'll know where they are, won't we?'

'That's all very well in theory, Captain,' Lanter responded, wishing he didn't have to burst the captain's optimistic bubble, 'but take a look on the screen and ask yourself what you see. The answer is vehicles—and lots of them. Yes, we'd be able to see them on our screen, but we wouldn't know if it was them.'

'I see what you mean, Lac,' replied the captain. 'I should've known life's not that easy.'

'And we also have to consider the fact that, if we did manage to locate their craft, we're then faced with a problem: Lara. We couldn't capture an airborne vehicle; we'd have to shoot it down. And I'm sure I don't need to remind you that she'd be on-board.'

'Undoubtedly, difficult,' Rowsell mused, 'but I really don't see you'd have any choice if it comes down to it. We've both lost many good people today for the greater cause. Everyone knows what's involved, and even we would have to accept we're expendable.'

'Yes, of course we all are—but with respect, Captain, you're rather missing the point here. The decision I see looming here is who's the most important in the long run when considering the greater cause: the chiefs or Lara? And mark my words, Captain: after this, the king will put everything possible behind the anti-matter project. Today has conclusively proved our technology now far exceeds his own, and he must deal with this fact at the earliest opportunity or lose the war. Undoubtedly, the three chiefs are important to him—they're his top commanders, after all. But, like the rest of us, he'll soon realise they're expendable too.'

Rowsell nodded his head, considering Lanter's words.

'Everything around his kingdom will need restructuring now, and they must've fallen from grace considerably by losing his homeland and letting us in. It's true they couldn't really be blamed for this, but it can hardly have improved their ratings, can it?' Lanter continued. 'If we eliminate them, have we gained much in the long run? They'll only be replaced with people equally as nasty eventually.'

'I suppose what you say makes sense,' Rowsell commented, 'but I'm afraid you're asking the wrong person here. I've always been in the position where longer term planning and the like are in the hands of higher authorities; my abilities lie more in the practicalities of the moment. With that in mind, Lac, it's your call.'

Chapter Twenty-Seven

'**W**hat's he up to now, I ask you?' demanded Maltor. 'He appears positively jubilant! It doesn't make any sense at all! Today has rocked our entire world to the core and changed everything around us for the worse, but he's perfectly happy about the whole thing?'

'Very strange indeed, Rak,' answered Aharmer, 'but it's not the worst possible outcome for us personally. We've escaped intact without incident, and the king's attitude is far from what we'd expected. The only way to find out what this is all about is to follow his orders. Collect Amis and his project from our ships at sea, fly to the Ra forsaken northlands, and meet him at the coordinates he's given us.'

'Which are approximately twelve hours' flying time away, allowing for collecting my dear friend on the way, one hundred miles from the fucking North Pole and totally desolate,' replied Maltor. 'At the moment, it's permanently dark and up to seventy degrees below freezing. Violent storms rage constantly and it's about as far as you can get from where I feel we should actually be going! I can only assume he intends to abandon us there, which possibly doesn't apply to Amis and his team, of course. I don't like the way this is shaping up, gentlemen.'

The reason for the chief's quandary had presented itself shortly before they'd escaped from Atlanta. They'd departed during the early hours of the morning, guessing their enemy would then be at their least effective. Using the cockpit of the king's Argotak as their base for the preceding time, they'd rerouted the reinforcements heading for Atlantis to Rammath. They'd discussed in-depth the situation in Mu with their regional commanders and were content they'd now stabilised the situation to a point where they were successfully making a counter attack. Communicating with all other areas concerning the military, they'd been both pleased and concerned with the information they'd gathered: despite Atlantis being a complete disaster, the remainder of the empire was damaged in parts but generally still under control—or it was rapidly becoming that way. Having little more than their instincts to follow, they'd assumed the resistance had no further surprises in store, considering they would probably have sprung them already if they had any.

If the chiefs were correct in all their assessments, on the face of it, things appeared to be retrievable.

Their escape had clearly concerned them, but there was nothing more they could do about it now. Providing their plan was successful, it seemed they'd have time to reorganise before the resistance launched another campaign against them.

Their investigations had led them to the point where they could more comfortably contact the king and present him with the facts. He pre-empted this by contacting them.

Though it could have been worse, it had been the blackest day the king had ever encountered, with an uncertain future looming before him. He'd lost his homeland, was under great pressure elsewhere and, as Aharmer had stated whilst planning the defences, 'the ramifications were indeed endless now.'

'Tiresome though it is, Maltor, small setbacks occur from time to time,' the king had said, a reaction they were not expecting. 'Nevertheless, on the whole, it's turned out to be a remarkably good day, I believe.' The men had been left totally speechless.

With no further explanation as to these bizarre comments, the king had issued them with their current orders and abruptly concluded the conversation.

'If he's going to do that, then it's completely out of character, Rak,' replied Neda. 'If he wanted to punish us, he'd make an example of us, in public. He'd also want to enjoy the spectacle himself, surrounded by his circle of cronies. How could that happen at the North Pole? Either the man's gone insane or he's found something in the area which has shed a new light on the situation for him.'

'It's possible, but we'd better watch our backs. I'm still not convinced,' Maltor warned. 'However, the world's riddled with surprises today, is it not? Maybe you're right; perhaps there is something lying hidden in the wilderness.'

'Whatever it is, it's important enough for the king to abandon his treasure. I realise we needed to unload one of these planes to accommodate Amis, but why all of them?' Aharmer noted.

Subdued and frustrated, the chiefs stared from the king's private cabin down at the trackless ocean, furiously waving beneath them. White willowy clouds decorated the deep blue sky, and the morning sun now reflected from the rolling waves to the far horizon. After a time, they became aware of their target heading for Rammath; dark smudges solidifying to solid steel, the ships emerged as they rapidly approached them. White wakes stretched for miles astern as they raced onwards.

Back on Atlantis, the conquerors were settling in, some enjoying the fruits of their labours whilst the less fortunate busied themselves with the awesome task of establishing the new order.

In the shattered streets of Atlanta, crowds of jubilant people rejoiced at their deliverance from a lifetime of oppression, which had prevailed until only yesterday. The taverns which had escaped damage overflowed with happy allied and resistance soldiers, all mingling with the equally joyful locals. Now a party atmosphere prevailed as the hot morning sun bathed the city, celebration the order of the day.

Captain Rowsell and Lanter strolled together across the square in the city centre, where surprisingly little damage had been inflicted.

'Well, I'll hand it to you all, Lac,' said the captain as a delightful young woman threw her arms around him and showered him with kisses, 'you certainly judged the mood of your people here correctly; their once beautiful city is sadly broken, but nonetheless it would appear they're still delighted to see us.'

'Does you good, doesn't it, Paul? You've no idea how many times I've dreamed of this—and it's even better than the best of them right now!'

'Would you care for some oats for breakfast, dear boy?' Jack asked with a smile as Mark and Tiea joined him and Rema. They were seated at a pavement table, outside the same tavern they'd left under very different circumstances a couple of days before.

'No thank you, Wing Co., already had some actually. We're hungry now,' he replied, completely unfazed by Jack's attempt to turn the tables on him.

Tiea shook her head laughing, and Jack and Rema smiled happily at each other, pleased their respective friends seemed to have also become an item.

'Look at those two strolling around as if they owned the place,' Tiea said, smiling at Captain Rowsell and Lanter. 'You'd think they'd have more to do than sun themselves right now. Just because they've parked their war buggy in the harbour doesn't mean they've completed their mission yet!'

'Oh, let them enjoy the moment like the rest of us; these things don't come around very often. And if they're anything like us, they're going to make the most of it too,' replied Rema.

CHAPTER TWENTY-EIGHT

Through the bitter arctic night, the Argotaks approached their destination. Hurricane force winds threw swirling snow against the black painted aircraft. Concerned and bewildered, the chiefs gazed from their cabin into stygian darkness as the giant machines were tossed by the elements.

'Holy Ra, this is terrible! I can't see a fucking thing!' cried Aharmer. 'I've rarely seen a storm this bad—even up here! What the fuck is he thinking, dragging us to this awful place? I'm thinking maybe we should have listened to you more seriously, Rak. If he leaves us here we won't survive long enough to realise we're dying it's that bad.'

'Hmm, it doesn't feel right, does it?' Maltor mused.

'We probably ought to be getting the Hades away from here. What do you think now, Rak? Should we turn back?' Neda asked.

'Fucked if I know what to make of it all, but if these planes get much more of this, I doubt it'll matter what I think really,' he replied darkly. 'I'll say one thing, though, bad as it is, dying up here is probably preferable to the alternatives. But then there's curiosity…'

Suddenly feeling the aircraft rapidly decelerate and lose altitude, the men knew they'd arrived at the king's coordinates, and before they'd time to look out, the pilot's voice came over the speaker in their cabin. 'Chiefs, you'd better come up here quickly, there's something you need to see.'

As they rushed to the cockpit, the main cabin filled with light and, as they entered, the reason was sharply etched through the Argotaks' windscreens. It hit them like a sledgehammer.

'What the…' started Maltor then, stunned into silence, stood speechless in horrified disbelief.

Below them, and encompassing several square miles, a blindingly brightly lit area had appeared in the otherwise total darkness. Immune from the arctic night surrounding it, unearthly creatures with coal-black eyes walked on seemingly bright green grass. Towards the centre, a portal stood open, revealing a nightmare red glow emanating from a vast cavern. Twisted shapes flickered darkly within, and brown tendrils of mist floated from its maw, appearing as wraiths rising to greet them. Parked around the perimeters, large circular objects with dark apertures ringing their metallic bodies stood closely together on the ground. Around each a shimmering aura bathed them with multi coloured light, and on every one a doorway lay open. An army of black suited large-headed humanoids, all with small stocky bodies and over-length arms, looked up into the sky through blazing yellow eyes towards the Argotaks.

From the communicator beside the pilots seat sprang a voice they all recognised. Deep, menacing and heartless as the arctic wind around them it froze their hearts. 'In one way or another, you have all totally failed me. I am less than impressed by your dismal performances—a subject, I assure you, we will revisit shortly. However, in the meantime, my new allies will undoubtedly deal with all the distress you have caused me.'

Looking down, the chiefs could swear they saw an evil grin spread over the king's countenance.

And standing before the portal, silhouetted menacingly against the sombre crimson glow, he was indeed grinning most evilly!

To Be Continued